fan base
A NOVEL

JANE HARTSOCK

HARTSOCK BOOKS

Copyright © 2025 by Jane Hartsock
All rights reserved.

This is a work of fiction. Names, characters, places, and incidents are either the product of the author's imagination or are used fictitiously, and any resemblance to actual persons living or dead, businesses, companies, events, or locales is entirely coincidental.

No part of this book may be reproduced in any form or by any electronic or mechanical means, including information storage and retrieval systems and/or scraping, or for use in training of or learning by AI or LLMs, without written permission from the author, except for the use of brief quotations in a book review.

No AI, LLM, or other generative technology was used in the conception, creation, drafting, editing, or revising of this novel. This novel is entirely and solely the work of its author.
Every fucking word of this is mine.

ISBN: 979-8-9916125-2-4

❦ Formatted with Vellum

For beach and lake lovers, alike.

For a while, it was one of the truths in my two truths and a lie: I fucked Austin Lewis. I can't remember the other truth—there aren't a lot of things about me that are beyond belief. I am —with the exception of the Austin Lewis encounter—spectacularly ordinary.

My lie was that I could roller skate backwards. I grew up in the 1980s when roller skating parties were all the rage, and I was pretty competent at the forward skating stuff. But I never could get the backwards skating. The kind where one leg glides in front of the other like some kind of otherworldly ballerina on wheels, and it looks like that should absolutely not move a person backwards, but it does. I could never do that. I never got past the figure-eight thing, which is nowhere near as cool, and you can't get any speed with it. I guess none of it's cool anymore. Austin Lewis sure as hell isn't cool anymore.

He's on social media, though. Instagram. I follow him, which, in light of our *encounter*, I admit is a little weird. We fucked back in 1997, so it was quite a few years later that I "followed" him. I hadn't forgotten about him; there just wasn't really any way back then to keep in touch, so to speak. But when social media arrived on the scene, I jumped on that, and after following the eight people in my family, and a few of the people I graduated high school with, and then a few randoms, I started in on the celebrities—current and past. He never followed me back.

Austin's star has long since faded, anyway. A nebula or something. I was pre-law in undergrad, so I don't really know the phases of a star. What I do know is that in 1997, when he asked me if I wanted a photograph, too, his star was burning bright, and the correct answer to that question was unequivocally *yes*.

Because I am unrelentingly socially awkward, I naturally responded, "That's okay. I'm fine."

I remember he looked at me then—he had these eyes. They're probably what made him a star (and then a nebula), but they were so incredibly clear and blue. They looked like they'd been special ordered from some child star parts catalog. I'm assuming the catalog also sold that haircut that parted down the middle and was long on the sides. He didn't have that haircut. His hair was too thick for that, and he opted for a southern California, short and spiky, fresh-from-the-surf thing. It was a good decision. He probably didn't make it himself.

He also was no longer a *child* star in the summer of 1997. He was, what, I guess twenty-five or so then. I was almost twenty, a rising junior in college. I was already dating Ryan, but not for very long, and the expectations were different then. You could be dating someone and be serious about them and not speak to them for a week because you'd run out of minutes on your cell phone (if you had one, which neither Ryan nor I did), or couldn't get a long-distance card. I remember that summer writing Ryan real letters. On paper.

Ryan's mother was, let's say, "overprotective," and Ryan wasn't allowed to call me from the phone in their apartment, so, he would go to the apartment complex clubhouse and call me from the pay phone there. That phone required thirty-five cents to make a call, but it was so old, it couldn't tell the difference between coins. Ryan would feed the metal slot two pennies, which it happily accepted in exchange for a thirty-minute phone call with me. Now that I think about it, that could have been my second truth—the pennies in a payphone. It sounds like a title for a book, Nicholas Sparks maybe, but that was actually how he called me. Each summer he was home. Maybe he'd call when he said he would, and maybe he wouldn't. He'd leave a message with a time he'd call back. Sometimes I was home. Sometimes I wasn't. That's just how it was.

The summer of 1997, though, my aunt and uncle invited my sister Margot and me out to California to visit. They were my dad's brother and his wife, and my dad left when I was ten and Margot was five. So, we didn't really know them. I think that's one of the reasons they invited us. They didn't have children and wanted to be the involved aunt and uncle, or to save us from the desolation of our unsupervised, single-parent household, or maybe they just felt like we were family, and they should know us.

I think, like a lot of older couples who never had children, they thought of nineteen and fourteen as somehow younger. They had it in their minds that Margot and I still occupied that little girl phase, and they could take us to the zoo, buy us stuffed animals (truly, each of our beds had a brand-new stuffed animal on the pillow), drown us in the pink cotton candy of gender-conformity, and have a little taste of parenthood. They hadn't counted on us being adults inchoate, with Sony Discmans, boyfriends, likes and dislikes. The allure of going to California was, well, not alluring. The phase of thinking the mere fact of being in Los Angeles was somehow, itself, cool had gone the way of roller skating (forward or backwards).

Their house was huge—the sort of house people with a ton of money and no kids have. Big empty bedrooms and acres of plush white carpet that had never had even a single drop of grape Faygo spilled on it. The dishwasher was always empty because they never cooked and never ate at home. We each had our own bedroom, and each bedroom had its own attached bathroom—luxurious by any measure, but particularly so for a couple of kids who grew up in a two-bedroom, one-bath walkup in Chicago.

The whole thing with Austin started with a simple enough question.

"Well, what *do* you want to do this afternoon, Barbara?" my Aunt Iris asked. She must have picked up on our general boredom and our accompanying resentment at having that boredom inflicted upon us.

Ignoring that she'd called me by my full name, which I detested, I suggested, "The beach?" thinking that's what people did in Los Angeles in the summer. It's what people did in Chicago.

Aunt Iris wrinkled her nose. "Hot," she said as if commenting on an odor rather than the weather.

"We could go see a taping," my uncle Leo volunteered.

To this day, I still don't know what he did for a living, what allowed them to have this huge house in whatever Los Angeles suburb, and what connected my uncle to *The Maple Street Martins*, but that show and Austin Lewis were, unbeknownst to Uncle Leo or Aunt Iris, Margot's favorite things in the entire world.

I'd seen it a couple times; it was good. Some primetime drama that targeted multiple age demographics at once. The Martins of Maple Street (as luck would have it) had four kids:

one in grade school, one in middle school, one in high school, and one in college. Later, the parents had a baby when the plots grew stale and the viewership declined. Then the show was canceled. That poor baby never even learned to walk. But this was my sister's favorite show, and Austin Lewis, who at age twenty-five played Bobby Martin, the high schooler in the family, was the love of Margot's life.

For me, though—in the days before streaming—a television show that aired at ten on a Thursday night was easy to sacrifice to frat parties, fake-ID-entry to Conner's Irish Pub, and making up for all those missed phone calls with Ryan. If there'd been anything else to do at all—including if Aunt Iris had agreed to drop me off at the beach—I would have declined the offer to go with Uncle Leo and Margot to see the show being filmed.

Seeing a set up close like that takes a good deal of the magic out of watching the show. Or it would have if I'd made a regular habit of watching. The house the Martins lived in was deconstructed to simply a sequence of boxes. Some of the boxes had to be next to each other because the rooms flowed one into the other. But the bedrooms were all life-size dioramas, self-contained closed ecosystems, not part of a house.

They were filming a scene in the kitchen that day, so the rest of the studio was dark, and the actors who weren't in that scene milled around, eating peanut M&Ms and making small talk that didn't make any sense to me. Austin wasn't eating peanut M&Ms and making small talk. He was sitting in a chair with (hand to God) his name on the back, reading his script. My sister spotted him and dragged us over.

The guide walking us around made the introductions. "This is Barbara and Margot Stewart. They're Leo Stewart's nieces."

"Babs," I said.

"What?" Austin put his script down.

"My name is Babs," I repeated. The guide didn't acknowledge the clarification.

"Can we get a couple of photos? They're here from Chicago," she continued.

"Sure," he said.

I remember thinking, *He seems like a nice guy.* He had an unassuming way about him. And I could see why Margot was so head over heels. Great teeth, great hair, those eyes.

"What part of Chicago are you from?" he asked.

"Lincoln Square," I said. My answer irritated Margot, who wanted to be the one to have the conversation with him.

"Oh. So, *in* the city," he said.

This was important to me because it meant he knew something about Chicago and about the way people would say they were "from Chicago," and you would ask them where in Chicago, and they would say "Aurora" or "DeKalb." He knew the neighborhoods.

"Yeah. You know the city?" I asked. I could feel Margot heating up next to me.

"He's *from* Chicago. His mom still lives there," Margot said.

Austin smiled a little self-consciously.

"Where in Chicago?" I asked.

Austin looked briefly at Margot. Maybe he thought she'd supply the street address. When she didn't, he said, "Evanston," which is not a neighborhood in Chicago; it's a suburb of Chicago, but the 'L' runs up there, so close enough. It's not Aurora.

"You want a photograph?" he asked, turning to Margot, who beamed openly. "Did you bring a camera?"

Margot took a black Kodak disposable out of her purse, and Austin stood from his chair. He looked taller than he did in the posters on Margot's side of our bedroom, and it seemed to me he really was too old to play a high schooler. If I'd cared to search AltaVista, I'd have found that the actor cast as his college-aged older brother was in his thirties.

Austin played the good sport and put his arm around my sister for the picture, smiling like he was happy to be there, and maybe he was. Some celebrities like being celebrities. The guide took the picture, and Margot, who could hardly breathe for having been physically touched by Austin Lewis, offered a barely audible "Thank you" before reaching to take the camera back from the guide.

This was when Austin asked if I wanted a photograph, too, and I offered the aforementioned "I'm fine" when I should have just said "Yes" like a normal person.

"Oh. Okay, then. Well, nice to meet you, Babs." He stuttered a little bit, which made me giggle, which made me feel stupid.

"Nice to meet you, too, Austin Lewis." I said both of his names. "Sorry. I don't know why I said that. I don't know any other Austins."

He chuffed and returned to his seat, reaching for his script. I could feel Margot's eyes searing into me as we headed back to the car, and I stopped talking. The meet-and-greet was over anyway.

In the car, Margot let loose. "You are so embarrassing. I swear to God, Babs."

I couldn't argue with her; it was true.

one

"I'M ASSUMING YOU KNOW WHY WE ASKED TO MEET WITH YOU THIS morning." Mark's doing the talking. Bruce is here, too, but they both know I like Mark better, so they're having him deliver the news, I guess.

"Is it to give me my productivity bonus?" I ask, knowing that it most certainly is not that.

Mark laughs. Bruce does not. So, Mark stops. His gaze shifts to the window behind me, which looks out on Upper Wacker and a thin sliver of the Chicago River. It's a window that speaks to my position at this firm. Or, more accurately, what my position once was.

"You billed seven hundred twenty-three hours last fiscal year, Babs." Bruce takes over. Laughing at the productivity bonus comment disqualified Mark.

"I thought the whole point of making partner was that you could finally back off, have a life."

They recoil at *have a life*. They know what's happened. I haven't billed an acceptable month in the nearly three years since Ryan died. While true that you can relax a little once you make partner, the average yearly billables for senior income partners at this firm still clocks in at fifteen hundred. I'm on pace to bill less than half that. For the third year in a row.

"It's not just the hours," Bruce continues. He's in the midst of getting a divorce. It makes sense for him to deliver the news. He has practice ending things. "You lost InterVids. That was your biggest client and this firm's third largest. And poof." His eyes flitter around my office at the imaginary explosion brought about by his *poof*. I look around too, but I don't see an explosion. Just a couple of assholes about to fire a widow.

"They were pretty clear, too," Mark cuts in, seeking redemption. "You stopped working on their files. You stopped returning their phone calls. You stopped reviewing their contracts."

Strictly speaking, this is all true. But InterVids had been on autopilot for years. I had associates reviewing the contracts because nothing ever changed in them. Year after year, they held the same repository of two thousand products and the same vendors for translation and dubbing. I'd ignored them, stopped wining and dining that pedantic woman who serves as their in-house counsel. But they also didn't need much. They'd never complained, and it's not like I billed them for work I didn't do. They were getting it cheap with the associates.

"Babs, you don't need this job. And we can't keep you around just because we like you." Bruce says this, but Bruce doesn't really like me. He never has. They should have assigned that line to Mark. "We're giving you two weeks," Bruce continues. "You can resign if you'd like. You've been a good attorney. I think things are just different for you now." He's become empathic. He probably thinks he knows exactly how I feel what with his divorce.

"I know it's not the same, but it's been hard for me with the divorce from Cathy—" he says, as if he's read my mind in addition to my billing entries.

I don't let him finish. "You're right."

He beams triumphantly for a moment—we understand each other.

"It's not the same," I say, and his smile fades.

"Two weeks, Babs. To tie up loose ends," Bruce says.

Mark grimaces. At least he has the good sense to know he's an asshole. I get the feeling Bruce thinks *they've* done *me* a favor. And I don't need two weeks. The nice thing about quitting your job while you're still employed is that there's not much to do when you finally leave.

"I think I'll just head out today," I say.

I get up from my desk and collect my messenger bag and the picture of Ryan, our kids, and me that sits next to my computer, and I leave.

They'll probably keep sitting there, wondering if I'll have to come back, if I forgot something in my office—a plant maybe, or at least need to enter my time. But I don't have any time to enter, and I don't want anything from my office except my messenger bag and the picture from my desk.

The thought of going home, facing that empty house, feels overwhelming, so I walk across the street to Starbucks. The late-morning line snakes through the confined space, but it moves at a reasonable clip.

"Venti blonde roast," I say when I reach the counter. I don't get the blonde roast because I'm blonde; I get it because it's less acidic, and Margot says it has more caffeine.

I take my coffee to a counter set up against a window looking out on the building I used to work in. The window has stools pushed up against it, and I set my messenger bag down on the counter next to me. Another stool goes with the space my messenger bag occupies, but I don't want anyone to sit next to me, and the bag serves its purpose as some guy takes a seat two stools down.

I stare out the window. I have just under five hours to kill before Penny and Colin need to be picked up from school. There's a CVS next to this Starbucks, and I consider buying a paperback. I can't imagine the selection of paperbacks at CVS is great, but it probably favors books that can be read in under five hours.

I take a sip of the acidic brew and am transported back to Paris with Ryan. We'd gone for our anniversary. It's the last time I had good coffee.

"I think I could live here, Bibs," he'd said as we sat outside one of the cafés by the Eiffel Tower. He always called me "Bibs" instead of "Babs." There isn't really a story behind that other than the ordinary way couples develop nicknames for each other to signify a kind of exclusion, like *She might be Babs to you, but she's Bibs to me.* Or sometimes Bibby. I adored it. I adored him.

Not that our marriage was perfect. Every marriage, every *relationship* as long as ours has low points. I continue staring across the street and remember the year I made income partner. I billed over 2600 hours that year, predominantly working for InterVids, the international client that just got me fired and for which the status of partner was enthusiastically conferred. Ryan spent that time alone, shouldering more than the lion's share of parenting, while I spent endless hours at the firm and a few too many of those hours around Mark.

Similarly, I got tired year after year of watching medical students and residents fawn and bat their lashes at a man who'd come to me more than twenty years earlier with wire-rimmed glasses, hair so bad he had to hide it under a baseball cap, and his cherry still firmly intact.

By the time he died, he was tall and broad. The glasses were gone, the hair taking the shape of soft, thick chestnut waves, just beginning to gray at the temples. I did wonder sometimes whether any of the batting eyelashes ever managed to move past flirting to an on-call room. If they did, you wouldn't know it by Ryan's attention to matters at home. He could walk up behind me with a promise that kept me in suspense for hours, waiting for homework to be completed and kids to go to bed. And then he would take me into our bedroom, and his lips would find mine, and his hands would be on my body, and then he'd be inside me, and I would know, for this man, I am the world.

Was the world.

I didn't appreciate how serious he was with the moving-to-Paris comment. His mom had died a few years earlier, and I think he was reassessing things. But the kids were in school; my mom and Margot were still in Chicago; we had the house. So, I pretended he was joking until long after it should have been obvious he wasn't. Then, he pretended he was joking, too, because it had gotten awkward.

He'd still be alive if we'd moved.

"Excuse me," says a woman, standing next to me. She's probably going to ask me to move my bag. There aren't a lot of available seats. I reach for it but she isn't talking to me; she's talking to the guy two stools down from me. I take a peek at them out of the corner of my eye, their conversation already more interesting than whatever paperbacks CVS sells.

I can't see the man because the woman blocks my view, but the woman looks just a little younger than me. It's gotten hard to tell people's ages. Everyone either looks twelve or eighty. She's probably closer to twelve than eighty, but it's a close call.

"Yes?" I hear the man say. He sounds tired to me. I know

what tired sounds like, and he sounds tired. Probably with the Chicago Board of Trade.

"Are you Austin Lewis?" the woman asks, and I nearly fall right off my stool. Or maybe spit out my coffee. A spit-take. Isn't that what it's called? If this were a television show—if this were *The Maple Street Martins*—I would spit my coffee all over the window in front of me, and the audience would howl with laughter. Actually, *The Maple Street Martins* didn't have a studio audience. Or a laugh track. That show was a drama. Still. Coffee on the window. I swallow instead.

"I am," I hear him say, and I can tell he's smiling, but he still sounds tired.

"Can I get a picture with you?" the woman asks.

"Sure thing," he says.

He sets his coffee on the counter and stands up next to his stool. The woman fluffs her hair—this picture is definitely going on Instagram, and she has to be ready. Her friend takes the photo. I get the sense her friend, like me, wasn't a fan of the show. She seems a little embarrassed by the whole ordeal. Other people start looking at them, then look away. Chicago is conspicuous in its disdain for celebrities.

Austin Lewis doesn't ask her friend if she wants a photo, too. He just says, "Feel free to tag me, and I'll like the post."

The woman smiles a smile that looks like it hurts, like a tooth cracked in the back of her mouth from the force of it. She examines the photograph her friend took, and her smile sags. Standing next to him makes her look ordinary. Which she is—probably mid- to late-thirties as I get a better look at her, brown hair that she wishes she'd curled that morning, but how was she to know she was going to run into Austin Lewis at a Starbucks in the Loop? Still, she'll post that picture to Instagram and tag him, and he'll remember to like it. All that will carry her through the next few weeks at least.

I continue peeking at Austin Lewis out of the corner of my eye as he sits back down, but I'm not very subtle, apparently. He catches me and sighs through his teeth, looking annoyed. He also looks pretty fucking good. I do the calculation; he's just over fifty, but he looks younger. Not young enough to play a high schooler, but younger than fifty. Maybe younger than me. He's wearing a navy-blue suit with a light-blue Oxford, no tie, open at the neck. His hair still has that sun-kissed, fresh-from-the-surf look. It's thinned a little, but not much. He's tan, which makes sense—late August in California. I assume he still lives there.

"Do you want a photograph, too?" he asks, and I laugh nervously. I screwed this up last time.

"No," I say, probably screwing it up again. "I know you."

"Yeah?" he says, but he returns his attention to his coffee with a movement that does not invite further conversation.

I scold myself. I should have said, *I met you,* not *I know you*. I don't know him. I've never known him. I did have sex with him once, and it was phenomenal, but I could understand if he doesn't remember.

"It was a long time ago." I add a hopeful, "Babs?"

He turns his head slowly back in my direction. "Babs," he echoes. The memory is pretty far off. He had to swipe through a few profiles to get to mine.

"Aganon. Well, Stewart then. Aganon now," I say, tripping over the words like it's a contest I want to win.

He silently consults my unadorned left hand.

"I'm widowed," I explain, even though he didn't ask. I've gotten used to this particular exchange. Next, people always ask what happened, and I always say, "A car hit him in a crosswalk," and they shake their heads in a nice way instead of in the way they shook their heads when Ryan told people his mother died of lung cancer. To be fair, the woman smoked like a chimney.

"I'm sorry to hear that. When did that happen?" he asks, a slightly less awful question than *how*.

"Almost three years ago." It sounds like a long time when I say it out loud, but it still feels like yesterday. "What are you doing here?" I ask to change the subject. I remember he has family here. His mother lives here. Or she did twenty-five years ago.

"My mom died," he says. "Two weeks ago."

Suddenly, it's my turn to say *I'm sorry to hear that.*

"I had to meet with her lawyers about her estate." He nods toward the building across the street.

"I used to work at a firm there," I say.

"Oh yeah? Which one?" He probably wonders if it's the one handling his mother's estate, which it isn't. We only do intellectual property—copyright, mostly.

"Daniels & Shay," I say.

"Is that a big firm?"

"No. Boutique. About fifty of us."

"How long were you there?" he asks.

"Oh gosh," I say, staring at the building. "I guess about twenty years."

He scrunches up his eyebrows. He can't make sense of it. "When did you leave?"

I consult my watch. "About forty minutes ago."

He leans his head back and laughs. "You just quit your job?" he asks as if he can't believe it, as if people don't quit their jobs every day.

"Not exactly," I say. "I was asked to leave."

"Babs!" He says it like we're old friends. "What happened?" He's still laughing.

I slide my messenger bag to my other side so I can see him better, but he misunderstands and scoots over to sit next to me.

"I lost focus. And I also lost a client. An important one." It's hard to explain what happened without getting dark, and I don't want to do that in Starbucks while sitting next to Austin Lewis.

"That's a rough day." He takes another sip of his coffee. "Why don't you let me take you to lunch?"

When he says this, his face becomes softer, not Austin Lewis's face, like he's selected a "human filter" for the camera-ready jawline, and he's just a person. A very attractive person. I think of the magazines in the grocery store checkout lines: *Celebrities, they're just like us.* They're not. But their mothers do die, and they do have bad days, and even the ones with millions of followers on social media still eat lunch.

"I have to pick up Penny and Colin—my kids—I—I have to pick them up from school by 4:30," I say.

I'm not sure whether I want to go with him, and even though picking my kids up is the only thing on my calendar for the day (given how my morning has gone), I still have to do it.

"We can probably manage lunch in—" he checks his watch "—four and a half hours. Where do your kids go to school?"

"St. Ignatius," I say.

"I didn't know you were Catholic."

For a minute, I entertain saying something like, *Why on earth would you?* But then I think, his comment probably has more to do with my not acting particularly Catholic the last time we met.

"I'm not very observant," I say.

He smiles. Yeah, that tracks.

"Let's head down to UIC. That's close to St. Ignatius and, as much as it pains me to say it, we're not likely to be interrupted for photo-ops on a college campus. I'll drive?"

The plan has momentum. He's already moving out of his seat, draining what remains of his coffee.

He reaches for my messenger bag—gallant—and I say, "I got it," because everything needs to slow down. But I get off my stool and throw my coffee away, and before I know it, we're walking toward a parking garage across from the Sears Tower.

two

"AFTER *THE MAPLE STREET MARTINS*," AUSTIN SAYS, TEARING OFF A piece of bread, "they considered a spin-off: Bobby, the college years. We filmed a pilot, but the network declined it. They said no one wanted to see Bobby Martin grow *old*."

We're sitting on the patio of an Italian restaurant just west of UIC's campus. I sniff inelegantly at the idea of college-aged as "old." Besides, I'm looking at Bobby Martin at fifty, and I'm pretty sure there would have been a market for this, but I'm just one person.

"And then there were the reunion shows." His voice falls with each word, a descending scale that seems to track the trajectory of his career. He pops the piece of bread into his mouth, chews it, then chases it with a sip of Pellegrino.

"Reunion?" I ask, encouraging him to continue.

"Reunion*s*," he emphasizes. "Three of them: a vacation to Hawaii, Rachel's wedding—everyone loves a wedding—and the sale of the Maple Street house. You know, so everyone would know there weren't going to be any more *reunions*." He's counted the episodes on his fingers but drops his hand back to the table. "The plots were irrelevant. The point was just nostalgia. For the fans."

The server interrupts us, delivering two salads, and the conversation stalls as water glasses are refilled and silverware is unfurled from napkins.

"You didn't like them? The reunions?" I ask, picking up on his tone.

"I don't know if I didn't *like* them. They were exactly what they were meant to be. I just thought they made the show look like it didn't take itself very seriously, and it had been a serious show." He takes a bite of the salmon filet that accompanies his salad, then brings his napkin to his lips. "You didn't watch it, did you?" he asks, remembering.

I shake my head apologetically, but really have no reason to feel guilty. Even if I hadn't been busy making up for lost time with Ryan, it wouldn't have made much sense to *start* watching the show in its fifth season. I suppose there might have been reruns of older episodes during the summers, but watching television was different in the '90s. There was no such thing as a "binge"—definitely not of a show that was still on the air.

"Well, I wouldn't have wanted you to start then anyway," he says, validating my good judgment. "It was losing its way. I think we were filming the fifth season when you were there. The next season they brought in the baby, and everyone knows that a new cast member—and a pregnancy plot line—means a show is over." He shakes his head with disdain, then stares at me wide-eyed.

"Penny," he says, setting his fork down on the edge of his plate.

"What?"

"The baby's name was Penny." He leans back in his chair and adds a single-syllable *ha*.

The baby's name was Penny? Did I know that? Margot

might have known that, but she's never said anything about it. I didn't mean to name my firstborn after a character on that show. I shovel a large forkful of salad into my mouth and make like I'd love to discuss this further but am unable to at present. He waits patiently.

"So, then what did you do?" I ask, pushing us past the topic of baby names.

"I did okay for a few years," he says. "I was able to ride that wave for a while. The parts weren't great, though. Lots of supporting this and side-kick that. And they all seemed like variations on a theme, just different versions of Bobby, which shouldn't have surprised me. I was so closely associated with that character, sometimes I'd show up for an audition, and the casting director would call me *Bobby*. Anyway, it was pretty obviously game over by the time I hit forty and I wasn't on either the leading man or rom-com shortlists," he says glibly, like he hasn't just recited his career's eulogy.

I remember this about him from that day, that he started sharing some fairly personal stuff—stuff I probably could have sold to a tabloid if I'd thought about it at the time. He's doing it again, though clearly by now it's a buyer's market when it comes to Austin's story.

"And now? What do you do now?" I ask. I hope it's not something I'm supposed to already know.

"Well, there's still a nostalgia market for *The Maple Street Martins*," he says. "That's why I agreed to the reunion shows. Gen-X loves their trips down memory lane."

Do we?

He reads my expression. "There's data to back that up. Look at the boy band cruises, the reunion tours, the quizzes and stuff on *BuzzFeed*. Our generation has trouble moving forward," he says, but I can't get past the "our generation" thing because I'd never thought of us in the same generation. He seemed so much older then. But he's right. He's six years older. Same generation.

The server comes over to check on us. "Is there anything else I can get you?" she asks. We've nearly finished our salads.

"Would you like dessert?" he asks me. "I—it's nice talking with you."

"Sure," I say, glancing up at the server, strangely embarrassed by Austin's comment. Her face remains neutral.

"I'll bring you a couple menus," she says.

"No reality TV stuff for you?" I ask as our server departs.

"I dodged all that. Melissa did a celebrity *Big Brother*, though," he says.

"Melissa?"

"She played Rachel on... the show you never watched." He drags over the last few words with a breathy laugh and goddammit those teeth and the eyes.

The server returns, hands us two menus, and collects our plates. I quickly scan the offerings, and we decide to split a spumoni gelato.

"Sorry, I've been talking a lot about me," Austin says. His cheeks pink up just a touch. I wonder whether he's actually embarrassed, whether he's over-shared. "What have you been up to?"

"Since my junior year of college?" Maybe I'm flirting, being a little coy. He ruins it, though.

"College," he says with a sly smile that absolutely refers to the moment he realized I was just some kid and not an adult in any real sense of the word. I'm immediately flustered, and I must be making some kind of face because he adds, "Hey, I'm just glad you were over eighteen. Considering."

He takes his blazer off and hangs it around the back of his chair. He's started sweating a little through the Oxford, and he unbuttons another button, revealing a sparse dusting of golden hair over a bronze triangle of exposed neck and chest. A few beads of sweat dot the patch of skin—it's too hot for a suit. The shirt clings to his shoulders, the humidity pulling the tightly woven cotton taut against the cut of his deltoids in a pronounced "v" that immediately refreshes my memory of the way his abs dropped into his hips below his navel.

Dessert arrives at the exact moment that an involuntary "oof" escapes my throat. The timing is so impeccable, I almost thank the server for saving me from myself.

"Too much?" Austin asks, referring to the generous serving of gelato.

"Definitely," I say.

"So?" he says, picking up a spoon.

"So, what?" I got distracted. I'm not sure what I missed.

"What have you been doing for the past twenty-five years?"

"Oh, right. Well, I graduated from college, and then went to law school."

"Congratulations on that," he says, with exaggerated pride, like he might have played some part in it. We are definitely flirting. "Where did you go for law school? You were out in Boston for college, weren't you? How'd you end up back here? Family?"

I shift uncomfortably as he seems to call back the pained conversation we had about whether he could fly out and visit me.

"Yeah. I thought about staying on the east coast for law school, but Northwestern offered me this enormous scholarship I couldn't turn down." I take a spoonful of the gelato, grateful for the cold shock it delivers to my mouth.

He takes a bite as well, then flips the spoon in his mouth and drags it over his bottom lip. I blink as I catch a glimpse of his tongue running over the curve of the spoon. He sets it down and regards me.

"What?" I ask, the last spoonful of gelato levitating in front of my face. I don't know how I'll answer if he asks me what I'm staring at. I'm staring at a memory, in a way, and the heat of it spreads over my chest under my blouse.

"Do you still run?"

Thank God, that's his question.

"Oh. Yes," I say, trying to hide how much I'm reading into the fact that he remembers I ran in college. "Every morning. First thing. Run then coffee."

"You look like you still run," he says. "You look exactly the same."

"I can't believe you remember that," I say, but I know. He has fully accessed the archives of 1997 and remembers everything.

"I remember," he says, and he does look just the slightest bit nostalgic. Definitely Gen-X.

"So, you moved back to Chicago, went to law school, got married, had kids..." It should sound boring, cliché. But his recitation is delivered with admiration, as if each thing is some extraordinary accomplishment rather than the very ordinary life of an infinite number of very ordinary people.

"I did," I say, agreeably.

He'd joked about being able to finish lunch in under four-and-a-half hours, but we could sit here talking for twice that long. Still, when he notes the time, I panic, because the drive down to UIC might have put me closer to my kids, but it's put me farther from my car, which is how I'd originally planned to pick them up. But we've completely lost track of time. It feels like we were just catching up, but that doesn't make much sense because we'd only spent that one day together. So, it's sort of like saying you have to run back to the grocery store because you forgot a few things, when all you got last time was a deck of Uno cards from the check-out aisle.

"When can I see you again?" he asks with a confidence that should offend me.

I hesitate, but not because I'm offended. It just seems like the same conversation we'd had all those years ago when I decided it was just too complicated. My life isn't any less complicated now. Arguably, it's more.

"How long are you in town?" I assume he'll say two or three days.

"As long as you want me to be." He stares at me like this is the most important conversation he's ever had, and I'm so locked into his gaze, I honestly don't know how to respond. "What are you doing tomorrow?"

"Nothing." I'm unemployed.

"How should I get in touch with you?" he asks, leaning forward against the table, pushing the empty gelato bowl to the side.

He has to have blinked, but I'm not sure if I have. "You could DM me if you'd follow me back on Instagram. I followed you." I realize I'm avoiding answering him.

"You did? When?" He releases me from his gaze.

"Like, ten years ago. It's fine though. You have about three-hundred-thousand followers. I can see how you didn't notice one more."

He picks up his phone, which has been lying face down on the table and fidgets with it. Then my phone vibrates.

"Let's set something up. I'll message you," he says.

"Yeah," I say noncommittally. "Sure."

After we leave the restaurant, Austin drives me to pick up my kids. On the way, I make a crack about his powder blue BMW, then have to suffer through the horror of him telling me it's his dead mother's car. I introduce him to Penny and Colin as "a friend from California," and they both seem as unimpressed with the reference to California as I'd been all those years ago. He returns the three of us to the parking garage in the Loop where my Volvo is parked. Door-to-door service. The kids call him *Mr. Lewis* and thank him for the ride.

At home, I start dinner while Colin does his homework at the kitchen island. I'm microwaving a bag of frozen broccoli when I hear the doorbell. I briefly wonder whether it might be Mark checking to see if I'm okay. Or Bruce, asking if I want to come back. I don't.

I open the front door to find Nathan Lasky on my porch. Lasky owns the three-flat across the street, which he's been renting out for as long as we've lived on this block. He's an odd duck with reddish-brown, curly hair that I determined some years ago he actually perms. His tenants are usually students—undergraduates at DePaul occasionally, but more often law or medical students.

In the fifteen years I've lived in this house, I have never had a single pleasant encounter with this man. When Ryan was alive, he mostly dealt with Lasky's never-ending litany of demands and grievances. That work now falls to me.

"Hi, Mr. Lasky," I say. I have no idea why I call him *Mr. Lasky*. He's in no position of authority over me other than some conceivable age-related seniority; he's probably approaching seventy.

"Good afternoon, Babs." There's a pause as he waits for me to invite him into the house. I don't, and he continues. "Anyway, I have a proposition for you. A mutually beneficial relationship."

It's the language of a sexual proposition, but I doubt he appreciates that. Besides, although it's been thirty-two months since I've had sex (but who's counting?), I can't imagine ever being desperate enough to fuck Nathan Lasky. I lean against the edge of the door.

"It's hot. Can I come in?" he asks with a conspicuous glance over his shoulder as if the weather is isolated there.

"No," I say, even though I can feel sweat gathering under my arms.

He purses his lips but gets to the point. "My tenants are getting more demanding. Millennials," he scoffs as if this will be a point of concordance for us. It's not. Plus, it's Gen Z in that building. "They want parking, and the city won't zone Seminary Avenue 'residential only' because of the business owners. I thought maybe you'd be interested in leasing the extra spot in your garage. You can keep that money, but it'll make it easier for me to rent my units, particularly the third floor. The kids really think they're entitled to parking—"

"The extra spot?" I interrupt.

"Yeah. The extra one." He raises his eyebrows in a manner that tells me he thinks he's being polite by not actually using the words "dead husband."

"You want Ryan's spot in my garage?"

"Fine. I'll give you a cut of the rent, too," he offers, like we're negotiating.

I blink—stunned—then say the only thing one can say in the face of such an offer: "Go fuck yourself, Lasky."

"I'm sorry?"

"You should be." I slam the door and hear a yelp on the other side. For some minutes, his silhouette remains visible through the frosted glass before I see him shuffle across the street back to his building.

I return to the kitchen and Colin has vanished—probably to the family room in the basement. His binder is closed on the counter. I walk out to the garage and stand between the two cars. Ryan's silver Audi. It hasn't been driven in nearly three years. I should sell it, I know I should. I take his keys from the pegboard next to the kitchen door, unlock the car, and slide in behind the wheel. I'm tall(ish)—5'8"—but my feet barely touch the pedals. I don't bother to turn the key; the battery is long dead, too. I wonder what the last song he listened to was. Wilco, maybe. Beck. Muse.

    I run my hands over the steering wheel, then pull the seatbelt across my chest, and suddenly he's in the car with me. The scent of his aftershave in the weave of the belt. I close my eyes, lean my head back against the head rest and tell myself I really have to stop doing this. My kids are waiting for dinner.

three

I GRAB MY PHONE FROM THE BEDSIDE TABLE. THE SCREEN GLOWS AN eerie blue-white, illuminating a spotlight around me as I lie in bed. I open Instagram and search @AustinLewis. I haven't done this in many years, and Austin's page is a kaleidoscope of images of filtered west-coast landscapes, contemporary art, posed photographs.

I click on his tagged posts, and the photograph from this morning appears with so many hashtags, the text takes up more space than the image. I follow the most straightforward hashtag: #AustinLewis. The screen populates with a mosaic of past and present as disorienting as it is unnavigable. Photographs of thirty-year-old magazine pages with Austin smiling beneath *BOP* and *Tiger Beat* logos contrast with blurry phone-camera shots of Austin eating at a restaurant, leaving a grocery store, or posing with fans in photos indistinguishable from the one this morning.

In the decades between, I see evidence of the sputtering career he described at lunch. Supporting roles, bit parts. Some of the images do look somewhat familiar, movies I've seen or at least seen trailers for, something that looks decidedly made-for-TV, an ad campaign for a cologne. I question whether I've seen these images before, or whether they are so perfectly of a time and genre, they evoke endless other similar images.

I return my phone to the nightstand determined to go to sleep, but it buzzes before I can take my hand away.

> Austin: I'm glad I ran into you today. Even if you weren't having a very good day.

> Me: ☺

A smiley face. I send him a fucking smiley face.

I've returned from dropping Penny and Colin off at school when I receive another DM from my new friend, Austin Lewis.

> Austin: How do you feel about baseball?

I associate baseball with taking clients from New York or Japan or Germany to Wrigley, buying them beer and hotdogs, and giving them the quintessential Chicago baseball experience so they'll give me their business. I consider whether, if I had to, I could approach baseball with Austin Lewis using the same strategy, then dismiss this thought as unforgivably naïve.

> Me: Depends on the team.

Not that I'd refuse to go to the White Sox, but I'm a northsider. So, if he says, "White Sox" I might be able to say, "That's not my team" and put him off a bit longer.

I'm not trying to tease him. We had a nice lunch; we caught up; it was flattering to have him sitting across from me flirting.

But Austin Lewis isn't some teen heartthrob with dreamy eyes and a dazzling smile who'd decorated the walls of my adolescent bedroom. That's who he was for Margot. For me, he's the man I cheated on my husband with—even if my husband was only my boyfriend at the time.

> Austin: Cubs of course! Where do you live? I'll pick you up.

I pace the dining room, then the living room. I walk upstairs to my bedroom and come back down. Every now and then, I pick up the phone and reread the message. A couple of times, I see three dots materialize in his texting window, then disappear. He's waiting for my response.

I walk through my closet, putting together imaginary outfits appropriate for a baseball game. The selection of shorts and a t-shirt has never seemed so formidable a challenge. I entertain dressing it up. A tunic, not a t-shirt. But no one gets dressed up for a Cubs game. You wear a Cubs shirt to a Cubs game. I consider a tank top and decide against it. I'd probably get burned.

I'm agonizing over how to respond when another text comes through.

> Margot: Hey. What happened yesterday? Is everything okay?

That's quite the question under the circumstances, but our exchange of texts above suggest she's wondering about something other than Austin Lewis. Yesterday morning, I'd texted:

> Me: Bruce AND Mark have asked to meet with me this morning. Should be interesting…

> Margot: Let me know if you want to talk.

I'd given her text a thumbs up, but that was my last communication and a lot has happened since then.

> Me: Can we talk? Too much to text.

> Margot: Give me three minutes.

Margot lives in an old Victorian west of Ridgeland in Oak Park. Her husband, Rishi, does something with money. I don't know what. Moves it around. Whenever I think of Rishi, I picture him standing behind three red Solo cups, figure-eighting them like a magician. Only, instead of ping-pong balls under the cups, there are stacks of cash. I'm grateful to know someone who moves money around, because when Ryan died, I turned over the whole wad of cash from the settlement and said I didn't want to know anything about it. Every quarter, I receive an electronic deposit into my checking account from some fund or trust or whatever he has it sitting in, and that plus my salary pay the bills. I don't have a salary anymore. I guess I need to talk to Rishi about that.

Margot and Rishi met at a gala auction thing that Ryan and I attended about five years ago. We sponsored a table and invited Margot. Rishi's firm had also sponsored a table, and he and Margot started talking at the bar. He asked her out that night, proposed six months later, and they married six months after that. He's a few years older than Margot, and I don't know what took him so long to get married, but I'm glad he waited. He's the perfect calm to her storm. Unflappable. Which is good, because Margot flaps a lot.

"I am officially unemployed," I tell her when she calls three-and-a-half minutes later.

"Fuuuuuuck," she groans.

"It was inevitable," I say.

"Babs, I'm so sorry."

"It's fine. I mean, it's not fine. But it will be. I don't know."

"Maybe this isn't such a bad thing," she says. "Finally take some time for yourself."

"I'm not sure I need more time for myself. It seems like time for myself is exactly what got me fired."

"I don't know about that." She pauses. "You want company today? Rishi's in New York again. I could bring Supriya over," she says, referring to her two-year-old daughter.

"Actually," I say with absolutely no idea how to broach this topic, "I might have plans."

"Yeah?"

"I... uh... I ran into someone yesterday. At the Starbucks across from my office."

"Yeah?" she says.

I'm not trying to build suspense; I'm trying to buy time, collect my thoughts, but her voice has shifted like she thinks we're playing a game.

"Neighborhood or high school?" she asks as if rising to a challenge I've set for her.

"Neither."

"Famous or blast from the past."

"Both," I say, knowing that can only mean one person.

"Shut the fuck up!" she says. "Is he here for his mom's funeral?"

"Yes. How do you know that? It's weird that you know that."

"The fandom is talking about it. Really tragic." I can picture her in her house, sitting on the couch, crossing her ankles, speaking on the matter with authority.

With her ebony hair and sea green eyes, we resemble each other only distantly, like vases made by the same potter from different clay. We looked more alike when we were younger. We *were* more alike when we were younger.

"The fandom is talking about his mother's funeral?" I ask.

There's a lot about this that unsettles me—that my sister is connected to Austin's fandom in any way, much less well enough to know what "the talk" there is, and that "the talk" includes something so personal as Austin's mother's funeral.

"Yeah," she says, leaving off the "duh," though it's there in spirit. "She died of breast cancer. There's a fundraiser for breast cancer research in her name."

"Who's hosting it?" I would go if it's in Chicago. I support breast cancer research.

"I don't know. Someone in the group. It's just a donation in her name to the American Breast Cancer Society."

"What's the group?" Does she mean Instagram? I don't understand any of this.

"On Facebook. It's Austin's Lewnatics." She spells it—clever. I pull the phone away from my ear and open Facebook as we talk. The 'Austin's Lewnatics' page has eight thousand members, but it's a private group. You have to send a request to join. I don't do that. I'm not a Lewnatic. But apparently Margot is.

"Did he remember you?" Margot asks after I've been quiet for a while.

"Not at first."

She grows silent, and I worry that we've been disconnected, but the phone keeps counting the seconds.

"Is this you?" she asks. The photograph from Starbucks pops up in a text. On the edge, I see one of my shoulders, my leather messenger bag, and the very edge of the profile of my face.

"Yep," I say. "That's me."

She's quiet for a beat, then explodes into my ear. "Did he follow you?"

"Yes, at lunch."

"You went to lunch with Austin Lewis?" She's basically started shouting. "Babs! He's liked a bunch of your posts."

I pull the phone away and open Instagram. Sure enough, I have four "likes" in my notifications all from @AustinLewis. He's "liked" a picture of me running by the lake and a picture of me from my law school graduation. He's also "liked" my *Super Lawyers* profile from a few years ago—probably won't be featured in that periodical again any time soon.

The final picture he's "liked" is of me at the lake house in Michigan. I'm sitting on the deck, drinking coffee first thing in the morning, right after a run. I'm sweaty, strands of dark blonde hair plastered to the sides of my face. Ryan took it. I didn't know anyone else was awake. I walked into the house after that first cup of coffee to take a shower and found Ryan enthusiastically waiting to join me. I'd assume @AustinLewis doesn't know that, or he wouldn't have liked that specific picture.

"Babs, are you there?"

I put the phone back to my ear.

"Are you—are you dating Austin Lewis?" she asks, like she's a little afraid of the question.

"No," I say decisively. "We went out to lunch yesterday, and he texted me this morning about going to a Cubs game today. But I haven't replied."

A part of me hopes she'll respond the way she did all those years ago: scream and yell and make it clear that if I go with him, it will be a personal betrayal of our sisterhood. It would simplify things. But she doesn't tell me not to go.

Instead, she offers an "Uh-huh" as if she thinks I'm lying to her about not dating Austin, as if I've been holding out on her.

"Margot," I say. "I'm not lying to you."

"I just think it's weird," she says. She has that tone. She doesn't think it's weird; she thinks I'm a liar. "You know. There are a billion Starbucks in the city of Chicago, and he just happens to be at the one across from your firm at the precise moment you just happen to be getting coffee."

Apparently, the intimation is that Austin and I have been dating for months, arranged to meet each other at Starbucks, and just now decided to fill her in. Or something. I don't know what she's after.

"His mother's attorneys are in the same building as my firm. Old firm. He had a meeting about her estate." I try to sound casual, like I might be talking about one of my own clients.

Margot doesn't say anything for a couple of seconds. Then she mumbles, "Well, I guess there are worse ways you could spend your first day of unemployment than at a Cubs game."

The nonchalance catches me off guard. "Wait. Do you—do you think I should go?"

"I have no idea what you should do, Babs," she says. "The whole thing is weird as hell. When does he go back to L.A.?"

"He didn't say."

She pauses. Then, "Think you'll sleep with him again?"

Fucking shameless, my sister.

"Probably not at the Cubs game. The seats are pretty small at Wrigley."

"Hey, are we visiting Mom this week?"

"Wait! What should I do?" The rapid-fire change in topics has me spinning.

"What do you mean, *what should you do*? You haven't had sex in three years. This is perfect. Go to the Cubs game. Fuck Austin Lewis. Get back on that train, Babs."

"I don't want to sleep with him. I'm not looking for all that."

"All what?"

"A relationship."

"Yeah. I don't think that's what you'd be getting. I'm pretty sure that'd be a no-strings-attached kind of arrangement."

"What's that mean?"

"You haven't been following his life at all, have you?" There's the razor's edge of condemnation there.

"I guess not. I follow him on Instagram. Honestly, I'm kind of surprised *you're* so well informed."

"Eh." I can almost hear her shrugging through the phone. "It's been deeply satisfying watching his fall from Hollywood grace."

"Jesus, Margot."

"What?"

I have no idea *what*. I think about reminding her that his mother just died, but instead I just say, "I'm going to go with him."

"Sounds good," she says, like she's just received an update from a repair man who's twenty minutes out. "Let me know how it goes."

"Really?" I ask.

"Sure."

I arrange for the parents of one of Penny's friends to bring her and Colin home from school. Then, I DM Austin my address. Within seconds, he gives me his cell number in case I need to reach him. I give him mine, then go upstairs to change clothes.

four

1997

"There's a boy on the phone for you, Barbara," Aunt Iris said with her hand over the receiver. The sly look she wore told me my secret was safe with her.

I assumed it was Ryan calling me out of earshot of his mother—not exactly a secret that I had a boyfriend—but I waited for Aunt Iris to leave the room before saying hello.

"Hi. Babs?" The voice wasn't Ryan's.

"Yes?"

"It's Austin."

It didn't escape me that this could have been a prank—Margot and her friends getting even with me for embarrassing her the day before at the meet-and-greet. But then he added, "Lewis?" As if maybe I knew more than one Austin, which we'd established the day before, I did not.

"Hi," I said, recovering myself.

"Listen, I wondered if you wanted to go hiking with me today. I don't know if you have something else planned with your family. It's fine if you do." He sounded nervous, which I found strangely reassuring. The tension in his voice soothed the tension in my body as I tried to make sense of his invitation.

I remember thinking, *Is he asking me out?* And just as quickly dismissing it. *No, this is a hook-up.*

Even so, the invitation was flattering. I wasn't a fan—of him or his show—but the invitation, whether date or hook-up, was flattering. He must have had to ask someone to track down Uncle Leo's phone number. There'd been effort involved in that phone call.

"Hello?" he said into the low hum of the receiver.

"Um… No, I don't have anything planned. But I don't have any clothes for hiking." I'd brought clothes for the beach, thinking that was what people did in Los Angeles before learning that the beach in July was "hot" and thus, we weren't going there.

"It's trail-hiking. Shorts and tennis shoes will work."

"Oh. I have that." I glanced down at my Umbros. It seemed I was already dressed for hiking. "My sister? She was there yesterday, too."

"Oh. Um. I was thinking—I thought just you and me. I mean, if you're okay with that."

"Oh," I said.

"Tom—my assistant—will pick you up at ten."

I hadn't quite said yes, but I sensed I'd nevertheless agreed, and the mention of his assistant added to my curiosity. *How does something like this work?*

I still thought this might have been Margot's doing—not Austin at all. So, when I got off the phone, I walked upstairs to her room and knocked on the door.

"Come in," she answered.

Inside the room, she lay on her back reading *Cosmo*, no obvious signs she'd been up to anything sinister.

"What?" she asked when I didn't say anything.

"I just wanted to see what you were doing," I said.

"I'm not doing anything because there's nothing to do here. The TVs in our rooms don't have cable, and Uncle Leo's watching golf in the family room."

"Right," I said. "Okay. Well." I closed the door and headed back downstairs to find Aunt Iris. Somehow, I knew that no matter how far into the wilderness I hiked, the most dangerous part of the day would be Margot finding out I was spending it with Austin Lewis.

"I can't go to the tar pits today," I explained to Aunt Iris. "I'm getting together with some friends." I'd counted Tom.

"I didn't know you had friends here, Barbara," Aunt Iris sang.

Neither did I, I thought.

"Why didn't you say something? We could have had them over." She looked up from her crossword. *The New York Times.* Saturday. She'd be busy for a while.

"I just got ahold of them. That was them calling," I said, which was sort of true.

"Is Margot going with you?"

"No," I said, feeling more than a little guilty about that.

"Okay, well. Just the three of us, then."

I think she liked the idea of my friends picking me up from her house, the way friends would have picked up their kids if they'd had any. She would have been a mom whose kids had lots of friends.

A black Jeep Cherokee pulled into the driveway at ten on the dot, and a man roughly my mom's age rang the bell.

"Miss Stewart?" he confirmed when I opened the door.

"That's me," I said. "Tom?" I wondered whether I should have called him Mr. *Something,* but I didn't know his last name, and he nodded in recognition, so "Tom" it was.

"Are you ready to go?" he asked neutrally.

I started through the door. "Hang on," I said, already turning back toward the stairs. "I forgot my wallet."

It seemed like if I were going to go on a date with a TV star, he would probably pay for everything, but I didn't want to presume. I sprinted up to my bedroom, grabbed my wallet from the top of the dresser, and headed back for the stairs just as Aunt Iris called from the kitchen.

"Are those your friends, Barbara? Have them come in and say hello."

"We're in a hurry," I called over the railing. "Want to get to the trail before it gets too hot." It seemed like a concern she might sympathize with, and she must have because she didn't push the issue.

I wasn't so lucky with Margot. She could smell the scandal from her cotton candy bedroom.

"Where are you going?" she asked, stepping into the hall, her eyes focused on the wallet in my hand.

"I... uh... hiking," I said.

"Where? With who?"

"It's... I..." I couldn't think of a way to explain it, and I couldn't think of a lie that was believable. "I'm going hiking with Austin Lewis." I said both of his names again. It was becoming a habit.

"WHAT?" Margot roared. "I want to go!"

"You weren't invited," I said and started to move quickly for the front door.

I heard her feet behind me, then her voice. "What do you mean, I'm not invited? We both met him. Why are *you* invited?"

I made a beeline for the car, rushing across the lawn toward the Jeep. The last thing I heard before closing the rear passenger door behind me was Margot's voice from the walkway in front of the house.

"YOU BITCH!"

"Everything okay?" Austin asked.

"Jesus Christ!" I hadn't expected him to be in the car. I thought I'd be meeting him somewhere. A hiking trail, for example.

"Sorry, I didn't mean to startle you," he said. That smile again.

"Yes, everything's fine." I tried to sound convincing but saw his confusion as his eyes slid in the direction of my sister, crimson-faced, on the front step of the house.

Tom glanced in the rearview mirror before backing out of the driveway. Our eyes met briefly, and I wondered what he must have thought of me. But, if Margot's performance made an impression on him, he wasn't letting on.

We drove for a while in silence as I struggled to think of what to say, finally settling on, "Do you go hiking a lot?" I did wonder if he had an established *modus operandi* for these things.

"Yes. Usually alone though," he replied. "I like the quiet. Relaxes my mind." Innocent enough. Though I suppose he could have been acting. That was, apparently, a talent he had.

"Well, I guess I should thank you for making an exception and taking me."

We drove for a while, the conversation taking the form of a recitation of my first trip to California, why we were there, what we'd done.

Austin handed Tom a CD. I don't remember what. I wish I did because I think music can reveal a lot about a person, and I'm still not sure I completely understand what happened that day. Sometimes I think if I knew the soundtrack to the day, I'd understand it better. And other times I think, it was probably Barenaked Ladies or Dave Matthews Band, which said more about the time period than the people in that car.

I do remember the scent in the car—sunscreen, the cucumber-melon lotion on my legs, a hint of whatever aftershave or cologne he'd used, body-temperature cotton shirts. I could have rolled the windows down; the breeze would have been nice. But I liked the smell of the car.

five

Austin (I've practiced using only his first name) arrives at twelve-thirty sharp. Parks the car, comes to the door, rings the bell. All very first-date. We take the 'L' and arrive at Wrigley with time to spare. He guides me to our seats along the third baseline behind the dugout, placing a hand on the small of my back as I step into the aisle in front of him. I feel touch-starved at the gentle pressure, as if it's been years since anyone has touched me like this. Then I remember, it has been. Nearly three.

"I like your hat," I say as he settles it back on his head after The National Anthem.

His hat is worn, vintage-logo Cubs. He's also wearing sunglasses, and I assume these two accessories are intended to hide him from more than the sun. He glances at me skeptically, as if to gauge whether I might be making fun of him. I'm not; I just can't think of anything to say. My brain is foggy, but I do like his hat.

"Thanks," he says as he rests the sole of his shoe on the empty seat in front of him. "My sister got it for me a few years ago. Dared me to wear it to an Angels game."

"Is that your team?" I ask.

"No, the Cubs are my team." He lifts two fingers in the direction of a hotdog vendor. "I always try to catch them when they're in L.A."

When the vendor arrives at the end of our row, Austin passes a generous bill before I can reach for my pocketbook, then waves off the change and hands me a foil-wrapped hotdog.

"Thanks," I say. "Beers are on me."

We're quiet for a while, watching the game, and I will myself to relax and be present. I casually throw the sole of my own shoe up to the empty seat in front of me only to notice immediately that I've mirrored his posture. I drop my foot to the ground.

A plastic cup of cold beer moves into my field of vision as yet another bill is extended to a vendor in the aisle.

"I was going to..." I trail off as the crowd erupts in a cheer. A fly ball to right field becomes a double play when the runner on third tags up, but a laser throw to home gets him out.

Austin's misunderstood my expression and eyes the beer. "Do you want something different?" he asks after the crowd quiets.

"No." I take a sip, not wanting to seem ungrateful.

He takes a sip of his own, then uses his lower lip to pull the foam into his mouth. I instantly realize there's no way for me to eat this hotdog without the obvious metaphor announcing itself. I try to tear off a piece of it, like a baguette, but the casing won't give, and I have to take a much larger bite than I probably would have if I'd just eaten the thing like you're supposed to.

A napkin comes my way, and I take it from his hand. His eyes are on the field, on a put-out at first, but he saw enough to know I'd need a napkin.

I wipe my mouth and fingers and tuck the balled paper into the cupholder.

"Have you gotten back to Chicago much over the years?" I'm channeling my client-entertainment self, using the standard questions.

"Not really," he says.

"Not even to visit your mom?"

"She didn't really live here," he says. "She mostly lived in a condo down in Florida."

"Oh." I move on to my next question. "What's your favorite thing to do when you *are* here?"

He gazes at me, an odd expression passing over his face. "Are you small-talking me?" Half a smile ripples the side of his face closest to me.

"Small-talking?"

"Yeah. You know. Running through the talking points you use when you're in a conversation with a stranger. Or clients, probably, in your case." The other half of his face has joined the smile, and even though I know he's teasing me, something like affection grounds it.

"Maybe," I admit. "I didn't know there was a phrase for that."

"Smalltalk?"

"Small-talk*ing*."

He bumps a shoulder playfully into mine. "Why don't you ask me something you actually want to know."

Is this a date? What do you want from me? Are we going back to your place after this? How good is my memory? Was *that day* really *that good*? Do I have mustard on my face? How did you find a t-shirt that fits you so well it looks like you were the fit model for the company that made it?

"We talked for four hours straight yesterday. What questions could I possibly have left?" I say.

He tips his head back and laughs. "All secrets revealed," he says with another shoulder bump. He follows this up with a sip of beer and does the thing with his lip again.

"Okay," I say, feeling that I've been challenged, even if lightheartedly. "Do you like it? Do you like this? Your job? Or whatever it is that means you have to wear a hat and sunglasses to a baseball game?"

"Well," he says, seeming to give it real thought. "It's not really my current job that requires this. It's the job I had fifteen years ago, so it *is* kind of weird. Some of it's habit, I guess—for a while, even a hat and glasses wouldn't cut it. But I don't want some random person, like that woman at Starbucks, interrupting us. I just want to spend the afternoon with you. You know. Watching the Cubs lose to the Pirates." He pauses, waiting for me to say something, then adds, "And you're wearing a hat and sunglasses, too, which I definitely don't like because it's making it impossible for me to tell what you're thinking."

I take off my sunglasses and rest them on top of my hat, so he can see my eyes. It's bright, and I have to squint against the sun, but I see his eyes moving over my face behind the dark shadow of his own sunglasses.

Then he turns and smiles out onto the field and says, "I think we might actually win this thing."

"What are you going to do now that you're a free agent?" he asks on the way home. We loitered, waiting for traffic on the platform to thin out, but the train is still crowded. Austin and I stand in the very back, by the door that runs between cars.

"I don't know," I say honestly. "Maybe I'll go to more baseball games." I only had one beer, but I feel a little buzzed, and I watch the progression of a barely controlled curl of his lips.

"Do you think you'll try to find another firm?" he asks.

I have to note—I've given him the perfect opening to ask me out again, and he hasn't taken it. But he seems distracted, his attention divided by the people around us. Maybe he doesn't want to be overheard.

"Not right away," I reply. "I might plan a vacation for Penny and Colin and me for fall break. Maybe I'll do a marathon or something. I guess I could probably get some work done on the house. Redo the family room." I'm just listing off random shit; I have no idea what I'll do. I wasn't really working before (as Bruce and Mark so helpfully pointed out), so maybe it won't be all that different.

We reach the Fullerton stop and get off the train. I usually avoid this stop, but that's definitely not a conversation I want to have with Austin on the 'L', post-Cubs Win. We walk the rest of the way to my house, stopping when we reach the foot of the stairs to my front door.

"Thanks for coming with me to the game," he says.

"I had a nice time," I say.

He takes my hand and swings it gently between us. I glance down, trying to figure out whose momentum is doing the work. When I lift my gaze back to his face, his eyes aren't looking at mine; they're focused on my lips.

The hand-swinging stops.

"Would you let me kiss you?" he asks.

"Yes," I say simply, even though it doesn't feel simple.

He hesitates, as if he didn't expect that answer, and I find myself eyes half-closed, bobbing forward in anticipation of a kiss that doesn't arrive. I open my eyes, and he's frozen, staring at me. The only part of him moving is his thumb, which brushes across the back of my hand. I'm beginning to wonder whether

I'd said *yes* aloud, whether maybe I should say it again, when he lifts his hands to the sides of my neck, his fingers teasing at the loose strands of my hair. He leans forward, and his lips brush mine so softly, I think maybe his earlier hesitation was indecision. When he draws back, I feel a heaviness in my chest that I recognize as longing. Have I been longing for him? I don't want to think about that.

My arms have been hanging limp at my sides, but I bring them to his chest, resting my palms against the impossibly soft weave of his t-shirt. He blinks, and his head moves almost imperceptibly as if to shake something off—nerves (I flatter myself), second thoughts (more likely).

I feel a sudden need to tell him it's okay. It's okay if he thought he wanted to kiss me but has changed his mind. The game was nice. We had fun. It doesn't have to mean anything. We can still be friends.

I open my mouth. "We—" But I hardly get the word out before his lips are on mine again. The soles of his shoes scuff against the sidewalk, and he leans into me, his waist to my navel as I open my mouth beneath his, and his hands seem to pull me up to him, tilting my head so that he can have more of me. I wrap my arms around his back, and I can feel the strength of his body through his t-shirt.

It's daylight, early-evening. Seminary Avenue is a quiet street, but there are still pedestrians and neighbors. Not to mention, my two children in the house. When I told them I was going to a Cubs game with Mr. Lewis, Colin seemed mostly jealous that he'd be in school while I'd be at a baseball game. Penny, though, saw through it immediately.

"That man from California?" she asked.

"Yes."

"He hasn't gone back yet?"

"No."

She didn't ask any more questions, but I have a sudden image of her, hands cupped around her face, trying to see through the frosted glass of the front door. I pull away from Austin and glance behind me. No one's there.

Austin shakes his head again, that same nearly imperceptible movement.

"What?" I ask.

He takes a deep breath. "You did this to me last time," he says, still focused on my mouth instead of my eyes.

I feel defensive. "Did what?" I ask, my voice sharp.

"Made me want you so badly I thought I couldn't breathe."

Oh. That.

He kisses me again, just the suggestion of his teeth against my lips before his tongue follows lightly. I must have made a noise of some kind. I mean, I know I did, because he pulls back and finally brings his gaze to mine. I get one more brush of his lips before he drops his hands from my face, kisses my cheek, and whispers into my ear, "Have a nice evening, Babs."

Then he turns around, tucks his hands into his pockets, and strolls back to his car.

six

Bankers boxes are the single most depressing object made of cardboard. I understand this probably can't be objectively measured, but I'm confident I'm onto something. My confidence in my theory grows as I return to the lobby of the firm I used to work at to take the fourth such box to my car. They wouldn't even loan me the dolly.

Although my dramatic departure earlier in the week had the exact effect I was going for—Stacey, who works reception, told me Bruce and Mark waited in my office for another hour and a half after I walked out—eventually the firm accepted that I really wasn't coming back and packed up my belongings. Then they sent me an email directing me to pick everything up in the next twenty-four hours or the firm would dispose of it. My diplomas, a series of framed covers of *The New Yorker* depicting judges, my books, desk organizers, my toiletries drawer—all is being returned in the bruised, commercial-grade, off-white cardboard boxes that evoke despair and are ubiquitous to law firms.

"Thanks, Stacey," I say as I sign a form acknowledging

receipt of the contents of my office, the adornments of my career.

She takes the pen and paper back from me. "Good luck, Babs," she says a little sadly. We always got along.

I heft the last box up off the floor—the box that holds my toiletries. It's not very heavy and will make for a fairly easy walk to the parking garage.

It's just after rush hour and the sidewalks have thinned. People in a variety of patterns and colors of suits walk briskly, with purpose, their faces bent over their phones or their eyes fixed straight ahead, claiming the space around them with each step. I am no longer one of them—I know—but it's disconcerting that they seem also to know, and they move around me as if I'm a parking meter, a tree, a sewer grate. I feel the quick steps of someone coming up behind me and look over my shoulder prepared to move out of the way. No one is there.

At the parking garage, a man materializes out of nowhere to hold the door. I don't need the door held for me—I can balance the box on my forearm and open it with my other hand.

"Have a nice morning, ma'am," he says as if he works for whatever company owns the parking garage, as if he's employed to hold the doors open. He's homeless, probably sleeps in the lobby of the parking garage; I'm supposed to tip him, but my wallet is in my car.

"I don't have any cash," I say.

He lets go of the door, and it crashes closed behind me. The compression hinge is broken. I punch the button for the elevator and step on when it arrives. As I select the eighth floor and the doors begin to close, I think I see movement outside the elevator, a silhouette on the marred tile floor. I tilt my head to the side—maybe it's the man who held the door for me—but the elevator doors are just inches from closing, and I don't manage a hand between them to hold them open.

At the eighth floor, I step off with the unsettling feeling that I am both alone and not. I hear voices in the distance echoing off the concrete and steel. It's mid-morning, but the oil stains, closely-packed cars, and city dust make the garage feel like it exists in its own ever-evening time zone. I pull my keys from my pocket and slip them between my fingers—a repurposed Wolverine claw.

The feeling has returned, and I spin this time, trying to catch whoever it is. But no one is there, and the voices I'd heard earlier seem farther away.

My car is parked about thirty yards from the elevator, and my legs itch to run to it, throw open the door, and sequester myself safely inside. I recall my mother's sage advice when Margot and I were children: Running only worsens panic; breathe instead, and keep walking.

I arrive at my car and open the trunk, depositing the final box alongside its companions. I'm certain now. The white lids catch the shadow of a figure behind me. I wrap my fingers around the tire iron along the side of the trunk and spin around fully prepared to bludgeon to death whoever is standing behind me.

"Stop! It's me!" Mark drops to the ground. "Fucking hell, Babs. It's me."

"Mark. You asshole. You scared the shit out of me." I'm crying, though honestly, I might have started in the elevator.

"I'm sorry," he sputters, rising carefully from the ground.

"What the fuck are you doing?"

"I just wanted to make sure you're okay?"

"By sneaking up on me in a parking garage?"

"No. I followed you—"

"Clearly—"

"I didn't want anyone at the firm to see..." He trails off then concludes "...to see me talking to you." He drops his gaze, looking truly ashamed. As he should. "I wanted to make sure you're okay. Would you let me take you to lunch?"

I snort.

"What's funny?" he asks.

"Nothing. Also, it's 10:30 in the morning."

"Coffee then?"

"I thought you didn't want to be seen with me."

"We could walk a few blocks east," he says as though it's a courtesy to me.

Despite it all, I agree, and we head to a coffee shop on Michigan Ave. We order and sit at a table across from each other in a corner of the café.

"How are you holding up?" he asks.

"I'm fine," I say.

"Really?"

"I don't know what you want me to say. Am I glad I was fired? No. And in any case, it would have been nice if you hadn't been the one doing the firing."

"I really wasn't," he says.

I roll my eyes. "My mistake. I could have sworn you were there."

"No. I mean, it wasn't my decision—either that you would be fired or that I'd be one of the equity partners to do it."

"It doesn't matter." I shake my head. My eyes shift to the wall beside us where an intricate wallpaper depicts a complicated geometric pattern of intersecting squares and triangles.

"It matters to me, Babs. *You* matter to me," he says.

So we're doing this again. I regret agreeing to coffee. He reaches across the table for my hand, but I pull it into my lap, and he looks at me disapprovingly.

"Look, Mark, I don't know what you're after," I do, actually; he's been after it for a while and almost got it once, "but whatever it is, you should look for it somewhere else."

"I'm not after anything. I just want to make sure you're okay. The way you left the other day—I was worried. You looked like you didn't even really grasp what had happened."

"I grasped it perfectly. My husband died, I stopped doing my job, I lost my biggest client, and I was fired."

"He died three years ago, Babs," Mark says, his gentle voice masking those violent words.

"Is that long enough? Do you think? In your estimation? That's enough time?"

"Stop. That's not what I mean."

He means that it would be helpful (from his perspective) if I could move on, so that he could move in. But it wouldn't matter whether I moved on or not. Mark's and my history amounts to one very brief exercise of poor judgment more than ten years ago. Well, it was once for me; I understand from Stacey that he's made a bit of a habit of it with the associates.

"What are you planning to do now?" he asks. "Will you go to another firm, do you think?"

"How am I going to do that? I'm a forty-six-year-old income partner with no book of business."

He takes a sip of his coffee, then pushes it to the side.

"I'll look for something in-house," I say reluctantly.

It's an empty promise, and the way Mark presses his lips together confirms he knows that.

"Listen," I say, expanding into some of the freedom that comes with being released from the law-firm-imposed hierarchy. "You don't need to worry about me. I'm going to be fine. I mean, if nothing else, I'm fucking loaded now. So, at least there's that."

"God, that's dark, Babs. Even for you," he says.

It's dark, but it's also true. I have a lot of worries at the moment, but money isn't among them. I take a long sip of my coffee. It's cooled since we sat down.

"Will you let me check in on you? Make sure you're okay?" he asks.

"I'd rather you didn't," I say. "And there's no reason for you to."

He flinches, wounded, but recovers. "Come on," he says. "I'll walk you back to your car."

On the Eisenhower, on the way to pick up Margot to visit our mother, I remember a short story by Richard Selzer that I read once in college about a little boy whose father dies. For a year after the death, the boy keeps thinking he sees his father on the street. He recognizes him by his fedora. But it's never actually his father; it's some other man in a fedora.

It escalates to the point that a police officer stops the boy for following a man and delivers him to his home, where his mother scolds him. The police officer says he thought the boy might be a pick-pocket "or worse." The reader is supposed to understand that "worse" is "crazy"—the police officer thought the boy might be crazy.

In the story, it all stops after a year, and the boy is both relieved and devastated.

I remember being twenty and thinking, "I'd just be relieved." I didn't really get it.

My professor got it, and she tried to explain it, but the only loss I'd known by that point was my father, and I wasn't exactly destroyed when he left. It was more disruptive than devastating.

I understand it now. It's the feeling I got while walking to the parking garage. The movement I saw from the corner of my eye as the doors of the elevator closed. The shadow on the tops of the boxes in my trunk. I'd hoped it was Ryan, but knew it couldn't be, so knew I was either in danger or worse. Turned out it was Mark, which is sort of worse.

I remember in law school, too—those years that Ryan and I weren't together—being so absolutely certain that he was just around the corner, in a bar, at a concert, in the library. But he never was. Well, until he literally was that night on my doorstep. Maybe that's why it was so easy for us to fall back in love with each other.

It just felt like he'd always been there.

"Are you okay?" Margot asks as she steps into the car.

"Yeah. Run-in with Mark."

"Dick." I'm not sure she's used any other word to describe him in more than ten years.

"How was the game?" she asks.

"It wasn't what I expected."

"Did you..." I can't see her with my eyes focused on the road, but I think she may have done the suggestive eyebrow-raise.

"No." I lift my fingers to my lips with the memory of his kiss as if some part of it can be felt tactilely, still.

"You want to expound on that?" she asks.

I take a half-second glance at her and put my hand back on the wheel. "It was a date." I attempt to explain it. The formality —he picked me up—the train, the privacy, the conversation. The kiss.

We're silent for a few minutes as I accelerate along the entrance ramp back onto the Eisenhower toward Wheaton.

Margot breaks the silence. "What did he say? 'I remember this from last time'?"

"No. 'You did this to me last time.'"

"Did he sound mad?" she asks.

"No. He sounded... maybe a little sad?" I realize I don't know him very well. Not at all, really.

"Are you going to see him again?"

"No, I don't think so. He hasn't texted."

"He's probably headed back to L.A.," Margot says. "And I'm pretty sure he's already seeing someone. Or lots of someones—that's been his general M.O. For. Years."

"Do you mind if we talk about something else?"

"Not at all," she says. But we don't talk about anything else. We ride the rest of the way to the nursing home in a thick fog of silence that doesn't relent until we reach the threshold of our mother's room.

I clear my throat as we both step into the room, and our mother turns in her chair. Her eyes scan over us as if she is looking at something and nothing all at once.

"Cindy, your daughters are here," says the nurse aid who accompanied us.

A smile breaks across our mother's face, but it's the ghost of a smile, an apparition of emotion, not the thing itself. "Come on in," she says. My spirits rise for a moment, then fall as our mother adds, "Margot. Not the other one."

"I'll wait in the lobby," I say.

Margot leans into me. "Stay," she whispers. "What does it matter?"

"That's okay. Text me when you're ready to leave." She doesn't really recognize either of us, hasn't for a couple years now, but it still feels like I'm disobeying her by staying. And there's always the risk she'll have a moment of lucidity in the middle of the visit. It's happened before; she remembers not just that she doesn't want to see me, but why.

"Okay," Margot says, stepping into the room as I walk wordlessly down the hall and continue out through the security doors to the lobby beyond.

seven

1997

It was Spring semester, just after our return from winter break. I was a sophomore; Ryan was a junior. I was working some Clinton-era work-study job at the Reference Desk of the university library, making $4.75 an hour. My responsibilities included opening all the mail, then filing anything that required filing. That meant taking all the Congressional Reports, the Standard & Poor's, the Federal Registers, all of those things to the specific three-ring binder to which they belonged and filing them.

I was terrible at it.

Since my practice schedule had me busy twenty hours a week and my classes had me busy another seventeen, I needed the work-study job to be exponentially more *study* than *work*. So a lot of what I did was my homework, which is exactly what I was doing when Ryan came up to the desk and asked me if I could direct him to the MCAT test prep books. Circulation told him the library kept them at Reference.

"Going to medical school?" I asked, glancing up from my used Norton's where I was reading Howells's *Editha*. It had been annotated by its previous owner, who, by the looks of it, had not done well in the course. This left me to erase his (a distinctly male script) markings as I read. Unnotating.

"I hope so," he said with a friendly smile.

We kept the MCAT, GRE, and LSAT test prep books behind the Reference counter because students kept stealing them. I imagine that a lot of students took the actual prep *courses*, but the courses were expensive, so those of us who didn't have thousands of dollars for prep courses had the books. And in order to get good at the tests, you needed a lot of time with the books. Which explained why they kept getting stolen. Until the previous semester when the librarians decided they should be kept behind the Reference Desk. That Ryan needed the library's copy of the MCAT test prep book told me we had similar points of origin.

"You can't leave this area with the book," I said.

"I know. Circulation told me," he said pleasantly. Much more pleasantly than I'd issued my directive.

"What are you reading?" he asked.

I showed him the cover of the anthology.

"Why are you erasing the annotations?"

"Because they're wrong."

He nodded and knocked on the counter, signifying the end of the conversation, but it echoed impressively throughout the quiet atrium. He winced, apologized, then took the book to one of the study carrels against the wall and began reading. As in, he opened to the first page of the MCAT test prep book and just started reading. Two hours later, he returned the book to me, said thank you, and left.

He didn't come back the next night, but he came back the night after that.

"MCAT book?" I asked.

"Please," he said.

I began to identify a pattern. Mondays and Wednesdays. After dinner. 7:00-9:00 p.m. MCAT test prep. It got so I knew to have the book ready for him. I'd be doing my homework, he'd come in, I'd hand him the book, sometimes without even looking up. Sometimes, though, I'd see him coming through the front doors toward the back of the atrium. Lanky. He was lanky then. He filled out later. But back then, he was tall and almost too thin. University cafeterias in the '90s weren't *a la carte*; you paid for a meal, not each individual item. So, there was really no explanation for his apparently not getting enough to eat.

He had dark brown hair that he didn't cut regularly, and as the semester wore on, it grew out in large soft waves. Curls really. Sometimes he tucked the mess under a baseball cap; other times it hung loose, and he would try to coax it back with his fingers while he read. Truly, it was sexy as hell when he got frustrated with it, and one hand would be woven through his hair, holding back that mop on his head while he read that goddamn book.

He wore glasses, so I didn't notice his eyes the first few times he came in, but one evening he walked up to the desk, asking if I could print something off the computer. I wasn't supposed to do that, but we were old friends by then. As he handed me the CD that accompanied the book and showed me which file to print, I noticed that he had gold flecks in his blue eyes. Gold flecks. Like a splash of whiskey in the ocean.

The Monday after we returned from spring break, he came in, and I had the book ready, but he didn't take it. Instead, he set a small plastic egg on the counter.

"What's this?" I asked.

"Look inside."

I did and found it filled with Jelly-Belly jellybeans.

"Happy equinox," he said, grinning.

"What?" It was kind of a strange thing to celebrate, though he didn't know then whether I celebrated Easter.

"What time are you off?" he asked.

"Nine."

"Meet you out front? We can get ice cream at Manny's."

I looked from the equinox egg to the whiskey-ocean-eyes in front of me. "What's your name?" I asked.

"Ryan. Ryan Aganon."

"I'm Babs Stewart," I said.

His gaze dropped to the name tag pinned to my shirt.

"Right," I said. "Nine?"

"Are you free?"

"I am," I said. And that was that.

After we were married, I loved reminiscing about those early days when we were just getting to know each other. Ryan told me that his heart was pounding so loudly in his chest when he handed me that candy, he worried it would, like the knocking on the countertop, echo out into the atrium.

We only got about six weeks together before the school year ended, but we made the most of it. The first night we had sex, which was the first night he'd ever had sex, I put him inside me and watched him beneath me, gazing up, his breath ragged with effort. I suppose he was old not to have dispensed with his virginity, but he didn't seem embarrassed, mostly just grateful.

When we returned to school the next fall, we didn't talk about what had happened in California, how I now wanted him to circle the tip of his tongue just so and direct his fingers just so and hold his rhythm just so. He never asked, he just did it, then commented almost sweetly, "I like that I can make you feel like that."

After we'd been back on campus for a week or so in the fall, and gotten *reacquainted,* he asked, "Is all this going to be okay?"

I thought he might have been asking then, what had

happened out in California, or maybe he wanted to know if I was on birth control (a little late to be asking, but of course I was). But I think what he actually meant was something more like, "Will we love each other forever?"

So, when I said, "We're good," it covered a lot of bases.

Grad school was the real test of it. Ryan was accepted to Duke for medical school while I still had one more year of undergrad. I'd done well on the LSAT—thanks to the LSAT test prep book kept safe behind the Reference Desk—and applied to Duke as well as the other law schools in the research triangle. I got into all of them. But a Northwestern scholarship made tuition there not much more than a song.

Ryan begged me not to take it, said we'd be making so much money when we graduated, we didn't need to worry about student loans. Just take them out and pay them back later.

I said—and I'm not sure it was entirely untrue, though it was a mistake to say it—that he was thinking only with his dick and not about what was good for me. And that was the only time he ever hinted that he knew something had happened in California.

He said, "I don't do that. I don't think with my dick. You must have my dick confused with someone else's."

We broke up. It was a real break up, not that "on a break" nonsense everyone joked about in the '90s. We sat down over spring break during my senior year of college as I was preparing to accept the scholarship-funded admission to Northwestern and agreed that we should go our separate ways. Mostly because it seemed like we already were. His first year of medical school had been the hardest thing he'd ever done in his life and, if the rumors proved true, my first year of law school would be equally hard. We'd have no time to visit each other and no money for it anyway. It seemed untenable.

A couple years later he showed up out of the blue at the

apartment I shared with three other law students, toting a small plastic Christmas tree full of Jelly-Belly's. He was in town for interviews for residency. He wondered if I wanted to grab dinner. He wondered if I was seeing anyone. He wondered if I sometimes thought about him. He sometimes thought about me.

Based on the rest of that night together, it really did seem like he'd been using his dick rather prolifically in North Carolina, but he'd also learned some things. So had I, for that matter—like that I could go months without seeing Ryan, but not months without talking to him. I needed him in my life.

Ryan matched for residency at the University of Chicago, and I started working for Daniels & Shay. We moved in together a year later and married a year after that.

Happily ever after.

Almost.

eight

PENNY AND COLIN HAVE FINISHED DINNER AND DISAPPEARED INTO THE nether-realms of their respective bedrooms. I busy myself removing the boxes from my car and am placing them on the same putty-colored metal shelves that hold the box of Ryan's belongings from the accident when my phone buzzes.

Austin: Are you free this weekend?

I tuck my phone back in my pocket without responding, but it buzzes again. Determined to settle the matter with an "It's just too complicated," I pull my phone out, but it's not Austin.

Margot: Sorry about Mom.

Me: Not your fault.

Margot: Kind of my fault. When you think about it.

Me: Not your fault!

The phone rings, and I answer it as I walk out of the laundry room and collapse onto the sofa in the family room.

"She doesn't even know what she's saying anymore," Margot says. "Halfway through her conversation with me, she started calling me Nancy."

"Who's Nancy?"

"No idea. A neighbor from when she was a kid? She started talking about paper dolls."

"I'm fine, Margot. Really. You don't have do this." I toss my feet up on the coffee table and accidentally kick a stack of magazines off the far end. "Shit," I mumble.

Margot misinterprets my swearing. "It was a hard visit."

"They're all hard," I say.

Our mother rarely recognizes either of us and can't remember my name, even though she apparently remembers Nancy. But she still knows why she's mad at me after nearly thirty years, and it's hard not to take that personally.

"Rishi just got home," Margot announces. "Do you want to talk to him?"

In the background, I hear him—*Is that Babs? Tell her I said hi.*

"Maybe another time. It's been a long day," I say. It's been a long week.

"Okay," Margot says, but I can feel her holding her breath on the other end.

"What?" I ask.

"Have you talked to Kelly about... everything?" she asks. I suppose it's an apt description. The week has brought quite a range. And Kelly was my work bestie for years—same age, both hired right out of law school. She was Bruce's associate; I was Mark's.

After Ryan died, there was a period of time when I was almost claustrophobic from how clingy she was—Mark, too, and parents of Penny and Colin's friends. Even Margot seemed afraid to leave me alone for too long. But grief eventually repels mere bystanders. As if they're afraid tragedy is contagious, they wash their hands, don their masks, and keep their distance. I can't pinpoint the exact moment that marked the end of Kelly's and my friendship, but it occurred well before she watched me carry my messenger bag and desk photo out of the firm without so much as offering a goodbye.

"I haven't talked to her in a while," I say, not elaborating on why.

Margot takes a contemplative breath and blows it out slowly.

The silence stretches until I break it. "Brunch Sunday?"

"Okay. See you then," she says, her words a surrender that ends the call.

I rise from the couch and meander back upstairs to my office. It's immaculate because I never use it. I *have* never used it. Ryan used it. But even he didn't use it that often. It exists because people who live in a single-family home in Lincoln Park have home offices. I sit down at the computer and wiggle the mouse. Nothing happens. It's been that long.

I press the power button and enter the password, and the screen lights up, assaulting me with a wallpaper background of Ryan, Penny, Colin, and me at Universal Studios four years ago—our last family vacation. The image is enough to siphon all the air from the room, and when I finally remember to breathe, I exhale like the air from my lungs tripped up the stairs of my throat.

I force back feelings of guilt, open the browser, and expand the window until it obscures the image of Ryan. Then, I search Wikipedia for "Austin Lewis." The Wiki picture is from 2006, but the entry runs longer than I thought it would. Longer than his highlight reel at lunch suggested.

Austin worked after *The Maple Street Martins*. He played the love interest of one of the supporting characters in a short-lived drama on Showtime. Not a huge part, but a recurring role from 2000-2002. The entry notes his trouble getting parts and details the smaller roles he'd mentioned, but doesn't end when he turned forty like his career just died, which is what he made it sound like happened. After the roles stopped coming in, he focused on producing and, according to Wikipedia, is understood to have a good eye for good television.

He began by purchasing the rights to *The Maple Street Martins* a few years after it was canceled when it was undervalued. He's since solely controlled the rights and syndication of the show. That's unusual for an actor but is seen as one of the reasons the show continues to have appeal.

I admit to myself that I wasn't aware the show still had appeal.

In his initial negotiations of royalties for himself and his fellow cast members, "Lewis seemed to have anticipated the power of the emerging world of streaming and ensured a lifetime of financial security for all six cast members." They forgot baby Penny. I can understand why. After purchasing the show, he carefully controlled use of the content, "thereby ensuring the show neither slipped into obscurity nor became one of the many clichéd examples of 'adolescent dramas' from the 1990s."

Since then, "Lewis has been obsessive" (Wiki's word, not mine) with distribution, shunting people who want to see it onto a platform he alone controls, driving up its value, as well as its demand. People want it, and there aren't many options for getting it, so they have no choice but to pay top dollar.

I read the section on his personal life. Short. Shorter than his professional life. He's estranged from his father who'd been his manager when he was with KidZone, Inc. His parents divorced because of a dispute over who should manage his career. His mom died of breast cancer two weeks ago and Wiki links her obituary. He's also been married, which feels like something he should have mentioned by now. The marriage only lasted two years, though, so maybe he doesn't think it's worth bringing up or thought I'd already know. It also feels like something Margot would have known, but for some reason didn't mention.

His ex-wife was a model, but when I click on her name, her Wiki page amounts to little over two paragraphs, and none of it interests me. Her "years active" are 1995-2008. I can't even find a clear picture of her, but Wiki says she's still alive.

"Hey, Mom."

I glance up from the computer to see Penny standing in the doorway of the office. It almost takes my breath away, her standing there, her brown hair holding the same soft curls her father's did.

"What's wrong?" she asks.

My expression must have revealed the pain I always feel when I look at our children, now—both of them, just the spitting image of Ryan right down to the small flecks of amber in Colin's eyes.

"Nothing," I say quickly.

Nothing can ever be wrong again. At the ages of twelve and nine, both of my children experienced a kind of *wrong* no child should have to experience. I feel the constant weight of that responsibility. The answer to the question "What's wrong" for the rest of their childhoods has to be "nothing."

"What are you doing in Dad's office?"

"I was just looking something up real quick," I say.

"Do you not have a browser on your phone?" she asks. Her voice conveys judgment and condemnation, which I much prefer to the worry that marked her words when she asked what was wrong.

"It's hard to read the text on my phone. It's too small. Did you need something?"

"Yeah. Esti invited me over tomorrow. Can I go?"

"Sure. What time?" I ask.

"After the cross-country meet."

"Oh. Right. Yes." Shit. I had completely forgotten.

"Did you forget my meet?" Her eyebrows shoot up with an expression that dares me to admit this unforgivable lapse.

"No," I lie and quickly move on. "Overnight or just for the day?"

"Just for the day," Penny says. "To watch *The Last of Us*."

"The whole thing?" How many hours of television would that be?

"I don't know. A few episodes, I guess."

"Oh." I get the sense this is all very obvious to her, and despite the fact I am clearly saying *yes,* I have still managed to underwhelm her with my failure to fully understand what I'm saying yes to. Probably also for forgetting about her cross-country meet—a transgression for which I actually do feel bad.

"Do I pick up after, or are they dropping you off?"

"Can I just text you? It probably depends." She doesn't say what it depends on, but it's not like I have plans for Saturday.

"Sounds good," I agree.

She stands in the doorway a moment longer, watching as I close the browser on the computer. "Do you need me to show you how to use the browser on your phone?" she asks.

"I know how to use the browser on my phone," I say, unsure whether the question is rhetorical.

"Do you need me to show you how to enlarge text on your phone?" There's an edge now.

"No."

"Okay," she says as she rolls off the doorframe, thrusting

her hand back toward me and miming the index finger and thumb movements that expand images on a touchscreen.

"Thank you, Penny," I call after her as she recedes into the hallway. "I appreciate your offer to help. I know it comes from a place of love."

A second set of footsteps follow, and before I can exit the office, Colin appears in the hallway.

"Is everything okay?" he asks. "I thought I heard yelling."

"Everything's fine, sweetie. Do you want to have a friend over on Saturday? Penny's going to Esti's."

By the time I turn out the light and close the doors of Ryan's office, my thoughts of Margot and my mother, Kelly and Austin have been cleared from my mind like so many dirty dishes after dinner. I need the mental space for more immediate concerns, like making arrangements for shuttling kids to and from friends' houses and ensuring that Penny's uniform is washed and dried so that she has it for the meet I very nearly forgot.

Grief has a witching hour. The night stretches out one minute at a time, teasing me with a distance from both sleep and morning that is nearly intolerable.

This doesn't happen to me very often anymore. Or it happens less than it did in the months after Ryan died. In those first few months, I would find myself as I do tonight, listening to the 'L' in the distance, trying to guess the hour by the interval at which its familiar clattering breached the night. In the morning, I would awaken on the floor of my closet, my head beneath the rows of Ryan's dress shirts. After a year, I boxed up his clothes and gave them to Goodwill. I don't know whether it was a coincidence, but after I emptied the closet, I stopped waking up in it.

Now, I just lie in bed until it's time for my run.

The train is due, and I start counting to see how many minutes, divided into seconds, it takes for it to arrive. I've bet myself that it's three hundred seconds, which I will count as ten sets of thirty. I have a pretty good sense of time from all of the interval training I did in college. Lawyers also have a good sense of time, but it doesn't help one count the intervals between trains in the middle of the night.

I flop onto my back, staring up at the ceiling, waiting. I'm on my fourth set of ten. I think. It might be my fifth. I'm repeating numbers.

Ten, nine, eight, seven, seven, three, five.

I'm jolted from sleep by a glass bottle breaking, and fucking hell if it doesn't sound like it broke against the side of my house. I climb out of bed and grab the baseball bat next to it. I used to sleep with it when Ryan was on call, but now I sleep with it every night. I carry it over my shoulder down the stairs. I don't want to wake Penny and Colin and frighten them. The streetlights leak through the vestibule into the front hall as I round the bottom of the staircase, casting a shadow as I slip through the living room, through the dining room, and into the kitchen. I hear what I think is the clap of the gate on the privacy fence that surrounds my backyard. I raise my elbow, lifting the bat just off my shoulder.

I'm wearing neither my contacts nor my glasses, which mattered less in the dark, but I want to see through the glass doors out to the patio, and all I can make out is the green of the grass against a tan fence so blurry it almost appears to be melting. The streetlights splice the night as if invisible fingers have pulled the beam apart, stretching it into both sky and earth.

"Fuck me," I whisper into the glass doors.

I squint, trying to force some definition on the slats of the fence. The gate should be locked from the inside, with nothing to grasp from the back. In addition to being locked, it should be impossible to see from the alley which part of the fence *is* the gate, though a minimally proficient criminal could probably guess it's close to the garage, which is exactly where it is.

I jog quickly upstairs and grab my glasses, then, still trying to be as quiet as possible, jog back into the kitchen, pause the alarm system, and journey into the backyard. I check the gate. Closed and locked. I open it and scan the alley in both directions. Brown shards of glass lie scattered to the side of the dumpster but no signs of life. In the distance, the 'L' rattles out of the Fullerton stop. I've lost track of time.

I lock the gate and return to the house, then arm the alarm and call the police. We engage in a brief game of semantics about whether I'm reporting "an intruder" or "a noise in the alley", and they promise to send a car around. I go to bed and listen for the 'L', counting the seconds, hoping for sleep and eventually finding it.

The landline rings, awakening me to the navy-blue hue of earliest, late-summer dawn. Nearly time for my run.

I reach for the phone. "Hello?"

Silence.

"Hello?"

Air moves between receivers.

"Mom?"

This happens sometimes. My mother calls—only me, never Margot—but can't remember who she called or why.

"Mom, is that you?"

There's no answer, so I hang up.

Pennies in the payphone. God, that was a long time ago.

nine

Margot's suggestion that I consult Kelly burrowed into my head like a beetle in the sand, until I finally acknowledged what Margot had actually said: I need friends.

I'd consider joining a running group, but I don't like to talk while I run. I like music and my thoughts while I run. A book club would be good—I love to read—but those seem to exist among already-formed groups of friends. Mom groups tend to skew young, and I know if I attempted to reconnect with my lawyer friends, it would only further highlight how unrecognizable my life has become since Ryan died.

I need a Tinder but for friendships. Friender, or something.

> Forty-six-year-old, newly unemployed, former workaholic widow seeks female friendship to discuss books, children, and the prospects of dating the former teen heartthrob she slept with once in college.

Jesus. I'd swipe myself left.

A different idea came to me after reflecting on the interaction I'd had with the homeless man at the parking garage last week—the tip he sought for holding the door open and my response that I don't carry cash. I thought about the disadvantage that an increasingly digital world must have on those who count out their livelihoods in coins. Those begging for change generally don't take Apple Pay.

So today, I find myself at The Basilica of St. Vincent DePaul, two blocks from my house, trying to locate a man named David, who Fr. Martin told me over the phone runs their soup kitchen on Wednesdays. They call it a "food pantry"; they don't serve soup.

David is easy enough to locate in the annex to the side of the nave, but as he gives me a tour, my hopes for new friendships diminish. I'd anticipated—strategized really—that volunteers at this church on a weekday morning would: (1) live in the surrounding neighborhood, (2) be predominantly women, and (3) probably not have young children at home, so be roughly my age. David appears roughly my age, but that's the only of my criteria he satisfies.

He shows me around the pantry—three spaces: a cafeteria with tables, a kitchen, and between the two, a serving counter with a long window through which food is passed. At the serving counter, he specifies the three stations: sandwiches, dessert, drinks. One person works each, he explains. He has just the hint of an accent, but I can't place it.

"We get our desserts from the grocery store down the street," he says, gesturing toward a countertop where plastic containers of pineapple upside down cake, white cake with pink frosting, and angel food cake line up like the last kids chosen for some confectionary kickball team. "They're expired —or close to it. Sometimes, we get a chocolate cake. Our patrons can choose which dessert they want, but they can't have two. Everyone would choose two desserts, and we'd run out."

I nod in what I hope conveys studious comprehension but is actually deepening disillusionment.

He next indicates three cardboard boxes under the food counter, each stocked with gloves and hats. "We got a winter-wear donation from a parishioner, too, so we'll hand those out till they're gone. It would be more helpful closer to winter. But, we take what we can get when we can get it."

"Makes sense." It doesn't really. It was over eighty yesterday.

"What made you decide to volunteer here?" David is friendly—I'll give him that. I hesitate, and he fills in the silence. "I just mean, most of our volunteers are students. For their service hours requirement."

His words expand my appreciation of the demographics here and further deepen my disappointment. Obviously, the other population with time to volunteer at a church on a weekday morning are college students. Unlike a summer donation of winter-wear, that makes perfect sense.

"I used to go to church here," I say. "So, I knew about the pantry. And I have a lot of free time right now and thought I should do something worthwhile." He starts to open his mouth, probably to ask why I stopped going to church, or why I have a lot of free time. Neither are topics I have any interest in discussing, so I cut him off. "What made *you* volunteer?"

"I guess it's sort of the same. My wife and I moved to Chicago about ten years ago, after our younger daughter was born. We started going to church here, and I just thought it seemed like a good thing to do. Only one morning a week. A small thing. Do you have children?"

"Yes. Penny is almost fifteen, and Colin is twelve." Maybe I'm a little clipped in my response. I see a stiffening across his shoulders and feel guilty. But I don't want to talk about me.

To assuage my guilt at rebuffing his attempts at being

personable, I explain the parking garage incident, omitting some of the details—why I was there, the uncanny sense I'd had that someone was watching me and that it would turn out to be my dead husband, the coffee with Mark, who'd actually been the one following me. I leave these details out, and the story comes out in small, disconnected shards. Still, David listens and seems to appreciate how it might leave an impression on a person.

When I don't say anything more, he says, "I'm ready to open. Are you?"

"Never been more ready for anything in my life," I say.

He smiles politely as he unlocks a door between the church and the pantry, and a line that has formed begins to shuffle toward the counter.

The uneven intervals at which patrons appear at the counter, and the repetitive task of placing food on plates, lends itself to meditation rather than conversation. Even smalltalk takes the form of no more than two or three exchanges at a time. From these, I learn that David is a civil engineer—designs and repairs bridges or some such, and there are a lot of bridges in Chicago, so I presume he stays busy. Except for Wednesday mornings when he works the food pantry at St. Vincent DePaul.

A man approaches the counter and holds up his hands. "Gloves," he says, his bare hands demonstrating his need, though I'd assume need is a given at the food pantry.

"Size?" I ask, almost singing the word. My strategy for making friends might have failed, but that doesn't mean I shouldn't be friendly.

"Extra-large," he says.

I hand him a pair of gloves from the "XL" box, then add a

sandwich to his tray, and he moves down the line to receive his one dessert. A college student, Haley, adds a cup of coffee. In contrast to my assumptions about the altruistic students who might work the pantry, she looks like there's no place she wouldn't rather be.

"Have a nice day, Charles," David says as the man takes his tray to an empty table.

"Charles," I repeat under my breath.

As the line continues, a rhythm soon develops as does my appreciation for David's familiarity with each of the patrons. He welcomes them, says *good morning*, and addresses them by name. If they're new or he doesn't know their name, he asks.

"Are you counting them?" David asks me.

"Hmm?"

"Are you counting them? The patrons?" he asks again.

He must have seen me mouthing their names. "Oh! No. I'm trying to learn their names."

"Ah. Well. Because counting them would be strange," he says with a voice that winks.

"It would?"

"Yes," Haley says, her upper lip curling back from her teeth. "They're not inventory."

"Maybe I just want to make sure we have enough sandwiches," I say.

"Is that what you're doing?" Haley challenges.

"No. I'm trying to memorize their names."

Haley turns with a scoff and starts organizing the sweeteners for the coffee.

David mouths a silent, "Sorry."

I assume the apology pertains to his getting me in trouble with Haley, though I hardly need the comfort. I doubt we'll see her again.

"Gloves and hat," says a woman from the other side of the counter. She's been waiting patiently.

"What size?" I ask.

"Medium."

I reach into the box marked "M" and hand her a pair of gloves and a hat.

"Irene," she says. "My name is Irene."

"Good morning, Irene," I say. "I'm Babs."

"Are you walking to your car?" David asks as he locks the pantry and we step out onto the sidewalk next to the church.

"No, I live in the neighborhood. I'll just walk home." I tip my head in the general direction of my house.

"I'd be happy to walk you home."

I glance up at the clear blue of the mid-day sky. It's a reflexive movement, but it must have conveyed some meaning to David. "Or lunch?" he suggests.

"Oh," I say, with a flinch. "Oh. Lunch." My Friender post flashes through my mind, and I wonder whether David may also have some strategy for volunteering. I nearly agree—he's friendly, personable, attractive. But something holds me back, some self-imposed restriction. *Lunch* is not why I'm here.

"I think I'll just eat at home," I say.

"Sounds good," he replies in a manner that causes me to reassess whether I'd read too much into what was a superficially innocuous invitation.

I begin walking west toward my house, and David falls into step beside me. I'm about to reassure him that I don't need a chaperone when he abruptly stops.

"Well, this is me," he says, standing beside a Volkswagen

Tiguan. He offers a friendly wave, and I wave back. Then, he gets in his car, and I walk the remaining half block to my house.

That night Penny, Colin, and I watch *Locke & Key*. Or they do. I was into the show last week—a rare series that held my attention just as well as my kids'. But tonight, I'm so turned in on my thoughts, I can't even hear the television in front of me.

My phone sits beside me on the couch, the message from Austin left unanswered and the lunch invitation from David still hanging in the air like a shirt on a clothesline that refuses to dry.

Three years. Not quite, but close.

That's a long time.

"What?" Penny asks.

I hadn't realized I'd said it out loud. "Nothing. Sorry."

Penny gives me a furtive look of concern then returns her attention to the television.

I lift my phone from the couch next to me and open the text chain with Austin. The entirety of it fits on a single screen.

Three years is a long time.

So is twenty-five.

> Me: I'm sorry I didn't reply to your message last week. What are you doing tomorrow?

Austin: You tell me. :)

ten

Austin has a meeting with a real estate agent at his mother's house in the morning, and we decide over texts that I'll bring sandwiches, and we can eat lunch on the deck. But an apathetic drizzle begins during my run and continues through the rest of the morning right up to my arrival at Austin's front step—sandwiches in hand—shortly before noon. He ushers me out of the rain into the foyer, then kisses my cheek, which feels both intimate and formal, but it doesn't seem he's given it much thought.

"She's still here," he says in a low hush. "I can't get her to leave." I presume he means the real estate agent, not some woman he slept with last night.

"I'll wait in the kitchen," I whisper.

I head to the back of the house, set the sandwiches on the island, and take a seat on a stool. Austin returns to his meeting in the living room.

I don't know what I expected from Austin's mother's house, but it isn't this. The house comprises easily six thousand square feet, updated within the past two or three years with nothing that says, *We lived here when 'W' was president.* No pictures of

Austin from his KidZone days hanging on the walls. No mauve carpeting or spruce-upholstered sofas. The house resembles the *after* segment of the HGTV remodeling programs my dentist's office always has on.

"We can probably get this on the market by the end of the month," a woman says.

"That would be great," Austin replies, but his voice is neutral, not really a voice someone uses when something is great.

The woman adds, "We'll do the open house, but I don't think we'll need it. This'll sell immediately. Real estate like this? Up here? I bet it doesn't make it twenty-four hours after it's listed."

She sounds a little breathy. I wonder if she's a fan, or if she just thinks she's sitting across from the best-looking man she's ever sat across from. I can't see her, so I don't know if she's the right age to be a fan.

"Thanks so much for thinking of us for the listing," she says.

"Absolutely," Austin says. Clipped. Perfunctory.

"Yeah," she breathes. "I should get going. Get back to the office."

"Sounds good," he agrees.

I hear people moving papers around, closing folders and messenger bags, getting ready to leave.

"Okay, then," Austin says as the front door opens. This is followed by a few more *thank-yous* and *nice-to-meet-yous* before the door *whooshes* closed. The house falls silent, except for Austin walking back to the kitchen.

"Thanks for being so patient," he says. He smooths the front of his shirt, then runs his fingers through his hair. He grabs a couple bottles of water from the refrigerator, then sits on the stool next to me. "I didn't realize that would take so long."

"It should sell quickly," I say, repeating the realtor as my eyes arc over the kitchen. I don't know anything about real estate, but I know the house will sell quickly—mostly because I have an actual crick in my neck from leaning toward the living room, trying to pick up as much of that conversation as possible. "It looks like it's never been lived in," I add—my own observation.

"It hasn't been for years," he says. He unwraps his sandwich and flattens the paper under it. "She had the condo."

"Right," I say, even though I'm incredulous at the notion of someone owning a six-thousand-square-foot house in Evanston and not living in it.

"Is this where you grew up?" I ask, partially because I harbor the hope that somewhere in this house hides a bedroom with grade-school-Austin's oak bunkbeds and his collection of Star Wars action figures.

"Here? No. I bought this for her in—" he gives it some thought "—maybe 1995." I wonder if he bought her the condo in Florida, too. Probably.

"I bet that makes it easier," I say.

"Makes what easier?" He takes a bite.

"Selling it. It would be hard to sell a house full of memories."

He looks at me curiously, his mouth paused mid-chew. Then, he takes a sip of water. "Yeah, I guess it would be."

Somewhere in the kitchen, an analogue clock ticks—a good decor decision. Every kitchen should have an analogue clock. I finally locate the one in this room over the French doors that lead out to the rain-soaked deck.

He sets his sandwich on the paper in front of him and swivels his stool to face me. "It took you a little while to respond to my text. I thought maybe you weren't going to." It's a question.

I lose my nerve and begin to babble. "My weekend got away

from me. Penny had a cross-country meet that I almost forgot about, and she and Colin both got together with friends. And I have brunch every Sunday with my sister."

One side of his mouth tugs upward as if against his will. "Sounds like a busy *weekend*."

Point well taken; it took me a week to reply to his text. I've managed to take a sip of water and wash down a thumbnail-sized bite of my sandwich. I'd plotted out what I wanted to say today, but as I sit here with him so close I can smell the sandalwood and amber scent of his aftershave, it seems there are decades of *what if*, and *what happened*, and *what now* standing in the way of the very ordered discussion I'd imagined on the drive over. With courage, I return to my original intention.

"I needed time to think." I pick at the edge of my napkin. "That day in 1997—"

"We don't have to revisit that," he says hurriedly and swivels back toward the island. "That was a long time ago."

"I feel bad about it, though." I say. "The whole thing."

"Why?" He looks genuinely befuddled.

I pause wondering if maybe he doesn't remember it after all.

"I felt bad about... after. I didn't realize." I clear my throat. "Honestly, Austin, it never occurred to me that you'd want anything more than that day. I... I thought that's why we were there. I thought that was something you did. You took women there. I didn't understand that it wasn't until later."

He offers an amused smile. "You thought I lured unsuspecting women out to Will Rogers State Park to have sex with them?" He doesn't seem especially offended, but as I hear my own thoughts repeated back to me, he would be justified if he were.

"I'm sorry. I know that sounds awful. In my defense, I was nineteen. I couldn't make any sense of what *you* would see in someone like *me*."

"No. No. Not *someone like you*," he says as if there's been a very serious misunderstanding. He gazes at me, his eyes full of concern, and pushes his sandwich back. "*You*. I thought *you* were interesting and funny and beautiful, and I wanted to get to know *you*. That's why I asked you hiking. So we could just walk and talk and get to know each other." He says this like it's the simplest most straightforward thing in the world. "I thought, depending on how that went, I'd maybe try to kiss you after dinner." His voice drops in mock seduction.

"Dinner?"

"I'd made a reservation... It doesn't matter. It was a long time ago." He glances at my sandwich. "Are you not hungry? Do you want something else? There's not much in the house." He checks the view beyond the kitchen window and frowns—still raining.

"I'm overthinking this. I do that sometimes." I give him a *be warned* look over the edge of my shoulder and hear a couple short breaths of laughter.

"I probably am, too." He moves off his stool, balling up his sandwich in its wrapper. "I really didn't think I'd ever see you again, and when I ran into you, it almost seemed like—I don't know—like a sign. What are the chances? It has to mean something, you know?" He reaches the other side of the kitchen and steps on the foot lever of the trashcan, then tosses the sandwich in. "That probably sounds ridiculous."

I smile weakly. It doesn't sound ridiculous; it sounds romantic.

He take a couples steps toward the counter and leans with his back against it, his hands on either side of his hips. "Honest to God, Babs, you were like no one I'd ever met before."

"Same," I say through my teeth, as I state the obvious.

"No. Seriously." I *am* serious, but he continues. "I asked you where you were from, and you were like, *Where are you from?* I offered to take a photograph with you, and you were like, *No thanks, I'm good.* I ask you out, and you tell me you don't have anything to wear and asked to bring your kid sister. Then we're hiking and you nearly fall off the side of a cliff." He's laughing now, the words coming out between breaths he can hardly control. "You left a bit of an impression, I have to say."

"I never would have guessed that." I laugh nervously, thinking it must be incredibly easy to forget one person in a sea of people over the course of two and a half decades. But he seems so sincere, I hesitate to argue.

"Well," he says with a shrug, but he doesn't extrapolate.

"There were other things, too," I say.

"Other things?" He brushes some invisible crumbs into his hands and delivers them to the sink next to him.

"That complicated it for me." That still do.

"Ah. I figured there probably were. You explained a little bit of it then. But I know the Hollywood thing is intimidating, and I thought you probably had a boyfriend or something waiting for you back at school. Was I right?"

My cheeks are on fire with how accurate a summary it is. I drop my eyes to the kitchen island, examining the thread of cranberry granite that traces through the opal-colored stone.

He tips his head forward, as if he can hook my gaze and draw it up. "Is that what's going on now," he asks, gently. "It's intimidating? Or maybe you're already with someone?"

"Sort of." I watch his face fall, the disappointment strangely familiar, if better controlled, all of it seeming to reside at the corners of his mouth. I course-correct. "I'm not with anyone. I haven't dated *anyone* since Ryan died."

"Oh," he says. "I see."

"And he was who I was dating then—when you asked me out then."

His lips part as he nods, which is a fair bit better than

having his whole mouth drop open, but he still looks a little stunned.

"I mean, not for very long. We'd started dating just before summer break, and he lived in Boston, and I lived in Chicago, so we hadn't seen each other all summer." I know I sound defensive, but it's still true.

He tilts his head to the side, pensive now. "Did you ever tell him about me?"

I stare at him across the span of the kitchen, thinking about how that day had been one of my two truths. How I came back and giggled and whispered with the girls on my cross-country team. How any time that show came up in conversation while I was in law school, I'd say, "I had sex with Bobby Martin. Out in the middle of a forest."

After Ryan and I got back together, I stopped telling the story; the more people who knew, the more likely Ryan would catch wind of it. And as Austin's star faded, so did the novelty of the story. "Who?" people started asking, and I'd have to explain more than just the sex, which was challenging, since I couldn't really say much about the show.

"Never," I say. And now I can't.

Austin nods again, though I don't know whether he means to acknowledge what I've said or agree with the decision I made. He ticks his chin at the barely eaten sandwich in front of me. "You done with that?"

"Yes," I say, and he pushes himself off the counter, grabs the sandwich from the island, and deposits it in the trashcan.

"Yeah," he says. "I can see how that would make this feel..." he searches for the word "... complicated."

"My sister was pretty pissed, too." I decide against fleshing that out.

"Have you told her we ran into each other?"

"Yes."

"What did she say?"

I shrug. "She said you have to go back to California, and that you're already seeing someone—or lots of someones—out there."

He chuckles. "Literally no part of that is true," he says, shaking his head. "Your sister is wrong."

"Austin," I say, finding the words I'd come there to say. "I really had fun at the game—"

"Me, too."

"—but I don't think I'm ready for this. To be dating anyone. To be dating *you*." The words come crashing down like a tray full of glassware on a tile floor. It sounded better in my head.

He blinks a few times; he heard the crash, too. Then, brushing the shards to the side, he says, "Look, I have a feeling Jenna's going to drag her feet on this sale. So I'm kind of stuck here for a while." He draws a breath. "I'd just like to get to know you. I'd like you to know me, too. That's all." He glances at me, checking in. "Maybe we stay friends. Maybe we become more. Maybe we find out we can't stand each other—nothing in common but a love for the Cubs—"

"I wouldn't say I *love* the Cubs."

"Well, now I know we have no future." He grins, and it's contagious. "Might as well go back to my... what was it? My *lots of someones* in L.A.?"

"Okay, okay," I say, with mock tolerance.

"No expectations, Babs." He steps forward and leans with his forearms on the opposite side of the island. "No pressure. You set the pace. You tell me what works for you."

"Am I scheduling the delivery of an appliance?" I ask.

He doesn't crack a smile. "We're doing whatever you want."

"I want a new couch," I say.

eleven

1997

"What were you going to do today?" Austin asked as we walked along a narrow trail beneath a canopy of thinly-leafed sycamores. The timbre of his voice reached me as a slow-moving, dark-amber honey. If voices were food.

"My aunt and uncle were going to take us to the La Brea Tar Pits," I replied.

"That's a good touristy thing." He sounded like he actually approved.

"I'd rather go hiking," I said honestly. "I run cross-country and track and haven't been able to do much since we got here."

"Where do you run?"

"For college. In Boston."

He stumbled and kicked out a cotton ball-sized puff of brown dirt.

"Are you okay?" I asked, coming to a full stop.

"Yeah, I... never mind." The corners of his eyes twitched as he attempted—and failed—a closer inspection of my face beneath my baseball cap. He'd thought I was older, I gathered.

We resumed hiking. "What are you studying in college?"

"I'm pre-law. Majoring in English." I tried to sound casual about it, even though I figured, ten minutes in, our hike was effectively already over. But he raised his eyebrows as if my answer impressed him.

"I graduate in ninety-nine," I said to help him out with the math. "Then it's off to law school."

"Do you know where you're going to law school?"

"Wherever I can afford to," I said, wryly. "I haven't applied yet. You don't apply until you're a senior, and I'll be a junior in the fall." I was trying to help him again, but his jaw tightened. Technically, I was still an underclassman.

I stopped again.

He took a couple of steps before realizing I wasn't beside him. "What's wrong?"

"We're not very far along the trail. Do you want to just call it a day? I would understand." I really would have. Not that I wouldn't have been let down. But I didn't have some elaborate Happily Ever Hollywood fantasy. That fantasy belonged to Margot. I was mostly flattered that *Austin Lewis* had asked me out and curious about what the day would hold.

"Do you *want* me to take you home?" he asked, looking down the trail where Tom and the Jeep had been instructed to wait.

"*I* want to go hiking," I said, in a manner that insinuated I didn't view Austin as totally necessary. "But I understand I might not be… what you're…" I faltered. "…used to?"

The phrasing was awful. It wasn't even exactly what I meant, and my only salvation was a tiny gecko nestled among the fallen leaves edging the trail, which gave me something to look at other than Austin's horrified expression.

"Used to," he repeated, hollow.

"That's not what I meant," I mumbled. Truly, it wasn't.

"No. It's fine," he said. "You're not what I'm used to. But you want to go hiking, and we're already here." It seemed he was buoyed a little with each word. "Let's keep going."

I think curiosity might have factored into his calculus as well.

We hiked for another hour or so after that, and if this was a place Austin brought his various conquests, he made them work for the privilege. He knew the trail well and kept the pace quick, and even though he said he liked the quiet, he talked all along the way. About how he was afraid of what would happen when *The Maple Street Martins* ended. About how he'd seen so many people who started as children in this business—he'd started as a child; he didn't know if I knew that—the business just chewed them up and spit them out as soon as they lost the fat in their cheeks. He'd been lucky to have had a career as long as he had, but it couldn't go on forever. He just didn't have that range. He was playing a high schooler. He couldn't do that at forty.

We talked about politics, too. He worried that Clinton was too moderate, that he'd move the Democrats to the right, which would move the Republicans further to the right, which would move the entire country to the right. He thought that was the wrong direction. I did, too, but wasn't accustomed to having lengthy conversations about it.

He asked me questions about myself—overly personal questions I probably should have told him were none of his fucking business. About my parents' divorce. About our tiny walk-up in Chicago. I told him I wanted to be a lawyer mostly because I never wanted to be poor again. I said I loved running, which was lucky because it was paying for school, and I was worried about paying for law school because there were no athletic scholarships for that.

"There are other scholarships," he said and seemed to know. "And there are loans and grants." He must have seen me looking at him like I didn't find him entirely credible on the matter, because he volunteered that his older sister was a lawyer, so he knew a little about the profession.

At some point, he took my hand in his, which I admit was weird—both that he did it and that I let him—and we weren't really hiking anymore. We were walking along the trail, holding hands and talking. Occasionally, the path became too narrow to walk beside each other, or a fallen tree or boulder presented an obstacle. In each circumstance, he'd drop my hand, placing his fingers lightly at my waist as he maneuvered me in front of him, before taking my hand again.

I stopped suddenly at the sound of rushing water.

Austin froze next to me, on alert. "What?"

"Do you hear that?"

"Oh. Yeah. There's a waterfall in that direction. Not a very big one." He nodded toward the oaks and sycamores to the side of the path—I couldn't see a waterfall.

I dropped his hand and took a step toward the trees.

"No," he said, reaching for me. "That's off-trail. The park doesn't maintain any of that. It'll be hard to climb back up."

"I'm in excellent shape, Austin Lewis. I don't know if you've heard, but I'm a Division One athlete." I raised my eyebrows in anticipation of his rebuttal, but I'd already made up my mind.

"Why do you keep calling me by both of my names?"

"Let's go see the waterfall." I tugged at his hand.

"It might be flooded," he protested.

I pulled my sunglasses off and put them on top of my hat. "It's July. When was the last time it rained here?"

"I don't know," he mumbled. "It's been a while."

"Come on." I didn't have to tug very hard—he'd made up his mind, too—and I led us in the direction of the sound of the water, weaving diagonally between trees, over rocks and fallen branches.

"I should be leading," Austin called from behind me. I could feel his hand—just the tips of his fingers—at the small of my back. "You could get hurt."

"I'm fine," I called over my shoulder, ducking under low-hanging branches and dancing between trees and shrubs in search of a viable way forward. I was nearly jogging, and the sound of Austin chuckling reached me just as the forest suddenly cleared at the sheered edge of a rock cliff, the scree falling away at my toes.

Austin's chuckling ceased immediately as he threw an arm around my waist, jerking me back into his chest in a single adrenaline-fueled maneuver.

I yelped, both at my "near miss" with the cliff's edge and at the strength of Austin's arm, a vise holding me so tight to his chest, I could feel the heat of his panicked breath against my ear, the solid wall of his torso against my back.

We stood frozen for what felt like hours, not more than a foot-and-a-half separating me from the edge of what turned out to be the top of the waterfall. Austin dropped his forehead to my shoulder as a shiver moved through him.

"Oh my God," he exhaled into my back, refusing to release his grip.

"Wh—where's the water coming from?" I asked. I'd expected to meet the stream *before* the waterfall.

Austin lifted his hand to one side where a creek lazily snaked through the trees, then turned sharply and poured over the cliff.

The air around us settled, and Austin loosened his grip, allowing us both to step back from the edge. The effort of the journey there, the fear just seconds before, and the heat of our bodies pressed together in the moments after had left both of us sweaty. The front of his t-shirt was speckled with perspiration, and beads tracked down from the edge of my baseball cap, dripping from my jaw to my tank top.

From our new vantage point several feet back from the cliff, I could see a more gradual descent to the stream below.

"That way looks safer," I said. It was sort of a joke—*any* way was safer—but Austin didn't laugh.

"I lead," he said.

twelve

"I'm noticing a pattern," I say as we sit on my back patio, following a productive excursion to Restoration Hardware.

Austin pulls a ruby-colored ice-pop from his mouth. "Yeah? Is it the one where you go radio silent for days at a time, and I chase you down and ask you if you want to get together?"

I give him a rapid fire tisk-and-scoff. "I didn't go radio silent. We've been texting since Thursday." If he'd pointed out that I hadn't initiated any of the texts, I would have been forced to agree with him.

He glances in my direction, then breaks off a piece of his ice-pop into his mouth and breaths over the cherry-flavored ice in an obvious effort to avoid brain-freeze. "Your lips are blue," he observes.

I could have guessed—blue raspberry.

"What pattern?" he asks.

"On the 'L'. The hat and sunglasses, and the decision—both there and back—to sit in the two seats behind the divider. Hiding. You—we did the same thing to and from the Cubs game. But not really at Starbucks and not at lunch. I can't figure it out."

"Well, look what happened at Starbucks." He lets his ice-pop slide down into the plastic wrapper.

"You don't like that? That your fans still recognize you?" I'm trying to remember what Wiki said about his last film. It's probably been at least ten years. Long enough, I'd have thought, for them to lose interest.

"It's a balance," he says like it's not a balance, it's an infectious disease. "For the most part they're fine, and I can manage it all pretty well. Plus, they've mellowed out a lot over the years. And every year I have fewer and fewer followers, which is—as you might imagine—both good and bad for me. Social media is a big part of how I make a living. It's how the show continues to make money. It's how I promote projects I'm working on, or that my former castmates are working on. Or products I'm asked to promote."

"Products?"

"Not always products," he says. "I did a campaign for MoMA a couple years ago that I'm pretty proud of."

I'm listening attentively as he explains a world I have only a superficial understanding of. Is this what an influencer is? Is he an influencer? He's not really; he's a retired actor with over three hundred thousand followers on Instagram. That's quite a platform; he's smart to monetize it.

"But it does mean I don't always know when they're going to pop up. It's hard to keep track of that many people," he says. "Sometimes I'd rather just be left alone to sip a cup of coffee or go sofa shopping with a friend. So, yeah, it's a balance." His ice-pop has melted to a cherry-colored slurry, and he tips the plastic wrapper into his mouth.

I sip my own melted ice-pop, and he goes on.

"It's a strange feeling though—that someone is watching you. More than forty years in this business, and I'm still not used to it."

I stare at him as he gazes out at the fence, then look away as it strikes me I'm doing exactly what he just described. But I can't help it, the way he explained it resonates.

"Does that sounds strange?" he asks, turning to me. I see a flash of something in his eyes. Embarrassment, perhaps.

"No," I say. "It doesn't sound strange." I hesitate, unsure how much I want to tell him. "I... sometimes..."

"What is it?" he asks, his head tilting to the side.

"I feel that sometimes. That feeling. Like someone is there." It's not enough not to look at him while I say it; I turn my head so I can't see him at all. The only other person I've told this to is Margot, and now I'm on my patio, eating popsicles, telling Austin Lewis I'm crazy.

"You've been through a lot," he says, his voice a blanket that wraps around me.

I exhale a heavy breath, relieved. "You have, too."

"I doubt it compares. And I had hundreds of thousands of people rallying to my cause. Hell, they raised a hundred and fifty thousand dollars for breast cancer research. In a week."

"It's not a competition," I say. "You get to just be sad when sad shit happens."

He smiles—and it's a sad smile. Then he takes my hand briefly in his own, squeezes and releases it.

"I like this," I say, closing my eyes, allowing the warmth from his hand to spread up my arm and through my body.

"I do, too."

"So, should I start hiding, too?" I tip the last of the ice-pop juice into my mouth.

He laughs a laugh that doesn't quite get free of him, tumbling around in his chest. "We probably have some time before you have anything to worry about. And I didn't mean to scare you. It's not like that. They mean well—most of them do anyway. There's a Facebook group that's fucking toxic, but it's really small, and they are *not* the norm."

I choke on the ice-pop juice, folding forward in my chair, leaning my forearms on my thighs as I cough against the blue raspberry syrup.

"Are you okay?" Austin asks with a hand against my back.

No. No, I am not okay. "Yes. Fine." I sit up and try to catch my breath. Austin pauses to ensure my recovery is complete.

"They call themselves the Lewnatics," he continues, confirming the worst of my fears. "And they are... something. Actual *lunatics*." I think he's spelling it differently, now. "They track my every move; they examine the background of every single photo I post or am tagged in and try to triangulate it with... who even knows. Another celebrity, a doctor's office, a gym. Once, there was a whole week where they were arguing about the position of the sun over the ocean in a photograph of me and my sister. They show up everywhere. One of them tried to visit my mother while she was in hospice."

"Oh my God, Austin. That's awful," I say. I think about Margot. Does she do this? I doubt it, but at the very least, she reads the reconnaissance reports.

"They spread rumors. They've harassed my girlfriends in the past, they still harass Samantha. That's—that's my ex-wife."

I already knew that from Wikipedia, but the sound of her name coming from his lips, the familiarity with which he utters it, rattles me for some inexplicable reason that makes me feel both possessive and ashamed.

He goes on, talking at quite a clip, one thought after the next barreling forth.

"You'd think they'd be happy that we divorced, but she's had to basically remove herself from all social media to get away from them." He shakes his head. "Fortunately, it's a small group. Only about eight thousand. I think. I haven't checked in on them in a while."

"Checked in? How do you check in on them?"

"My lawyer—Micah—he has a fake Facebook account and is a member of their group. Gives me a heads up if he sees anything he thinks I need to know about."

I immediately wonder whether Micah gave him a "heads up" about Margot. Surely, Austin would say something if he knew *my sister* was in that group. Or maybe he's waiting for me to say something. Maybe this is a test.

"Should I be worried?" I ask. It's the kind of question that asks a lot in only a few words.

He doesn't say anything right away, which is its own answer, I suppose.

"Not *worried*. No." He turns his head, staring at me with an expression that flirts with desperation. "I just want a few more weeks of no bullshit. From *any* of them." He says it like he's trying to convince me. But I don't need convincing.

"Okay," I say with resolve. "Anything else you think I should know?"

He sighs, then, "Your lips are still blue."

"Yours are still red."

"Lips are supposed to be red." He pouts them out and crosses his eyes as he attempt to see them.

"I'm not sure they're supposed to be *that* shade of red."

He delivers another quick squeeze to my hand and releases it. Well, he lingers a bit.

thirteen

"Babs! Take that off the burner!" Margot yells from the kitchen table where she's adjusting a bib around Supriya's neck. Supriya squawks, which I assume constitutes an attempt to scold her mother for daring to scold me in my own kitchen.

In Margot's defense, I'd drifted off into a replay of my week with Austin and nearly burned the bacon. I lift the skillet off the heat just in time.

I set a plate of blueberry pancakes and a side of bacon in front of Margot and join her at the table. At the aroma of food and the sound of plates, Colin and Penny burst into the kitchen.

"Hi, Aunt Margot," Colin says. He takes the plate from my hand, then kisses her on the cheek.

"Did you cut your hair?" Penny asks.

Margot gleams. "I did. Thank you for noticing."

I didn't notice. I've always been bad at noticing things like that. But Penny thinks Margot is the most glamorous woman she's ever laid eyes on, and she notices everything Margot does. The way she holds her coffee cup, the color of her lipstick, the way she crosses and uncrosses her legs. And her hair.

"I like it," Penny says.

"Thank you," Margot says with a delicate sip of her coffee.

Penny takes a plate of food, and she and Colin head to the family room downstairs to eat and watch TV. I tear up a blueberry pancake and put it on Supriya's highchair. She is delighted. Nearly two years old, she goes after the pieces of pancake like they contain the answers to every single one of the world's problems.

"Hey," Margot says between bites. "What ever happened with Austin Lewis?"

I pause mid-chew and stare at her warily.

"What?" Her eyes widen with concern.

I try to collect my thoughts. There's a lot to catch her up on.

She drops her fork to her plate and leans against the table, piercing me with a stare. "Did something happen?" She leans in closer, as if trying to protect Supriya. "Did you sleep with him again?"

I try to picture Margot as a Lewnatic, triangulating the location of the sun over the ocean in a picture of Austin and his sister.

"No, I didn't sleep with him," I say, being deliberate with my words. "We're just... getting to know each other."

Margot sits back, stunned. I see her lips twitch as if preparing to say something, then reconsidering. "What does that mean?"

"It's friendly. Nice."

"Friendly?"

"Yeah. He helped me pick out a new couch for the family room." I take a bite of pancake.

Margot's face puckers—eyebrows clenched together, lip curled. "You went *furniture shopping* with Austin Lewis? What do you have planned for this week? Romantic getaway at the gyne?"

I laugh. Supriya glances up from her pancakes and laughs, too.

"It's a nice color, the couch. You'll like it," I say, thinking maybe it's best to just leave the Austin conversation behind for a bit.

"What color?" Margot's voice has dropped with the conversational pivot.

"Burnt caramel," I say. "It's a deep umber, but it's Restoration Hardware so they named it after food."

"Ooh! That'll look really nice." She follows this with a sip of coffee. "Are you going to change out the rug? It won't match."

"Yes. Eventually."

"I think they're having a promotion for September. You should buy the rug soon."

Supriya appears to agree as she slaps her high chair tray with a squeal.

"So that's it? Just the couch?" Margot ribs. "You didn't follow that up with—I don't know—a trip to Lowe's to pick out a new dishwasher?"

I allow a smile, along with a tisk of my lips. "He's out of town. He won't be back until Tuesday."

Margot takes a sip of coffee. She picks up a strip of bacon but puts it back down. "Is he not going back to L.A., then?"

"He said he's staying here for a while."

"How long's *a while*?" She shakes her head, like the words are confusing, maybe an entirely different language. Supriya offers a protest at being restrained in her highchair, and Margot grabs some baby wipes to clean the syrup from her hands.

I offer what I hope is a plausible explanation. "His realtor is dragging her feet selling his mom's house."

"Huh," she muses as she lifts Supriya from the highchair and sets her on the floor, then returns to her seat. "Well, I guess that explains it."

"Explains what?"

"They were wondering why it was taking him so long to go back to California."

"*They* who?"

"The Lewnatics." She says it with an air of boredom.

"About that," I say, dipping my toe in the water. "I don't know how much time you spend in that group, but Austin said they're pretty..." I struggle to find a description that captures Austin's unmitigated contempt for them without offending my sister, who evidently is one of them.

"Yeah, it can be like watching a train wreck in there sometimes when they get going. I can*not* look away. The group is aptly named," she says with a laugh.

I glance at her curiously. "Is that why you're there? For the entertainment value?" I'm not sure whether I want her to say *yes*. The group's behavior sounds an awful lot like stalking, though I suppose I don't know that she's doing any of the stalking.

"Sure?" She's got one eye on Supriya who's taken *The Joy of Cooking* from the bookshelf on the side of the island and is flipping through the pages. "When I joined, I just wanted to see if I could get their admission trivia question right."

"What was the trivia question?"

She clears her throat and recites: "What was Travis Sorrell's make and model of motorcycle in *An Octave Above*?"

"Austin Lewis was in that movie?" I remember it vaguely, though I never saw it. It looked terrible, like someone tried to take *Save the Last Dance* and set it in a music conservatory.

"Yeah. He was a teacher at the school. He had, like, four lines. But it's a trick question." She lifts her chin with what I think is pride. "His character's name was Trevor Samuel, and he drove a Honda Civic. Anyway, I knew the answer, and they let me in."

"And now you just sit back and watch the train wreck? You don't feel... guilty?"

"Eh. Not all of them are like that. And there are crazies in every fan group. If you're a celebrity, I think it just goes with the territory."

"Well," I say, pushing back. "He's not really a celebrity. He's a *former* celebrity."

"Is that what he told you?"

"No. But he hasn't been in a movie in more than a decade. He mostly just manages the rights to *The Maple Street Martins* and works as a producer on other shows. I guess people think he has a good eye for television."

"That sounds like a Wikipedia entry, Babs. He's a celebrity. D-list, but still. At worst, he's an influencer." She gets up from her chair again—Supriya's found the red ribbon bookmark and is trying to free it from the spine of the cookbook. "Honey, stop pulling on that." Margot takes the book from her daughter's lap and pulls her into her arms. "I still don't understand; you're dating but you're not sleeping together?"

"I wouldn't say we're dating. I'd say we're getting to know each other."

"What do you think *he'd* say?"

"That *is* what he said—that he wanted us to get to know each other."

Margot regards me from beneath two perfectly sculpted, arched eyebrows.

"This is a lot for me," I confess. "I haven't dated anyone since Ryan died."

"I know," she says softly as she sways Supriya back and forth, peppering her tiny hands with kisses.

"It would be a whole lot simpler if he were just a guy I'd met in a running group or something."

"Are you in a running group?"

"No."

"Well, that does narrow the odds of meeting someone that way."

Penny returns to the kitchen with her dirty plate and places it in the sink. At the sight of her big cousin, Supriya reaches her arms out and Penny obliges, seeming flattered that she's been chosen.

"Want to go downstairs and watch TV?" Penny asks Supriya.

"Please!" Supriya says gleefully. She'd follow Penny to the ends of the earth, but she doesn't have to go that far to find the toys in our house.

Penny takes Supriya downstairs, and Margot begins putting the books back in the bookshelf.

"Just leave them," I say. "I'll get it later."

Margot ignores me and continues cleaning up after her daughter. "You should invite him over for Supriya's birthday next weekend," she suggests. "We'll cook out. Not meat, you know. But something."

I have mixed feelings about that as soon as she says it. I suspect part of the reason Margot suggests it is because she wants to meet Austin again. But it's also a good idea. I'm not sure where this is going, but it would be smart to introduce him to Penny and Colin, and a small family birthday party could be a good way to do that. There'd be a normalcy to it, relaxed, low key.

"Would that be weird for you?" I ask.

"Oh please, Babs," Margot says with a dismissive wave of her hand. "I'm forty years old. It's been a long time since I was pining after Bobby Martin."

Her comment seems at odds with her earlier remark about "the fandom," but I let it go. I have no interest in talking her into renewing her obsession with Austin Lewis.

"I'll ask him."

"Just text me and let me know so we have enough food," she says.

> Me: Good morning. Any interest in attending my niece's birthday party on Saturday? Just family. Low key. No gift necessary.

I stare at the phone waiting for some response. It's 6:30 pm in Germany; my timing's not great. The dots show up immediately, but the text doesn't follow. I watch as the seconds tick by.

Austin: . . .

"Fuck," I breathe at the phone. It's a terrible idea. Meet my sister, meet my kids. What was I thinking?

> Me: Please don't feel like you have to go? I would completely understand if you had something better to do.

Austin: No.

. . .

For a minute I don't know whether it's "no," he doesn't want to go, or "no," he doesn't have something better to do. I slide my thumbnail between my teeth, biting. There are some big differences between those things, and I'm not really sure how to respond given the ambiguity.

Austin: This seems like something we should talk about.

> Austin: I want to make sure you're completely comfortable with me meeting your family.

Oh, God. He's seen right through it.

> Me: Call whenever it's convenient.

The phone rings within seconds, and I take a deep breath before answering.

"Hey," I say, doing a fairly decent job of holding it together.

"Hi."

"How's Germany?"

"Good." It's obvious he's waiting for me.

"So, my niece is turning two, and we always have a small family party on kids' birthdays. Hers is this Saturday. I wondered if you'd want to go."

"Sure. I'd love to. Have you talked to Penny and Colin about this?" he asks.

"No. I didn't want to go through all of that if your answer was going to be *no*."

"Why would my answer be *no*? Hang on," he says. "I'm going to move somewhere quieter."

Voices echo in the background on his end—like he's at a restaurant—and it buys me some time. The noise fades, and he goes on. "I don't want you to feel rushed. I meant it when I said you get to set the pace."

The silence hangs, precarious, unbalanced.

"Why don't we do this," he says, finally. "Why don't you talk to Penny and Colin? If they seem okay with it, I'd love to go."

fourteen

I go to Colin first—under the covers reading the latest Rick Riordan. I kiss him on the forehead, and he ignores me but doesn't push me away. A reasonable compromise. When I loiter, he sets his book down and glances up. I sit on the edge of his bed.

"I was thinking I might invite a friend to Supriya's birthday next Saturday," I say.

Colin's cheeks inch up toward his eyes. His brows narrow. "A friend?"

"Mr. Lewis."

The confusion remains.

"You remember Mr. Lewis? I went with him to the baseball game a few weeks ago."

"Oh. Right," he says weakly. "I forgot. Does he know Uncle Rishi and Aunt Margot?"

There's a complicated answer to that question, but I decide to simplify it. "No."

"Oh."

"We've seen each other a few times since the baseball game."

"Oh." A look of discomfort slides down Colin's face, taking the corners of his mouth with it. "Oh." His voice slides down, too.

"Is that okay?"

"Sure," he says and lifts his book again.

"Hey." I place a hand over his, gently pushing the book back down. "If it's not okay, you can tell me."

"Why wouldn't it be okay?" His voice suggests he doesn't know there are answers that some kids might offer to that question.

"I just wanted to make sure you were comfortable with it," I say.

"It's Supriya's birthday," he points out. I see his point—maybe I should consult the birthday girl.

"Margot invited him, so I don't think Supriya's going to have a problem with it."

"Okay, then." He makes another attempt to lift his book. I allow it this time and give one more kiss to his forehead, which he again ignores.

I tell him to sleep well and have a good night, and he nods. Then, I leave his room and knock on the door across the hall. Penny doesn't respond. I open it to find her sitting on her bed with her headphones on, watching something on her tablet. I have an errant thought that it might be *The Maple Street Martins*, then remember that not only do we not own the right streaming service for that show, but there'd be no reason in the world for Penny to be watching it.

She looks up as I open the door and pushes her headphones off one ear.

"Hey, kiddo," I say. "Can we talk?"

She shrugs but touches the screen of her tablet, pausing whatever she's watching. I walk into the room, close the door behind me, and sit on the bed. She sets the tablet down, her face tightening.

I approach it the same way I did with Colin, the same opening line, but there's a lot of distance between a high school freshman and a seventh-grader, and before I can get the words out, her eyes take on the watery prologue to tears. I pull her into my arms, and she rests her forehead against my shoulder. She doesn't say anything, doesn't make a single sound, but her fractured breathing makes it clear she's crying.

"I knew it," she whispers after some time.

"Knew what?"

"That you were dating that man."

"We've only been out a handful of times."

Penny leans back from my shoulder. "What's a handful?"

"I don't know. We had lunch a couple weeks ago. He helped me pick out the new couch..."

"I thought he lived in California," she says.

"He does. But his mother just died, and he has to get things sorted out with her estate here."

"And then he's going back?" She sounds hopeful.

"I don't know when he's planning to go back," I say. "But you and Colin are my first priority. You two are the most important things to me in this entire world. I like spending time with Austin, but it matters to me what you guys think about that."

"Would you not date him if I said I don't like him, and I don't want you to date him?" Penny lifts her head from my shoulder. She's ready for a fight but doesn't really want to have one.

"Yes," I say. "There's nowhere for a relationship to go with someone you guys don't like."

"He's nothing like Dad," she says, a comment that nearly knocks me over; she's met him once, and I hadn't imagined she'd inspected him quite so closely.

I give her observation some thought. The temptation to comparison is strong. And Penny is right that he's nothing like Ryan, so I'm left agreeing with her.

"He seems nice, though," she says—a concession of sorts.

"Is that a good enough place to start?" I ask.

"I guess."

I flop onto my side with an annoyed grunt as if it's the pillow's fault I can't sleep. I pull my phone from my nightstand and check the time: 12:11 a.m. I open the texting app and re-read the last message from Austin.

> Austin: Beautiful day here, but I miss Chicago.

I'd hearted the message. I probably should have given it a thumbs up. That's friendlier. A heart means love, and I don't love him.

> Austin: Are you awake?

I must have activated the text box.

> Me: Yes. Can't sleep.

> Austin: Want to talk?

> Me: No. I want to sleep.

> Austin: LOL! What's on your mind?

Margot. Penny. Colin. Kelly. And a new song by Sabrina Carpenter that is on a loop in my brain.

> Me: Nothing. This just happens to me sometimes.

> Austin: Try to get some rest. I'll see you when I get home.

Home. He adds a sleeping face emoji, and I give the text a restrained thumbs up even though I miss him in a way that I'm not entirely comfortable with.

I pull my laptop from the floor and flip through Netflix. The "Movies we think you'll like" bar reflects a particular state of mind over the past several years—not exactly a selection of uplifting rom-coms. I type *The Maple Street Martins* into the search bar and am surprised to find that it returns a single result: *The Maple Street Martins-Pilot.*

"Shut the fuck up," I say into my utterly still bedroom. I select the tile, and the description provides an original air date of September 1993.

I've seen a couple episodes of the show—reruns in the summer, a random episode during college—but never had the desire to binge the whole thing. Then I was informed by the unimpeachable authority that is Wikipedia that the show was expensive and hard to get. But this is just the pilot.

I press play.

It takes me about two minutes to see exactly why the show had the following it did. There's something that, despite its contrived premise (one character in each sought-after viewer demographic), is so profoundly authentic, it pulls me in immediately.

The pilot introduces what I assume will be the plot lines for the main characters throughout the show, or at least throughout that first season. Daniel Martin, the eldest Martin child, is "troubled." The viewer knows this because he's starting college but has to live at home; his grades are only good enough to get him into the local commuter college. We might also know this by the way he's dressed.

In contrast to the Gen-X "grunge" look that a lot of early- and mid-nineties shows attempted to emulate—a flannel over some overtly threatening t-shirt, some Doc Martins, a pair of ripped jeans—Daniel dons a well-worn black t-shirt with "DEAD KENNEDYS" fading off the front. His jeans are ordinary blue jeans tucked into a pair of black combat boots. No Doc Martins here, his boots came from the Army-Navy surplus store. In place of the cliché flannel, he wears a green canvas 7-UP delivery man jacket with the name "Mac" embroidered under the 7-UP patch.

The dialogue with the Martin parents indicates worry about Daniel, not reprobation. The tension in his arc will be his parents' love for their son, not their unmet expectations. They ask him if he needs anything for his first day of college. Mr. Martin tells him he's proud of him. It all takes place in the kitchen I saw twenty-five years ago when I visited the set of the show.

Sitting at the kitchen table eating breakfast are middle-schooler Rachel, who keeps trying to talk and keeps being interrupted (middle child struggles), and grade schooler Katy. Katy is precocious. She's nervous about her first day of school because she thinks she'll be bullied. She confides in her parents that her strategy is to make sure the teachers don't know she's smarter than they are. She says "know" instead of "think." She recommends that Daniel adopt the same strategy.

"Don't correct the teachers," she tells him. It's cute, and funny, and just a little bit sad.

Austin, I mean, Bobby enters the kitchen, and I can't breathe. Bobby is starting his freshman year of high school. He just got his braces off over the summer, and his objective for the school year is to be one of the popular kids. He tried out for the football team and made it. This will be his year. He hints that his pursuit of popularity will be more difficult because of Daniel's reputation at the high school.

The opening scene revolves around Daniel. The show is an ensemble cast, but the writers clearly anticipated that the actor playing Daniel would be the breakout star and have focused the first season on his arc.

But I'm enthralled by Austin. When he steps into a scene, the camera wants to turn to him. He plays a fourteen-year-old in the first season, but he's nineteen—the same age I was when I met him. His plot is objectively uninteresting, but he delivers his lines with a sincerity that draws me in. I feel something for "the younger brother of the troubled sibling." When he says his year will be harder because of Daniel's reputation, he doesn't say it with a foot-stomp, even though I suspect it must have been written with something like that in mind. He delivers it with tenderness and sensitivity. He doesn't want to hurt Daniel's feelings, but he feels trapped by expectations he didn't set for himself.

My God, he is good.

It's evident from the pilot that the writers wrote the season for the wrong actor. The actor who plays Daniel—whose name I don't know and whose face I barely recognize—won't be the breakout; Austin will be. Actually, neither of them will be. Neither of them will move on from this show, but Austin will dominate it while it runs.

The credits begin to roll, and the "next" tile in the lower corner counts down, then bounces to the pilot episode of *Beverly Hills: 90210,* and the music from the opening credits wraps itself around my memories so tightly, I can almost smell the Delia's catalog.

I return to the search bar and type in *The Maple Street Martins*, but I'm presented with a single result: the pilot episode

I just watched. It's a smart move, making it available for free across platforms. Hook people with a freebie and let them purchase the rest. I google the show and see that the streaming platform that carries it is something called *Mapletown Productions,* which I assume Austin owns. I'm tempted to make the purchase, but hold myself back—the weirdness of giving my credit card information to Austin so that I can watch a show that first aired when I was in high school. I suppose I could just ask him to get me a copy of it; he owns it. But I don't want to watch the show. I don't want to be a fan. I don't want to be Margot.

fifteen

I've lost myself in the din of voices in the St. Vincent DePaul pantry, and the repetitive movements of placing squares of nearly-expired cake onto Styrofoam plates allows my mind to unfold. Within the landscape, I explore thoughts of Austin, the Lewnatics, my sister, Ryan, my firm (well, not *my* firm anymore).

I inadvertently plate a square of Funfetti cake a little too carelessly, and the Styrofoam snaps in half. The cake falls to the floor.

"Are you okay?" David asks and hands me a wet-wipe for the floor.

I glance up at him to see his face full of concern. "Yes. I've just got a lot on my mind."

"Hmm. Yes," he says. "Sometimes this work clears your head, and sometimes it causes you to become lost in it."

I stand and toss the wet-wipe in the garbage, tucking my lips against my teeth in that smile Midwesterners offer when they're not really smiling. Then, I return full-throttle to the task at hand, finding some enjoyment in getting to know the people. Already more of the patrons look familiar.

My phone buzzes in my pocket, and I check it during a break in the line.

> Austin: Any chance I might see you today?

> Me: I'd like that.

> Austin: Lunch? Picnic?

> Me: Sounds nice. What time? I'm working until 11:30?

> Austin: New firm?

> Me: No. I'm volunteering in the food pantry at St. Vincent DePaul.

> Austin: Is that where you go to Mass?

> Me: I don't go to Mass. I'm lapsed.

How many times do I have to have to have this conversation?

> Austin: Your Catholicism confuses me.

> Me: It's probably all the saints. And the veneration of Mary. That can be hard for some people.

> Austin: LOL! I'll pick you up from St. V at 11:30.

> Me: Where are we going?

"Good morning, Babs." It's Irene, politely trying to get my attention.

"Good morning, Irene," I say.

Her face is flushed, and her upper lip glistens with sweat even between the cool tile and dark wood of the pantry. It's always hard to know when winter will arrive in Chicago, but the late-September air outside is unmistakably summer at present. I hope she opts for the bottle of water when she gets to Erin (our student volunteer), but I know she'll choose coffee or hot chocolate. All the patrons do.

She points to a piece of white cake with coconut frosting. "That one."

I hand it across the counter, and she places it on her tray.

"Thank you," she says.

"Of course."

I pick up my phone again.

Austin: Beach?

He's spent too much time in California. No one in Chicago says "beach" unless they're naming a specific one; they say "lake."

Me: Hot.

Let it be said that if you are the only person "in" on an inside joke, attempting to involve a second person is asking for problems. I realize within about a tenth of a second of hitting send, that Austin's first thought upon receiving my text will not be, "Oh, that's what her Aunt Iris said when Babs was in college visiting L.A. and asked to go to the beach. That's how she ended up on the set of *The Maple Street Martins*."

I close my eyes willing him to at least connect the reference to the ongoing heatwave; it was over ninety yesterday.

Austin: That's up to you.

Well, shit.

I haven't been unemployed since I was fifteen years old, but with nearly an entire Wednesday splayed out, the status is quickly growing on me. Austin picks me up, kissing me on the cheek when he meets me at the side door of the church. I determine this is something he does. Charming—sort of French.

Smartly avoiding North Avenue or Ohio Street where everyone goes, he suggests Promontory Point, the cove down by the University of Chicago. Promontory Point definitely isn't a beach; there isn't even sand. It's a cove with a perimeter of enormous boulders that step down into the water.

He parks his car, and we walk under the viaduct along the path that leads to the lake. The last time I walked along this path, I was holding Ryan's hand, and the fullness of that memory momentarily augments Ryan's absence.

I'm sorry. The words whip through my head, and I feel a compulsion to say them aloud, even though I don't know exactly what I'm apologizing for. Spending time with Austin? Not moving to Paris? A strange day in 1997? Selling Ryan's car? Moving on.

"Did you say something?" Austin asks.

Did I? "No."

The look he gives me is an assessment, but I don't know what conclusion—if any—he reaches. He offers a slow, reassuring circle of his palm against my back. I take the opportunity to pull my hair back with a hair-tie from my purse. After we agreed on a time, Austin texted to say he'd take care of getting food, and we both knew the lake would be too cold to swim in, so I didn't go back to my house. Even with the air temperature over eighty, the lake this time of year is low sixties. All I brought is my purse.

Austin brought a backpack, which I presume holds a blanket and our lunch. Maybe he also brought some water wings. I really don't know. Walking side-by-side, we are teenagers in the bodies of middle-aged adults. He may feel more comfortable with that than I do since he'd managed to build a career around it. I feel simultaneously juvenile and ancient.

We drape a blanket over the grass just back from the boulders that border the lake. A shelter with restrooms and picnic tables separates us from a bike path, but sitting on the blanket makes it feel more like a picnic. The cove is largely deserted. A few people here and there. Older. Older even than us. Every once in a while, I hear a cyclist on the other side of the shelter. They like this area for the same reason we do: it's deserted.

One brave soul swims in the lake—breaststroke—his head out of the water, his chin jutting forward with each stroke of his arms. His wetsuit gives him an amorphous, seal-like appearance accentuated by his rather seal-like figure.

"How do you know about this place?" I ask, setting my purse on my side of the blanket. I know about it because my husband did his residency down here.

"My mom's neighbor suggested it," he says, and describes a conversation so banal I have trouble picturing *him* having it. "I asked him which beach is the quietest, and he said it's not really a beach, but down here by U Chicago."

I lie back on the blanket, propping my shoulders up with my forearms, and look out at the water. Austin adopts a similar pose. The one guy out in the water is still doing breaststroke, still not getting his face wet. After a while, he swims toward the boulders and climbs up, stepping carefully from surface to surface until he stands on the grass. A pile of clothes lie next to a tree, and he strips down to a Speedo, throws on a pair of running shoes, then grabs the street clothes under his arms and starts walking toward the lake path, his wetsuit draped over his shoulder.

"He's just going to drive home like that," Austin says as if he admires the man.

I suppose his confidence is admirable; he hasn't even put on a shirt. "He might live around here. He might *walk* home like that."

"Or take the 'L'."

I snicker. "If he's on the 'L', I hope he stands."

"He's carrying jeans. Did he come here in jeans?" Austin asks.

We fall silent as we watch the man slip under the viaduct and out of sight.

"Hungry?" Austin asks. He reaches into his backpack and pulls out two bottled waters and a bottle of Chardonnay. Then he removes a plastic container of fruit, along with one caprese and one turkey focaccia sandwich. "Which one?" he asks, holding them both up. "I wasn't sure what you liked."

"Turkey," I say as I sit up.

He hands it over with a fork for the fruit, then pours the Chardonnay into two small plastic cups. "I would have gotten a little more creative, but it was sort of last-minute, so I had to just go with what the grocery store had on hand."

"This is really nice. And it was nice of you to organize it all," I say as I twist the cap off my water. "Is there dessert in there?" I make an effort of trying to see into his backpack.

"There might be," he replies, pulling the backpack back so I can't peek inside. "What's your favorite dessert?"

"Like ever? Or that you might find at a grocery store?"

Austin grins. "I didn't realize I had to be so specific. Both, I guess."

"Pretty much any type of cake will work for me. But my favorite dessert is the sticky date cake at the Armitage Alehouse."

"Sticky date cake?" He seems equal parts perplexed and amused.

"Yes."

"Well, clearly we have to go there."

I laugh and bite off half a piece of grocery store pineapple I've forked from the plastic container. He pops a piece of watermelon into his mouth.

"I'd like that," I say. "What about you? Favorite dessert?"

Behind us, the high-pitched *fzzzpp* of a road bike flies down the path. I peer over my shoulder to watch the cyclist disappear, then turn back to see Austin gazing at me, his eyes narrowed in thought. I find myself examining the line of his jaw, the way it dances nearly imperceptibly. I don't think he's really focused on desserts anymore.

He clears his throat and directs his gaze back out across the lake. "I believe my official answer is German chocolate cake." He chuckles.

"Official answer?"

"Yeah. Favorite color, green. Favorite food, lasagna. Favorite band, the Pixies—"

"Your favorite band is the Pixies?"

He turns back to me. "I mean, maybe. I don't really have a favorite band. My agent put all that stuff together for interviews and fanzines."

"Ahh," I say, picking up his train of thought. "So do you actually have a favorite dessert."

Half of his face lifts in a smile. "I don't really like sweets. I never have." He shakes his head as if the whole topic is absurd. I guess it is.

"Well, more cake for me, then," I say, reclining back on the blanket and crossing my ankles.

His phone buzzes, and he taps out a quick reply. "Jenna—the realtor," he says. "She wants to meet to talk about staging."

"I thought you already did that." I fight to restrain a knowing smirk.

"I thought I did, too." The phone buzzes again, but he ignores it.

"What's your house in California like?" I have a picture of it in my mind—grand, yards and yards of cold marble tile and a curved staircase sweeping up to a bunch of bedroom suites all with reclaimed rare-wood floors.

"It's cozy. A bungalow. As close as I could get in L.A. to something that looked Chicago." He pauses for another bite of cantaloupe, then continues. "I bought it years ago, right after the show took off. I always thought of it as a starter home, but I never really had a reason to get anything bigger."

"Hmm," I muse.

"I don't need much space. Though I guess my mom didn't either, and I bought her a house three times the size of my place in L.A."

I take a sip of wine. "Why did you buy it for her?"

"She asked for it," he says, lifting a shoulder. "We were really close. I'd have given her anything."

"I'm sorry she's gone," I say.

For the first time, I have some real sense of his loss. He's been, thus far, fairly subdued about his mother, referencing conversations with her attorneys, the process of emptying her house and preparing it to sell. I've never really heard him talk about their relationship.

"A death like that makes you re-examine things, you know?" he says.

I do know but ask anyway. "How so?"

"I think when you lose a parent, even if they've lived a good long life—I mean, my mom was eighty-two—but when your parents die, you can't help but think, *I'm next. And what do I have to show for this life?*"

I didn't know his mother was eighty-two when she died. Margot would know that. But I think Austin has an awful lot to show for his life. Some legacies are more permanent than others. As much as it pains me, I accept that within a year of Ryan's death, he'd been replaced by his practice group, his patients transferred to other physicians. And while his loss was cataclysmic to me, it probably was an initial shock followed by a short-lived inconvenience to his colleagues and patients.

"Sorry, I shouldn't talk. I can't imagine everything you've been through." He shakes his head and stares out at the water.

I think maybe this is an invitation to share—an I-go-then-you-go thing. I don't want to go, so I just nod.

"And she'd been sick for a while," he says. "I had some time to prepare for the loss."

"How long was she sick?" I ask. Questions seem like a good way to keep from having to talk about how I'd had no time to prepare and how, yes, that had been a particularly brutal cruelty in it all.

"Several years. And there was a relapse in there. So we sort of knew, once that happened, how things would go."

His hands rest on either side of his hips as he reclines on his forearms, and I slide my hand over, placing it on top of his. The conversation makes the gesture feel more intimate than I'd anticipated, and because of that, I can't bring myself to look at him. He flips his palm and weaves his fingers between mine, and I can feel his eyes on me even as I refuse to return his gaze.

"I could fall asleep like this," I say lazily as the lake laps at the stone perimeter of the cove. I might have, too, but he rolls to his side, and I feel his lips against my cheek, the same place he'd kissed when he met me at the side door of the church.

"Tell me to stop, and I will," he whispers.

The warmth of his breath tickles my ear. Honestly, it might be his tongue. I hardly know, as gone as I already am. I pull back so that I can see him, his words still hanging between us. *Tell me to stop.*

I don't, and the kiss that follows suggests he's glad I agreed to come to the lake with him. I'm glad, too. I drop a fork holding half a bite of pineapple and wrap my arms around his shoulders, and the sound that comes from his mouth flutters against my lips and echoes through my body. I glance behind us to see what amount of privacy our little corner of the cove affords—some.

We recline onto the blanket, and I pull his mouth to mine again. He opens his eyes as if to make sure he's read the situation correctly. He has, and his hand moves slowly from my back across my stomach, which flinches at his touch.

He breaks the kiss, his palm flat against my abdomen, as his thumb grazes back and forth, back and forth. I draw a breath with each pass.

"That tickles," I say.

He stops and watches my face, his own becoming serious, almost contemplative. Then he brings his lips to mine again, and I coax him on top of me, grateful for at least some of the modesty a woman's anatomy provides, because it has been a long damn time since I've held a man between my thighs, and my body has missed it—the pressure of his body against mine, the obvious effect of it all on him even as my own body cleverly hides its secrets.

He groans against my mouth as I arch my back forcing my hips hard to his.

"Babs," he breathes, dropping his head to my shoulder and burying his lips against my neck. "God."

He finds an angle against me, and the pressure is exquisite as I grip his waist, increasing the friction until my breath comes in short bursts, and I can feel the heat of his own breath against my neck, and his teeth against my earlobe.

My body seems to hold the memory of a similar moment from years ago—the lead weight of need low in my belly, the resistance of his waistband against my fingers as I recognize the tightness in my throat, the heat concentrated in my chest until the earth is no longer cool against my back, it is a devouring fire that consumes in all directions. And I am ash.

The high-pitched buzz of a cyclist brings me back to the cove, to him. They're moving at quite a clip—a blur of black and red as I twist my head awkwardly to see behind me. But the intrusion, however minimal, is enough.

"This isn't a good idea," I say. I hear my heart beating in my ears and feel it beating in a number of different places.

"No. Probably not," he agrees, the effort of his restraint obvious enough from the flush that has bloomed over the neck of his t-shirt and into his cheeks.

"I'm sorry," I say bringing my hand to the side of his face. He closes his eyes against my touch. "I really am. That wasn't fair to you."

"Don't apologize," he says, shifting to the side of me. "I told you no pressure and then..." He gazes at me, his pupils crowding out the blue-gray irises that halo them.

"I wish the water were warmer," I say just to say something.

Austin doesn't reply. He lies back on the blanket, taking my hand in his and holding it between us. We stay like that, staring up at the sky, which has become overcast, like it might rain.

sixteen

1997

We slipped and slid, down the steep incline, dropping our hands to the earth and arriving at the basin covered in streaks of mud, moss, and the decomposing vegetation of the forest floor.

Austin reached the stream first, removing his shoes and socks before splashing into the shallow water and holding a hand out to me to ensure safe landing. I joined him in the ankle-deep stream, and the icebox-temperature of the water transcendent soaking between my toes and around my legs.

I sighed heavily, closing my eyes and turning my face up to the sky where the sun fought in vain to break through the protective canopy. At some length, I realized Austin still had my hand in his, and I opened my eyes to find him staring at me, wide-eyed, as if some danger threatened us still.

His Adam's apple bobbed down with a hard swallow as he released my hand—set it to my side, really. "I'm going to rinse off," he said with a gesture to the waterfall.

"Good idea."

We sloshed over to the cascade where we scrubbed the

muck from our hands and arms and splashed the cool, clear water over our faces. Austin took off his shirt and tucked it into the waist of his shorts, and I followed suit, grateful that the end of the twentieth century had deemed sports bras "fashionable."

"That side looks easier to walk along," he said, eying the far side of the stream.

We didn't make it that far, though. The minute I held out my hand—force of habit by that point, I'd expected to find his waiting—he wrapped an arm around my waist and pulled me to him with only slightly less force than he had twenty minutes earlier.

"You are not what I'm used to," he said, voice hoarse, our stomachs pressed together, his face an inch from my own.

"I'm sorry I made us come down here." It did seem like I'd caused an awful lot of trouble.

"Don't be," he said. "I'd follow you anywhere." He brought his index finger to the edge of my jaw and traced the line to my chin, where his thumb floated up to tug at my lower lip.

The sound that came from my throat was something between a squeak and a sigh, and my cheeks flushed when Austin replied with an affectionate laugh.

The kiss that followed was a kind of question—and I understood what it asked. The way it began with the gentle, tentative press of his lips to mine—he'd have stopped there if I'd drawn back, if I'd hesitated, if the hands I brought to his chest had pushed him back, rather than fanning across his damp, tan skin, before they reached up to his shoulders and slipped around the base of his neck.

He pulled my baseball cap from my head and tossed it with his to the bank before dropping his lips to mine again. My mouth parted as I slipped my fingers between the dewed strands of his hair, and he responded, his tongue tickling at my lips, carefully, carefully, as if I might change my mind, I might pull away. But I leaned into him, his desire obvious enough between us, until he cradled the back of my head in one hand, tipped my mouth up with the other, and crashed into me.

It was far from my first kiss, but it was the first time I'd been kissed *like that*, by someone who knew all the things a single kiss could say and wanted to say them to me. I wanted to know how to do that as much as I wanted it done to me, and when he finally drew back, I felt nearly bereft in my need for him.

He led me across the stream and freed his shirt from his waist, spreading it over the soft earth. I arranged mine similarly, and reclined onto the cotton, my hair fanning out on the leaves and grass beside the stream.

"Jesus Christ, you are beautiful," he said, kneeling between my legs.

"What?" I lifted my shoulders up, trying to get a look at his face, see if he was serious. But his eyes were cast down, his cheeks glowing with the early hint of too much sun and the unmistakable hue of wanting.

He kissed the top of my abdomen, and I threw a forearm over my eyes in mortification when I quaked with that simple intimacy.

He lifted his head, his eyes finding mine in the shadow created by my forearm. A gentle hand wrapped around my wrist and removed my arm from my face, setting it on his shoulder. He leaned down and kissed the side of my neck, and my legs lifted against his hips in response—an involuntary movement he rewarded with a caress along the side of my body, until he met the waistband of my shorts, slid a hand beneath, and gripped a cheek, pulling my hips against his.

Another sigh floated out into the space above us as Austin flipped my sports bra up and brought a hungry mouth to my nipple.

"I'll take it off," I said, feeling desperate and ridiculous.

He leaned back on his heels while I shimmied the Lycra over my head and threw it on top of our hats, then he brought tentative hands to the waist of my shorts.

"Can I?" he asked.

I remember thinking he must have slept with all these women with these perfect bodies, with these amazing breasts and these incredible asses. But somewhere I found the courage to nod, and Austin pulled my shorts and underwear down, discarding them to the growing pile next to us.

The trees overhead shivered, their leaves like iridescent minnows in an ocean of air as a breeze gathered the vapored tendrils of the stream, and skimmed them, ice-cold, across my body. I pinched my eyes closed with such force that tiny orbs of gold and pink bounced behind my eyelids.

Austin sucked in a breath. "Oh my God. Where did you come from?"

"Chicago," I said, not really thinking about it.

He laughed—genuine, joyful—as his hands glided slowly down the inside of my thighs.

I was afraid to look, afraid of what I might see in him, in myself, as his lips brushed the paths his hand had taken, first one thigh, then the other. And the ache, the ache, and then his touch, the tip of a finger, maybe two, I don't know, I couldn't tell, and it didn't matter, as it slipped inside me curving with a gentle pressure. My hand slapped over my mouth to muffle the absurd noises coming from my throat, but Austin again coaxed it to his shoulder, and I sank into the earth, wondering if the women he was used to were fully shaved, if they were used to feeling like this, if they knew how to purr sounds that were tantalizing, instead of the throaty, unintelligible syllables I couldn't stop making.

Before I could give much more thought to that, I was levitating as his tongue traced the line from his finger up, adding a swirl, then a flick at the top. I gripped the shoulder he'd put my hand to with such force, I worried I'd hurt him as his tongue continued its unbearably marvelous circling and his fingers continued their movements, slow and purposeful, as if to say, *Come here. Come with me. Come.* And I did.

I reached down to his shorts, frantic, fumbling with the button and the fly, frustrated by my own desperation. But I needed him, wholly. All of him. Immediately. My eyes met his as I managed to get the button free.

"We don't have to do this," he said, and I thought I had never disagreed with someone so much in my entire life. "We can wait. There's no rush."

"What?" Had he confused me with someone else? I was the college student. From out of town. I was going home the next day.

"We don't have to do this now," he said.

"Yes we do," I said, trying to push his shorts from his hips. "I want to."

"I just didn't think..." he continued.

How could he not have thought this might happen? *I* thought this might happen. *I* thought that was the whole reason we were there.

"Okay," he said and kicked his shorts and boxers to the side.

It wasn't until we were done, until I'd wrapped my legs around his waist, and held him in my arms as he came, his breath in short staccato rasps against my ear and my whole body shaking beneath his, that I realized I'd made a terrible mistake.

We both had.

He didn't have me confused with someone else. He wanted to see me again. He wanted to know how long I'd be in town. He wanted to visit me in Boston. Would I come back and visit him in L.A.?

"I—I can't," I said, stunned. "How would I do that?"

"I would make it happen. I would... for you... I would make it happen." He was sitting up, both of us still naked as the day we were born, clothes strewn about the bank of that stream.

"I'm—you don't understand." I almost told him. I almost told him I was seeing someone. But it didn't matter. Even if I'd been as single as a one-dollar bill, I'd have said *no*. It was too complicated. I needed to finish college and get through law school and... do things. I couldn't imagine myself in a relationship with Austin Lewis. I could never be one of the perfectly sculpted women who constantly surrounded—and had probably slept with—him. It was wholly incompatible with everything I knew about myself, about my life, about where I was headed.

seventeen

THE FOUR OF US STAND SILENTLY ON MARGOT AND RISHI'S PORCH AS I ring the doorbell. The car ride proved more than a little uncomfortable, so Margot can't answer the door fast enough.

Thirty minutes earlier, Austin met us at my house so we could drive together. I re-introduced him to Penny and Colin as "my friend from California" and immediately understood that a significant chasm resided between Penny thinking Austin "seems nice" and Penny behaving in any way that might be misconstrued as welcoming.

She waited until we were in the car to begin her interrogation. I assume she wanted to make sure neither of us could escape.

"So, how exactly do you know my mom," she began from the backseat. Her voice cut and jabbed with each word, asking questions not merely to get answers, but to send a message.

"We knew each other when we were younger," Austin replied amicably and, it must be said, imprecisely.

Austin sat in the front passenger seat, not entirely visible from the back of the car. I could see Penny looking into the rearview mirror, but that gave her a view of me, not the subject of her inquisition. I narrowed my eyes in warning.

"My mother just died. Now I'm sorting through some of her things," Austin volunteered.

Colin looked up from his Switch. Our family has experienced the death of a parent, and Colin knows this is serious. "I'm sorry to hear that," he said, which is the customary response when someone tells you someone in their family died. We know because every single one of us has heard it more times than we can count.

"Thank you," Austin replied.

"How long are you staying?" Penny cut in, offering no condolences.

"I haven't decided yet."

Her eyes narrowed to slits. She didn't like the response. "Do you have a family in California?"

"No. I have a sister in New York."

"Do you have children?"

"That's enough, Penny," I soothed. "That's enough questions for now."

"It's okay," Austin said as if the questions weren't being hurled at him like a verbal axe-throwing competition. "No. No children. Just two nieces."

"Are you a doctor like my dad is?"

"Penny!" I couldn't keep the scold out of my voice. I also felt sick to my stomach at her use of the present tense.

"No. I'm an actor." Austin still sounded unperturbed. I imagined both that he was hopeful this fact would impress her and was certain it would not.

"What have you been in?"

"I was in a couple of TV shows in the 1990s and the aughts."

By this point, Colin was on full alert. He'd deduced from Penny's questioning that there was some reason to be particularly interested in Austin, and the rapid-fire inquisition was enough for him to put his Switch down and watch the volley taking place in the car.

"Do you play any sports at school?" Austin asked when Penny paused. He probably thought he could disarm her with some questions of his own.

"Yes," she said without volunteering the sports, then she turned her head, facing the window.

She didn't speak to us again for the remainder of the drive. Every now and then, I heard a whisper from the back pass between her and Colin. I assume Colin was asking her what "all of that" was about. I couldn't hear Penny's answer.

When Margot finally opens the door, Penny and Colin push past her into the house; they don't want to be standing out here any longer than I do. Margot laughs at their rush into the foyer, then smiles at Austin and me.

"Come on in," she says, sweeping back from the door.

As I walk into the foyer, she takes me by the shoulders and kisses my cheek, then does the same thing to Austin. What's important to know about this is that in all the years my sister and I have been going to each other's houses, she has never once greeted me by kissing me on the cheek.

"Austin, it's so nice to finally meet you," she says as if they've never met before.

"Likewise," he says warmly, commenting that he loves her house. I imagine he's relieved by her easy acceptance, while it's exactly that easy acceptance (along with the head-tilt-with-smile at the house compliment) that has me on edge.

Rishi walks into the foyer from the kitchen holding Supriya. He extends his free hand to Austin, and the two introduce themselves.

Margot tucks an invisible strand of hair behind her ear, then places her well-manicured hand on her hip. She offers a

Cheshire Cat grin at both Rishi and Austin. Rishi seems thrown, and I see his eyes pose a silent question: *What's going on?*

She takes the salad I brought and makes a production of inviting everyone into the kitchen, apologizing for how messy the house is, even though I can smell the wet-Swiffer before she even sashays across the threshold.

"What are you doing?" I hiss in her ear as we walk into the kitchen.

"What are you talking about?" She looks genuinely confused. I wonder if she's even aware she's doing it. The fawning, the preening. I question whether she actually *is* doing anything. Maybe I'm imagining it. I sneak a peek at Austin to see if he seems uncomfortable. He doesn't. He's already fallen into conversation with Rishi about the weather—overcast, but a nice break from the heat.

Parts of the rest of the afternoon are blissfully normal. Rishi and Austin share a couple of beers while Rishi makes Beyond Burgers and Brats on the grill. I glance up from where I sit with Margot and think, *They might actually like each other.* I don't know what they're talking about, but occasionally one or the other of them laughs, and it seems genuine, relaxed. Rishi always liked Ryan. Really, Rishi likes most people—everyone's a potential friend.

But other parts of the afternoon are dreadful in ways that defy description.

I set the table and Margot joins Rishi and Austin at the grill, wrapping her arms around Rishi's waist in something that's not quite an embrace. He plants a kiss on the crown of her head and throws an arm across her shoulder, and the two of them exchange a look so fleeting and so familiar, my body recognizes it before my mind does. A wordless, casual reminder: *I love you; I love you, too. Forever. Forever.*

She moves toward the patio door—I assume to get condiments and toppings—and Rishi is frozen in place as if a spell has been cast. He watches her walk up to the house, open the backdoor, and disappear into the kitchen. His hand, still holding the tongs, hovers over a brat as Austin takes a swig of his beer and absently flips a couple burgers.

I know the expression Rishi wears even though my view is limited to no more than a few inches of the side of his face—I remember what it felt like to be regarded so, to be missed when I wasn't even gone, to be admired and wanted. To be loved in that remarkable, ordinary way.

I finish setting the table and scan the backyard. Penny has Supriya on a swing suspended from one of those elaborate backyard play sets. Colin swings sullenly on the other swing—the "big kid" one—next to Supriya. He's watching Austin talk to Rishi like his dad used to talk to Rishi, which breaks my heart.

I walk over to the play set, and stand behind Colin, giving him a little push every once in a while. Seventh graders don't usually want their moms pushing their swings. He drags his toes against the wood-chips until the swing stops, but I keep holding the green plastic-encased chain that suspends it from the set.

All of a sudden, Colin leans back and rests his head against my torso. I wrap my arms around him, and he wraps his arms around mine, and we stay there for a minute not talking until finally he asks, "Are you marrying that man?"

Penny stops pushing Supriya and swivels her head, but she doesn't fix her gaze on me, waiting for an answer; she directs it at Colin, angry at him for asking the question. She must have put it in his head.

"I really am just getting to know him," I say to Colin (and to

Penny, who is clearly listening but still not looking at me). "Is that okay? For now?" I lean down and kiss Colin on top of his head. He's too old to be kissed on top of his head by his mother, but he doesn't flinch, doesn't pull away. He lets me keep my lips there while I breathe in his sweaty boy hair.

"I think that's okay," he says finally. He needed some time to weigh the matter. "For now."

He steps away from the swing and away from my arms and walks toward the house. I hear Rishi say something to him and follow him into the kitchen, leaving Austin standing alone at the grill. I make my way from the play set to the grill to keep him company.

"What's Rishi doing?" I ask.

"Helping Colin set up video games inside the house," he says as he rotates the brats with a pair of tongs. He seems content, happy almost. He glances at me, smiling absently, then does a double-take as I smile feebly back. He moves the brats off the heat, takes my hand, and walks me briskly into the kitchen, past Margot, and onto the front porch. By the time we get there, I'm crying. Not ugly crying, but the kind I'd really rather he didn't see.

"Hey. Hey. It's all going to be okay," he says, taking my face in his hands.

"My sister..." I say, even though that's really the least of it.

"What about her?" His eyes are intent on my face, on the details of it, like he's trying to pick up any hint, any clue that might help him understand how we've gone from cooking brats to crying on the front porch.

"This is hard on my kids," I say, a confession that's much more on point, and because of that I have a hard time looking at him when I say it. He doesn't reply at first.

Then he says, "I thought it might be."

He coaxes my chin up so that I have to meet his eyes.

They've become darker, the blue irises have shifted like a mood ring from the contentment they held in the backyard to the deep worry they convey now.

"It's going to be okay, Babs," he says. He so convincing I think maybe I believe him.

He still has his finger hooked beneath my chin as if I might refuse to look at him if he doesn't hold my head up. Or maybe he thought I didn't have the energy to hold it up myself, which it feels a little like I don't. When he pulls it away, I rest my forehead on his shoulder, leaning into him, and he encircles me in his arms, hugging me tight.

"I bet the food is just about ready," he says.

I lift my head off his shoulder, and he takes my hand as we go back into the house.

Rishi comes down the stairs at the same time. He sees my face, and his expression shifts to one of understanding. When he joins up with us, he puts an arm around my shoulder and gives me a side squeeze. He waits to say something until we get outside when he moves the brats and burgers back onto the heat—they only require a few more minutes of cooking. "It's going to be okay, Babs." It's become a refrain.

Dinner forces attention on the kids, including the birthday girl who is overjoyed at the festivities in her honor.

Penny makes a valiant attempt to steal the spotlight from her cousin—though not for herself—by informing the table that "Austin's a movie star." She adds an "I guess," in case anyone mistook her for being impressed with this fact.

"I heard something about that," Margot says in a voice that wobbles between defusing the tension and flirting with it. "I understand he's very talented."

Austin appears to have Margot's stamp of approval, which has Penny shifting from agitation to curiosity. And because Penny's darkness has relented, the gloom has disappeared from my son, and he's listening and interested, if also cautious.

"What were you in?" Colin asks.

"The show most people know was called *The Maple Street Martins.*" He offers this fact carefully, humbly it would seem, as if he has no expectation that Colin would be "most people."

"What was it about?"

Margot volunteers the explanation. "It was about four kids and their parents and just kind of the ordinary stuff kids face. I guess in a way, it wasn't really *about* anything. But it dealt with important issues that other shows weren't really talking about. Any teen drama you watch today probably owes its existence to *The Maple Street Martins.*"

"I think I'd probably agree with that," Austin says.

Margot smiles, satisfied, like she's the star pupil in Austin's twentieth century pop culture history course.

There is a tragically short period of time during dinner when I allow myself to believe that everything is fine. Margot's "fan-girling" is almost endearing. Rishi seems tickled to learn that he's dining with someone famous. Penny has let go of her hostility, and Colin looks like he's ready to proceed with a thousand questions, none of which carry the threat of physical violence that accompanied Penny's interrogation in the car.

Then, predictably, it collapses.

When it's time to sing *Happy Birthday*, Margot delivers to the table a three-tiered German chocolate cake. She sets it down in front of Supriya and lights the two candles in the center.

"Supriya's favorite," she says, then pauses a moment, and I know she's waiting for Austin to enthusiastically announce that it's his favorite, too. What a happy coincidence.

I feel his hand reach for mine on the arm of my chair, and I happily allow him to take it, twining my fingers between his as he delivers a small squeeze to my hand. I turn to offer a smile and am confronted with a look of aching fatigue.

After cake and presents and a respectful period of time, we rise to leave, wishing Supriya a happy birthday. She's been over-served on everything from attention to chocolate frosting and is in countdown to detonation. I probably am, too. So, I gather our four plates to take them into the kitchen on the way back to the front of the house, and as I do, I notice that Austin hasn't taken a single bite of that cake. Not one.

eighteen

THIS IS HOW MY SISTER AND I FIGHT.

When she comes over the following Sunday, we don't talk about the fact that we're fighting or what we're fighting about. We don't talk about the fact that we haven't talked to each other for a full week. I was only 50-50 on whether she'd even show up for brunch, but I went ahead and made a breakfast strata with spinach, sun dried tomatoes, and feta.

I set a serving of it down in front of her and Supriya. Penny and Colin come to the kitchen and help themselves. I sit across the table from Margot, who's talking about Rishi. He was traveling for work all last week. I'm not sure what she's saying. My mind is focused on the speech I've rehearsed to address the birthday party—the result of my conversation with Austin after, when I informed him that Margot is not merely a fan, she is a Lewnatic. I'd prepared myself to hear that the relationship was over. But instead he asked simply that I be "judicious" in what I share with her. Then, he asked if I thought Oktoberfest might be something my kids would enjoy.

Margot continues on, now talking about her mother-in-law who stayed with them while Rishi was out of town. I take the opportunity to review my key points: I get it; Austin was her teen celebrity crush; I could imagine it would be strange. But that was years ago—decades. It's time to tuck away the *Tiger Beat* fantasy cult and—

"Anyway, enough about me. Did you see Austin last week?" she asks. She follows her question with a delicate bite of the strata. Supriya looks up as if she's hoping for an answer to the question as well.

"Yes," I say without offering any further details. "And I wanted to talk to you about Supriya's birthday party."

"Happy Birthday!" Supriya exclaims, throwing her hands in the air, then promptly returning her attention to her breakfast.

"What about it?" Margot lifts her coffee mug with two hands, elbows resting on the table, and follows the question with a sip. All very casual.

"The cake," I say.

She blushes and drops her gaze to her lap.

"Margot."

She sets her mug on the table and glances up at me. "Sorry?" she cheeps.

"What was that about? I don't understand."

"I don't know," she says in a way that really does sound like she does not know.

"Did Rishi say anything?"

She shakes her head. "I mean, before last week, he had no idea who Austin Lewis was. He just thinks it's cool that someone famous came to Supriya's birthday party. I think he's following him on Instagram now."

I take a sip of coffee.

"Did—did Austin say anything?" she asks.

"No. I did. I apologized to him. It made him really uncomfortable. He doesn't even like cake."

"He doesn't?" The way she says it, it's beyond belief.

"No. He doesn't. And all that stuff is thirty years old. What the hell, Margot?"

"What kind of person doesn't like cake, though?" she mutters into the table.

I can't help it—a couple bursts of laughter bubble out of me.

"Maybe I should have made some paleo frosting or something," she says, obviously grateful for the levity. She moves some of the food around on her plate, then sets her fork next to it and turns serious. "It's... it's hard to be normal about this," she says. "I really thought he'd already be back in L.A. by now."

"Honestly, so did I."

"And I thought you said you were just friends."

"I don't know what we are," I say into my plate full of untouched food. "I guess we're dating, right?"

I watch as she struggles with something she wants to say, but must think she shouldn't. "Babs, he doesn't really *date*. Or, he hasn't in a long time. He just kind of cycles through women. A few months here, maybe a year there."

I try to call back the Instagram photos I've scrolled through. They predominantly document his travels, products he endorses, projects he's involved in, castmates' projects. I haven't followed his career, certainly not as closely as Margot apparently has. And my own social media footprint is limited—my last post was five months ago at Colin's birthday. For a long time, I simply didn't have time for all that, and since Ryan died, it only reminds me of his absence. If grief has an enabler, her name is *nostalgia*.

"I'm just seeing where it goes," I say. It's a wastebasket of a response, intended to contain anything tossed in its general vicinity.

Margot lifts her fork, but I'm assuming the skepticism she wears so openly is not intended for my flatware.

"You think I'm making a mistake," I say.

She turns the handle of the fork slowly in her hand, the tines flipping, blurring. "Not a mistake," she says carefully. "But I'm not sure this is the best choice for your first foray into the dating world in twenty years."

I can't help but wonder whether there might be more than one motive at work with this advice, but her eyes hold only worry, and I have no reason to doubt that the worry extends to me. Still, the description she's providing is irreconcilable with what I've experienced of Austin over the past month.

"It might be better if I just didn't talk about it with you," I say.

"Yeah. That wouldn't be weird at all." Her voice roils over the words. "Be serious, Babs."

I was being serious, but she's right that it's a ridiculous strategy. We talk multiple times a day and see each other every week.

Colin reappears in the kitchen before I can agree with her. He liberates Supriya from her highchair, and the two head downstairs.

"What did you do?" Margot asks once Colin and Supriya have departed.

"About what?" I glance around the table wondering if I dropped something.

"This week. With Austin. You said you've seen him a few times this past week." She's moving on, though the question doesn't feel like a complete non sequitur, more like an olive branch.

I take it at face value. "We went to Oktoberfest."

"You weren't worried about a crowd that big?" she asks. It's the same question I'd asked Austin when he suggested it.

"Can't hide forever," he'd said. Though when he arrived at my house to catch the 'L', the hat and sunglasses were back.

"It seemed mostly fine," I say, finally relaxing enough to enjoy some of the breakfast I'd made. "It was a Sunday, so the crowd was smaller."

"Mostly?" Margot picks the word out like she's plucking a spec of dust from a glob of wet paint.

"The biggest issue seemed to be that I had the temerity to suggest Colin get his face painted. The way he—*and Austin*—looked at me, you'd think I'd offered meth."

Margot laughs but sides with Colin. "He's kind of old to have his face painted."

"He was younger the last time we were there." Three years. It had been three years since we'd been to Oktoberfest. The pandemic, Ryan's death. "Other than that, it was really nice. Penny and Colin seem to be warming up to him." It might be more accurate to say that Colin is warming up to him; Penny mostly tolerates his presence in the manner of someone who likes to camp, but hates mosquitoes. Fortunately, one of her friends had been at Oktoberfest, too, and they spent the evening together, which probably mitigated Penny's desire to swat Austin away.

"I think some people recognized him, though," I say. I decide to venture back into perilous terrain. "Have you—have you seen anything... in that group you're in?"

I watch her, attentive to any sign. But she shakes her head. "I haven't checked in there in a couple days." She reaches for her phone.

"You don't have to look now. And I'm not sure—I don't know what it was. It was more just a feeling."

I shiver as I recall. Austin had an arm around my shoulders, and I had an arm around his waist, and we'd settled into a cadence so natural and ordinary, it was as if we'd known each other for years. I felt his hand leave my shoulder and travel to my neck where the tips of his fingers dragged along the line of my spine under my hair from the base of my skull to my shirt and back. Goosebumps prickled out along my arms and legs, and I struggled to continue walking a straight line.

I glanced at him from the corner of my eye, but he gazed straight ahead behind his glasses, not at all conscious of the effect this particular caress was having on me. I exhaled, trying to keep my breath even and controlled, but failed miserably as a shudder ran through my body.

Austin's hand stopped immediately, and his head snapped toward me. He clearly thought he'd find me upset, but the heat that had risen into my cheeks must have set the matter straight. He reached a hand across the span of my shoulders pulling me into his side and placed a kiss at my temple.

"I'll have to remember that," he whispered into my ear, then took my hand in his, and it was then that I felt… I'm not even sure what. Observed. Inspected.

I scanned the crowed but before I could say anything, Colin called to me, asking if he could have a pretzel.

"Yeah, bud. You can have whatever you want," I'd said.

"Are you okay?" Margot asks, and I realize I've wrapped my arms around myself, my hands slowly moving up and down my biceps. "Did you tell Austin about it?"

I drop my hands to my lap. "No. I wasn't sure what it was. I thought maybe…"

"I thought that had stopped," Margot says. She's the only person who knows, the only person I've told, and I've sworn her to secrecy.

"It wasn't the same feeling. It was different," I say.

She nods, but her eyes rove over my face with precision, every line, every crease under inspection.

I change the subject. "We had brunch on Thursday and went to dinner and a movie on Friday."

"Where'd you go for dinner?" Margot asks into her coffee.

"Armitage Alehouse," I say.

"Did you get the sticky date cake?"

"Of course."

She laughs, and the tension eases out the room like an uninvited guest trying to sneak out of a party without being noticed.

"Can you promise me something?" I ask.

"Sure."

"Promise me you'll keep all of this off Instagram?"

"The group's on Facebook. But I never post in there anyway," she says.

nineteen

1997

I walked into the living room—shellshocked from the day and from the way I'd left things in the car with Austin. I'd worn my sweatshirt, attempting to conceal some of the damage to my clothes, but underneath, I was covered in mud. It streaked my shorts, my sports bra, my socks. I had to throw every article of clothing away, including my tennis shoes.

"How's Margot?" I asked. I probably didn't have any right to be, but I was worried about her, and as I examined my aunt and uncle, their faces were sufficient to answer the question.

"She won't come out of her room. She hasn't eaten all day," Aunt Iris said.

"Is she upset about your father? That son of a bitch. What kind of man makes a family and then just walks away from it?" Uncle Leo stormed.

"I don't think that's it," Aunt Iris said.

"It's not," I said. "She's upset because she wasn't invited to go hiking with me."

"She's upset because she wanted to go hiking?" Uncle Leo

asked. "Why didn't she say so? We could have taken her. There are some great trails over in Will Rogers. Is that where you and your friends went?" He sounded baffled.

"She's upset because I went with Austin Lewis." I watched as both Aunt Iris and Uncle Leo's jaws dropped nearly to their chests.

"You went hiking with Austin Lewis?" Uncle Leo asked. "When... how... How did we not know about this? Why didn't you say that's who you were going with?"

Aunt Iris put a hand on his arm, quieting him, and turned to me, regarding me with kind eyes. "That's who called this morning?" She brought the tips of her fingers to her mouth and patted her lips lightly as if to further soften the words.

"Was it a date?" Uncle Leo asked, still not quite getting it. He glanced at me, expectant of an answer.

"I don't know what it was." I felt stunned, dizzy from the conversation that followed and from Austin's words as we sat in the car in front of my aunt and uncle's house just ten minutes earlier.

"Just give it some thought," he'd said. "And call me if you change your mind." He'd held my hand in both of his as he said it, then brought my hand to his cheek, closing his eyes as he rested the side of his face against my palm. I could feel the warmth of him even as I stood there in front of my aunt and uncle.

"I think it's best if we just stay friends," I'd said.

It was a lot easier to say shit like that back then because it was a lot harder to stay in touch with people back then. So, when I said, "We can still be friends" what I meant was, "We will be nothing ever."

"Are you okay?" Aunt Iris asked. "Did he... try to..." She looked up at Uncle Leo whose eyes had grown wide.

"No. No. It was nothing like that. It was—" I searched for the right words, but nothing came to mind.

Aunt Iris continued examining me. I could understand her skepticism.

"I think he wanted to see me again," I said as if I weren't quite sure.

"Well, how would that work?" Uncle Leo demanded. "He's a twenty-six-year-old man. You're a college student." I thought he was twenty-five. Margot would know.

Aunt Iris's chest rose and fell with a labored sigh.

"I said no."

Uncle Leo nodded, in agreement with that evidently sound decision.

"You look tired, Barbara," Aunt Iris said.

She was right. I was exhausted. Exhausted enough that I didn't even care what she called me. She could have called me Janice, and I'd have answered to it.

"Why don't you go upstairs, and we can talk more about this tomorrow?"

We were leaving for the airport tomorrow, so I knew what she really meant was that we weren't going to talk about it because it was irrelevant.

I climbed the stairs and stopped in front of Margot's door. It was nearly ten at night, which could have allowed me to continue walking to my room with the plausible excuse that I'd thought she was asleep. Certainly, there was no noise coming from her room.

I knocked.

No answer.

"Margot?" I whispered.

I tried the handle and was surprised to find it unlocked. I cracked the door, then pushed it open when I saw that the room was dark. I couldn't tell whether Margot was even in it, and I panicked that she'd run away. Or worse. Then, I heard her shift on the bed.

"Margot?"

She sat up as my eyes adjusted to the dark, and I walked into the room.

"Oh my god. You smell like shit," she said, as I closed the door behind me.

"Okay," I said, not at all interested in a fight. Plus, I probably did. "I just wanted to say good-night. Make sure you're okay."

"Make sure *I'm* okay?" she said. "You're the one who smells like she went hiking in a toilet."

I came slowly toward the bed and sat down on the edge of it. Margot brought her knees to her chest and wrapped her arms around her shins. Even in the dark, I could see that she'd spent most of the day crying—her eyes so puffy I wondered if she could see.

"Why did you get back so late? You've been gone all day." Her voice softened.

"It was a long hike," I said, leaving out why. I had no hope of being able to fully discuss and process what had happened with Austin Lewis with a freshman in high school, much less this specific freshman. But Margot had questions.

"Did he kiss you?" I still remember the small sound of her voice as she asked that question. Now, with all the years in between, I know she was asking because she needed the answer to be *no*.

"Yes," I said.

She hiccuped a sob and dropped her face into the small valley between her kneecaps. "Did you have sex with him?" she mumbled without lifting her head.

"Margot—"

"Did you?" She lifted her head then.

"Yes," I said.

She stared at me in icy silence for several seconds, her chin quivering, new tears tumbling down her cheeks. "I'm going to tell Ryan," she said, her bloodshot eyes squinting into daggers.

"Don't you dare," I said. All previous sympathy for her fell away.

"Do you love him?" she asked.

"Who?"

"Austin, you stupid ho."

"No. I don't," I said. "And I'm not a ho. It just happened. We got lost, and it just happened." As I said it, I could hear how ridiculous it sounded, but I went on. "Neither of us planned that part of it."

I watched as Margot's face hardened, the tears still wet on her cheeks, which had become flushed not with sadness, but with rage.

"Get out!" she shouted. "Get out of my room. I don't ever want to see you again."

Honestly, the rage terrified me; I'd never seen her so angry. I headed for the door, and Margot flew off the bed, following close behind me.

"I will never speak to you again, Babs. Never! I hope you die. I hope Austin Lewis gave you AIDS. And when you die, I'm not coming to your funeral because I fucking hate you."

By this time, I'd opened the door and backed into the hall. Aunt Iris and Uncle Leo were rushing up the stairs, no doubt in response to the shouting they'd heard, but by the time they reached the top, Margot had slammed her door shut, and it was just the three of us in the hallway.

"I'm going to bed," I said and skulked off to my room, locking the door behind me.

The next morning, Aunt Iris drove us to the airport. I was grateful for her mindless prattling in the car, her running commentary about what a wonderful trip it had been and how she hoped we'd visit again and how meaningful it had been to have us stay with them. Then she walked us to the gate and made sure we safely got on the plane.

    We never visited them again.

twenty

"Jesus Christ." I cover the lower half of my face with my sweater as Austin opens the front door of his mother's house, releasing an overpowering, fetid odor that brings bile to the back of my throat.

"What are you doing here? I told you not to come. It's not safe," he says, stepping out onto the front porch and lowering an N95 to his chin.

"I know it's not safe. I was worried about you. I came as soon as I got your text." The same text that told me not to come over.

Austin starts to laugh. "I should have told you everything is fine."

"*Pfft*. I wouldn't have believed that for a second."

"Mr. Lewis?" A man in a hazmat suit steps out onto the front porch, smelling every bit as bad as the house behind him. "We've scoped the line and—" the man glances at me. "This your house, too?"

"No. I'm just here for moral support."

"Neither of you should be here at all. I'm sorry, Mr. Lewis. I know you were hoping to put this on the market this weekend, but you're not going to be able to do that."

Whether I'd forgotten or just pushed it out of my mind, the fact that Austin planned to sell his mother's house and return to L.A. is an event I've not thought about in quite some time. That he evidently planned to start that process in a matter of days—and had not said a word to me about it—freezes me in place, the cold weight of dread landing in my stomach.

Hazmat Man continues. "From what I can see, the blockage is about mid-way between the house and the street. It looks like a tree root on the camera. Sometimes, you know, it's just a collection of tampons or maxi-pads—" he looks at me when he says this.

"I don't live here," I remind him.

"Just the same," he says. "One time, some kid shoved a bunch of Beanie Babies down a toilet, but we were able to push that out into the city lines and avoid a major repair."

"I take it it's not Beanie Babies," Austin says, dryly.

"No, sir. I can't say with certainty what it is. But we're going to have to dig up the line." He surveys the front lawn to underscore his meaning.

"Are there any other options?"

"Not unless you like a basement full of raw sewage and no running water. I don't judge. In my line of work, you can't. You wouldn't believe some of the things I've seen in people's basements. One time—"

"Mr. Lewis!" The voice belongs to Jenna. She's arrived in heels and is trying to negotiate a hypotenuse from a grotesquely large SUV (parked behind my car, which is parked behind the plumber's truck) across the spongy lawn toward the porch. "Are you the plumber?" she asks when she reaches us.

"Yeah. You the realtor?"

She nods.

"You're not selling his house this week," he says.

"Yes, I know that," she snaps. "What happened?"

I feel myself growing dizzy as my eyes bounce from Austin to the plumber to the realtor.

"We're going to have to dig up the line out to the street. It's got to be replaced."

"How long will that take?" Austin asks.

"A project like this? Plus the remediation? Three weeks, at least. Probably more."

Jenna groans and puts a hand up to her forehead in exasperation. "We've already printed the open house info."

I glance at Austin again. It's Monday. Was he planning to mention this to me at some point?

"I should go," I say, feeling the god's honest truth of that statement.

"Wait," Austin says. I see him reach for—and miss—my arm as I head toward my car. "Hang on. Where are you going?" he calls after me. His forehead creases with confusion as I reach my car and open the door to get in.

"Sorry," I say. "I didn't realize there was so much happening here today."

"Do you need me to move my car?" Jenna calls as she tiptoes her kitten heels back across the yard and *beep-boops* her SUV.

"Yes, thank you," I say tightly. All I can think is that Margot was right about Austin's temporary status, that he cycles through women, and that I only narrowly avoided becoming one such cycle.

"Hey, hey," Austin says, like he's calming a frightened animal. "Tell me what's going on." He holds the top of the car door, his knuckles turning white from his grip.

My eyes burn with tears I refuse to unleash, and I have to bite my teeth together to prevent my voice from shaking, which it does anyway. "You're ready to sell. You're going back to L.A."

Jenna backs out of the driveway but, probably imagining I'll be leaving in short order, angles back and waits patiently so she can pull her tank back in behind the plumber's truck.

"What? Why would I be going back to L.A.?" He seems disoriented, like he's lost something and doesn't even know where to begin looking for it.

"But you didn't say anything," I point out. "So…"

"So, it looks like I was planning to leave without telling you," he says, dropping his hands to his hips as he focuses on the concrete driveway between his feet.

"No?" I ask, sensing that I'm the one who's missed something.

"No," he says. "Absolutely not. Selling the house has nothing to do with how long I stay in Chicago. It's not part of the equation."

Jenna rolls her window down and sticks her head out. "Are you leaving?" The two rows of gleaming white teeth she bares imply impatience.

"I'm staying," Austin says. "For as long as you want me to."

"Hey, Mr. Lewis. I'm going to need you to come sign this work estimate if you're agreeing to replace the line." The plumber lifts his watch to his face.

"Okay. In a minute," Austin says over his shoulder.

"Where were you planing to stay?" I ask—a version of *where were you planning to go*, which was the question, as phrased, in my head.

"Well, I thought the house would sell whenever it sells, and then I'd look for an apartment before the closing. I'm sure Jenna will be more than happy to help me with that." He laughs, a single *huh* at a sort-of-joke. "I guess this mess is going to require me to get a jump on the apartment hunting, though." He directs a regretful glance at the house.

"Where are you staying tonight?" I ask.

"What?" he stutters, his eyes snapping back to me.

"You can't stay here."

"I—I haven't had time to think about it. A hotel, I guess."

"We have a guest room off the family room in the basement. It was my mom's room when she lived with us. Has its own bathroom and everything."

"Mr. Lewis!" the plumber calls with a tap to his watch.

"Give me a second, Paul," Austin shouts back to the porch without taking his eyes from me.

"Just until you find a place." I need to pick up Colin and Penny from school, talk to them about all this, but it looks like Austin's going to be busy here for a while.

I glance behind me at Jenna in time to see her roll her eyes, then she rolls up her window and pulls back into the driveway.

"Are you sure that's a good idea?" Austin asks.

"No," I say.

Austin laughs. "Well, thank you."

I hear Jenna clear her throat and find her standing to the side of us. My open car door blocks her path up the driveway, and she's disinclined to walk across the grass once more.

"We need to amend your contract," she says to Austin.

"Right," he says.

"I'm going to talk to Penny and Colin," I say. "Come over when you've sorted things out here."

"Okay," he says.

I turn to Jenna, wincing. "I actually need you to back out again."

She stares at me, then her eyes shoot to Austin as if he might save her, but he's already walking back toward the plumber.

"You must be fucking kidding me," she says, but heads back to her car as I step into mine.

At the sound of the garage door closing and Austin's duffle bag hitting the floor, Penny and Colin sprint into the kitchen. I've spoken with both of them extensively, explained Austin's unfortunate circumstances. I'd thought I'd meet with resistance, and was hopeful his situation would engender sympathy. Instead the description seems to have endowed them only with lurid curiosity.

"Like the whole basement is just full of..." Colin trailed off, his lips pulling back from his teeth as I explained the situation a couple hours earlier. We'd been eating dinner, and he pushed his plate back in disgust, but he'd already eaten everything on it, leaving the gesture—along with the plate—empty.

"I don't know. I didn't go into the house," I said.

"Like how many feet do you think?" Penny asked.

"I have no idea, Penny. Enough that he can't live there while they're fixing it."

"This has got to be the most disgusting thing I've ever heard of in my life," Penny said.

"I bet I can come up with something grosser," Colin said.

"Nope," I said. "Nope. I don't want to hear it. Find another place in the house to have that contest."

They departed the dining room, taking their plates and gross-out contest to the kitchen where I could hear them talking, but tried exceptionally hard not to hear what they said.

Now that Austin stands in the kitchen, entering the competition in the flesh, both Colin and Penny gaze upon him with awe. The things he must have seen. The horror laid out before his very eyes.

"Follow me," I say.

Austin picks up his duffle bag off the floor, and I lead him into the hall and down the stairs to the basement.

"This is incredibly generous of you," he says, trailing a respectful distance behind me.

"I put fresh sheets on the bed and clean towels in the bathroom," I say, feeling strangely awkward about whether the hospitality is *incredibly generous*. It had seemed, amid the chaos earlier, that it was the only appropriate thing to do—a simple matter of manners. But as he follows me into the guest room and sets his bag on the floor, I feel the electricity of his presence.

"Are you hungry?" I ask. "I saved you a plate from dinner."

"Thank you. Do you mind if I shower first? I changed my clothes back at the house, but there was no running water."

"Not at all. Really, just make yourself at home," I say, employing the standard language for house guests.

He hesitates, and I wonder if I'm supposed to leave. Probably.

"Do you have a garbage bag?" he asks a bit reluctantly. "I think I'd be better off throwing most of this away." He glances down at himself.

"I'll put one on the bed for you while you're in the shower," I say. We stand stiffly for a moment more, then I start for the door.

"Babs," he says.

"Yeah?"

"Just... thank you."

"Don't worry about it," I say—all business—and close the door behind me.

I return to the kitchen. Colin is seated at the island busy doing homework.

"Is Mr. Lewis okay?" he asks. He seems worried.

"Yes, honey. Of course he is. He's just flustered." I assume the flurry of activity when Austin arrived unnerved Colin.

"Penny said he could have *e. coli* poisoning," Colin says. "He might get really sick."

"No, Colin. I don't think so. I think he's going to be okay. He's taking a shower right now. Then he's going to eat dinner. He'll be fine."

Colin's shoulders relax, and he returns to his homework.

About twenty minutes later, Austin comes up to the kitchen barefoot in sweatpants and a t-shirt, holding the garbage bag I'd placed on the bed. "Where's your dumpster?" he asks.

"Here," I say, reaching for the bag and eyeing his bare feet. "I'll take it out."

"No, you will not," he states firmly—strongly enough that Colin, who'd been examining every square inch of Austin (probably for signs of *e. coli*, dammit Penny) turns to me to see if I'll argue.

"In the alley, against the fence."

Austin departs through the garage and returns a couple minutes later, heading directly to the sink where he washes his hands. "Definitely not California out there," he says.

"No," I say, feeling some of the shock of the day set in. "It's October. In Chicago. Do you need socks?"

"I brought some," he says.

"Are you hungry?" I ask, walking toward the microwave where I'd kept his plate.

"Yes," he says, with a sigh.

I heat his dinner and lead him into the dining room, both so that we can have some privacy, and so that we won't disturb Colin. I set the plate down and sit at the head of the table, while Austin takes a seat adjacent to me. He takes a few bites, then sets his fork down.

"I'm so sorry about this afternoon, about all the confusion," he whispers. "I was worried for a minute there that you were going to leave, and I'd never see you again. Again." He lets a smile play with his lips.

"Well, you can decide how grateful you are when you're

awoken tomorrow morning at 6:30 to the sounds of teenagers tromping around the kitchen. It's the one downside to the location of that guest room."

"I bet I'm still grateful," he says, then takes another bite.

Austin finishes dinner, then helps me load the dishwasher before excusing himself to his room to make some phone calls and respond to emails.

"My sister needs to know about the house," he says as we stand at the top of the basement stairs.

"Okay. I'll probably straighten up down here and then head up to bed."

"Okay. Good night," he says.

"Good night," I return and walk back to the kitchen to wipe down the counters before going to bed.

As I straighten the kitchen, I hear Austin's voice, the low baritone rumble of it as he speaks to someone on the phone. I move into the living room, straightening up there before climbing the stairs, checking on Penny and Colin, and crawling into bed for the night. I read for a while, then turn out the light. If Austin is still on the phone, he's keeping his voice down. The house is a tomb.

twenty-one

I WAKE TO THE SOUND OF TIRES SCREECHING BEYOND THE WALLS OF MY bedroom. My phone reads 2:00 a.m. on the dot, which makes me question whether the screeching was nightmare or reality. I sit, alert, listening for sirens, but none follow as I concentrate, inviting the night in—listening for the 'L', attentive to voices out on the sidewalk. Waiting. No sound arrives.

I feel the chill of autumn sweep in around me like an invisible fog. Our house is a gut-rehab from the early aughts, but the cold still seeps in, making the hair on my arms stand at attention, my skin cool to my own touch. Across from my bed, the door glows like the entry to a portal. I suppose, in a way, it is.

I tiptoe out of my room and down the stairs. I could pretend I don't know where I'm going, like maybe I just want a glass of water, even though there's plenty of water available from the taps upstairs. I don't break left at the kitchen. Instead, I take the stairs down to the basement. In my mind, I've established a fatalist coin toss: if he's asleep, which I fully expect him to be at two in the morning, I'll march right back to bed.

I round the corner at the foot of the stairs. In the silver light, my new couch clashes loudly with the area rug beneath it. I head toward the hallway beyond, laundry room on one side, guest room on the other. The door is open but the room is dark, and for a second, I think he's one of those strange people who sleeps with the door open. Then I see him in the doorway, his shoulders, the length of his legs, the breadth of his chest, cutting a shadow against the ambient city light that sneaks in around the shades.

I catch a breath and begin to stammer. "I—I couldn't..."

"I couldn't either," he says. His hair suggests he put forth an effort, however unsuccessful. Mussed on one side, a tuft out of place along his forehead, he gives the appearance of restlessness.

He also gives the appearance of a man who takes care of himself. The broad, tan span of his abdomen and chest rises out of a pair of navy-blue, jersey sweatpants low-slung on his hips. His chest rises and falls with shallow breaths, and I am moved —compelled—to touch his skin, to put my hands against the heat I know resides there.

I lean into a step, but lose my nerve as his jaw tenses, a tic just below his ears, and I drop my heel back to the floor. I am paralyzed, stuck, like the dreams where I want to run, but my legs simply will not obey my command. Move, move. Go, damn you.

Austin's legs must be more obedient. He steps into the hall and throws an arm around my waist, plucking me from the carpet like a clover from the grass. He backs slowly into the bedroom, holding me tight to his chest, and tosses the door closed with his free hand. He releases me, and I slide down his body, my t-shirt furling up against my stomach which twitches as I come to rest against his waist and feel the movement of his breath, expanding into me, then withdrawing.

He brings his lips to mine, and I hear him draw in a breath at the touch of my mouth to his, as if he didn't anticipate this—

it's been more than a month since that kiss after the Cubs game. My hands find his chest—as warm in the night-cool of my house as I'd thought he'd be—and I slide a hand around the back of his neck encouraging a deeper kiss. He obliges, and the force of his kiss pushes me against the back of the door, which isn't an entirely unpleasant circumstance for the leverage it allows as he places a hand under my thigh, pulling my leg to his hip. This provides a similar pressure to that he'd exerted at the lake, and my hands drop to his hips, seeking more.

Our lips part as I lean my head back against the door, arching my hips towards his, as his mouth finds my neck, my earlobe, the sensitive skin below. A hand glides up the side of my ribs, and I shiver from that light touch and the heavy weight of his hips against mine. His thumb traces an arc up across my breast, pausing at my nipple until I find that my hands have formed fists around the waist of his sweatpants, and there is nothing I can do to stifle the guttural sounds that emerge from my throat.

I open my eyes in a futile effort to exert control and find his eyes searching mine. It's dark, but I can see his cheeks are flushed, and I assume mine are, too.

He takes my hand without saying anything and walks me back to the bed. I recline on the covers, and he lifts my shirt over my head, then quickly tugs my pajama pants down, and I blink up at him, naked under his gaze in an act of courage so monumental it deserves its own limited run series. He shoves his sweatpants to the floor, and the only sounds in the room are his breathing and the thrum of my heart in my ears.

A stray thought about his model ex-wife floats through my head, and I scold myself again for how stupid I'd been to feel self-conscious when I was nineteen. I should have saved some of that for now, when most of the women he's known have been replacing the parts of their bodies like Theseus's fucking ship, and here I am with the same damn parts I've had my whole life. I'm thinking about that when suddenly I can't think about anything at all because his mouth is between my legs, and his hands are everywhere on my body, and my voice fills the room.

When I come, he scales up my body, kissing a trail up to my breasts, which hurt for how much I want him to touch them again. Then he does, and my hands are in his hair, and I need him inside me, that needs to happen.

"Now," I say. "Please," because they're really the only words I can form, and he looks up at me. We've had a version of this conversation before followed by unmet expectations and misunderstandings about motives. But that is our past, and this is something new, and I want that residue of confusion and loss washed clean.

"I want this," I say. "Do you—"

"Yes," he says without pausing. "Hang on. I have condoms in my bag."

"It's fine," I say because of the tubal after my c-section. I also haven't slept with anyone other than Ryan in more than twenty years.

"I got it," he says and moves off the bed to pull a condom from his duffle bag. Maybe he wants to protect me from himself. He's probably slept with a lot of people in the last twenty years.

He takes the corner of the wrapper between his teeth and tears it open, then sheaths himself with a look of concentration so absolute, I worry something might be wrong. Regret? Reluctance? I extend a hand downward, intent on reassuring him. But he intercepts me, clasping my wrist.

"I need a second," he says hoarsely. Not reluctance, it would seem.

That wayward tuft of hair vibrates against his forehead as

he leans over me and closes his eyes. I feather it back, and he acknowledges the kindness with a kiss, pulling my lower lip into his mouth, assisted by a nip of his teeth.

When he's ready, I guide him in, and I am half satiated, half ravenous as I wrap my legs around his hips wanting only more, whatever this is, more, but he becomes still. He props himself up on his elbows, brushes the hair back from my cheeks, and holds my face in his hands not like a clover plucked from the grass but like Emerson's Rhodora.

I reach up for his shoulders, and he's fully in my arms. He rests his forehead to mine, then with a kiss, starts to move inside me, his eyes closed, the corners of them creasing with the effort, his jaw tight, burying himself in me like he's burying a secret. His breath in my ear stutters and stumbles and mixes with his voice which mixes with my voice. I don't remember this. I don't remember him being like this. Or not exactly like this. I guess neither of us is *exactly* who we were then.

When he comes, after he's already heard me call out for him, and I'm clinging to him like there's some risk I might fall off the bed, he doesn't whisper in my ear that I'm beautiful or ask me where I came from.

He whispers, "All of me is yours. All of me."

We lie next to each other in a tangle of covers. He holds my hand between us but brings it to his lips at intervals. I turn my head to look at him, his eyes closed, his breathing returning to normal. Beads of sweat have popped out across his chest, at his hairline, across his upper lip.

"Babs," he says, but he isn't really calling for me. He's practicing my name. "Babs. What do I have to do to keep you this time?"

I have no idea what to say. So much is different now. *He's* different. I curl into his side, and his arm encircles me as the intervals between his chest rising and falling, rising and falling begin to lengthen. His breathing becomes heavy. It's a state I remember belonging to someone else even as I know the body my cheek rests against is Austin's. It's his skin and heat and the faint scent of his deodorant and aftershave, mixing with the scent of sex and clean sheets and the laundry detergent across the hall.

I hear a raspy breath draw into his throat and assume I am relieved from answering his question.

I allow my eyes to close, drawn into him, wrapped in him.

"Whatever it is, I'll do it," he mumbles in his sleep.

At least, I'm pretty sure he's asleep.

twenty-two

Austin's belongings arrive at his condo—the top two floors of a three-story walk-up—in the form of eight large boxes, one moving truck full of furniture, and a black BMW i7. The furnishings comprise a hodgepodge of things he decided to keep from his mother's house, along with furniture he either bought or had shipped from California.

In the week that Austin spent at my house, we quickly grew accustomed to each other—more so than I would have thought given both the short time we've known each other and the short time he resided there. But I began to recognize the routine of his days, and an intimacy developed from learning the rhythm of his time.

I ran in the mornings as I always have and arrived home to find he'd already made coffee for us both. Then, I took Penny and Colin to school while he went to his personal trainer in Wrigleyville. On Wednesday, after my shift at the food pantry, I made lunch to the sound of Austin in the guest room with the door closed, his voice audible but barely from the other side. I came to appreciate that he has a job. He manages his projects, collaborating with the studios he's still connected to and responding to requests related to *The Maple Street Martins,* as well as several other shows he's smartly bought the rights to.

When he called Jenna and asked her to inquire about finding a rental, I was grateful to him for saving me from the tortured process of trying to decide whether to ask him to officially move in with me or tell him he couldn't, both paths seeming outsized in their significance.

"I want to be careful with this. It's so new, fragile, you know?" he'd said. "I want to give you time to miss me," he'd added a little more light-heartedly.

By the time I arrive with lunch for both of us, the moving truck has departed, and Austin has begun the inventory-and-unpacking phase of the project.

Most of what he's received are winter clothes, which makes sense given he plans to stay in Chicago for "a while." The sight of jeans and sweaters, NorthFace and Columbia attire is enormously reassuring, even if watching him open the boxes feels like an invasion of his privacy.

He already has a system down. He immediately takes six of the boxes upstairs to the master bedroom and bathroom, another box to the office, and the final one he places in the kitchen.

"I feel like I'm under your feet. I'm going to leave," I say as we stand together in the kitchen. I've set Potbelly's on the counter, but it's too early for lunch.

"No," he objects. It doesn't seem like he's just saying it to be polite. "Stay. Keep me company. I like having you here."

He gets up to start on the box labeled "kitchen." At first, I wonder whether he's just very particular about his toaster and salad tongs and that's why he had them shipped from California. But I see, as he begins emptying the box, that it contains protein powders and vitamin supplements, a blender and what looks like a juicer. I briefly entertain teasing him about it before

I remember what he looks like without any clothes on and think, *You just keep on doing whatever it is you've been doing.* I consider whether maybe I should get a juicer, too.

"Can I help you in some way?" I ask.

"You want to organize my underwear drawer?" he asks, winking at me over his shoulder as he continues stocking what I can only describe as his men's health cupboard.

"I will, if that would be helpful." It's not like I've never put away laundry before, and I certainly saw his underwear during the week he stayed at my house. Boxer briefs. Usually black, sometimes gray.

"How about this?" he says, closing the cabinet. "Why don't you empty the box in my office while I start on the boxes in my bedroom. When you're done, we'll eat lunch and figure out what to do next."

"That sounds like a reasonable plan," I say, though I have a pretty good idea what we'll do next.

I've spent the better part of the last twenty years in an office, so setting one up is a good task to assign to me, and it's all straightforward enough. Two computer monitors, which I place on the desk along with the charger cord that I assume goes with Austin's laptop. A docking station and some additional cords accompany that, and I arrange them in a way that makes sense, to me at least. The box also contains some photographs and knick-knacks, all carefully wrapped. The built-in bookshelves seem like the logical place for them.

As I unwrap the items, I see that they are quite personal: a framed photograph of Austin and his sister (or I assume it's his sister) from her wedding. I can't help but stare at Austin in the picture. Taken shortly after the show was canceled, he looks almost unchanged from that day back in 1997. Other photographs include him with his nieces and with his sister and mother.

I expected more vanity bric-a-brac—awards, pictures from sets, letters from fans, something that roughly resembles an ego shelf, but none of that is here. Either he doesn't have any, or he left it all in California. Most of the objects seem to be souvenirs from travel, photographs of family, a couple framed prints that I set against the wall—suggestions for where they might hang.

All told, it only takes about forty-five minutes to get his office up and running.

"I'm done," I call from the bottom of the stairs.

"Already?" he calls back.

I hear his feet on the floor above me, then he appears at the top of the stairs.

"That was fast," he says, starting down.

"There wasn't much to it. One box."

He lands at the foot of the stairs with a hop—jovial, kid-like. We might go skipping off to the park to climb trees next. We might sing *See See My Playmate*.

We walk into the kitchen, and Austin surveys his new residence. "It's not very homey here, is it?" His eyes dart off the walls—bare, like the walls of his office.

"Need a nightlight? Colin just outgrew his."

He laughs and sits at a small kitchen island with a posture that claims some ownership of the room, expanding his arms over the granite as he reaches for the sandwiches.

We eat for bit, the process of unpacking boxes proved meditative, and we're both content in each other's company as Austin takes in his surroundings.

Finally, he turns to me, his eyes staring directly into mine. "Well, Babs, what should we do?"

I falter for a couple of seconds, trying to read his mood. "We could go hiking," I say.

For a second his face doesn't move, and I worry that I've offended him. But then he tips his head back and laughs with his whole body. He throws an arm across his chest, trying to catch his breath.

"Where should we go hiking?" he asks, grinning so brightly it's like someone brought the entire goddamn summer into his kitchen.

"I don't know. You're the hiker," I say, and he laughs again.

"I don't think there are any trails in Old Town," he says.

"I don't think so either," I say, letting him off the hook.

The smile fades a little, but his eyes don't. They're doing the thing where instead of focusing on my face, they focus on my lips. I bite my bottom lip nervously, but I'm not trying to be sexy. I'm not good at being sexy, and in the past, trying has made it worse.

He scoots off the stool, and I pivot my body toward him as he steps between my legs and wraps an arm around me, pulling my waist to his. The height of the barstool invites this, but so do I, because I can't quite figure out what to do with my hands, so I grab the belt loops of his jeans.

He kisses me, a soft sweep of his lips to mine. "I don't think I like hiking anymore," he says.

"I gotta say, I did kind of like the hiking." I feel myself growing lightheaded as his lips brush against my cheek, my temple, my earlobe.

"I think you might be confused about what hiking is. A lot of it's just wandering in the woods." The words float into my ear on a warm feather, followed by the touch of his tongue against the sensitive skin just below.

"Oh. Yeah. No. That wasn't my favorite part," I stutter, and I feel his ribs flutter with laughter against my hands.

He takes my hand in his and pulls me off the stool. "I think I remember your favorite part," he says and guides me up the stairs to his bedroom, where I'm fairly confident I won't be organizing his underwear drawer.

We're lying in bed, languid after exertion, talking about first crushes. He's intentionally nonspecific about the object of his first affection, I presume because I might know of her. I tell him about Brandon, first grade. Our teacher had arranged the desks in the classroom into groups of four, and we were seated together along with two other students.

"Not for long. We talked too much. The teacher separated us," I explain.

Austin snuggles me closer and kisses the top of my head. "I'm not sure that would have been enough to keep me from talking to you."

A phone buzzes, and both of us reach for our respective nightstands. I glance at mine—the buzz must have come from his. I return it to the nightstand and roll back toward him just as he sits up, taking his phone in both hands. His face is creased with concentration as—I assume—he replies to a text.

"Something with the house?" I ask.

"No," he says, the word sharp as a spear.

I sit up as well, pulling the sheet to my chest, suddenly cold. "What is it?"

He shows me.

> Micah: Following up on this.

"Who's Micah?" I ask.

"My attorney," he says.

"Oh, right."

Below the message is a series of screenshots that make very little sense to me.

They appear to be from a bizarre webpage with a distinct DIY HTML aesthetic, like the first iteration of MySpace pages before everyone migrated to Facebook. The initial post is deleted, but the remainder of the thread cascades down from a single seemingly random question from a poster with no name and a pink daisy for her avatar.

[deactivated]

✽ I think it's this woman. Does anyone know who she is?

There's a photo within the line, which skews the replies below, pushing them to the far right of the screen and making them hard to read. The photo is Austin and me at the Cubs game. He's standing up as I walk into the aisle after coming back from the restroom. We could be strangers but for his hand on the small of my back.

✽ No idea about that woman. But that's Wrigley for sure. Who's on the field?

[deactivated]

[deactivated]

[deactivated]

✽ That's the last week of August.

🍄 I think this is them too.

Toadstool's post embeds a photo from Oktoberfest that's a little harder to make out. Whoever took it got a decent shot of Austin (albeit clad in hat and sunglasses), but only managed to capture the back of my head looking away.

"I knew it," I say, nearly biting at the words as they slip from my mouth.

Austin turns to me, evidently expecting more.

"I just had this feeling..." I say.

"Did you see someone? What did they look like?"

"No. No, I didn't see anyone. I just had this feeling, like... like someone was watching me." I drop my gaze to my hands on top of the sheet. Even as I say the words, I'm assessing in my head: How much do I say? How much do I tell him? It will sound crazy. He'll think I'm crazy.

I peek up at him, but he doesn't look like he thinks I'm crazy.

"Why didn't you say something?" he asks.

"I thought I was just imagining it."

"I wish you'd said something."

"What would you have done?" I ask.

"Ducked into a tent," he says. The question has an answer—an obvious one from his perspective.

"Oh," I say, chagrined. "Is it the Lewnatics?"

He glances at the phone again. "I don't know," he says. "Probably. Though this isn't Facebook."

> Austin: What website did you pull this from?

Micah: Something called Scuttled.com ?

> Austin: Lewnatics?

Micah: Probably.

"You seem worried," I say. I'd have thought he'd be accustomed to this, but he seems unnerved.

"The date on the first post, the deactivated one," he says,

pointing. "That's two days after the lunch at Tufano's. That's fast for them to be asking questions. *Really* fast."

"Should... Do I... Tell me what to do, here," I say.

"I'm not sure, yet," he says. He climbs out of bed and begins to dress. "I'm going to give Micah a call."

I watch him as he pulls his underwear and jeans on and rakes his fingers quickly through his hair. His mind is turned inward, his eyes shifting around the room, never settling on a single point of focus.

"Austin?" I pull the sheet tighter to me. "You're scaring me a little."

He snaps back to me, his eyes locking with mine, then softening. "Don't be scared. They've probably just figured out that I have someone planted in their group, and they moved their bullshit off Facebook."

"Maybe they figured out that Margot—that my sister's in there?" I suggest.

He puffs out a lower lip. "Could be. What do you think she'd say if you asked her what she knows about this?" He sits on the edge of the bed, regarding me over his shoulder.

"It would depend on whether she actually knows anything about it," I say.

twenty-three

Margot saves me the trouble of having to ask. The next morning, as I'm gathering old clothes that Penny and Colin have outgrown and organizing them for donation, she texts.

> Margot: The Lewnatics are talking about you.

I don't reply; I call.

"What are they saying?" I ask.

"Well, not really *you*," she says. "They're just speculating that Austin must be seeing someone out here."

"Okay. That's different," I say, exhaling my relief as I collapse into Penny's reading chair.

"Different than what?"

"What makes them think Austin is seeing someone?" I ask.

"They think he moved to Evanston," she says. "Why are you acting like this?"

"He moved to Old Town," I say.

"I know," Margot says. "They assumed he moved to Evanston, since his mom's house still isn't on the market."

"Did you correct them?" It sounds like an accusation, and I regret my tone immediately.

"Why would I correct them? It's none of their fucking business. Plus, I'd have to tell them I'm your sister to do that, which seems like not a great idea."

"I'm sorry," I say. "Apparently, there are some photographs of us circulating, and it's making me nervous."

"The one from Oktoberfest?" she asks. "Yeah, That's in there. It's on Instagram, too."

"No. There's a photo of us from the Cubs game and maybe from lunch back in August."

"I haven't seen those. Where are they?" she asks.

"Some weird website. They're trying to figure out who I am."

Margot takes a deep breath on the other end of the line. "Hey Babs," she says—a warning shot. "I think this is kind of the deal. I don't mean to be uncaring, but it's not like you have paparazzi following you into bathrooms or something. There are a handful of photographs of you two circulating among fans. They want to know who you are. You seem awfully worked up for what sounds like an entirely predictable development."

"You said they can be mean," I say by way of rationalizing what she apparently sees as an overreaction.

"Yep," she agrees, unimpressed. "They can be."

I get up from Penny's chair and go downstairs to the living room. From the window, I see Lasky's car parked in front of his building. Maybe he's showing one of the units. I've seen how much he lists those for, and the issue isn't that I won't give him my "extra" garage space. Even with the desirable location, he's overshooting the market. Especially considering how little he does to maintain the building. One of the students who lived there last year told me that when the railing in the entryway fell off the wall, Lasky epoxy-glued a bunch of water noodles to the wall and tried to call it a handrail.

"What are they saying right now?" I ask.

"Just what I told you—that he must be seeing someone and that it's probably the woman who was at Oktoberfest with him. This will shock you," she says sarcastically, "but they are speculating that it'll burn out fast. The over/under on when his mom's house will hit the market is nineteen weeks."

"That's very specific," I say as I sit on the couch. Austin is probably on his way over from Wrigleyville.

Margot doesn't respond, and although I can't hear her shrugging, I'm pretty sure she is. "Are you still there?" she asks finally.

"Yeah. I just don't know what you want me to say."

"I don't want you to say anything. You asked me a question, and I answered it." She's frustrated with me. I guess she's entitled to be.

"Where are *you* on the over/under?" I ask.

"Babs," she says, making no attempt to conceal her irritation, but also not answering the question.

"Well?"

"I hope it's more than nineteen weeks," she says. "I want that for you."

"But you don't think it will be."

She doesn't reply.

"I have to go," I say.

"Hey, don't hang up. I can tell you're upset with me, but I'm doing my best here."

"No. It's not that. I have to go. I think I see Austin's car pulling up across the street."

She pauses briefly, then offers a reluctant, "Let's talk later" and ends the call.

Across the street, Lasky steps out of his building and calls to

Austin. Austin turns, looking annoyed, and he and Lasky exchange a few words that I can only assume have something to do with where Austin is parked—legally, but directly in front of Lasky's car. Lasky probably wants that spot kept open for prospective tenants. Austin shakes his head and turns toward my house, looking downright pissed.

I open the door and shout across the street, "You need a place to park, Austin? I have an extra space in my garage." I should have let him keep the garage door opener.

Lasky shoots a glare in my direction that I appreciate is intended to convey his intense animosity toward me but only succeeds in making him look near-sighted as he squints his already beady eyes under that clown wig of permed and dyed hair.

Austin crosses the street, which makes my heart drop fully into my stomach as a car slows to allow him to cross. I shake off the panic as he throws a friendly wave to the considerate driver.

"Was Lasky giving you a hard time about where you parked?" I ask as he strolls into the living room.

"Yeah. How'd you know?" His eyebrows narrow in a ridge over his nose, and one side of his mouth curls up into an uncomfortable smile.

"He's an asshole. I've been dealing with his weird idiosyncrasies for almost fifteen years now. In August, that man came to my front door and asked if he could rent Ryan's parking space to one of his tenants. You know, since no one was using it anymore."

"What?" Austin stammers in disbelief. "Who does something like that?"

"That guy," I say, ticking my chin in the general direction of the building across the street. "He's been trying to get tenants for months now, and I'm guessing between the shitty job he does maintaining that building and social media, the word's out not to rent from him. Is he showing it today?"

"I guess so. He wanted the spots in front of the building kept clear—"

"Yeah, that's what I figured. Fuck him."

"I'd rather not. Are you ready to go? You look upset. Is everything okay? Just that guy?" He inclines his head toward the other side of the street.

"I talked to Margot," I say as we walk into the kitchen to grab my purse. We're headed back to Restoration Hardware. I need to finish the family room. The rug down there is hideous.

"Yeah?"

"I just got off the phone with her. She said..." I struggle to explain and decide to leave some details out. "The Oktoberfest photo is circulating, but not the Cubs game or Tufano's."

"That's what Micah said, too." He opens the refrigerator and pulls out a can of sparkling water, then leans back against the sink, his legs outstretched in front of him.

"She wasn't especially sympathetic." I peek at him from the corner of my eye but see only anxiety where I'd expected annoyance. "Why do you look like that?" I ask.

"Like what?" He pops the tab of the water.

"Anxious?"

"Because I can tell you're not telling me everything your sister said. Which worries me."

I take a couple of seconds to think about whether I want to invite this particular conversation, but Austin has set his can down next to him, and his posture, the tilt of his head, the cross of his arms say we're not leaving this kitchen until I tell him the rest of it.

"Margot says they're speculating that you moved here because we're dating—"

"I *did*," he says insistently.

I'm not sure who he's arguing with. Not me. He takes a sip of water, and that seems to calm his nerves.

I go on. "And she said there's a bet—an over/under, on how long it takes until you put your mom's house on the market."

"Three weeks, hopefully," he says.

"No. That's not what they mean. They think that's where you're living right now and that you haven't put it on the market because we're dating. The bet is that that you'll put it on the market when we break up. The over is nineteen weeks."

I watch as every muscle in his body tightens, his cheeks flush, and for a moment, I think he's angry. Maybe he is, but as I evaluate him further, I see something more, something I can't place.

"Margot told you that?" he asks. Hurt. He's hurt, the clench of his jaw visible from where I stand on the other side of the room.

"She did."

He nods, the kind of mindless bobbing not of agreement, but of speechlessness. He sets the can of water on the counter next to him and spins it in slow circles.

"Micah didn't say anything to you about that?" I ask.

"No. That's not the kind of thing he pays attention to unless it starts taking on some kind of life outside that group. How many people are betting under nineteen?" he asks, his eyes roving the kitchen.

"I—I don't know."

"How many people are betting total?"

I shake my head. "I didn't ask."

"Was it, like, one post with a handful of people joking around, or is that whole fucking group wagering that this is nothing?" He waves two fingers between us.

"Austin, I don't know. I didn't ask." I proceed with caution.

"But it's not the first time Margot's brought up your dating history."

A flash of true anger moves across his face, replaced just as quickly with resignation.

I continue. "I'm sorry if it sounds... what... clingy or something, but I've been through an awful lot in the past few years." I laugh wryly at my understatement, and Austin drops his gaze to the floor. "I have Penny and Colin to consider, too. I think Margot's just looking out for me."

I'm no longer confident that's her only motivation, and Austin peers up just in time to catch my effort at hiding my ambivalence. I take the few steps that separate us, which places me between his outstretched legs. He loops his arms around my waist and weaves his fingers together at my tailbone.

"There's a reason I have Micah filter that shit for me instead of just reading it myself," he says, seeming to calm.

"I figured you didn't have time to comb through it," I say.

"Well, that, too." He places a kiss on my nose. "But I'd drive myself crazy if I knew every awful hypothesis they had about me or someone I'm dating. I'm sorry I told you to ask Margot about it. That was unwise. From now on, I'll let Micah tell us if there's something he thinks we should be aware of."

"Okay," I say, placing a kiss on his chin.

He lifts my chin, bringing my lips to his in what I think is going to be a sweet, playful kiss but quickly becomes significantly more. I'm wondering whether we're still going to Restoration Hardware, when he draws away.

"Nineteen weeks," he grumbles. "Fucking Lewnatics."

My phone pings on the nightstand and delivers a "sleep well" text from Austin. I reply in kind and turn out the lamp next to my bed.

Despite Austin's suggestion that we allow Micah to curate our social media information, I open Instagram. I haven't looked through it in quite a while. I have three new friend requests: two men with obviously AI-generated profile pics and a woman I don't know. I delete and block all three.

My last search was for #AustinLewis, and when I repeat it, the photograph from Oktoberfest populates amid the array of photos I last saw. The Oktoberfest photo was posted by MsJess-Marie three days ago, long after it was taken, I'm assuming by some phone other than hers. The caption reads "Who remembers this guy? Out wandering Chicago, living his best life. Pour one out for Kurt. #TBT #AustinLewis #MapleStreetMartins #LaminatedList #90sChild #Gen-X #BabyBlues"

"Kurt?" I say aloud. My empty bedroom provides no response.

The photograph has garnered forty-seven hearts, though I don't know whether that reflects Austin's reach or MsJess-Marie's. The picture's a repost anyway. Beneath, are maybe ten or twelve comments. Several are simply emoji: hearts, flames, lips.

One person has commented, "That photo is old he's not seeing her anymore."

Another person replied, "That's Oktoberfest. That's like two weeks ago."

Someone else has commented, "If they were together they'd be holding hands. He always held Chloe's hand in public."

The comment below that is a single eggplant.

Is that supposed to be in reference to the commenter or to Austin? Water drops would make more sense for the commenter. Unless it's a man. I suppose there are men who had crushes on Austin Lewis.

I groan and close the app. I hope Micah is well compensated for his time sifting through all this. I set the phone on the nightstand and flop onto my side just as the landline rings.

"Hello?" I say, but I already know. My mom is the only person who still calls the landline.

"Mom?"

I can hear her breathing.

"I love you, Mom. Sleep well," I say.

"You sleep well, too, Babs," says a smooth feminine voice on the other end, completely clear, and not my mother's.

The line goes dead before I can demand to know who it is. I check the caller ID, which lists the caller as "unknown." I dial *69.

Your call cannot be completed as dialed. Please hang up and try again.

I sit up in bed and turn on the light. My heart is beating so quickly, it's causing my t-shirt to pulse in time.

I pick up my cell phone and call Austin.

He answers, groggy, confused. "Babs?"

"Someone just called me," I say, fighting to keep from screaming.

"It wasn't me," he says.

"No. I know it wasn't you. It was on the landline. It was a woman." I try to explain, but the description fails to capture the menace in her voice, the sneer, the taunt.

I start to cry.

"What did she say?"

"She told me to sleep well."

"Okay," he says, restrained, cautious.

"But I didn't recognize her voice." I force myself to be calm, coherent.

"Would you like me to come over?" he asks. I hear him rustling around in the background.

"Yes," I say. "Please"

"I'm on my way," he says. "Do you want me to call the police?"

"Can you just get here?" I ask, feeling my rational self slip away as fear forms a noose around my neck, choking out my breath.

I hear a car door close and his phone fades out, then back in as it transfers to bluetooth. "I'll be there in ten minutes."

He arrives twelve minutes later, pulling into the garage, then taking the stairs—by the sound of it—two at a time. I worry he'll wake Penny and Colin, but he's both deliberate and conscientious as he opens and closes my bedroom door, climbs quickly onto the bed and takes me into his arms.

"Okay, okay," he whispers into my ear. "It was just a prank phone call."

I heave sobs into his gray t-shirt, which smells faintly of sleep—that mixture of warm body on cotton sheets.

"My mom is the only person who calls that line."

"It wasn't her?" he asks, confirming.

"No. She can't talk anymore. She just waits for me to say something."

"Do you want to text Margot and see if she got a call tonight?" He uses the pads of his thumbs to brush away the tears from my cheeks.

"No. It wasn't our mom, and she only calls me, anyway." I don't say it, but we're both thinking it.

Austin takes a heavy breath. "I'll talk to Micah in the morning," he says. "And I'm staying here with you tonight."

twenty-four

1997

Margot stomped through the apartment and slammed the bedroom door, prompting Ula—the Polish woman who lived below us—to hammer a warning against her ceiling, our floor. Much more noise and she'd be at the door to our apartment. She barely spoke English, but she knew how to make herself understood. Usually, it was our music she complained about. Whatever hundred-year-old insulation existed between floors was insufficient to muffle the notes of Phish Bouncing Around the Room or Ani DiFranco letting the world know she was Not A Pretty Girl.

"Margot," I said through the door. I rattled the handle but she'd locked it. "Margot, let me in."

"Fuck you, Babs!"

I could hear her thrashing about on the other side of the door and tried to picture the scene that would eventually present itself once she emerged. I could imagine significant property damage—my clothes, my trophies and ribbons, maybe my furniture—would be involved. I started inventorying the losses.

I rattled the handle again. "You better not touch my stuff."

Ula's broom knocked through the floor again. I wondered what she'd do next. Complain to the landlord? Call the police?

"What's going on?" our mother asked, returning from parking the car. She'd picked us up at the airport—Sunday evening, she wasn't at work—and the car ride home had been mostly her talking. That suited me fine as it masked the impassable tundra of silence between Margot and me. She hadn't even spoken on the plane. When she had to pee mid-flight, she got up and stepped over my legs into the aisle, kicking my thigh in the process, then repeated the acrobatics when she returned.

Our mother walked up to the door, standing beside me, both of us staring at the grain of the wood as if it might become transparent, providing a view of whatever was happening beyond.

"She's mad at me," I said, an obvious explanation that was met with a look of sharp rebuke by our mother.

"What about?"

"It's a long story."

"Tell the short version," our mother said. "Kevin is on his way over, and I don't want this to be his first impression of you two."

"Who?"

Things seemed to be quieting on the other side of the door —though it was hard to say whether that was a good sign or not.

"I told you about him in the car." She stepped back from the door, her face hard. "Fix it," she said through clenched teeth and with a nod to Margot's and my bedroom door.

I stared back at her, mouth gaping open. "I—how?"

"I don't care how, Babs. Just fix it." She looked at her watch.

"Cindy?" came the voice of a man from the living room.

I glanced down the hall, finding—I assumed—Kevin standing just inside the door. It took about three seconds to size up that relationship. The brown leather jacket, the expensive jeans, the black leather shoes that I suspected cost more than our monthly rent.

He works in the Loop, I suddenly remembered our mother saying in the car.

"What's going on?" he asked. His eyes slid over me.

"It appears my daughters have chosen *this* moment to... I don't even know." She threw a hand in the direction of the bedroom, and Kevin's eyes followed. "It's locked," she added.

Kevin strode across the living room into the hall, pushing my mother and me to the side, and pounded on the door with the flat end of his fist. The pounding was echoed by Ula's broom, but all noise from the bedroom ceased instantly.

"Open the door!" Kevin shouted loudly enough that my body bounced back against the wall behind me, and something slithered deep through my belly, then crawled down my legs into the floor.

The handle turned, and the door inched open, revealing Margot's face, blotchy, streaked with tears. Behind her, the room lay in tatters. The contents of the top of my dresser had been swiped to the floor. Our closet doors had been ripped open, one accordion panel hung to the track precariously from a single roller. Hangers swayed in the half-empty closet, the chaotic *tinging* symphony of metal floating out into the hall.

I scanned the room. The open window over Margot's bed made clear the exit path my clothes had taken.

"Have you lost your mind?" our mother hissed.

Margot glared at me. Then her eyes roved up to Kevin.

"Clean it up," he said.

It was a kind of voice I'd never heard before. A simple and

not unreasonable request, delivered in a tone so smooth, so steady, it could have been used to sharpen an axe.

I tried to step back further, but met the wall behind me; I had nowhere to go.

Margot stood in the doorway unmoving—unable to move, it seemed to me.

"I said, clean it up," Kevin repeated in that same lathe voice. He took a deliberate step to the side, making room for Margot to pass. Her eyes shot to our mother, whose face I couldn't see. Then Margot walked past Kevin, out of the apartment.

He pivoted, his gaze falling on me. "You, too."

For a split second, I thought about arguing. I hadn't made this mess. I hadn't opened a window and thrown half a closet's worth of clothes out of our bedroom. But the chance to get as far away as I could from this man, from his voice, from the set of his shoulders and the weight of his stare, prevailed, and I ran down the stairs and out of our building to join Margot.

I found her stooped over a pile of tunics, hoodies, my high school letter jacket, all piled on the sidewalk between our building and the one next to it.

"We have to stay away from him, Margot," I said as I crouched across from her.

She glanced up at me, eyes full of wrath, but said nothing.

I gathered as much as I could in my arms, trying to minimize the number of trips up and down the stairs, in and out of the apartment. She did the same. And as the clothes cleared the sidewalk, I saw what lay beneath them—the shredded glossy pinups of a two-dimensional Austin Lewis.

"Leave it," Margot said.

I stared down at the serrated strips of paper, already flapping with the breeze that whipped through the narrow walkway, like fish released from a net onto the deck of a boat.

"Leave it," she said again, and brushed past me, a pile of my clothes heaped high in her arms.

Our mother was already gone by the time we got upstairs.

"We should sleep with the door locked," I said when I came to bed later that night, but Margot was already asleep under the scotch-tape refuse that clung to the walls around her bed.

twenty-five

ALTHOUGH MICAH IS UNABLE TO CONCLUSIVELY CONNECT THE Scuttled.com posts to the Lewnatics, Austin and I proceed under the assumption that it's them. We further operate under the assumption that if Micah isn't informing us of any Lewnatic-related drama, there's none worth reporting.

Over the course of the next month, we develop a routine of sorts—the routine that had started to announce itself during the week Austin lived in my guest room. Either I text him after I drop off Penny and Colin at school or he texts me after he finishes with his personal trainer, and we decide what to do for the day. This is the part of the day when I feel the most tension. If he's busy with work, I won't see him. And since I'm not working, I *feel* that absence. I get bored, restless. There are only so many Netflix series I can binge. I reach out to a few old friends to catch up, but most of my friends are attorneys. That was my world for twenty years. They all work during the day. I'm suddenly a stay-at-home mom of kids who aren't at home during the day. I'm a decade late for the job.

I miss working and offer to help Austin, but he gives me an "Absolutely not" and says he doesn't ever want to be in a position where he's telling me what to do or paying me a salary. But this means that occasionally an entire day goes by with only a couple of texts or a phone call. I guess that's normal. We don't live together. We're dating. People who are only dating don't see each other every day.

Sometimes Austin has to return to L.A. for work, or sometimes he travels to New York, or overseas. When he comes home, I pick him up from the airport, not because he couldn't get a car to bring him home, but because I miss him when he's gone for these stretches—a few days, a week or more. I miss him so deeply, the pain feels physical.

He returns home hungry for me as well, and I notice that the trips become fewer and further between, and shorter. The first trip of October was a week and a half to Los Angeles. The longest trip he's planned for November is three days. One trip was overnight to Luxembourg. There for a meeting, then immediately back. Who does that?

Sex with Austin is the best sex I've ever had in my life, and I feel guilty even thinking that, but it's true. He's inventive, curious, passionate, attuned. He has a confidence that accompanies his experience and while I'm not thrilled with the extent of his experience, I'm appreciative of the lessons he's learned along the way. We become comfortable with each other's bodies, or maybe he was always comfortable with mine, but I stop worrying about his model ex-wife or the actresses he knew before me. I stop worrying about the scar from my c-section, the imperfections in my thighs. None of it matters.

He tells me stories of his strange childhood and listens with rapt attention when I tell him stories of mine—a childhood he never had. We talk about books, we talk about music, we go for walks, we do blissfully boring things like hanging a new towel rack in his bathroom and buying a vacuum cleaner. And by the end of October, he's spending Friday nights at my house in my bedroom—fully liberated from his former residence in the basement.

The first time he does this is awkward as hell. He brings an overnight bag, which makes it feel like a slumber party. We don't have sex that night because I'm afraid Penny or Colin will walk in or hear us. The next morning, I wake up to him plastered to my back, his fingers already between my legs, promising he can be quick, and I'm not worried about him being quick, I'm worried about him being quiet, but he's both with his mouth buried against my neck, moving the entire length of himself no more than ten or twelve times, as if each thrust is a separate thought, its own experience of me.

Margot and Supriya come over for brunch on Sundays, but I find myself increasingly more circumspect in what I share, and although Austin and I have reached the point in our relationship where he occasionally drops by unannounced, he has never once dropped by on a Sunday morning.

On Saturday mornings, though, he wakes up in my bed and sits at my kitchen table, drinking coffee and talking to me about politics and his business ventures and my favorite topic: us. He tells stories to Penny and Colin about how television is made—not petty behind-the-scenes gossip, but details of a craft we know nothing about, and it's like listening to an artist explain how a painting is made, from the weave of the canvas to the weight of the brush strokes.

This time between Austin and me is a perfect, blissful, early courtship. It's fantastic sex and sweet exchanges of affection, lingering kisses and learning each other's favorite songs. It's lying on the couch in the middle of the day and obsessing over his absence during a business trip. It's me telling him he makes me feel beautiful, and him telling me I am. He starts calling me "Bee" for no reason other than the ordinary way that couples develop nicknames for each other. I forget that he was once every poster on my teenage sister's half of our bedroom, in the bedrooms of teenage girls all over the country. I forget that some of those women now comprise a group of adults who willingly refer to themselves as "Lewnatics."

I receive the picture in a DM through Messenger in the first week of November. It catches me off guard for a number of reasons one of which is that I'd just received a text from Margot. She reached out today, just as she did last year and the year before.

> Margot: Hey sis. How you holding up? 🤍

>> Me: Fine, I guess. Not my favorite day of the year.

> Margot: Would you like company? I hate to think of you being alone today.

>> Me: 🤍 Austin's on his way over. I won't be alone today. Thanks for checking in.

> Margot: I'm glad to hear that. Let me know if you need anything.

>> Me: Thank you. I will. 🤍

I walk over to the living room windows just in time to see Lasky standing on the front step of his building. He has his hands on his back—the posture women adopt in their eighth month of pregnancy. He's not even overweight. His attention is focused on two guys, who just stepped out of a car parked in front of his building. He calls to them, and one of them spins—

startled—in his direction. They exchange words, and the other guy offers a middle-finger salute. Lasky glowers at them as they walk toward Fullerton.

When my phone buzzes again, I'm distracted by the scene across the street and mostly just disoriented by the image in the DM. It takes me a good five seconds or so to process that the message isn't even from Margot.

It had been my firm profile picture for probably a good ten years, so isn't the most current photograph of me. My hair was shorter then. I would have thought the firm took down my bio page within minutes of me walking out the door. I haven't checked though, so maybe not.

In the photograph, I'm wearing a black suit per the specifications of the firm—black, gray, or navy suits for the website. A light green silk turtleneck peeks out of the blazer. My earlobes are dotted with a pair of small silver earrings from Tiffany—a gift from Ryan. They match a silver necklace he also gave me. I face the camera but at an angle, a pose that, for some reason, those who photograph attorneys for their firm websites love. The image is touched up, though, and the end result is a waxy plastic-ness to my complexion.

And then there are my eyes, which have been replaced two large, red X's. Across the center of the photograph, the sender added the words "Die You Fat Bitch!" The same color of red as the X's—a nice touch.

I take a screen shot of the message and text it to Austin.

> Me: They've figured out who I am.

Austin: Fuck. I'm on my way over.

There are a lot of things about the message that bother me: that it ends the illusion I'd had of normalcy with Austin; that there was effort undertaken in finding the photo; that an actual death wish accompanies it. But the "fat" part inflicts a particularly vibrant sting as well. It may be vain of me, but whoever sent the DM probably has very little effect over whether I live or die, yet, as it turns out, has considerable effect over whether I feel that I am fat.

I'm evaluating all of this when Austin walks into the kitchen. He's parked in the garage, in the empty space left when I sold Ryan's car. He has a key to the house, too, but doesn't need it because he has Ryan's garage door opener. For some reason, I'm aware that there are milestones at work as he enters my home.

He finds me in the living room, sitting on the couch, pretending to read a paperback—one I've read before so it doesn't matter how closely I pay attention or if my mind wanders as I read. He's kneeling by me within seconds.

"Are you okay?" he asks. His hands reach for my face.

"Yeah, I think I just got used to things, and this feels like they leveled it up."

"Definitely," he agrees.

I'm taken aback by how readily he agrees, and I attempt to temper it. "I guess it probably wasn't *that* hard to find me. Frankly, I'm surprised it took so long."

He doesn't take the bait. "Was it just the one?"

"Yes." I hand him my phone.

He sits on the couch next to me and enlarges the photo. He clicks through to the profile of the sender, but it's clearly a fake account. They didn't even bother with a profile picture, and the account was created yesterday. He hands me my phone and takes out his own, texting a quick message to Micah, then leans back into the couch, pulling me with him. I settle against his chest.

"This seems... aggressive," I say, "Personal." I close my eyes as his fingers slide up and down my arm.

He's still for a moment before he offers a fatigued, "Yeah. It does."

"Resourceful little fan club, too, finding what has to be one of the more unflattering photographs a Google images search would return."

Austin startles under my cheek. "They found a photograph that was easy to find, Bee," he says. "And it's not unflattering. What are you talking about?"

"Never mind," I say.

"No. Don't do that," he says, pulling me back from his chest. "Tell me. I don't understand."

How can he?

"This is what I was afraid of *then*," I say. "That it would be obvious that I'm just... I'm not like the women you're..."

"Used to?" he fills in.

A fire crackles in the fireplace, but the room has turned cold.

"I'm not like the women you usually date," I say, without conviction.

"Do you *know* what kind of women I usually date?" It's a little argumentative. An echo of the past causing static in the present.

I sit back further from his chest and force myself to make eye contact. He doesn't blink, his face tight, his mouth drawn down.

"I have no idea," I say, defeated. "But I'm confident they aren't middle-aged mothers of two, who've spent the past twenty years in a desk job."

He shakes his head, not like he's disappointed in me, or even frustrated really. I think maybe he's sad.

"My God, Bee. Have I done something to give you the impression that I don't find you absolutely perfect?" Yeah, it's sadness. Maybe even sorrow. "I'd be happy to provide you with some very specific feedback *right now*, but I get the feeling you're not really in the mood." A low, mirthful vibration moves through his chest.

I already feel the wear of this corrosive doubt, the way I instantly start to pick apart aspects of myself that I've never given any thought to. This will be their refrain—of course it will be. I'm old. My clothes aren't stylish enough. My haircut is out of date. I'm boring. I'm *fat*.

"It's not true, though," Austin continues. "I want to make sure you understand that. They said it because it's mean, not because it's true." He looks for me to agree with him, so I do, but I don't believe it. I'm already creating a mental inventory of other pictures that might be out there.

Without thinking, I reach for my phone.

"Did you get another message," he asks, apparently thinking my phone buzzed.

"No. I just... I want to look through my profile. I want to make sure everything is private."

"Here. Let me see it," he says, gently.

I hand him my phone, unlocking the screen, and he sits back and gets to work.

"How many accounts do you have?" he asks.

"Just Instagram and Facebook. Well, Twitter's on there, too, but I don't use it anymore."

"I'm going to deactivate your Twitter. Is that okay?"

"Yeah, totally fine."

He returns to his work. "Your Threads is public. And you have TikTok." It sounds like an accusation.

"For BookTok. I don't post anything," I say.

"I'm locking all of this down," he says as he runs a hand down his face from forehead to chin. It takes him about three or four minutes, all told. I watch as his eyes flit over the screen and his finger scrolls up and down. His thumbs select this button, then that, before he hands the phone back to me.

"The only things that are public now are your current Facebook and Instagram profile pictures. All of your posts are set to private; your friend list is private; and no one can message you unless they are already a friend. You're locked down," he says.

I glance at the screen. "Thank you," I say, though it looks unchanged to me.

"Now I have a question for you," he says.

I put the phone down on the cushion next to me and turn toward him.

"Who's Mark?"

"Mark?"

"Mark," he says.

"Like from my firm?" I ask.

"I don't know. I just know that he texted you twice while I was changing your privacy settings, and he wants you to describe what you're wearing."

I blush. It's the kind of blushing that burns under my skin and brings out a very thin film of perspiration above my lip. "What the fuck?" I growl at my phone as I review the texts. There's actually a third one that just came through.

> Mark: Loving your life of leisure?

> Mark: I bet you're still in your jammies. Actually, I like that idea. Please describe. ;)

> Mark: Sorry. Was that too much? It's a slow day here and I miss my work wife.

That last message probably isn't going to help matters so I pretend it's only the two Austin has already seen.

I weigh how much of this I want to explain, what I want to say about the darkest chapter of my marriage. I decide, not much. "Mark is an equity partner at my firm. He's harmless."

"This doesn't seem harmless," Austin says. "Is he married?"

"He doesn't mean anything by it. He thinks he's being funny. You'd probably like him if you met him," I say.

"I don't think I would," Austin replies without hesitating. He's right, of course; he would hate Mark. Ryan couldn't stand Mark. And I would put Mark's wife on the list of people who possibly sent that DM but for the fact she's probably thrilled I'm off the market.

I'm quiet for a moment. I don't know what else to say. If Ryan had seen those texts, he would have been furious. Of course, things had been different then; there'd been some emails first.

"Do you *want* him sending you messages like that?" Austin asks.

"No. But... it's a really complicated relationship," I say, peeking up at him.

"Relationship?"

"He was my mentoring partner for twenty years," I say. "For my entire career," I add sadly.

"That makes it *more* inappropriate," he says.

"If it makes you feel any better, he's one of the attorneys who fired me."

"Why would that make me feel better?"

"I should block him," I say. I should have blocked him the minute I walked out of that firm, but somewhere deep inside, I'd hoped he'd call to invite me back. Plus I might need him as a reference when I start looking for another job.

I select his contact and block the number, muttering mindlessly, "If you think *my* firm photo is unflattering, you should see Mark's."

Austin doesn't miss a beat. "I *don't* think your firm photo is unflattering. *You* do." Good catch.

"Right."

"Listen," Austin says, and in a moment, he's become so serious, so fixed on me, I'm afraid to blink. The pupils of his eyes deepen, darkening as if they mean to swallow me. "I don't want to fight. But this Mark guy seems like an asshole. Who fires someone and then sends them a text like this?"

Mark. That's who.

"Are we fighting?" I ask. It doesn't really feel like a fight; I'm not mad. Austin's reaction to a man who is not him, sending me sexually suggestive messages is entirely reasonable.

"I hope not," he says.

"We're not fighting," I say. "And I blocked Mark."

"Good," he says. Then he pulls my legs down the length of the couch so that I'm looking up at him, and I know he's preparing to make it clear that he very much thinks I'm perfect.

twenty-six

Margot: Hey Barbara! We need to talk about Thanksgiving.

"Is that Mark again?" Austin asks.

We're lying on the couch under the blanket that I usually keep draped across the back. The fire casts a soft orange glow over the living room. Outside, it's gray and cold. I wish time would stop. I wish we could lie here all day, our legs crisscrossing on top of each other, my head on his bare chest, his fingers feathering back the hair at my temple.

"Tell him you're not wearing anything because that's how I like you."

"I told you; I blocked him," I say, rolling my eyes as if his jealousy is completely unfounded. "It's Margot, and she's called me *Barbara*, so she must really want a response."

"Barbara," he repeats, his chest fluttering with laughter. "What does she want?"

"To talk about Thanksgiving."

"Do you usually celebrate together?" he asks.

"Yes. It's my turn to host. I'll respond to her later," I say, tossing the phone onto the coffee table in front of the couch. I make sure it lands face down. It's caused enough problems today.

His phone is the one to start buzzing though, and he picks it up lazily as if the weight of it might be too much for him.

I laugh at our dueling cell phones, but Austin tenses next to me. If not breathing makes a noise, he's making it.

"What's wrong?" I ask.

"Fuck," he groans as he continues reading whatever text has just come through. Finally, he asks, "Do you—do you know how active Margot is with the Lewnatics?"

"She said she never posts. She's just a lurker."

"Have you told her that Micah watches that group?" he asks.

I slide up his body, resting my forearms on his chest so I can see him better. "No. I mostly try not to talk to her about any of this. Why? What's going on?"

"She's not a lurker, Babs," he says. He hands me his phone, open to a text that just came through.

> Micah: Let me know how you want to handle this.

Below the message is a series of screenshots—Facebook posts, obviously from the Lewnatics page. The original post is a screenshot of Zillow—Austin's mother's house: "sale pending." "Who had under twelve? Austin's gonna Austin. LOL!" reads the accompanying post.

Several posts beneath that comment on the house—the sale price, the pictures of the interior. But it's a post by Margot Sinha that chills the blood in my veins: "That's not where he's living, you idiots. He has a condo in Old Town."

There's a flurry of people telling her she's wrong, telling her Austin has no reason to both keep his mother's house and rent a condo half an hour away from it. One person suggests he's moved in with "the girlfriend." A reply says: "That's over. There hasn't been a photo of them in weeks." Someone else accuses Margot of trying to stir up drama—as if the entire group isn't a restaurant-grade KitchenAid mixer of drama. Another post calls Margot a shill, a bot, a troll. Someone calls *her* an idiot.

Margot replies: "His girlfriend is a retired attorney in Chicago. They've been together since August." Below this, she's linked my Super Lawyers profile from five years ago. I feel physically ill. A noise slips from my mouth, like someone waved a plateful of rancid meat under my nose. Which they sort of have.

I'm overwhelmed with shame, embarrassment, disappointment, anger.

Austin's phone rings. It's Micah. He declines the call. "Why would she do this?" he asks.

I shift to the end of the couch, taking the blanket with me, and Austin sits up, bringing his feet to the floor. "If I had to guess, she just wants to be the one with the information, the one in the know."

"But why would she send you that message?" he asks. He glances for emphasis at my phone still lying on the coffee table.

"No. No. She didn't send that DM," I say with conviction. I am certain of it.

Austin glances around the room anxiously. I watch as he chooses his words, but I beat him to it. "She would never send a message like that. Today of all days."

"What's today?" he asks as he flips again through the screenshots from Micah, his head sagging between his shoulders.

I take a breath and close my eyes. It's easier to say in the dark. "November second. It's the day Ryan died. Three years ago."

He visibly shudders.

I go on. "I don't think she'd do this *any* day, but definitely not today. She texted me this morning to make sure I was okay, offered to keep me company if I was going to be alone. It's not possible." Even as I'm saying it, I know how it must seem—the personal attack, the meaning behind the day, that specific photo.

He reaches for his underwear and pulls them on then grabs his jeans. "It seems like it's someone who knows you," he says, then adds, "Really, really well." He buttons his jeans, then pauses gazing at me as though he knows what he's about to say will hurt. "How many people know the number for your landline? How many people know you *have* a landline?"

I lurch with a grunt as if the couch is a boat tossed on a raging wave. Austin picks his shirt up off the floor.

"Please don't leave," I say, shrugging the blanket from the couch over my shoulders.

"I have to get back to my office," he says as he brings his shirt down over his shoulders. "I have to call Micah. Can we talk more about this after dinner? That'll give me time to figure out how we want to handle it."

"We," I say under my breath.

He stops his movements. "We," he repeats, firmly. "You and me. Together."

"Okay," I say.

He finishes tying his shoes and pulls me to my feet, tugging the blanket snug around me. "Don't stand naked in front of the windows," he says. "The last thing we need on top of all this is for that weirdo across the street to see you."

I look past his shoulder toward the living room windows. The only light in the room comes from the fireplace. I doubt anyone can see in unless they're using binoculars.

"I'll text you when I'm on my way over tonight," he says while I'm distracted with thoughts about the visibility of my living room. He kisses me quickly—he's in a hurry—then pauses and groans again before taking his time on a second attempt.

"We'll figure this out," he says.

I manage to put Margot off until Austin returns that evening. He's had a chance to talk to Micah and tells me, from Micah's perspective, the issue isn't so much that they've figured out who I am—they would have eventually anyway. The issue is the DM—what they did with that information and how quickly they did it. Austin says "they" even though I know he remains unconvinced that it's anyone other than Margot. I can understand why.

"I usually go to my sister's house for Thanksgiving," Austin says as we sit across from each other in my kitchen. "You and the kids are welcome to come with me—Ellen would love to meet you—but I think under the circumstances, it might be best if you just do what you and your sister always do."

"Yeah?" I ask. He's probably right, but even if Margot didn't send the DM, I feel strongly disinclined to smile politely at her while eating sweet potatoes off of my wedding china.

"Micah thinks—and I agree—that it's best if you don't say anything to her about the DM or the Lewnatics. See if she gives anything away."

I don't like the plan. But truthfully, it doesn't require me really to do anything I wasn't already planning to do. I cook a meal. I have my sister's family over. I'd hoped that Austin would be joining us, but I understand why that can't happen now.

He sees my discomfort. "If you're right and she didn't send the DM, it might be as simple as just asking her not to post in that group anymore. I mean, eventually, they're going to figure out who *she* is, and she won't be able to be in there anymore anyway."

"Okay," I say. "I'll miss you though, while you're away."

"It'll be a short trip," he says and brings my hand to his lips. "I'll miss you, too."

twenty-seven

Margot comes over for Thanksgiving with Rishi and Supriya. I've found excuses to cancel the last three Sunday brunches, which means it's been nearly a month since I've actually seen my sister—the longest we've gone without seeing each other since I was in college—and she's on to me.

"Is Austin not coming?" she asks as she joins me in the kitchen.

The kids are downstairs with Rishi, and it's clear Austin is nowhere in the house. I'm peeling potatoes at the sink.

"No. He's with his sister and her family in New York," I say.

"Oh," she says, coming alongside me. "Is everything okay between you two?"

"Oh yeah," I say casually. "I guess he just always goes there. He invited us to join them, but I didn't want to leave you hanging."

Margot grabs a potato and a knife and starts peeling. "I could have managed," she says.

"Well maybe next year his sister will come here," I say, though I can hear the inauthenticity in my voice, and I close my eyes against the slow turn of Margot's head as she takes me in.

"Are you going to tell me what's going on?" she asks.

"What do you mean?" I ask at a pitch not at all suited to the exchange.

My first thought is that she has convinced herself that there's an issue between Austin and me. It dawns on me that depending on how this day goes, there might never be a time when I can talk to Margot about Austin the way I could talk to her about Ryan, when I can share my insecurities without fearing that she'll betray the confidence, when I can relate anecdotes that make me smile or bring me joy. But she doesn't say she wants to know more about Austin. She asks me why I'm "so fucking jumpy."

"What? I'm not jumpy." I laugh to indicate the assertion is ridiculous, totally unfounded. But even the laugh sounds jumpy.

She regards at me like I've proven her point.

"I think I'm just going stir-crazy. I need to start looking for a job." It *would* be better if I had a job, that much is true.

"Are you sure everything's okay between you and Austin?" she asks.

"Yes," I say curtly.

"Can I be honest with you, Babs?" she asks as if I have any choice in the matter. She doesn't wait for me to answer. "I'm worried about you. You really don't seem like yourself, lately. Three Sundays canceled?"

"I cannot do this today, Margot," I warn.

"Look, I'm not trying to ruin Thanksgiving, but you're obviously not telling me something. You can't even peel a potato without your hands shaking, and... I'm just going to say it... you're too thin. Whatever diet you're on, you need to get off it."

It probably looks sudden to her, but I've been smart and methodical, losing the last little bit of grief weight (plus admittedly just a bit more) over the past month.

"I weigh the same now as I did when I graduated college," I say like I'm reciting a fact about the ideal pH balance for laundry detergent.

"You were training twenty hours a week in college. I'm not sure it's a good thing that you've managed to get yourself down to that weight again."

"Well, you're the only person who's said anything about it." Actually, David made a comment at the food pantry, but when I told him I was training for the Chicago Marathon, he dropped it. Okay, he asked if I wanted a running partner. I said no. *Then* he dropped it. I toss my peeled potato into the colander. I can feel her eyes on me as I grab another and begin peeling.

"I'm not trying to be mean, Babs—" she begins, but I don't let her finish.

"Please just drop it," I say, pivoting to face her. "Please just be happy for me. Can you do that? When Ryan died, he left me with two children and a world that felt incomprehensibly empty." I turn back to the sink and start peeling the potato like it might have had some role in that, the strips flying off and slapping the back of the sink. "And now I'm with a man I'm crazy about. My kids are happy. I'm running faster than I have in decades. I'm having some of the best sex of my life, and you're upset because I've finally lost the grief weight." I throw the potato into the colander, and the metal collides with the side of the sink.

"I'm sorry. I'm sorry," Margot says over the clatter of the colander. "I shouldn't have said anything. You look great. I'm glad your kids are happy and that you've found someone who makes *you* happy and that you're having the best sex of your life."

"You leave that last part off Facebook," I say.

Her mouth clamps shut, and she looks at me wide-eyed. I

was supposed to use today to assess her, but I've blown it. I should have been smarter than to blurt something like that out.

"I already told you, I don't post in that group," she says. Her eyes pose the question before her mouth does. "Did something happen?"

I fumble for a way to extricate myself from this conversation without giving away my position. "They've figured out who I am," I say.

The color drains from her face so abruptly, I look to the floor to see if it's puddled at her feet.

"What makes you think that?" she asks, and now *her* hands are shaking.

"Austin saw something on Instagram," I lie. "A reference to my old firm."

She sets the potato in the colander like it's a hardboiled egg she's trying not to crack.

"It won't be long till they figure out who *you* are," I say, hoping to shift the spotlight off of me.

"Different last names," she mumbles and swallows with some effort. She flinches like she's about to follow up but Rishi enters the kitchen.

"Do you two need any help?" he asks cheerfully.

"If you can put these potatoes in there, that would be helpful," I say, gesturing toward a pot of boiling water. Rishi comes up behind us and grabs the potatoes, dropping a kiss against Margot's cheek as he does so.

"The sweet potatoes could probably also go in the oven, now," Margot adds, and Rishi manages that task next.

When dinner ends, and pie has been served, Margot packs up before Penny and Colin have put the last fork in the dishwasher. Rishi seems confused—we usually sit around, rubbing full bellies and making the kind of small talk that comes from wine, turkey, and too many carbohydrates. Not so this year.

Margot offers a hollow excuse about an upset stomach and ushers her family out of the house.

The next message arrives via email the following morning. I have no idea how they got my personal email address, but I suppose they could have called the firm and asked for it. Pretended to be a former client or a colleague from another firm. It's a feeble threat from an email address comprised entirely of numbers plus the percent sign. It instructs me to "Stay away from Austin." The message itself is lame. That they've managed to get my personal email address is the concerning part.

After that, I wake up on eight separate mornings to grammatically and syntactically chaotic emails calling me fat, calling me ugly, pointing out the ripple in my thigh from some picture of me running, asserting Austin can, and eventually will do better. They call me a gold-digger (don't they know I'm loaded?) and a celebrity whore. The email addresses are never the same and have the randomly generated appearance of the passwords websites suggest, which everyone ignores in favor of using the same password they've been using since college.

I show the messages to Austin and he tells me, "Everything is going to be okay."

I want to believe him, but I see the way he draws the corner of his lip between his teeth. Even he's not convinced. And the messages are out of line with the "hot-takes" that make their way onto Instagram: Will I go back to work? (*She can't; Austin's job is too demanding*); Will we move in together? (*Undetermined, but Austin would never leave L.A.*); How did we meet? (*Maybe through his sister?*).

The emails aren't hot takes; they're cruel. They don't sound in vapid speculation; they seek to wound and know where to aim. And they target only me.

twenty-eight

"How is your training going?" David asks as we stand behind the counter at the food pantry. I'm on sandwiches; he's on desserts.

It's the Wednesday of finals week at the university which means we lack student volunteers at the exact time the pantry is at its busiest. We've been stacking food on top of plates and handing it over the counter so quickly my forearms are sore. There's also something about the holidays that makes the patrons edgy. I suppose the holidays are hard for me, too. Maybe I'm edgy.

"Pretty well. It's hard, you know," I say. "I remember what my times used to be, and I'm not even close to that now."

David laughs as he passes a brownie across the counter. "That's the freedom of it, though," he says. "You get to start over. All new PBs."

"I get to start over," I whisper into the top of a ham and cheese sandwich.

He pauses, though only momentarily—the line doesn't allow one to pause longer than that. "I understand. Starting over can be hard," he says in a way that suggests he knows what he's said has meaning beyond personal best times.

"Hey!" one of the patrons calls out, interrupting our conversation. "There's a line. You can't cut in the line!"

"Go to the back!" calls out another man.

This is followed by a high-pitched yelp as David and I lean over the counter just in time to see one of the larger men shove a woman out of the line. She falls to the floor with enough force to cause her to slide back on the tile. Her purse flies off her arm, landing behind her. I watch as a man, Mitchell, rises from his seat and picks the purse up.

"My purse!" my sister cries out.

"I'm not trying to steal it, ma'am," Mitchell says as he hands over the shoulder bag.

Margot's eyes meet mine, brimming with shame as she accepts the bag from Mitchell, stands up, and dusts off her coat.

"Do you know her?" David asks.

"That's my little sister."

"Is she a volunteer?" he asks.

"She is now," I say, stone-faced. "I'll let you back," I say when Margot finally reaches the counter.

I open the door to the kitchen and usher her in, directing her to the closet where she can drop her coat and purse.

"We need someone on drinks." I say brusquely.

"O-okay," she says, too flustered to argue.

We step back out to the counter to find David moving at double time, trying to keep up with the line.

"David, Margot; Margot, David," I say, introducing them with all the enthusiasm of someone receiving a demerit for a high school dress code infraction.

"It's nice to meet you, Margot." David extends his hand. "Your name is French? Is your family French?" He glances at me as if I've been holding out on him. I haven't; we aren't French. At least not that I know of.

"We're not French," I say. "Our maiden name is Stewart."

"Too bad," David says. "I was hoping maybe you spoke French."

He said it to me, but Margot just can't help herself. "Désolé, David. Je ne parle pas Français, mais je parle très bien Anglais."

David laughs as I try not to vomit. "Your accent is quite good," he says. Margot beams.

"Hot chocolate," one of the patrons requests.

"What?" Margot looks across the counter.

"Hot chocolate, please," the woman says again.

Margot scans the counter, then sorts the situation out and hands the woman a Styrofoam cup of hot chocolate.

"What are you doing here?" I ask as I place a sandwich on another woman's tray. Margot's station on the other side of David means we have to talk around him. He politely keeps his eyes straight ahead, handing out desserts and pretending he can't hear us.

"I wanted to get coffee with you, but Austin said you were here. Is he living with you, now?"

"No," I say, pushing the word out between clenched teeth.

"Well, he's at your house right now. Did you know that?"

"Yes," I say. "On Wednesdays, Austin and I eat lunch together when I get home from the food pantry."

"Oh." She sounds dejected. I haven't been talking to Margot about Austin lately.

"What's wrong?" I ask.

"I was going to suggest we get coffee when you're done here." She seems to be catching on to the rhythm of the food service. Not that there's much to it.

"I already had my coffee for the day. Run then coffee," I say.

"You can have more than one cup of coffee in a day, Babs,"

she says. "Or lunch. We can get lunch," she adds when I remain silent.

"I already have plans for lunch."

David must have noticed my tone because I see from the corner of my eye that he's subtly inclined his head, first in my direction, then in Margot's like he's following a tennis match of words.

"Can you… make an exception?" she asks, turning to face me, placing David awkwardly in the middle.

David clears his throat politely as if trying to remind us that he's still there.

"It's almost Christmas, Babs," she says, ignoring the line bottlenecking at her station.

"You're holding up the line," I say, but Margot doesn't budge.

"Coffee?" says one of the patrons, probably for the second time.

"Coffee?" Margot repeats in my direction.

"Fine," I say. "Coffee." I'm pretty sure I hear David exhale.

When the pantry closes, David locks up and walks with us out to the side of the church.

"It was nice to meet you, Margot," he says, holding out his hand.

"You, too," Margot says. She shakes his hand but adds an "à bientôt" as he turns to walk away.

"Jesus Christ," I mutter.

"What?" she asks, flipping the collar of her coat up around her ears as we head for a café located diagonal from the church. "David seems nice." She's pronounced it Da'VEED.

"You're married," I remind her.

"You're not," she says.

"Margot," I warn and start to turn back toward the other side of the street, in the direction of my house.

"Stop. I'm sorry," she sputters, grabbing my arm and hooking it in her elbow. "I'm sorry."

"He pronounces it DA'vid," I say as she pulls me toward the coffee shop.

"He doesn't, Babs. He's just being polite." She opens the door and ushers me in ahead of her.

"Where's Supriya?" I ask as we step up to the counter. Between the approaching holiday and the time of day, the place is nearly empty.

"I asked Rishi's mom to watch her so I could run some errands in the city."

"What errands are you running?" I ask as I hand the barista a package of Madelines.

"Is that all you're having?" Margot asks.

"Austin's getting lunch for us." I figure she's getting ready to assess my diet again, but I soften when she tells the barista, "Just add these to my coffee. Large dark roast. Room for cream."

We sit at a table by the window, and I eat one of my cookies as Margot takes a couple sips of her coffee.

"How's Rishi?" I ask.

She sets her coffee on the table. "I know you know," she says. "I know you know what I did. And I'm sorry, and I miss you. I miss Sundays. I miss talking to you and texting with you. I miss my sister."

I'm her errand. She asked Rishi's mother to watch Supriya so that she could drive into the city unannounced, not giving me a chance to cancel or hide or ignore her.

"I left the group," she says. "It was too much temptation for me—all their stupid theories and analyses."

"I don't even understand why you were in there to begin with. I thought you hated Austin." When we returned from L.A., she'd refused even to watch the last two seasons of the show.

"I do—I mean, I did. Or not hate him, but just..." She

glances around the café like the rest of her thought might be trapped behind the bookshelf stacked with logo mugs. She returns to me, contemplative. "Austin thought he was such hot shit back then, basically picking women out to sleep with like he was choosing an ice cream flavor—*I'll take that one.*"

"That's not what happened," I say, and frankly it's insulting to *me* that she believes it is.

"Isn't it?" It's less a challenge than a sincere question, and I realize, for the first time, how removed her understanding of that day is from what actually took place. It seems trapped in its moment in 1997 for her, while, for me, it's grown and evolved as I've gotten to know Austin.

"No," I say, resolute. "I understand how you would assume that; *I* assumed that when he called that morning."

She takes a sip of her coffee, her face neutral, open.

"He wanted to see me again. He wanted to start seeing me. That's why he didn't invite you. And I think I hurt him—then. I didn't understand what he wanted, and I didn't treat him very well... in that moment," I mutter into the table. I'm leaving out quite a bit—the confusion beside the stream, the strained conversation in the car that night—but decide those details probably won't actually help matters here. They might make things worse.

I glance up to see Margot wholly confused, creases formed at the corners of her eyes and a tension around her lips as if she's holding back words.

"Look," she finally says as she sweeps a strand of ebony hair behind her ear. "I'm old enough and have enough insight to know that, absent some serious pathology, a twenty-five-year-old man was not going to call up some fourteen-year-old for a hook up."

I clench my teeth as she ignores that I just explained it was not a hook up.

"But at the time, it just felt like... I was the ice cream flavor he didn't choose. So, yeah, for a while, it was pretty satisfying watching all kinds of people not choose him."

I stare at her from the other side of the table and open my mouth to speak, but no words form. I finally manage a low, hollow, "Wow."

"You have to understand," she begins. It seems the conversation is not going as she planned, and her voice carries an anxious tremor. "Before his mother died, I hadn't checked in on that stuff in *yearrrs*." I don't ask her to be more specific. "We both have a lot going on these days. That breast cancer fundraiser for his mom showed up on Instagram, and I popped over to the Lewnatics, who were at fever pitch, and then two days later, you call and tell me you're going to a baseball game together? It was a lot to get my head around, Babs."

"I can understand that. I can see how that would be true," I say sincerely.

Margot sips her coffee and scans the sidewalk outside the café. She sets the cup down and leans against the table, forcing me to look at her. "All of this is just to say: I'm sorry I outed you. It was a shitty thing to do. Stupid. I really am happy for you, Babs. It's weird, and awkward, and it's going to take some getting used to. But I'm happy for you."

The tension in the room begins to defuse as Margot lets out an audible sigh. I realize I've been holding my breath, and my sigh joins hers.

"How did you leave things, then?" Austin asks, crushing some wasabi into his soy sauce.

"I thanked her for apologizing—I know that must have been hard—and I asked her if we could just take things a little bit at a time. I think it will probably be a very long time before I feel like I can confide in her about my relationship with you."

Austin takes a sip of water and regards me carefully, his eyes taking on that inquisitive quality they hold from time to time.

"What?"

"You're so... decisive. When you make a decision, that's it, isn't it?"

I get the feeling we aren't talking only about my sister anymore. And probably not the new décor in my family room either. I set my chopsticks down.

"I'm not saying it's bad." He dips a piece of sushi into his soy sauce. "Granted, it hasn't *always* worked to my favor."

"Do you disagree?" I didn't ask him so much because I believe he has any expertise in relationships between sisters, but he certainly has expertise in negotiating the balance between a need for privacy and his continued interactions with his fan base.

"No. Not at all. I think it would be incredibly sad for you to become estranged from your sister. And I'd feel awful if it was because of me—"

"It's not *because* of you," I argue.

"Well..." he equivocates, "I do think boundaries are smart. I'll be honest Bee, this stuff, these messages—"

"It's more, isn't it?" I ask. "It's worse."

He inhales a slow breath and exhales it as his head sags into his hands. "It's worse," he concedes.

"What do you think is going on there?" I ask, choosing to overlook that he's tacitly implicated my sister.

"I don't know. I wonder—" he stares across the span of the table and out beyond the glass doors to the patio. "—I wonder whether they can sense... it's... you and me..."

"I don't know what you're trying to say, Austin."

"They can tell this is different. It's going to be over nineteen weeks."

twenty-nine

1998

My roommate, Amanda, brought me the phone. "Your sister," she said, handing me the receiver.

This was back when I answered the phone every time it rang. Instead of *not* answering the phone unless I was expecting a call, I answered every call I received, unless I was specifically avoiding someone. Everyone did.

Ryan was racked out on the couch, his legs resting across my lap as we watched something—I don't remember what—on TV.

I must have looked as absolutely stunned as I felt, because Amanda offered a *don't ask me* expression, and Ryan slid his legs off my lap and sat up. He'd never met Margot and knew only that we'd had a huge fight out in California because I'd gone hiking with friends and didn't take her, and she hadn't spoken to me since.

"Hello?" I said.

I was greeted in return by a muted sniffle.

"Margot?"

Another sniffle, and a quick breath in. "Babs, something happened." Her voice was so small, I could hardly hear it.

I covered the receiver and turned to Ryan. "Mute the TV," I mouthed. "What's wrong, Margot?"

"This is all your fault," she said.

I glanced over at Ryan and threw out a gesture of helplessness, cradling the phone against my shoulder and tossing my hands to the ceiling.

He shrugged his shoulders—helpless—and got up. "You want anything from the kitchen?" he asked.

I shook my head.

"If you hadn't gone away, this wouldn't have happened," she said, a comment that didn't map on well to the events over summer break, during which she'd made it clear I couldn't return to Boston fast enough.

I leaned forward. "What wouldn't have happened?"

She inhaled a stutter.

"What happened?" I demanded.

"Kevin," she squeaked out.

As soon as she said his name, I felt sick. "Kevin," I repeated.

She had trouble explaining it—at the time, I thought she was hiding something, but as an adult, I know she was worried no one would believe her.

It started with a kind of proximity—him standing just a little too close, finding a way to be in whatever room she was in, though with the plausible deniability that there really weren't many rooms in that apartment. It was his eventual presence in her bedroom—in his underwear, in the dead of night—that prompted the phone call to me.

"He tried to kiss me," she said. "He tried to do more than kiss me."

"When did this happen?"

"Last night."

"Did you tell Mom?"

Ryan returned to the living room but froze next to the couch at the sound of my voice. I waited for Margot to respond.

"Margot. Did you tell Mom?"

"Yes," she said. "This morning."

"And?"

"She said he must have gotten lost."

I fought the impulse to catapult up from the couch, catch a cab to Logan and... what? I couldn't afford a same-day flight to Chicago.

"Is she there right now?" I asked.

"No. She's still at work."

"Is he there?"

"No."

"Is there somewhere you can go?"

"Can I stay with you?" she asked so softly, I hardly heard it over the sound of my own panic.

"How would you get here?"

"I could take a bus?"

"Go stay at Kira's," I said, referring to her best friend from her dance squad.

"And tell her what?" She began to cry again. "Everyone will know."

"Call me back as soon as Mom gets home," I said.

I spent the intervening time with Ryan and Amanda trying to think of a way to get Margot out to Boston. Would our mother allow that? Would it be kidnapping if I took her anyway? Would I be her guardian? I finally determined to call the police but was told I needed a statement from either our mother or Margot herself.

Two hours later, the phone rang again.

"He's home," Margot whispered into the phone.

"Is Mom home, too?"

"No."

"Put him on," I said.

Ryan was eating takeout on the chair next to me, both of us studying—well, he was studying; I couldn't concentrate. He dropped his chopsticks into the container, his eyes fixed on me as if he could see through the phone to whatever room Margot was calling from.

"What?" Margot asked.

"Put him on the phone, Margot. Give Kevin the phone."

There was a long pause followed by the muffled sound of a door opening and an exchange of some sort.

"Hey, Babs. How's Boston?" Kevin's cheerful greeting cut through the line like a guitar string badly in need of tuning.

"Cold. You have forty-eight hours to leave that apartment and get away from my sister or I'm calling the police," I said.

Ryan looked on with an expression that betrayed his appreciation for the risk of this bluff.

"Look, I don't know what Margot said to you—"

"Forty-eight hours," I repeated.

"Babs, this is a misunderstanding—"

"There's no misunderstanding. My sister's fifteen."

Ryan got up from the chair and sat next to me on the couch, taking my free hand in his. I was shaking like a leaf, fighting to keep my voice even.

"She's not like any fifteen-year-old I've ever met," he spat. "What did she tell you? Did she tell you about the other times?"

I almost asked, almost tumbled right into that question, but I managed to shake off the accusation. There was no way. Not that I couldn't imagine Margot being precocious with the boys, but she was chasing high school adulation: homecoming court, a class ring, a boy's varsity basketball letter jacket. A middle-aged CPA wouldn't have stood a chance with her, let alone been the actual object of her affection. No matter how nice his shoes were.

"That sounds like a confession, Kevin," I said. "That sounds like you admitting to me that you've been fucking around with my sister. Who is a freshman in high school."

"Fuck you," he said. "Fucking white trash, both of you."

"None of that sounds like a denial," I said.

A click punched through the line, followed by the dial tone.

"He hung up," I said to Ryan.

"You have to call the police again," Ryan said. "She can't be alone with him."

"Ula," I said. "I'll call Ula."

I called information for her phone number, then dialed and waited as it rang.

"Ula," I said when she answered. "Hi. It's Babs Stewart. From upstairs. Well. Not now. I'm in Boston right now. I'm wondering if you could go upstairs and check on my sister—"

"I already call police," she said.

Ula's English wasn't great, but—I learned later—the sound of Margot screaming evidently didn't require translation. While my phone call had not been sufficiently persuasive, Ula's description of "peoples fighting" in the apartment above her was.

Kevin spent eighteen months in prison following a misdemeanor child abuse plea. Not surprisingly, the statutory rape charge never saw the light of day—this was the 90s, and it was her word against his. But the x-rays of Margot's two broken ribs and broken nose, along with Ula's testimony ("I never like him from beginning," she'd said; me neither, Ula)—that was enough to put him away. At least for a few months.

It was also enough to both reconcile my sister's and my relationship and permanently fracture my relationship with my mother.

thirty

Next to me in bed, Austin rolls onto his back. One hand rests on his chest, the other is tucked under his head. He takes a breath deep enough to tug the sheet.

I roll to my side. "Are you going to tell my what's bothering you?" I ask.

He jolts, his head quickly turning toward me in the ink-black dark. "I didn't realize you were still awake."

"Is this about Margot?" I ask.

He rolls to his side, his cheek pressed against the pillow, which he pushes down. "No," he says.

I reach behind me and pull my phone off the nightstand. It reads: 2:12 a.m. "How long have you been awake?" I ask. He usually falls asleep—dead to the world—after we have sex and doesn't wake up until I get up to run.

He lifts a finger to the bridge of my nose and traces it down the center, adding an extra tap when he reaches the end.

"I'm not going to want to hear this, am I?" I say.

He looks at me for a moment, then says, "There's a book coming out." His eyes are black, and I can't tell whether that's because the room is dark or his mood is.

"About the show?" What else could it be about? Well, it could be about just him. He was the unequivocal star of that show.

"Sort of," he says. "It's a memoir."

"Yours?"

"No." His tone is dour. "But I'm in it."

"I see." I adjust my head on the pillow, trying to see him more clearly.

"It's not flattering." He reaches under the covers for my hand, which I place in his.

Kurt Alison, he explains, is the actor who played Daniel, Bobby's older brother, and Kurt has written a "tell-all" memoir. Pre-orders currently available; the book will be released the week of Christmas. Happy holidays, I guess.

"Have you read it?" I ask.

"No. But Micah got his hands on an advanced reader copy, and it paints a pretty ugly picture. Mostly of me."

"Why you?" I ask.

"It's an incredibly long story," he says. "But after season four, Kurt threatened to quit if he didn't have more screen time, and the studio said *fine, quit*. He played chicken with the showrunners of one of the most popular shows on television. And he lost."

"Weren't you," I'm choosing my words carefully, "one of the… show runners?"

"No. I had producer credit those last two seasons, but no. If I'd had control over the show *then*, I'd have done things very differently."

"So why is he mad at you?"

"I'm not sure *mad* is the right word. More bitter. He got fucked there in the end," Austin says as though he's not sure that's the right word either. "The show *did* focus too much on me, though that's not my fault; I wasn't a writer, and I wasn't a producer until after Kurt left. But I was a lot more careful than he was with those relationships—I wanted to have a career after the show ended and knew it was going to be tricky for me with my age, so I couldn't afford to burn bridges. I don't think Kurt anticipated what would happen, so when the scripts weren't going his way, he just went scorched earth, and they wrote him out completely."

He takes a breath and goes on. "I don't know what his financial situation was—more precarious than mine, I guess, because when I decided to purchase the rights to the show back in '03, I asked all of them if they wanted to go in on it with me. Melissa, Chloe, Susan, Scott, and Noelle did, but Kurt *couldn't*; he didn't have any money. I put up fifty percent and lent him enough for an eight percent interest, which is what the others were throwing in. But then he didn't even pay *that* back and forfeited his share."

Austin shakes his head as if he still can't believe it. "You know every single one of my cast mates is financially set because of the good business decisions *I've* made over the past twenty years. Everyone but him. I really don't think he could believe it was over, that he wasn't going to get something just as big as that show—or bigger. But none of us ever did. That's not my fault. And neither is the fact that he can't pivot to some kind of productive life now."

This seems undeniably true. The whole thing smacks of sour grapes from an actor who left the show thinking he was going to land something better and ended up landing nothing at all.

"Can you stop him from publishing it?" It sounds like a lot of it isn't true—maybe defamatory.

"Micah says Kurt's been pretty clever. The way he's written it hedges *just enough* for him to probably be able to get away with it," Austin mutters bitterly.

"What else?" I ask, thinking that can't possibly be the sole explanation for his tossing and turning in the middle of the night.

"The book includes some details about my private life." Austin's voice is steady, strong, assured, but his eyes are not. His eyes glint in the dark, examining mine.

"What kinds of details?" I ask, even though it doesn't matter. I won't read Kurt's memoir. Although Margot probably will, and that will be its own problem.

"He says that I haven't been very discriminating in my dating habits, which probably is true. But also, that I cheated on Chloe—"

"Who is Chloe?" It's the second time he's mentioned her, and I remember one of the Lewnatics said something about him always holding her hand in public.

"The woman who played my girlfriend on the show. We dated after the show ended—not for very long, but still, I never cheated on her." He pauses to see if I have any additional questions. I don't, so he proceeds. "And then, he's going to say that I married Samantha solely for publicity. Which arguably *is* true. But he will say pretty much anything he can to damage my reputation. It's just one hundred percent a vendetta."

"Sounds like it," I say sourly.

Austin offers a heavy sigh. "So, I'm going to have to do a little bit of press in response to this," he says, moving on. "Just a couple of daytime talk shows, some of the late-night shows. Just clean it up a little bit."

"It matters that much to you? A memoir?" I ask. I wonder whether people will even believe it. Much of it sounds like a man-child's temper-tantrum.

"In the age of cancel-culture? Yes. Parts of it are already leaking. I have to clean it up. The show continues to have appeal—and continues to make money—because people have this warm, fuzzy feeling about it. They aren't going to feel that if they think I was cheating on my girlfriend, acting like a prima donna on the set, and fucking everything that moved."

I could have done without the itemization of the last thing, especially since that part of the memoir is arguably true.

"Wait. When are you leaving? Christmas is in ten days."

"Tuesday," he says. "Come with me." He promptly kisses me, which I know he's doing to prevent me from saying no, which I have to say.

"I can't go with you. Penny and Colin can't be home alone."

"Can we bring them with? We wouldn't be gone for very long," he suggests.

"The week before Christmas?"

He grows solemn. "I'm afraid to leave you here alone," he says. "I'm afraid something will happen while I'm gone, and I won't be here."

"Nothing's going to happen to me, Austin. What on earth would happen to me?"

He's quiet for a moment, his thumb passing over the back of my hand. "Listen," he says, "I'm going to tell them in the interviews not to ask about who I'm dating. I just don't feel safe giving them any more ammunition."

"You can do that? You can tell them what they're allowed to ask?" The things I'm learning about his world.

"Oh yeah. These interviews are so scripted. I can tell them what *to* ask, what *not to* ask. That's why those funny anecdotes at the beginning of the interviews always sound so canned. *They are.*"

"Huh. Interesting." I say.

"It's the least interesting part of the entire business," he says, but I think this might be something I'd watch. Plus, I'll miss him, so it would be one way to see him while he's gone.

"I think you're more worried about this than I am," I say. "We should get some sleep. We can talk more in the morning."

He nods.

"It's going to be fine," I say. "Maybe there will be a lull."

Austin's preemptive strategy against Kurt's memoir does not occur during a lull. Over the three days before Austin leaves for New York, I receive a barrage of emails and message invites, and have already started to consider closing the email account I've had for nearly twenty years. The messages are, at turns, incoherent and frenetic, threatening and specific. The senders embed modified, distorted photographs from wherever they can get them: a friends' social media accounts, old pictures still left on the web, races I've competed in, and increasingly, photos Austin is tagged in and in which I now appear.

Austin is at his house packing when the worst of them comes through my Messenger app. By this time, Messenger is chock full of friend requests, some of which are probably legitimate—from people I knew once. I've managed by sheer force of will not to open a single one. I only open the one I do because it looks like it's from Kelly. Along with the demise of Kelly's and my real-life friendship, came the inevitable "unfriending" on both Facebook and Instagram. We didn't interact with each other much on social media, but it still hurt when I realized she'd severed even that tenuous tie.

I accept her friend request, and a message promptly follows, but I know as soon as I open it that this isn't Kelly.

On the screen in front of me, under a text that reads "You're one in a million. LOL!" is a picture of Austin. Not just Austin. Austin and a woman. A woman I don't recognize. Her face isn't visible as her head is cast down, her raven-colored hair falling over the sides of her face. She is positioned on all fours with Austin positioned (I guess you could call it) behind her, one hand wrapped around her shoulder, the other grasping her hip. The expression on his face is one I know well, by now; there's no mistaking it's him or what he's doing. The only thing I can't be certain of is when it was taken. A business trip last week? A honeymoon a decade and a half ago? I have no idea. From the background, I know it isn't any of the rooms in his condo or my house. Which leaves pretty much every other room on the planet.

Something constricts around my neck, and I lift my hand to my throat, legitimately surprised to find nothing there but my sweater. I want to be unbothered by the photograph, to scoff at the sender—*You think I'm surprised? That I don't know? Nice try.* But knowing something and seeing it are two different things.

There's so much about the picture that disturbs me, I can hardly order it. The clarity of the photograph, the angle, the closeness of the image, suggest it was not the result of a telephoto lens or clandestine paparazzi; the people in the photograph knew they were being filmed. Austin's face is an unrestrained ecstasy I'd allowed myself to imagine he only ever felt with me. The woman in the photograph resembles me in no identifiable way. She's younger, her skin the milky white of youth, not a freckle, not a flaw in sight. She's reaching between her legs to hold him as he comes, and this is what he's told me he likes, what he told her he likes. I am not special. I am one in a million.

Austin picks up the phone immediately.

"Hey Bee," he says cheerfully. "I was just getting ready to call you. I'm almost done packing and thought we could grab lunch before I head to the airport."

"I got another one," I say flatly.
"Oh," he says, somber.
"Can you... do you have time to come over?"

thirty-one

Austin remains in the office for a while—Facebook open, Messenger pulled up. I'm not sure how long. Maybe fifteen minutes, maybe three hours. Probably closer to fifteen minutes. Either way, it's clear he needs the time to compose himself. When I walk back toward the office, after going to the kitchen and making a pot of coffee then drinking none of it, I hear only the loud exhaling of someone trying to calm himself.

He steps out of the office and crosses the hall to the living room where I sit, staring out the window.

"I don't know what to say." He sits down next to me on the couch. "I think this is the worst thing they've ever done." He offers this observation as if he's still weighing some of the other things they've done.

"When is that picture from?" I ask. It isn't the only thing I care about, but it's up there.

"Um..." he hesitates. "About eight years ago, judging from —" I assume he was going to say *the woman in the photograph*, but he doesn't finish the sentence. *Judging from* is sufficient. That's of some comfort, though I hardly have the capacity to impeach him. It could be from last week, and I'd be none the wiser.

"You don't believe me," he says, reading my face (and apparently my mind).

"I don't have any reason not to," I say.

"I can tell you who the woman is, and that will date the picture," he offers, but I don't want to know who the woman is. I really just want her not to exist.

"Where did the picture come from? Is that something you did? Like you recorded... yourself. Or... I don't understand how a picture like that came into being."

He stares at me, something akin to terror in his eyes, then puts his face in his hands. "Yeah. I mean, not a lot. A couple of times. Isa... she wanted to. It was stupid. I shouldn't have done it."

I have to give him credit for telling the truth, but the confirmation that it's him, it's real, it's not some AI-generated...

"It was on *her* phone, though," he says, interrupting my thoughts. "I don't know how... maybe she was hacked or something. Maybe she sent it to someone, and now it's circulating somewhere. Maybe she sent it to *you*. She wasn't real happy when we broke up."

"No. She didn't send it," I say, fairly certain that's true. "It's whoever's been doing the other stuff. They pretended to be a woman at my old firm." Whoever this is, they know enough about me to know who my friends were there.

"Bee, I'm so sorry. I'm so sorry this is happening." He takes my hand in his, and the warmth of it is enough to leech out every ounce of anxiety I'd managed to bottle up, bringing it to the surface as something between a breath and a sob that moves through my chest and out between my lips.

"I think we should call the police," he says.

My experience with the police in the past suggests they

won't be exactly helpful. I can't imagine them caring that there's a photograph of Austin Lewis naked, circulating on the internet.

"Stay," I say as if it's an alternative to his suggestion. I know I ask the impossible. So, I say it again. "Stay, please. Don't go to New York."

"Bee..."

I lift my eyes to his and feel a panic so strong, it makes me exhale through my teeth as if the problem is too much air, rather than not enough. I see the answer in his face, in his eyes, in his silence, and I deflate, my shoulders slumping inward.

"I'm going to call the police," he says.

"They won't do anything." I wipe my cheeks with the backs of my hands.

"Then I'll hire a private investigator."

"You think a private investigator would be able to figure something out that Micah can't?" I ask.

"I don't know. Maybe."

"Did you forward it to Micah?" I ask.

"Yeah. He's following up with... her," he says.

"That sounds like a good place to start," I say.

I get up from the couch and walk back into the office. There's Kleenex on the desk, and I need one. After I've blown my nose and tossed the tissue in the trash, I take a look at the computer. The screen is dark. I wiggle the mouse, and it lights up. My messages reappear, though fake-Kelly is blocked, her messages gone with her. Austin follows me and stands in the doorway.

"Come with me to New York," he says again, taking his phone from his pocket like I've already agreed. "I'll get you a ticket right now."

"I can't!" I explode. "I can't just drop my life and run off to

New York with you." I bring my palms forcefully against the desk, leaning into the top, staring at the keyboard.

Austin silences. He takes a step forward, then, evidently reconsidering, steps back again. "What do you need from me," he asks, a tremor in his voice. "I'll do it. Anything."

"I don't know. I can't even logon to my email without sifting through a bunch of bullshit about how someone hopes I die, or thinks I'm hideous, or that Chloe—or whoever the fuck—was hotter than I am. What if this gets out at Penny and Colin's school? I just want this to end; it's fucking exhausting." I realize I'm only about three and a half months into this relationship, so if I'm exhausted already, that probably doesn't bode well long-term.

Austin must see the direction of my thoughts. "What do you mean, *end*?" he says, his voice a low gravelly whisper.

"Nothing," I say, closing my eyes against all of it. "Nothing. What time is your flight? You're going to be late."

"You must be joking," he says, almost a guffaw. "I'm not leaving things like this." He steps just over the threshold. "Are you breaking up with me?"

I glance up over the top of the computer to find him drained of color.

"What? No," I say, shaking my head. "That's not what I'm saying."

"What *are* you saying?" He takes another step into the room, and the only thing dividing us is the desk.

My head sags, my chin resting on my chest. "I don't know, Austin. That it's hard and weird and my sister doesn't like you—"

"Still?"

"Well more I think she doesn't like *us*. But that's just it, isn't it. None of them do. They hate *us*. And I thought an old friend was trying to reconnect—Kelly and I were friends, and then we weren't, and I thought she was trying to reconnect—but instead it was just more. More bullshit. In my face. First thing in the morning—"

"Okay, okay," he says coming around the desk. "First of all, it isn't true that *none of them like us*. The Lewnatics are just one group, and they're small—"

"Small but mighty," I mutter.

"Fair enough," he says. "But it's still just one small group."

"The way I felt when I looked at that picture—" I say, staring at the computer instead of Austin, "—it's exactly what I was afraid of when we started this. It's what I was afraid of way back then: the constant comparisons with models and actresses, with girlfriends and one-night stands and sheer numbers I can't compete with."

"It's not— it's not a competition," he says as if he finds the whole idea not merely false, but incomprehensible.

"Yeah... well..." I lift my head. Austin appears stricken. I close my eyes.

"Look at me," he says.

I don't. I'm not sure why. An exercise in defiance, perhaps. The comfort of darkness. The image of his face, drawn down, eyes full of sadness—it's enough in my mind.

"Look at me," he says again.

I feel the fingers of one hand twine with mine, and his other hand lifts to the side of my face, the pad of his thumb moving across the apple of my cheek. I open my eyes.

"There you are," he says. He smiles—a twitch of his lips that slips away as his eyes sharpen. "I'm sorry."

"It's not your fault—"

"No. Listen to me."

I bite my lips to keep myself from interrupting.

"I will figure out who is doing this, and I will stop them. I'm going to report it to the police, and if they can't help, I'm going to hire someone who will. I'm going to do that, Babs, because I love you."

It takes me a minute to register what he's said. I'd followed along with the plan, the strategy, the police, the private investigator—the plan is a good one. The words at the end linger in the air between us for some time before I recognize them for what they are.

"Do you understand me?" he asks. "I love you."

I nod, dumbly.

"Okay," he says, apparently unbothered by the fact I haven't returned an *I love you, too*. He kisses my forehead, then pulls me into his chest. I feel myself settle into him as another kiss lands on top of my head.

"I love you, too," I finally manage to squeak out into his neck.

His chest expands and contracts with a heavy sigh. "That's good to hear," he says. "I was starting to wonder."

The press junket begins with a late-night show, which I decide to watch. I can't remember the last time I watched one of these shows, but it's the same man hosting who hosted then: Nate. He doesn't even look older. How do they do that? Is it the lighting? The only way anyone would know it wasn't a rerun from fifteen years ago is the cut of his suit.

The first guest is an up-and-comer from a new series on Hulu about a man whose mind is split between two different bodies. He simultaneously experiences two separate realities. Austin would call this a "concept show." It has an amazing premise but will be nearly impossible to build a plot around. It will run for one season. Maybe two if they can throw in a twist at the end of the first season. As I listen to the young actor enthusiastically promote the show, he teases a second season. My guess is that the twist will be twins. He's actually a twin.

Then Nate introduces Austin.

"You might remember him as Bobby Martin. But ladies, he's all grown up now!!"

He was grown up then. It's so canned, I feel embarrassed watching it. There's a thirty-second clip from *The Maple Street Martins* that precedes Austin's appearance. It's from the season that won him the Emmy. It's impassioned. Bobby is fighting with the principal of his high school for a boy who is HIV-positive to be allowed to play on the football team.

Jesus, this would have been 1995? I have to watch this show.

When Austin walks out from behind the curtain and strides across the stage, I almost don't recognize him. He waves to the audience, and by the squeals coming from the seats, I think at least a few Lewnatics managed to score tickets. His clothes have been picked out for him: a leather jacket that I have never once seen before, and jeans, just barely too tight. He sits down in the seat and takes a sip from a mug on the edge of Nate's desk.

As I watch him settle in, lean back, cross his legs, I'm amazed at how much he looks nothing like the man I know and yet exactly like the man I know. Under his too-tight jeans, I know he's wearing black boxer briefs. Small chance they're gray. He smiles out into the crowd at a spontaneous *whoop* that erupts there. Dazzling. He's so fucking good at this, I think I'm developing a crush on him.

Nate starts with the script, which I know because Austin and I practiced it on the phone. They begin with "small talk," with Austin commenting that he's been in Chicago for the past several months, managing his mother's estate. Then Nate pivots to some "difficult questions," but they aren't actually going to be difficult because they've been fed to him, and Micah has already prepared answers.

"So, there's a book coming out that has some things to say about the show and about you. Not very nice things. Have you had a chance to read it?" Nate asks.

"I haven't, and I don't plan to," he begins. "I'm basically approaching it the same way I do any time gossip comes out about me or about *The Maple Street Martins*." He's managed to drop the name of the show, just in case anyone is up late watching and doesn't know it. Now they do. Now they can buy it. Just in time for Christmas.

"I can hear legitimate critiques of the show—and critiques of myself as an actor," he goes on. "And I think I've grown a lot as a person over the past twenty years. I'd assume most people would rather not be judged for something they said or did more than two decades ago."

The audience murmurs their agreement, and Nate nods amicably.

"It must be especially painful, though. All this coming from Kurt. You two were close, weren't you? Can you think of any reason why he would do this to you?" Nate asks.

This question is absolutely not on the list. Austin wanted to address the content of the memoir broadly, not Kurt specifically.

He takes another sip of water and glares at Nate over the top of the mug. I wonder if anyone else can see it, or if I just know him, so the slight deepening of the creases around his eyes is perceptible to me but wouldn't be to others.

Nate makes no attempt to retract his question.

"I couldn't even begin to comment on Kurt's motivations. He was a very dear friend of mine for a very long time."

"That's it? Nothing else to say about your big brother trying to torpedo your career?"

Jesus Christ. Who is this guy, and what does he have against Austin?

"No. Nothing else to say about that."

I twist the sheets under the duvet leaving them wrinkled and damp from the sweat on my hands as the silence extends from the studio into my bedroom.

An audience member saves him with a shrill, "I LOVE YOU!"

Austin chuckles and looks out into the crowd, which seems to snap both Nate and Austin out of their standoff, and Nate moves on to another topic.

"I see you've still got that Bobby Martin magic. I hear there's a little bit about that in the book." A reference to the description of Austin's sexual exploits, but Austin ignores it. Simply refuses to respond, and Nate is forced to connect his comment to an actual question. "You've managed to age pretty well." A titter runs through the audience—as if they're embarrassed at having their collective mind read. "What's your secret?"

"Diet and exercise," he says. "I wish I had a more interesting answer. I think Melissa may have better advice on that front. Her book has quite a bit on healthy living in it."

That's a nice plug. Push another cast-member's project.

Austin tosses Nate a disarming smile, but he's trying to make it awkward. Stick to the script or the answers won't be interesting.

"Melissa Miller. Your co-star from the show," Nate says for anyone in the audience, who might not know. "You two stay in touch?"

Austin does this thing with his shoulder where he slowly rolls it back, then rolls it forward. Because I know him, I know it's a tell. He isn't happy. I wonder if he'll walk off the set. I check the time. The show ends at 12:30 a.m. It's 12:26. Four minutes is a long time depending on what one is doing.

"We do," he answers without elaborating. I didn't know they stayed in touch. Maybe they really don't.

"Now, you two used to be a thing, didn't you? Back in the day?" Nate asks.

There's a twitch at the corner of Austin's eyes, but I also know that Nate is confusing the on-screen sister with the on-screen love interest. This will work in Austin's favor.

"We were not. I think everyone would have found that pretty strange—probably not a lot of people *shipping* me and my sister."

The audience laughs, but even they sound nervous.

"Well, she's not really your sister," Nate says, defending his question, but he's just revealed that he doesn't really know the show. Of course, I don't either. Austin is silent.

"It's a good question, though. You're not married. At least not anymore. How have you managed to stay single this long?" Nate asks. "Or maybe you're not. Apparently, it's not Melissa Miller. Do you have someone else in your life?"

Nate has strayed from questions that are not on the script to questions that are on the "don't ask" list. Austin struggles to answer. There are fans in the audience, clearly—Lewnatics, probably. They know he's seeing someone; they know he's seeing *me*. I also don't understand what Nate is getting at. What's his motivation for all this?

"Yes, I am seeing someone," Austin finally says and takes another sip from the mug.

"What's the story there? Is it as good as the ones Kurt tells?"

I can see Austin weighing the risks, evaluating his next move. But he pauses for too long. The silence stretches. He knows enough about television to know that's bad for the show. *Everyone* knows enough about television to know that's bad for the show.

"She was in a coffee shop," he says, breaking the tension, and it's weird because I see him again. Through the leather jacket and the jeans and the too-styled hair, I see him. "Across the street from the firm that was handling my mother's estate after she died." Good call mentioning the dead mother. "I was feeling pretty low, and we started talking, and we just... we didn't stop talking for four hours."

"She had you at hello?" Nate asks.

Hardy-har-har. Fucking cheeseball horseshit. The audience groans, but I want to cry. I feel so awful for him. He betrays nothing, though, and the audience is on his side. They like the story even though it's really two stories wrapped into one.

"Not quite hello but not long after."

Some of the audience offer an "Awww."

I'm disgusted but also riveted. He was right when he said not everyone hates us. This audience, at least the majority of them, likes us.

"Well, who is she?" Nate asks, and just fuck that guy and his smug little face.

"She's a very private person. I don't feel comfortable saying more about her than I already have. As you know, I promised her that there wouldn't be any questions about our relationship, so I've already broken that promise." He delivers the line with an icy stare. He's read the audience, too, and I'm not even sure he cares if people notice the hostility.

"Well, thank you for dropping by, Austin," Nate says. The transition is awkward, clunky. Nate turns to the camera. "That's all we have time for tonight. Thanks for watching, friends. We'll see you after the New Year!"

Austin faces the camera, smiles and waves, but I see the emotion behind his eyes. Fear. Confusion. Maybe anger. I'm not sure about anything other than that he needs to come home.

thirty-two

"I'M SORRY. I'M SO SORRY. I DIDN'T KNOW WHAT TO DO." He hasn't left the studio yet, by the sound of it. I can hear voices in the background and the sounds of heavy objects being moved about.

"Where are you?" I ask.

"Walking down to my car," he says, confirming my suspicion.

"It's not a big deal. You handled it really, really well," I say. "I guess I don't understand what he's got against you. Why did he do that?"

"He's friends with Kurt," Austin says. "I wouldn't have even done his show, but it would have looked weird to leave him out."

> Margot: Are you awake? Did you see Late Night Live?

"Margot's texting me," I say.

"Oh God. They're going to have a field day with this," Austin says. I hear a door slam. He must have gotten into his car.

"When do you get home?" I ask.

"Friday. First flight out. Fuck!"

"I think it went about as well as it could. I think it's fine," I say.

"Yeah. Okay, okay," he says, seeming to catch his breath. "You're not mad?"

"Not at *you*." I say. "Nate is obviously a giant chode."

He laughs.

"Do you want me to pick you up on Friday?" I ask.

"That would be nice," he says. "I miss you," he adds, dropping his voice.

"I miss you, too."

"I heard back from Micah about the picture," he says. "I'll talk to you more about it when I get home, but it wasn't her. She didn't send it. She's horrified."

"I assume you can't speak freely about the matter right now?" I say, imagining that there is, at the very least, a driver who might overhear.

"That's right," he says.

"Understood. Are you still thinking it's the Lewnatics?"

"Even more so," he says.

"Are you going to the police?"

"Yes. When I get home."

> Margot: Why aren't you responding? What happened? Is Austin pissed?

"Margot won't stop texting me," I say.

"I don't think we should talk to her about this, Babs," Austin says.

"I agree," I say. I don't even have to think about it. "She'll be coming over for Christmas, though," I remind him.

"Do you want me there?"

"On Christmas Day? I'd kind of hoped you'd spend the whole weekend with me."

My phone buzzes; Margot is calling. I send it to voicemail, then promptly realize she now knows I'm awake. It rings again. Then another text.

> Margot: Are you talking to Austin right now?

"That would be nice," he says.

"I'll leave it up to you. What you're comfortable with."

"I'm almost at my hotel, and I'm beat. Can I give you a call tomorrow, and we can figure out plans for Christmas?"

"Sure," I say even though I suspect that *figure out plans* means he wants to be back at his condo by the time Margot and Rishi arrive at my house.

"Hey!" he says, as though he just remembered something. "I love you. Sleep well."

"I love you, too," I say feeling oddly self-conscious as I utter the words, though I can't explain why. They must have sounded a little uneven coming out because I hear the suggestion of laughter on the other end.

"I'll take it," he says.

"I mean it," I say, with more confidence.

"Good. So do I. I'll talk to you tomorrow." He ends the call before I can dig myself any deeper.

I set the phone on my nightstand only for it to ring before I manage to take my hand away. Margot. She's just going to keep calling, and I'm not going to be able to sleep, so I might as well take her call.

"Did you just see that?" she asks as soon as I answer.

"I did," I say.

"Were you just talking to him? What did he say?" She's nearly breathless.

"Not much. He thinks it was about ratings." A fib.

"He fucking annihilated Nate. Oh my god, that was amazing," she says.

I don't know that I would have phrased it quite that way, but I'm reassured that she would. I think she might be cheering for him.

"I bet it's a fucking blood bath in the Lewnatics. *I met her at a coffee shop?*" Margot is laughing so hard, she's cackling.

"Hey, Margot," I say. "I'm going to let you go."

"What's wrong?" she asks. "Does Austin not think it went well?"

"It's not that. It's just hard for me to laugh at this kind of stuff right now." I turn off the light and slide down under the covers.

"Were there more mean messages?" she asks. "You'd think they'd have moved on to his movie deal."

"His what?" I say.

To my knowledge Austin has not so much as been offered a supporting role in a commercial in the time I've known him. All his work, the work that occupies his days, involves managing the ongoing business related to projects he completed years ago, or working behind the scenes as a producer. Occasionally, he consults on a script or something.

"The movie," Margot repeats. "Some Sorkin film about QAnon. He's supposed to play this ordinary guy, who gets sucked into that world, and he loses his wife and kids and job over it. It was just announced last week on Instagram. I'm assuming that's why he's so upset about this memoir. It pretty much couldn't land at a worse time."

I'm silent. I know nothing about this. How do I not know anything about this?

"It's based on a true story," Margot adds hesitantly.

"It's based on a lot of true stories if my 2020 Facebook feed was any indication," I say.

"He hasn't said anything to you?" Margot asks, not a taunt in sight. Since we had coffee together, she's been careful with her words. She thought I knew, or maybe she thought the information would be helpful, informative.

"I'm going to bed," I say.

"Are you okay?" Margot asks.

"I'm fine," I say. "It's late. I'm going to bed."

"Sure. Okay," she says. "But let's talk tomorrow."

"Fine."

I set the phone on my nightstand and punch my pillow down under my face. I've been avoiding social media when at all possible and didn't see any movie announcement. But that doesn't explain why Austin hasn't mentioned it. I try to concoct some passable explanation for why he wouldn't that doesn't involve me sitting—cast off—in Chicago, while he goes back to his life in California. I come up empty.

I'm about to call him and ask when my phone buzzes again on the bedside table. I suspect it's Margot with just one more thought, but I pick it up on the (very) off chance it's Austin.

It isn't Austin or Margot, and a yelp escapes my throat at the image contained within the text. I managed to stifle it only by my fear of waking my children, who sleep safe and sound in their bedrooms down the hall. I sit up fully in bed and turn on the light next to me, then examine the image again, trying to decide if it's real. Am I awake? Is this a nightmare?

The phone vibrates in my hand and three texts follow the picture.

I.

See.

You.

Reflexively, I throw the phone across the room. It could be a snake I'd mistaken for a twig that tried to bite me. It ricochets off the corner of the dresser and clatters to the hardwood floor. I stare at it for a few moments, waiting to see if it slithers back to life, but it remains motionless.

I crawl out of bed and cross the room. It's landed face up, the screen shattered, black. I'm tempted to nudge it with my toe to see if it's still alive. I pick it up and tap the obliterated screen. No response. It's dead. For a second, I'm relieved before I remember that my laptop syncs with my phone, as does the desktop in the office.

The photograph itself was a single picture sent from a phone number in the western suburbs (area code 630), but I suspect if I call, I'll get an outgoing message telling me I have reached a number that is no longer in service.

At this point, I'm used to seeing pictures of myself sent through various messaging apps and email. Sometimes they're altered, usually they're unflattering. But this picture is neither, though there's no question it's me. I'm standing in a pair of pajama bottoms and a t-shirt in front of the sliding glass doors out to my patio. I'm holding a baseball bat over my shoulder, and my eyes squint as I stare across the backyard. The photograph is blurry; it must have been taken at some distance. But I remember that night, and suddenly what I can't remember is when it was. After the Cubs game? I'm pretty sure.

My hands fumble as I reach for the landline next to my bed, but I don't know Austin's number by heart. Fucking cell phones, no one memorizes numbers anymore. I panic, then remember that his number will be in the texts on my computer. I grab my laptop from my reading chair and open my last text from Austin. I call from my landline, and his phone rings three times, before he sends it to voicemail.

Fuck. He doesn't recognize my number.

I call again, and it goes straight to voicemail.

I open the texting app on my computer.

> Me: That's me calling. Answer. I'm calling from my landline.

I decide to send him a screenshot of the photograph and the texts, but when I open them again, the screen is blank. The messages have been deleted by the sender.

My landline rings in my hand, and I nearly throw that phone, as well.

"Hello? Austin?"

"It's me."

"I just got a text," I say, between panicked breaths.

"I know. I got it, too," he says. "I'm packing now and catching the first flight out. I've asked Micah to cancel the rest of the interviews."

thirty-three

Colin and his piano teacher are in the living room. Austin is probably in the air at this very moment. He should land late this morning. I open my laptop to check my text messages—my phone is dead-dead. The first flight out of New York was at 5:30 a.m., but Austin had to wait standby through two flights before he managed to get a seat.

I spent most of the night trying to decide what we should do about the photograph. I entertained calling the police, but what would they be able to do about a text with no content? Austin must have been thinking along the same lines, because I received a text from him shortly before he boarded his flight, stating that he'd retained a security service for my house.

The first guard shows up just as Colin is settling into Chopin's Nocturne in E-Flat Major. The guard steps into the vestibule and in a low voice, introduces himself as "Mike, ma'am." He explains that they're a twenty-four hours service. Six-hour shifts. Today will be two Mikes, Tyler, and Drew.

He gives me a small black plunger with a red button on top. "If you press this, I respond."

"Can't I just call you or something?" I ask.

"You can do that, too, but if you press this, it tells me there's an emergency, and I respond." He touches his hip, where I see his coat does not lay flat against his side.

"Can you have that in the city limits?" I ask.

"Yes, ma'am," he says. He hands me two more plungers: one for Penny and one for Colin. Each has a braided lanyard. I briefly rehearse a version of the truth that I can bear to tell them. *This is just what it's like when your mom's dating someone famous.* Colin will think it's cool; Penny will not.

"Thanks," I say, and Mike steps back out on the front step.

I walk into the office with my panic plungers and text Austin from the desktop.

> Me: Security service is here. I'm not crazy about a guy with a gun standing on my front step.

> Austin: Coming straight to your house from airport. Will text when I land.

I have a feeling this is not really up for discussion. I return to the kitchen.

Colin's lesson ends, and I should walk out into the living room, thank his teacher, pay her, and confirm we'll see her after the holidays. Instead, I sit at the kitchen table, staring at my laptop, watching the minutes tick by.

I hear a voice. Colin's. He's in front of me. His presence snaps me out of my head.

"Is your lesson over?" A most obvious question.

"Yes." He inspects me, suspicious. "Ms. Grayson is in the living room waiting for you."

I rise from my seat and slip into the familiar routine: pay Ms. Grayson, then help Colin make lunch. Outside, it's started snowing. It's cold. Not Chicago-cold. Not as cold as it will be in February, but too cold for me to suggest some fun (and distracting) activity for Colin, Penny, and me to do. They seem content in the leisure of their winter break anyway.

An hour later, I receive a text that Austin has landed.

> Austin: On my way.

He arrives directly from the airport roughly forty-five minutes later. The snow is falling in large, wet flakes, melting against the windows, but accumulating on the patio and in the backyard. I hear the garage door, then his footsteps in the hallway, and I stand as he enters the kitchen. He looks like himself again, dressed himself, I see. He's wearing a black turtleneck sweater and a pair of black jeans that actually fit. He takes the distance in four long strides and pulls me to him so tightly it hurts.

"I can't breathe," I gasp.

"Is there a place we won't be interrupted?" he asks. I'm not even sure he said *hello*. It's possible he whispered it against my cheek.

"Penny and Colin are both up in their rooms. They probably don't even know you're here," I say, thinking that I officially have two teenagers in the house. Well, Colin isn't a teenager yet, but he's started to adopt the persona. "We can go downstairs, though."

We sit next to each other on the couch in the family room, and Austin sets his phone on the coffee table in front of us. He presses a few buttons, calling Micah.

"Austin?" the voice on the other end says.

"Yeah. It's me. I've got Babs here." He reaches for my hand and brings it to his lips.

"Hi Babs," Micah says. "How are you, kiddo?"

It's strange to hear the man's voice. When I pictured him in my mind, I'd imagined someone roughly Austin's age, in an expensive Italian cut suit, flawlessly tailored. But he sounds older than that, and now I'm picturing someone my mother's age, gray-haired, grandfatherly. And the way he greets me—it feels like he's known me for years. My blood pressure descends, and I am immediately at ease.

"I've been better," I reply. Austin tightens his grip on my hand.

"I bet," he says. "Here's what I know." He launches into the meat of it. "That post on Scuttle went up within days of you two going to lunch. That's fast. There are two possibilities there. One is that it's just coincidence—a fan happened to be at the restaurant, snapped the picture, and started asking questions. The other possibility is that it's not a fan."

He lets that sit for a minute, and I mutter the obvious: "Margot."

"Well, maybe," Micah says. "But if it's not a coincidence, then it's someone who was following one of you."

"Why would anyone be following *me*?" I ask, then instantly realize that is not at all a rhetorical question. "Oh fuck. Mark."

"Who?" Micah asks.

"A colleague," I say. Austin would probably describe him more colorfully but doesn't get a chance.

"Did you text anyone before the lunch?" Micah asks.

"No," I say. "I didn't even tell Margot until the next day."

"Have you told her about the photograph from last night?" he asks.

"That photograph isn't *from* last night," I say.

"It's not?" Micah and Austin chirp in unison.

"No. It's from September. I'm pretty sure the night of the Cubs game. I called the police because I heard something in alley. They sent a car around, but said everything was clear."

"That raises another question," Micah says. "Do you want to go to the police with this? I *would* recommend that."

"I was already planning to," Austin says.

"Austin, I know you want to make a statement on Instagram asking people to leave you two alone. I would strongly counsel against that—"

Austin cuts in, "But—"

Micah doesn't allow the interruption. "If this *is* a fan, she is someone who sees herself *in a relationship* with you—parasocial though it may be. You're essentially addressing her individually if you post something on social media, and that's an awful lot of attention going to someone who's seeking exactly that—your attention."

Austin remains silent, but I'm certainly persuaded by the argument.

"Margot left the Facebook group," I say. It sounds completely disconnected from the conversation when said aloud, but it made sense in my head.

"I saw that," Micah says. "You don't think she's gone off to some other shadow group?"

"Shadow group? I have no idea. She didn't sound like she knew what was going on with them anymore. I talked to her last night after the interview, and the only thing she said—" I glance over at Austin; there are better times to bring this up, but here we go. "She said she'd have thought they'd have enough to talk about with Austin's new movie."

Austin goes rigid next to me.

Micah doesn't respond for a couple seconds. Then I hear him take a breath. "Because of the Instagram announcement?"

"Yes," I say.

"I was going to tell you," Austin whispers weakly. "There's been a lot going on."

"Babs," Micah continues. "I'd also recommend you get a new email address. And a new phone number."

"Yeah," I say, with a slouch into the couch. "I kinda knew that was coming."

"That's it for now," he says.

"It is?" I look to Austin. It feels abrupt, but I guess I can't think of what more he could offer at this point.

"Let me know what the police say," Micah says, I think mostly to Austin. He ends the call, and the family room plummets into uncomfortable silence.

Austin clears his throat. He's still holding my hand.

"Do you want me to come with you to the police station?" I ask.

"I think you probably should," he says. "Um... about the movie."

I turn toward him, holding my face steady. "Do not try to tell me you thought I already knew."

"No," he says. "I knew you didn't. It's a project that's been in the works for a while—couple of years, actually—and I auditioned before my mom died. I wanted to tell you before it went out on Instagram, but all of this..." He looks around the basement like we might be talking about the redecorating I did in September, but I know what he means. "I couldn't find a good time. It just felt like everything was going to shit, and I'd be piling on."

"When does filming start?" I ask.

"May," he says, closing his eyes as his shoulders slump forward.

"Is this why you're so concerned about Kurt's memoir?"

Austin nods, reluctantly. "I really can't afford to have any negative press right now."

He pivots on the couch, turning his whole body to mine, and takes several breaths. He's still holding my hand, tighter it seems than he was before. Maybe he's holding me to the conversation. "Would you consider... moving in together?"

I feel dizzy. "I don't know what to say." I want to say yes. Having him sitting with me in my house is the safest I've felt in days. Maybe years. "I don't want to leave Chicago," I say. "Ever."

"I don't want to leave Chicago, either. I would sell my house in L.A. Plenty of people in the business live outside of L.A. We could buy something together in the city." He's been thinking about this.

I don't want to sell my house. I love this house. It's all I have left of Ryan.

"Babs," he says, and his voice has dropped to just above a whisper. His pupils have done that thing where the blue of his irises haloes around the black of his pupils. "I hated being away from you these past two days. And I'll hate being away from you while I film this movie and while I do the press for it afterwards. I want to come home to you. I want as much of you as I can possibly get in the time in between." He smiles almost shyly, like he thinks I might not be on board with this idea—him having as much of me as he possibly can.

It's a lot to think about. "I don't know what to say." This is the second time I've said it, so it must be true. "I need to talk to Penny and Colin."

"Of course," he says.

He slides closer to me, our knees touching, and he rests a hand on my thigh. The warmth and pressure against my body is intoxicating. I feel woozy, like I haven't had enough to eat.

"I don't think I'm ready to sell this house," I say. "I'm worried what that would do to Penny and Colin." And to me.

"Bee, I... I don't know what's going on with all of this. I want to be able to protect you, and I don't feel like I can do that, definitely not from L.A., but not even from Old Town."

His thumb brushes back and forth over the top of my thigh.

He brings his hand to my face, cupping it against my cheek. I close my eyes and lean into his palm, and it slides to the back of my neck. He leans forward, resting his forehead against mine.

"I worry about you constantly," he says, his lips so close they nearly brush against mine as he speaks the words. "I can't concentrate on anything else. If something happened to you..." He looks at me with eyes so wide I think perhaps he's seen something I haven't, a future I haven't. Or, more worrisome, a number of messages I haven't. In either case, I understand what he's afraid of. I loved someone, and something happened to him. I know what that is.

His thumb stops brushing against my thigh, and his hand slides down along the side of my leg, hooking behind my knee.

"Okay," I say, not that I think I could talk him out of it. "I feel safer with you here."

A constrained smile fights through at least some of the tension. "I hope I make you feel more than just safe."

"Austin," I breathe, realizing how guarded I've been with him, how protected, while he's laid himself before me again and again. "Austin, you make me feel more than I thought I could." I can hardly look at him as I say it. I feel more naked than I did that first night together in the guest room. "I love you," I say with a shrug.

There's not much else to say, so I lean forward and kiss him, and I can feel in him the effects of our absence from each other, the past twenty-four hours of worry, the past thirty minutes of conversation. He breathes in as if I've surprised him, then he finds himself again, and his mouth opens, and I feel his tongue against my tongue, his lips pulling at mine.

I take his hand, the one that rests behind my knee, and I lead him to the laundry room, the only part of the basement that is unfinished, the floor a cold, gray cement under my socks. A stack of towels sits on top of the dryer, waiting to be delivered to the second-floor linen closet. The room smells like Tide. I close the door behind us and lock it. Then I watch as he peels off his clothes and throws them to the ground without a shred of modesty. I do the same, and he has me pulled to him, his body against mine, hard and urgent.

He lifts me against the back of the door, and I wrap my legs around his waist as he enters me, and he is tight arms and hungry lips, and his hands are rough against my breasts, against my hips, along the back of my thighs. His tongue is in my mouth, against my earlobes, at my neck. My fingers are in his hair, my hands on his shoulders, and I need him like this so badly it takes my breath away.

"I love you, Babs," he says against my neck, and I am losing myself in the pressure of him deep inside me and then the wave that crashes over me, and I hear him above the wave. "Tell me again. Tell me you love me. Tell me you're mine." And I want to tell him, but I can't; the air has left my lungs. All I can do is hold to him as he follows me, shaking under my hands, his forehead dropping to my shoulder, and he loses his words. I am ahead of him; I'm coming out as he's going under. I'm returning, and he's still away.

"I love you," I say as he calms in my arms. "I'm yours." I feel the words physically, as if they move out of my body and into his, a part of me for him, in him. "Don't go home. Stay with me. Here," I say as he releases me and I stand, not entirely sure-footed, on the floor. "I love you. Stay."

He kisses me again, a sweet contrast to the frenzied moments that preceded. He's a little winded, and I remember a line from *A Farewell to Arms* about "the masculine difficulty" of making love while standing up. It really does seem challenging.

"I'll stay for as long as you want me to, Bee."

Forever. Stay with me forever. But I swallow the words before they can sneak out into the space between us.

We collect ourselves and return to the kitchen. He still has his suitcase in his car and brings it into the house. That night, he's in my bed, and his lips are so sweet against mine, I'm reminded of the boyfriends I had in high school who kissed like *that* was an achievement in itself. Second base, or whatever.

thirty-four

I'm standing in my closet, staring at the rows of useless suits—"business professional" as the dress code at my old firm stipulated. I need to go shopping. Even the blouses correspond with a life that no longer belongs to me.

"What are you doing?" Austin asks, strolling into the closet.

"Trying to figure out what to wear," I say.

"What's wrong with what you've got on?" he asks with a smirk.

What I have on is one towel wrapped around my body and another on my head. I've skipped my morning run—notwithstanding how much I needed to clear my mind. But I showered, then stepped out to the aroma of Austin brewing coffee in the kitchen.

"Here," he says, handing me a mug. He kisses my cheek. "As soon as you're ready, we can head to the police station." He's already dressed and pulls a pair of shoes from the floor on what I suppose is his side of the closet.

Last night, he'd returned to his condo to empty his suitcase and gather some clean clothes for the next few days. I'd used that time to sit down with Penny and Colin.

"What's he going to do with his apartment?" Penny asked—a question that really asked, how permanent is this?

"He'll use it as his office," I said.

"I don't want to move to California," she said.

"Are we moving to California?" Colin asked, looking suddenly worried.

"No. We're not moving to California. He's going to sell his house out there. He's moving here."

"For us?" Colin asked.

"Yes," I said.

"It's going to be weird," Penny said. "Like, he'll be here all the time."

"We'll do it slowly. He won't just move in overnight. And I can understand, yes, it will be weird at first," I agreed. "But I think it'll also be nice. He really likes you two."

The conversation ended with what I think was an agreement to a time-limited trial.

I watch now as Austin grabs a sweatshirt from *his* shelf. He's in motion, efficient, task-focused, moving through this space as if we've shared it for decades. I can't explain it, the way I've settled into him, as though I've known him for years and years, when really I spent less than a day with him years ago. The way it feels to share this space, though, to have his body so close to mine, the comfort of it. He is not *Austin Lewis.* Maybe he never was. At least not to me.

"What?" he asks, freezing in place, his eyes growing wide. I suppose he's wondering whether some additional awful thing managed to transpire in the brief time he was making coffee.

"I love you," I say.

The tension eases from his shoulders. He takes a step forward, closing the distance between us. "I love you, too," he says and places a kiss against my lips, lingering and restrained.

I should feel vulnerable standing in my closet, naked

beneath my towel, a paid security guard at my door, and probably an inbox full of hate. But all of that melts away like the snowflakes against my bedroom windows. All that's left is this man, who loves me when I'd thought there'd be no chance of ever having that again.

"Penny's up; Colin's not. I'll get her breakfast. Come down when you're ready to go." He walks with purpose out of the closet. I listen to his feet on the steps down to the kitchen, then hear some soft exchange of words between Penny and him.

On the other side of the closet, I run my fingers across the five or six shirts he brought over last night. I pull one to my face, breathing it in, the scent of him filling my nose and the image of him filling my mind as I close my eyes. Then I throw on a pair of jeans, a long-sleeved t-shirt, and a sweater and head downstairs.

With the snow soft on the ground, it's almost romantic, the two of us hand-in-hand, strolling along Webster toward Halsted. We're tucked into our coats even though the frigid Chicago winter has thickened our blood. A gust of wind whips around us, and I drop my head into Austin's shoulder, bracing against the force of it.

"You sure you don't want to move to L.A.?" he asks as the gust dies down and we resume our previous postures.

I laugh—the first time I've felt anything approaching levity since I received the text. Austin lets go of my hand, wrapping his arm around my waist and tugging me into his side. He attempts a kiss to my forehead but meets with my wool hat instead.

"I'll collect that kiss later," I say, feeling myself returning to normal. Something about the cold, the wind, the sights of the neighborhood with its brick and limestone, its wrought iron, waist-high fences surrounding Victorian architecture—it returns me to myself.

Austin bats playfully at the ball on top of my hat and says, "I'll hold you to that."

We've already gone to the police station and reported the text messages. They said they'd increase patrols in the neighborhood, but there's nothing really they can do about it. They asked us to be vigilant, keep monitoring it, let them know if anything else happens. Maybe file a complaint with the internet crime center of the FBI.

Our next stop is the cell phone store, where I explain to the clerk—Shane—that I accidentally stepped on my phone and need a new one. He glances at the phone, then at me; he doesn't buy the story, but it doesn't seem he cares much what caused the damage. I select a new phone and case, and Shane prepares to guide me through the familiar routine.

"Hang on," I say as he asks for my Apple ID in preparation for transferring my data over to the new phone. "I want a new phone number, too. And a new Apple ID. And a new email address—"

"That's not a good idea," Shane says.

"I didn't step on my phone," I say.

"Yeah. I know," Shane says, bored already.

"I—I've been getting these texts and emails and stuff and..."

"Like cyber-stalking?" Shane asks, his interest piqued. "That's a felony, cyberstalking. You know who they're coming from?"

I take a peek at Austin and see him shift uncomfortably next to me. It will be hard to explain.

"No," I say. "I don't know who they're coming from. It might be more than one person. The one last night had an area code of 630 but—"

"Probably spoofed," Shane says with authority.

"I want to start over. I want to delete everything and start over."

"Micah just said phone number and email," Austin puts in.

"Getting a new ID won't start you over. Your apps will still be there. You have to deactivate those separately. But I can get you a new phone number and ID and all that, and then you can deactivate your other stuff."

"Thank you. I'd like to do that," I say. I glance at Austin. "I'm just going to delete it all."

Austin places a hand against my back. I feel the pressure of it just barely through the down of my coat, but the reassurance, the love conveyed with that small gesture is simultaneously fierce and tender.

When we get home, I log onto my laptop and the computer in the office and deactivate every social media account I have. I hesitate at Goodreads, then remember even that has a messaging function and deactivate it, too. Then I text Penny, Colin, and Margot my new number.

thirty-five

Margot steps into the living room from the front hall and eyes the foot of the Christmas tree, the wrapping paper refuse of the morning long gone. Rishi follows her and places their gifts for Penny, Colin, and me under the tree where they keep company with our gifts for Margot, Supriya, and him.

I hadn't warned them that Austin would be here, mostly because he and I were still discussing it until about half an hour before Margot and Rishi arrived. I'd left the decision entirely up to him, but he sought my advice anyway. Ultimately, he thought it would be confusing to Penny and Colin if he absented himself every time their aunt came over. Plus, irrespective of Margot's history with the Lewnatics, we both think it's unlikely she's behind the crescendo in harassment, especially now that Micah has confirmed her departure from the Facebook group. On the off chance she *is* responsible, showing a unified front, we hypothesized, is even more important.

The result, though, is that this is the first time we've all been together in the same room since Supriya's birthday party. I knew it would be uncomfortable, but had not adequately predicted *how* uncomfortable.

"Hi, Margot. Rishi. Merry Christmas. It's nice to see you both again," Austin says, stiffly. He extends a hand, which Margot takes reluctantly.

"Merry Christmas," Margot echoes, looking over his shoulder, directly at me.

Rishi holds out a hand as well. "Merry Christmas, Austin." Rishi's effort to remain neutral makes the tiding something less than merry. Even the scramble to find seats in the living room is tense. Rishi sits in an arm chair next to the Christmas tree, while I sit between Austin and Margot on the couch.

"Who's that guy out front?" Margot asks.

"I think it's Damion out there today," I say.

"I hired security for the house," Austin says, not quite an accusation.

"Because of the—" she begins.

"Just to be on the safe side," I cut in, aware of Penny's eyes on us. "With Austin's movie coming up and the way the sidewalk just runs right in font of the door. It's just a precaution."

"I see," she says. "I'm sorry that's something you even have to think about." It's clear she'd say more, but appreciates the need to be vague.

Attention on the kids pulls some of the tension away from the adults. Supriya sits in Penny's lap as Colin reaches for a gift and hands it to her. She rips the paper off enthusiastically and reveals a cloth book, each page containing small tasks of daily life: a page all of shoelaces, a page of snaps and buttons, one with various dials. It came with a strap, which Supriya promptly throws over her shoulder, sliding off Penny's lap to stroll about the living room with her new "purse." She is delighted. So is Austin for that matter, his baritone laughter reverberating through the couch.

Margot and Rishi exchange gifts with Penny and Colin—the perfect sweater and jeans for Penny, tickets for Colin to see the

Chicago Symphony Orchestra playing the entire soundtrack to *Harry Potter*. Smaller gifts follow—a couple of bracelets for Penny and me that Margot saw at an art fair in Oak Park. A new video game for Colin's Switch (undoubtedly selected by Rishi).

As the gift-giving dies down, so does the conversation. Supriya is distracted, spinning the rotary phone dial in her activity purse, and the tension in Margot's and my relationship announces itself into the void. In years prior, this part of the festivities would have involved a relaxed conversation about books, movies, our mom, some politics, some early discussion of spring break plans.

"Oh! I almost forgot the coffee and cookies," I say, popping up from the couch.

Austin rises with me. "I'll help you."

"I'll help her," Margot says, less offering and more instructing.

Austin's eyes meet mine, a silent exchange, and he sits back down. At the sound of her aunt's tone, Penny's head snaps up from *The Inheritance Games*, a gift from Austin. I can feel her eyes on me but refuse to acknowledge it. Margot smiles sweetly, and Penny's attention returns to her book as we head to the kitchen.

"Which trays do you want to use?" Margot asks as we begin opening Tupperware containers full of Christmas cookies.

I pull three from a cupboard and place them on the island for her to choose from, then turn my attention to the coffee maker. I don't see Margot until her arm wraps around my waist, pulling me to her. She rests her head on my shoulder, and I smell the clean, floral scent of her shampoo.

"What's that for?" I ask as she pulls away.

"I'm just happy you're so happy," she says, though the words are put forth with effort.

I close the filter door on the coffeemaker and press "brew."

"It's been a nice Christmas," I say, intentionally understating it.

"Yeah?" she asks. "I didn't expect Austin to be here. I thought he'd be with his sister and her family."

I glance at her, trying to evaluate any potential agenda, but she doesn't look up from organizing thumbprint cookies on her tray. "His sister spends her holidays with her husband's family," I say.

Margot nods. I wonder whether this is something she already knows, something all the Lewnatics know.

"Did you and Austin exchange gifts already?"

"Yes. He's hard to shop for. I bought him a Cubs hat—"

I see Margot's face, the disorientation, almost disgust.

"It's an inside joke. Our first date," I say.

"Should have gotten him hiking boots," she says, then promptly sucks her lips between her teeth, attempting to silence whatever words might next launch forth.

I laugh. Truly, the comment, and the fact that she has to restrain herself physically to keep from saying more, are both funny. Plus, I'd also bought him a coffee table book of the best hiking trails in the Midwest, so she isn't totally off the mark.

"What did he get you?" she asks, moving on to some Russian tea cakes.

"Earrings," I say and brush my hair back from the side of my face. "They're snowflakes."

"They're diamonds," she says matter-of-factly.

"Is that okay?"

"I wouldn't be mad about them."

I pinch my eyebrows together, trying to read into the sentiment behind the comment.

"Those are nice earrings, Babs," she says, not so much in an *ohmigod* gush, as in a voice that suggests she thinks maybe I don't quite understand how nice they are.

I knew they were nice as soon as the red box peaked out of the wrapping paper. They came with a pair of airplane tickets, too. Austin is taking me to Rome in July, after filming. I don't mention this to Margot. I begin pulling the Christmas mugs from the cupboard over the coffeemaker and setting them on one of the trays.

"They're beautiful," she says, in the manner of a conclusion reached with difficulty. "Do you—" She drops her eyes back to the cookie tray, toying with the candied orange peels. "Do you love him?"

I'd reached for the small china Christmas tree that the half-and-half goes in, but nearly drop it when she asks the question.

"Yes," I say, setting the star-and-treetop lid on the creamer and placing it on the tray.

"And he loves you."

"Yes," I say.

"It wasn't a question."

"Oh," I say with a light touch to my earlobe.

"Not because of the earrings, Babs. Because of the way he looked at you when you stood up to leave the room." She steps back from the cookie tray, admiring her work, the arrangement of the cookies in their neat little rows.

"Looks good," I say as I set the coffee pot on my tray.

"It does, doesn't it? It's nice that we still do this. Still do Christmas cookies on Christmas day."

I smile nostalgically, and we start toward the living room.

Margot begins to giggle next to me. "A baseball cap?" she whispers.

"Cubs. Because that was our first date."

Margot shakes her head as if experiencing the shame on my behalf. "You're going to have to give a lot of head to make up for those earrings if all you got him was a baseball cap."

thirty-six

2020

We didn't go to my house after the funeral; we went to Margot and Rishi's house. Our mom stayed at home. Even then she couldn't go out much. There wasn't much of a gathering. Fucking pandemic. People dropped by, standing on the porch six feet from me—a metaphor if ever there was one—bundled in their coats as they offered condolences, and I was numb as I replied, "Thank you. So kind of you to come."

They said, "He really was such a special man." As if maybe I didn't know.

Margot for the most part stayed inside. She came out occasionally, stunning in funeral attire and a COVID mask. I don't know how I looked, but I'd imagine it was a different sort of stunning. That morning, Margot had brushed my hair back into a ponytail before the funeral Mass and dusted the top of it with dry shampoo because I hadn't showered in close to a week. The grease had turned my hair the color of dead grass. It was probably good that people offered their condolences from six feet away.

Car versus pedestrian. That's how they describe these accidents in Chicago. Ryan had gotten off the Red Line at Fullerton and was crossing the street. The driver who hit him said Ryan had his head down, looking at his phone, and stepped out against the light. Late at night, he'd been delayed at the hospital. He was tired; it was dark and rainy; he was distracted. But it wasn't a car that hit him; it was a truck hauling chunks of jackhammered sidewalk cement. And it drove fully over him. It didn't just hit him and bounce him back into the street. It hit him, then pulled him under, and the wheels of the jackhammered sidewalk truck drove over his beautiful body—this man who was my world, and I was his—and took him from me and from our children.

He was dead before the ambulance arrived.

The driver was hysterical—or so the police report stated. He'd disappeared long before the attorneys started showing up. A subcontractor of a subcontractor of the trucking company, no one seemed to be able to find him, which my attorney told me was a good thing, though I knew he meant it in the money sense and not the Martha-Stewart-pumpkin-centerpieces-at-a-wedding sense. My attorney was right though. Even after accounting for "the pedestrian's own negligence," the insurance company paid out the full policy, and the excess insurer paid out on top of that, and Colin, Penny, and I walked away with more than thirty million dollars.

But without Ryan.

So, not a great deal in the end.

"Are you ready to come inside?" Margot asked from behind me.

It had grown dark. People had stopped coming to the porch.

"You're shivering," she said and pulled her sweater tight around herself as if her warmth might transfer to my body.

"I want to go home," I said. I didn't know if I was cold, but I hadn't been home all day, and I wanted to go home.

Margot examined me for a minute, maybe trying to decide whether I was allowed to go. After some time, she made a decision and said, "I'll help Penny and Colin get their things."

At my house, Margot walked us all in. In the foyer, she set down the Bankers box of Ryan's belongings that the hospital gave the funeral home and the funeral home gave us. Then she helped me settle my broken children down for bed. We laid out their pajamas. We made them brush their teeth. We tucked them in.

"Where would you like me to put the box?" she asked as we stood in the hallway between Colin and Penny's bedrooms.

"In the basement," I said. I had no intention of ever opening it. If I'd been thinking clearly, I would have buried it with him.

Margot went downstairs, and I crawled into bed, pulling the duvet over my head. Several minutes later she returned to my room.

"Mom's watching TV," she said.

"Okay."

"She called me Nancy."

"She's started doing that." With my head under the duvet and my eyes closed tight, I could almost pretend I too had been buried. Margot's voice sounded far away, muffled, above the earth, and I was beneath it.

"She can't keep living here," Margot said.

"She doesn't want to anyway," I said.

She had never wanted to. She wanted to live with Margot and Rishi, but it made more sense for her to live with me. Margot and Rishi were just starting out. They were newlyweds. They wanted to start a family. Plus, I had a doctor in the house, a pediatrician, and our mother had been reduced to something like a child. Though now my husband was something like a ghost, so maybe the arrangement didn't make sense anymore. And why should it? Nothing really made sense anymore.

"I'll start looking for places," Margot said. "You don't need to think about any of that right now."

I was glad she said that because, whether I needed to think or not, I couldn't; the marshmallow Xanax walls were collapsing around me. My bed swayed like a porch swing. We didn't have a porch swing. Margot had a porch swing.

"Babs?" Margot called from the doorway. I heard the click of the switch and knew she'd turned out the light. A couple of seconds later, her weight rested on the side of the bed, then the duvet floated off my face and gathered around my shoulders.

"We don't have a porch swing," I said.

"That's okay," she said from inside the marshmallow walls. "How many pills did you take?" she asked.

"I can only have two. To help me sleep," I said, recalling Dr. Metz's very specific—and, it seemed, unnecessarily draconian—instructions.

"How many did you take, though?" she asked again.

"About that," I said.

"I think I'll stay with you tonight," Margot said.

thirty-seven

After dropping Penny and Colin off at school, I head to Target.

> Me: At the grocery store. Need anything?

There's something both incredibly intimate and entirely unsexy about buying groceries for someone you live with. But over the weeks since Christmas, Austin has made his home with me, as we quietly, slowly braid our lives together, and so if I am at the grocery store, I should ask—as I once did for someone else, as Austin always does for me—whether there is anything he needs.

> Austin: Blueberries, peanut butter, chicken breasts. Please and thank you. I promise not to eat them together.

I laugh right there in the cereal aisle—loud enough to have to apologize to the other woman in the aisle.

"It's my... I'm laughing at a text," I say, pointing to my phone.

The woman nods but backs out of the aisle. Probably just as well, as I re-read the message and my face breaks into a grin, the left side inching up just a smidge higher than the right.

Austin: OH! And kale.

Me:

Austin: Thank you!

I'm texting a "no problem" when I hear my name and see Lauren, my mentee from my old firm. Her cart holds an infant car seat containing a baby roughly the size of a butternut squash.

"I thought that was you," she says. "God, you look amazing." She glances down at herself. She looks like she's the mother of a baby roughly the size of a butternut squash: yoga pants, sweatshirt, ponytail. The shadows under her eyes tell me that baby has not yet learned that nighttime is for sleeping.

"How are you? Who is this?" I coo into the carseat.

"This is James."

"Hi James, sweetie," I say. To his credit, he makes eye contact, then returns his attention to his fist, which he shoves into his mouth with enough force that I worry for his gums. "He's hungry?" I suggest, aware of a vicarious anxiety at a countdown my body seems to recall.

"Yeah, I'm trying to get in and get out, but I don't think I'm going to make it." She starts rolling the cart forward and back. There is zero chance that baby is falling asleep without a meal, but I admire her optimism. "What are you doing now?" she asks.

Just being periodically stalked by my '90s heartthrob boyfriend's groupie cult fan club. Actually, since I ditched the phone number and email address, things have been pretty quiet on that front.

"Mostly relaxing," I say. "Taking some time for myself."

"Any chance you might come back?" she asks. James *meeps* as his fist falls out of his mouth, but he manages to find it again.

"No. I don't think so. I think I'm done with private practice." I don't ask her, but I know she's thinking about it—whether to go back.

"I wish you were there. It's not the same without you. I'm working under Geoff now, and he's terrible. He never lets me do anything. I can barely make my hours. You were so good, Babs. You were such a good mentor. Honestly. I didn't even realize it until you were gone. I know things were really hard for you after Ryan died, but I miss you so much—" James interrupts her with the first burst of what will be an opus.

I eye the back of the store. "There are rocking chairs in the nursery section," I say.

She glances in that direction and wheels the cart around.

"Hey," she says, turning back, "I think Northwestern is hiring an adjunct in intellectual property. Starts in the fall. You should apply. You would be an amazing teacher."

I don't ask her how she knows about the academic listings at Northwestern. I did the same thing after Penny was born. "Thanks, Lauren. It was good to see you again," I say, but she's already wheeling the cart away.

She's right though, about the teaching job; Northwestern is hiring. And when I tell Austin about it later that night—after checking the listing and seeing that I have nearly twice as much experience as they're seeking—he quotes Lauren. "I bet you'd be an amazing teacher. You'd be perfect for that."

I submit my C.V. the next day and receive an email inviting me to interview in March. Someone will reach out shortly to schedule.

"Where is everyone?" I ask David. I count only eight patrons in the entire pantry.

"They're at the shelters. Because of the cold," he says.

Typical late-January weather. Yesterday, the high was 14, the low 3. That doesn't include windchill. It's double that today—a balmy 28 and 6.

"So, it's actually good that there aren't very many people here. It means they have somewhere to go," I say optimistically.

David leans his head to the side. "The ones who are not here probably have somewhere to go, yes."

I accept his qualification; that still leaves those in the cafeteria, few though they are. My optimism evaporates further as Irene approaches the counter. She has on the hat and gloves we gave her in September, but her cheeks and nose are raw with cold and wind, her lips cracked, one thin fissure dark red with blood.

"Good morning, Babs, David," she says as if she's greeting us at a PTO social. "Chilly out there this morning."

"Stay as long as you'd like, Irene," David says. "There's no wait for tables, and we don't close until 11:30."

"Thanks," she says, and I put a sandwich on her tray. David adds a dessert, and Kaelyn, the student, provides coffee.

"Hang on," I say as she begins to head to one of the numerous empty tables. "I think I have some ChapStick in my purse that I haven't used yet."

Irene pauses, and I dash back to the kitchen digging through my purse for the unused tube in the three-pack I'd bought last week at Target.

"Here you go," I say and set it on the tray.

"Thank you," she says a little self-consciously. I hope I didn't embarrass her. If I did, it doesn't stop her from using the

ChapStick. She opens it and traces it across her lips as soon as she sits down.

"Do you have plans for Valentine's Day?" David asks.

Kaelyn looks at him suspiciously. I, too, wonder if he has an ulterior motive, but his face looks innocent enough.

"I don't know yet," I say. "Austin and I will probably do something, but we haven't settled on anything yet. It's still three weeks away, I guess."

David nods. "Austin. Is that your boyfriend?" he asks. "The man who meets you here sometimes?"

"Yes," I say. "How about you? Plans?"

"My girlfriend and I will probably do something the weekend before. I haven't figured out what yet. I was hoping to be inspired by whatever you'd planned."

"I'm terrible at that stuff," I say. "I got Austin a baseball hat and a coffee table book for Christmas."

"What did he get you?" David asks, withholding judgment as to whether I am terrible at "that stuff."

"A pair of diamond earrings and a trip to Rome."

That gets Kaelyn's attention, and I hear her cough under her breath. She definitely thinks I'm terrible at "that stuff."

"Oops," David says, chuckling.

"What did your girlfriend get you? I'm sorry, I don't remember her name."

I actually don't remember him ever mentioning a girlfriend. He's mentioned running, his engineering firm, his education (which brought him to the United States), and he's definitely mentioned his divorce. He moved to Chicago for his ex-wife's job, but within two years of settling in the city, she moved to Seattle with the man she left David for and is now married to. I recall those details because when he told them to me, it seemed they still caused him pain. I've avoided telling him about Ryan because I don't want to have the exchange where he says my grief is worse than his. I hope he thinks I'm divorced, too.

"For Christmas?" he asks, bringing me back to the conversation.

"Yeah."

"We weren't dating then. So nothing. We've only been dating for a couple of weeks, so Valentine's Day is awkward. I don't want to overdo it and scare her off or underwhelm her and make her think I'm a bad boyfriend."

"Tickets to the symphony," Kaelyn says. David and I both snap our heads in her direction. "They're expensive and fancy. It's a special night out, but it doesn't signify any particular relationship status."

Jesus Christ, that is a sophisticated analysis for a twenty-year-old, but she's right, and I wonder whether I should get Austin tickets to the symphony, too. Though I'm not concerned about suggesting any particular status. I can't imagine what I could get him for Valentine's Day that would scare him away.

"Pair it with a nice dinner beforehand. You probably need to get tickets, like, today, though," she adds.

"Well, there you go," I say, directing my praise in Kaelyn's direction. "Problem solved."

David and I step out to the side of the church as he locks the pantry door. I scan the sidewalk, the area across from the church. I don't know what I'm looking for—someone hiding behind a tree, curious eyes peering from a restaurant window? I pull my hood over the hat I'm already wearing, dig my hands into my pockets, and drop my head.

"Are you okay?" David asks.

"Hmm? What?" My hood falls back as I lift my head.

"You seem... not yourself," he says.

"It's just the cold," I say. "I feel bad for Irene." This, at least, is true; I do feel bad for Irene. In the four minutes David and I have been standing outside, my face has already grown numb enough that I have trouble speaking at my usual quick clip. Still, David looks at me like he doesn't quite believe me.

"Why don't I walk you home?" he suggests.

"You don't have to do that," I say. "I'm sure you need to get to work."

"It's fine," he says, already turning in the direction I usually head when I leave the church.

"Thanks," I say as we begin walking together. I do feel better not walking alone.

It's a short distance to my house, three-and-a-half blocks, and we arrive at the foot of the steps to my front door just as Drew—today's security guard—returns from his hourly lap around the property. He'd call it a *perimeter check*, but I prefer something slightly less evocative of a military operation. He reclaims his post at the foot of the stairs.

"Hi Drew. This is my friend David," I say.

"Hi Ms. Aganon. Mr..."

"*David* is fine," David says, his eyes skittering over the front of the house, then sliding to me, obviously troubled.

The front door opens and Austin steps into the doorway. He's wearing a navy blue Oxford and a pair of gray flannel pants. He must have a Zoom meeting. I see it's at least cold enough for him to put on socks.

"Hey, Bee," he says. "Everything okay?" He makes a quick assessment of David.

"Yeah, I just got a little weirded out as we were leaving the church, and David offered to walk me home."

"David," Austin says, connecting the dots. His face relaxes, though I know he'll have questions for me. Weirded out, how?

Did I see something? Are the new email and phone number still working? Still no contact? No texts?

"Come on in," I say to David as I start up the stairs.

"It's cold," Austin adds. "Join us for lunch."

"Oh no, no," David says. "No. I have to get to my office. I have a meeting at one." He holds up his phone as if to confirm his excuse, an act that creates the opposite effect. Then he bids a strained farewell, offers a "Nice to meet you" to Austin, and returns in the direction of the church where his car is parked.

I step into the vestibule with Austin and am met with precisely the questions I'd predicted.

"I don't know," I say. "I can't explain it. I didn't see anything. It was just a feeling. Did you have a meeting this morning?" I ask to change the subject.

"Several," he says as we walk into the kitchen. "Including one with the police."

"The police?" I say, hopeful.

Austin shakes his head, and my hope dissolves. "Quick phone call. They wanted to know if there'd been any more attempts to contact either of us. I told them no, and they said to reach out if there were any further episodes."

I sit down at the kitchen table, and Austin sets two plates of salad Niçoise in front of us.

"Thanks," I say, both for making lunch and for the update from the police.

Austin takes my hand, rests it against his cheek, and closes his eyes. "I love you," he says.

"I love you, too," I reply.

thirty-eight

"Hey! I got an interview for the Northwestern job," I say to Margot, who sits with Supriya, eating omelettes and cinnamon rolls in my kitchen.

"Of course you did! When?"

"March-something. They're going to call to set up the date."

"That's almost a month and a half from now," she says.

"I'm assuming they have to leave the position open for some specific period of time. Get a pool of applicants."

We're interrupted by Austin coming up from the family room into the kitchen.

"Good morning, Austin," Margot says, a formal greeting for a distant acquaintance.

"Good morning," he replies, then turns to me. "I've been directed to bring the cinnamon rolls down to the basement."

"All of them?" I ask.

He shrugs.

"They can have one more each," I say.

Austin walks over to the island and removes two cinnamon rolls from the baking dish, placing each on a paper towel. He's Sunday-casual in a pair of blue jeans and a gray hooded sweatshirt, his feet bare. I catch Margot examining him too, but her face holds no fondness for his California idiosyncrasies. She catches me evaluating her and tucks away her disapproval.

"What are you guys watching down there?" I ask as Austin turns back to the two of us.

"*Locke & Key*," he says. "Have you seen that show? It's incredibly good."

"I know!" I say. "It's one of the few shows I can actually stand to watch with them."

Austin strolls back to the table, palming a cinnamon roll in each hand and drops a quick peck on my cheek. "Want me to take Supriya down?" he asks Margot. Supriya looks up at him, then back at her mother.

"That show's too scary for her," Margot says, with a hint of condemnation. "Plus your hands are full. How would you pick her up?"

He silently shifts one of the cinnamon rolls, palming both in one hand.

"She's two, Austin. That show would terrify her."

"Okay, Margot," Austin says with affected tolerance, and he returns to the basement.

I stare at my sister, waiting for some explanation for her frost.

"What?" she says.

"He has nieces," I say.

"Then he should know better."

I shake my head. "You have zero reason to be upset with him."

"And he should be over his issues with me," she says. "Yes, I made a bad choice in the Lewnatics group. *Once. More than three months ago.* And I left the group. *And* the result was *one mean picture*. But he's basically refused to so much as be in the same room with me for the last three months, and he's only doing it now because he lives here," she says.

Supriya has stopped eating her cinnamon roll and watches her mother closely. I've adopted a similar pose.

"What?" Margot demands again.

"It's more than one mean picture," I say, keeping my voice low on the off chance one of my children is coming up the stairs.

Margot regards me closely.

"He didn't hire twenty-four hour security for *one mean picture*. I didn't get a new phone number and email address for *one mean picture*."

"What do you mean?" she asks carefully. She pulls a wet wipe from her diaper bag and wipes Supriya's hands.

"It's been constant, Margot. Constant. And some of it's pretty scary."

She lifts Supriya out of the highchair and sets her on the kitchen floor where Supriya promptly makes a break for it in the direction of the stairs to the family room. Margot gets up from the table and brings her back to the kitchen.

"I—I didn't realize," she says, her eyes cast down as she focuses on Supriya and, I suspect, hides her shame. "You could have said something."

"If I said something every time I got a text or a DM or a mean email, I'd be texting you almost every day."

She looks up. "It's that bad?"

"It's not great," I say. "He canceled his interviews last month to get back to Chicago because one of the messages was so threatening."

"Threatening?" she repeats as if it's a word she's never heard before. "He said he did that because he was prioritizing his family for Christmas."

"Well..." I say, "he kind of was." I'm not exactly his family, but he definitely reshuffled his priorities over the span of about ten minutes.

"It's not like that on Instagram," she says.

"I'll have to take your word for it. We let Austin's attorney tell us if there's anything we need to know about on social media these days."

"It wasn't even really like that in the Lewnatics," she adds. "I mean, they're batshit crazy and mean as fuck, but I never saw them actually threaten anyone."

I hear the groan of a tread on the basement stairs, and Margot and I cease talking immediately. The top of Penny's head pops up into the hallway as she makes her way into the kitchen with three dirty plates. She drops them into the sink, then turns to Margot and me, her eyes sharp, perceptive.

"Were you talking about me?" she asks.

"No," I say.

"Why did you stop talking when I came upstairs?"

"Because the conversation ended," Margot says, reminding me of the kinds of excuses high schoolers offer when they get caught talking behind a friend's back. She should have told Penny we were talking about a *different* Austin. "We were talking about how lame social media is, and the conversation ended."

Penny looks at me accusingly. "I wouldn't know," she says. Neither of my children is allowed to have social media, and to the extent I might have been talked out of that rule a year ago, I'm definitely not flexible on it now.

"Consider yourself lucky," Margot says, much more convincing than I would have been.

Penny abandons the opportunity for debate and turns to her cousin. "Do you want to come downstairs, Suppi?"

Supriya lifts her arms up to her cousin, and Margot strolls

back to the table. "Try to keep her back to the TV. That show is kind of creepy," she says, reclaiming her seat.

Austin's fingers sweep against my neck as he lifts my hair back and places a kiss under my ear. I sigh and lean into him, feeling the solidness of his chest against my back.

A woman in the line next to us coughs and glares at me with reproach as I turn my head in her direction. A fair judgment. We're at the symphony not Northerly Island. And we're old enough to know better.

"Sorry," I say and step away from Austin's lips.

"For what?" he asks, oblivious.

"People are looking."

"It's because you're so fucking beautiful," he whispers into my ear.

"No. It's because I'm *thisclose* to dropping this dress and letting you take me on one of those cocktail tables," I say, trying to keep my voice hushed.

Austin laughs. "They're too tall. Might work for oral, though."

"Babs!" A familiar voice calls.

I glance across Austin to see David and a woman I presume is his girlfriend inching forward in the line next to us.

"David. How are you?" I ask, feeling even more self-conscious for Austin's and my behavior now that the audience is someone I know.

"Very good. It's so nice to see you both again. A good idea, the symphony," he says with a wink. I gather he hasn't told his girlfriend where the idea came from.

David and Austin shake hands affably, and David introduces Madison.

"Are you enjoying the performance?" David asks.

Next to him, Madison wraps an arm through his, pulling herself into his shoulder. It's a sweet sign of affection, but her dress is short and sleeveless and her legs bare, so she might just be cold. David takes his blazer off and wraps it around her shoulders, suggesting he read the move as "cold."

"Yes," Austin says. "You?"

"Yes. I was thinking I should make more of an effort to follow their schedule. They had a piano performance in November that was nearly all Liszt."

"Are you enjoying the performance, Madison?" Austin asks.

"I didn't realize it was going to be all classical music," she says, which I take to mean no, she is not enjoying the performance. The look of dejection on David's face indicates he interpreted the comment likewise. "I would have liked the *Harry Potter* concert better, I think. That would have been fun." She peers up at David hopefully.

I hadn't examined her very closely before—the lighting in the lobby is the subdued yellow of sconces and chandeliers set to dimmers. But upon closer inspection, she is much closer to twelve than to eighty. She's probably closer to Colin than to David.

"You look familiar," she says to Austin, her eyes narrowing. "Have we met before?"

"Not likely. I just moved here from L.A. in August," he says.

"Oh yeah?" she says. "What do you do out there?"

"Nothing anymore," he says with a self-effacing chuckle. "I used to be on a television show in the mid-nineties—"

"That's it!" Madison says with enough exuberance that the woman who had been judging Austin and me for necking in the refreshments line is now judging Madison for using her Soldier Field voice at Symphony Center. "That's where I know you from. My mom loves that show. She has the whole collection on DVD. I can remember watching it when I was still in diapers."

"That's a good memory," Austin says, drolly.

"What's it called? *The Maple Leaf Family* or something?" Madison asks. "Was it set in Canada?" she adds as if that connection just dawned on her.

David looks dizzy, trying to follow the conversation, but his eyes flick to mine, a question settling over his face. This seems like something I should have mentioned to him, perhaps when I introduced him to the armed guard at my front door.

"*The Maple Street Martins*," I correct.

"Set in Ohio," Austin adds, his shoulder rolling back and then forward under his blazer. "Our line's moving a bit faster than yours. Babs, do you want to chat with David and Madison, and I'll get drinks for all of us?"

"Can I get a photo with you?" Madison asks, ignoring Austin's offer. "My mom is going to freak when I tell her I ran into you."

"Something red," I say to Austin, both of us now ignoring Madison.

"Same for us, please" David says, already guiding his girlfriend out of the line and over to a cocktail table. "Thank you," he calls over his shoulder in Austin's direction.

"I thought about getting her a juice box. They had them. Apple and grape," Austin says. "But I didn't want to be rude to David. He seems like a nice guy."

I flick my tongue over Austin's nipple, and he reaches for my bra, unhooking it expertly and tossing it to the side of the bed where my dress lies in a pool on the floor.

"She got a picture of you," I say as he runs his palms over

my ass, pushing me against him. He groans against it, tilting his head back, his eyes closed. "She pretended she was using her phone to touch up her lip gloss, but she was taking a picture over her shoulder. It wasn't even subtle."

"Put me inside you," he says, his eyes still closed, his hands running along the tops of my thighs.

"Already?" I tease as Madison and her selfies fade like the dimmed lights of the symphony hall. I lean over and bring his earlobe between my teeth and feel the exquisite pressure of his hands as they tighten their grip on my thighs.

"It's not *already*," he protests, encouraging a gyration of my hips against his. "I've been waiting for this for hours. I watched you put that dress on, and all I could think about was when I would get to take you out of it."

The dress is a fitted black maxi-dress with a bustier top, over a white Oxford. It's sleek, minimalist, and modern, but hardly the stuff that inspires hours of lusting.

His hands grab and pull and push against me. "I know what you were wearing under it."

I pause, my brows pinching together in confusion. Austin opens his eyes, gazing up at me, then his face breaks into a grin. Nothing. I'd worn nothing under it.

"If you won't do it, I will," he says, reaching between us. And he does.

thirty-nine

It's weird because yesterday was Valentine's Day and... no flowers, no card, no earrings. Nothing.

"Do you want to do something special today?" I'd asked when Austin returned from the gym.

"Sorry, Bee. Today's a work day for me. I have back-to-back meetings until dinner. Time change," he added, referencing the two-hour difference between Chicago and L.A.

"Oh," I said. "I just thought... because... Valentine's Day..."

He locked eyes with me, looking a little frightened. "I thought—I thought we did Valentine's Day on Saturday."

"Oh. Of course," I said, trying to sound unbothered, flipping my hair back over my shoulder.

I'd arranged for the tickets to the symphony, but he'd arranged for dinner, and he'd pulled out all the stops on that front, including having sticky date cake waiting for us when we got home. He'd picked it up earlier in the day, apparently. And certainly, we'd celebrated that night like it was Valentine's Day. As I thought about it, I didn't have any reason to expect something on the actual day itself. I hadn't gotten him anything beyond the tickets. Well, I got him a card.

"Is that okay?" he asked. His eyes moved over me, an evaluation taking place.

"Yes. Yes, of course. Are you working here or at your condo?"

He smiled at me reluctantly, which was its own answer.

"Are you okay?" David asks as we prepare the pantry to open.

I'm pulled from my rumination. "Oh yeah. Just thinking. Did you and Madison enjoy the rest of the symphony?" I ask busying myself organizing plates.

His expression is politely weary. "I think it just wasn't her thing."

"It's not everybody's," I say. "I haven't been in years and wouldn't have gone on Saturday if Kaelyn hadn't suggested it."

"I'm sorry if she made Austin or you uncomfortable," he says.

"Don't worry about it. We're used to it," I say.

"I don't know what's worse, that she asked for a selfie or that I didn't recognize him at all." The plates are getting a heavy dose of David's attention as he avoids making eye contact with me.

"Neither is bad. Please, don't give it another thought." The request for the selfie was definitely worse.

"You're being very gracious," he says.

I've run out of ways to be polite and can only shrug as I pull the bagged sandwiches out of the refrigerator.

"How was the rest of your Valentine's Day?" he asks.

"Oh, it was really nice," I say, not mentioning that I actually only saw Austin for about four hours total yesterday. "When we got home from the symphony, Austin had my favorite dessert waiting for me. He'd picked it up from the restaurant earlier in the day. And we went to a really nice dinner beforehand. How about you? Did Madison get you anything?"

David's head jerks up from the rows of multi-colored desserts. "She umm... she... sort of."

"Did she forget?" I ask. Maybe I can disclose yesterday's strangeness. Not even a card.

"No," David says, dashing my hopes for a chance to vent and maybe elicit the male perspective. "No. She didn't forget. She... Yesterday. She umm..." He drops his voice, and all of a sudden, I feel like I'm talking to one of the women on my college track team. "We work together—"

"She's an engineer?" I admit, I hadn't imagined Madison making the kinds of mathematical calculations that lives quite literally depend on.

"Yes. She just started last summer."

I feel deservedly shamed. Be better, Babs.

"What did she get you?" I ask as I press *brew* on the industrial-grade coffee maker.

David fidgets with the rows of multi-colored desserts. "She umm... she... sort of. Never mind. Nothing."

"What? What happened?"

He shifts from one foot to the other. "She came to my office before lunch and..." He widens his eyes as if the rest should really go without saying.

My mind sorts through the options: candy-gram, office full of balloons, catered lunch... "Oh!" I say, as his cheeks turn the pink of candy hearts. "Oh my God. Well. That's hot."

"Is it? I was terrified. What if someone walked in?"

"Isn't that the fun of it?"

"I'd lose my job. I'd have to go back to France. I haven't lived there in thirty years. My kids don't even speak French." I hadn't pegged him for a catastrophizer, but he's doing a marvelous job of it. "And it all seemed very theatrical. The desk and all that. I think she saw it in a movie or something and thought it would be fun." He pauses, reflecting. "Do they watch movies?"

"Who? Engineers? You'd know better than I."

"No. Gen Z or whatever generation she is," he says.

"Oh. Yeah. They watch movies. They just watch them on their devices instead of going to the theater. Or at least my kids do."

"Your kids," David says, sounding thoroughly defeated.

"Hi." The voice belongs to our student volunteer. "I'm Nick. I was told to ask for David?"

"That's me," David says, shaking off his fatalism.

He directs Nick to the drink station, explains the rules of the pantry and the general flow, then unlocks the door at nine sharp. The line is long, snaking well back through the pews of the church. The handful of days with above-freezing temperatures have encouraged an increased number of people to make the trek.

"We're going to run out of trays," David says as he places a piece of cake with pink icing on one. "And we're going to need to turn the tables over faster."

The patrons hate that. In the winter, it means being turned out into the cold faster, and in the summer, it means being turned out into the heat. Either way, putting a time limit on the meal is unpopular.

"Babs?" inquires one of the patrons standing in front of my station.

"Sorry. I was distracted," I say. "Peanut butter or turkey?"

"Turkey, please. Also, this is for you."

"What?" I hear the tiding as if on delay. I'd already placed the sandwich on his tray.

He smiles and hands me a rose so orange it almost resembles candy.

"What's this?" I ask, but he's already moved down the line.

"Turkey," says the next patron, and my attention returns to keeping the line moving.

"Peanut butter," says a woman. "Also, here you go." She holds up a yellow rose, the petals edged with crimson.

"Who gave you this?" I ask, but the woman just shrugs and requests cake with pink frosting from David. I lean over the counter and crane my neck, trying to see back into the church. The line continues, but all the usual patrons populate it.

David notices the two roses. "Austin?"

We don't have much time to discuss it before another orange rose makes its way across the counter. "For you."

A red rose joins the growing bouquet, then another yellow, until I have a pile of two dozen or so roses the color of the sunrise. I scan the cafeteria, following the line back into the dimly lit church. It has to be Austin trying to make up for yesterday. I'll have to pretend he's overdone it. But I don't see him anywhere.

The line pauses as tables fill, and we have to wait for people to finish in order to make more seats available so we can serve more people. I step back from the counter.

"I guess I'll go put these in some water while we've got a minute," I say.

"There are vases under the sink," David says.

I locate the vases, select one, and fill it with water, putting the roses in and stepping back to admire the arrangement. The kitchen is dark, the same green subway tiled walls as my grade school cafeteria. But even within that gloom, the bouquet glows.

"Line's starting again," Nick calls back.

I jog out to the counter to find Austin standing at my station, an unrestrained grin spread across his face.

"They're beautiful," I say.

"You're beautiful," he says without missing a beat.

"They remind me of the sunrise."

"They're supposed to."

"You didn't have to do this. I'm not upset about Valentine's Day," I say, delivering the speech I half-rehearsed while handing sandwiches over the counter.

"I didn't do it for Valentine's Day," he says.

"I don't understand," I say. "My birthday's in July."

"I know when your birthday is." The corners of his mouth twitch against his smile.

The cafeteria grows quiet, though I can hear some chatter back in the church from people wondering why the line has stopped.

And then he reaches into his pocket and drops to his knee. "The sunrise," he says. "The start of each day. I want you at the start of each of my days, as the brightest point in my sky—"

"Yes," I say.

"I'm not done," he whispers. "I haven't actually asked you yet."

"Right."

Laughter skitters out in the cafeteria.

"Like the sun, I cannot live without you. Like the sun, I cannot explain you, why I have been so lucky to have crossed paths with you. Twice. But I'm smart enough to know when to stop asking questions that can't be answered and start asking questions that can. Will you marry me? Now you can say yes."

"Yes." I don't hesitate. I lean across the counter, reaching for him, willing him to rise so that I can kiss him, and pull him into my arms, and we will begin our life together at this moment.

He slips the ring onto my finger. "Babs," he murmurs as he buries his lips against my neck. "I have been waiting for you for my whole life."

"I love you," I say again and feel it so deeply I can barely muster the air needed to push the words from my throat.

"I love you, too, Bee," he says. "So much."

Distantly, I hear clapping, but mostly I just hear my own

joy, a heady ringing in my ears, and the muffled sound of his voice telling me again and again that he loves me.

Marrying Austin Lewis is a lot more complicated than marrying Ryan. We talk with Penny and Colin that night at dinner. Both seem nervous, which I would expect of any kids who have been through what they've been through. They have questions. When? We don't know. Where? Here in Chicago. Are we moving to L.A.? No. I don't mention that we might sell the house. I just can't.

I tell Margot the following afternoon. She offers her congratulations, but I can tell she doesn't mean it. I ask her to be my maid of honor. She was at my last wedding.

"Matron of honor," she says. "I'm married now."

"Right," I say. "Matron of honor."

"Yes, Babs. I'll be your matron of honor," she says, straining to convincingly convey excitement. "Do you have a date yet?"

"No," I say. "We haven't gotten that far in the planning."

"Okay. Well, let me know when you settle on a date," she says, then, perhaps realizing her performance has left much to be desired she adds, "I'm glad you've found happiness again."

I *am* happy; I'm so happy my jaw hurts from smiling. Austin approaches our engagement in a manner I assume is similar to the way he approaches his projects. We set a date by the end of the weekend. We decide that the following February, while somewhat cliché, makes the most sense. If we marry in Chicago, it's likely to be cold as hell, but it gives us—and Penny and Colin—time. Austin doesn't say so, but I know some of that time will be spent deciding where to live, how to integrate our lives.

My exodus from social media, along with my new email

address and phone number also continue in effectively thwarting my stalker(s). Not a single taunt, photograph, or hostile message in weeks, though Micah says Madison's pictures from the symphony have made the rounds on social media with some enthusiastic, if not universally flattering, commentary.

On the Sunday after we set the date, Margot comes over with Supriya, and Austin makes coffee for us while I scramble eggs.

"You up for visiting Mom later this week?" I ask from the stove.

Margot exhales a sigh. "Yeah, I guess we probably need to."

"She's getting worse," I say, though this is hardly news to Margot, and she responds with a subdued, "I know."

I don't say it aloud—I probably don't have to—but I'd like to tell my mom I'm in love. I'd like to tell her I'm engaged. If I go with Margot, there's a chance—thin though it may be—that I can tell her I'm getting married and she will have *some* awareness of what that means. But it feels increasingly like the clock is ticking on all of it. I'm slipping away. Or she is. Hard to tell.

Austin slides over from the coffee maker and kisses my cheek. I lean into his side—the corporeal substance of him—and find an intangible solace in his knowledge that this is one of my sorrows. His nose brushes against my ear followed by one more kiss. Then he returns to his task, pulling mugs from the cabinet.

"Some time this week?" Margot asks. She too understands the way time constrains us.

"Yeah, that would be good."

"Hey!" Margot says, cutting through what had become a dower mood in the kitchen. "Did you see Wikipedia updated its entry to note your engagement?" She offers a high-pitched impersonation of whoever edited the entry. Apparently, she assumes it was a woman. "In February, Lewis became engaged to retired attorney Barbara Stewart Aganon of Chicago, Illinois, whom he has been living with since December." She winks at me giggling. She's trying to be funny, move on to happier topics.

"Retired," I say, a bit mournful at the description.

"Who updated the page?" Austin asks, his tone contrasting with the lighthearted way Margot had quoted the entry.

"I don't know." Margot says. "How would I know that?"

"You can track the changes on Wikipedia, see who entered what when. What was the username of the person who updated the page?"

"I have no idea, Austin. I didn't look. It wasn't me."

"I didn't say it was you," Austin shoots back.

"Hey, take it easy." I'm not sure which of them I'm talking to, but Austin leaves the kitchen, and I hear him close the doors to the office, so I assume he decided to look into it himself.

"I thought you said things had calmed down," she says after he leaves the room.

"They have. But we still don't know who was behind the stuff over the holidays."

"It wasn't me, Babs," she says again.

"No one thinks it was you," I say, but Margot's expression is dubious.

"Do you have a plan for what you'll do if that movie takes off? You're probably going to need to move."

"We've talked about a few options," I say.

She shakes her head and casts her eyes up to the ceiling, disapproving of my ambiguousness.

"Also, I'm not retired," I say. "I have the interview at Northwestern."

Margot feigns exhaustion—with me, undoubtedly. "It's Wikipedia, Babs. I'm impressed they spelled your name right."

Austin returns to the kitchen.

"Any luck?" I ask.

"No. I guess it's no surprise they didn't use a real name to enter the info. They updated the page on Thursday though, which is one hell of a turnaround time."

"Jesus," I agree.

"I'll have Micah draft a formal announcement for Instagram," he says with an air of efficiency.

forty

2021

When our mother put the Lucky Charms in the microwave, Margot and I knew it was time. There'd been soft signs before that—signs that the current arrangement would not be long-term. Our mother had originally occupied the extra bedroom on the second floor of my house, but as her world shrank, the greatest danger she faced on any given day—during much of which Ryan and I were not home—was falling down the stairs on her way to the TV in the family room. We decided that putting her in the bedroom next to it cut those odds. And we were able to place some safety features in the attached bathroom.

But the Lucky Charms.

"It was almost fine," I said to Margot as we sat in the lobby waiting for Jessica, the director of Millwood Manor, to give us a tour of the memory unit.

"It wasn't," Margot said, dragging her finger up the center of her phone, flipping through a technicolor waterfall of filtered realities.

"If the compass hadn't had a metal dial, the only consequence would have been melted marshmallows." The prize in the cereal—intended to assist in locating pots of gold, I suppose—nearly set the entire kitchen on fire.

"That would have been bad enough," Margot said with a tap at the screen—an image she must have liked. She set her phone on her thigh and glanced at me. "Why do you even have Lucky Charms in your house. My teeth hurt just thinking about eating that."

"They're magically delicious," I said.

Margot regarded me, unamused, before picking up her phone again. The truth was, I'd been at the grocery store, and they looked good, and I wanted to taste what it was like to be ten years old again. Then I brought them home and put them in the pantry with the rest of the breakfast cereal and the cans of soup and bottles of water and never touched them.

> Kelly: Where are you!!!! Everyone's here for the dep?

"Fuck," I groaned.

Margot's head swiveled in my direction, inviting explanation.

"It's nothing."

> Me: I asked Danni to cancel that.

> Kelly: No you did not! That's bullshit. It's a court ordered dep of your fucking client. Where the fuck are you?

My stomach twisted, and I began to sweat. I opened my calendar on my phone seeing the deposition entered clearly with a 10:00 a.m. start. This prompted a distant memory of one of my associates returning from court and advising that we would not be permitted any further extensions for completion of party depositions. I didn't have a memory, though, of scheduling Monika Flessing's deposition for any particular day.

> Me: Who set the dep? I have a family obligation this morning? I wouldn't have agreed to that date.

> Kelly: I have no fucking idea who set the dep. Why would I know that. Do your fucking job!

> Me: Can you cover?

I waited as the minutes ticked by—no response. I was preparing to call when Jessica appeared in the lobby.

"Margot? Babs?" she asked as she approached us with a hand extended.

Over the next hour, we wandered the halls of Millwood Manner, to the soothing, documentary-grade narration of its director—a recitation of facts and figures endorsing our good decision, providing assurance that this particular residence was the very best among several we could have selected.

All the while, my phone continued its periodic buzzing, reminding me that my mother might have put a box of cereal in a microwave, but I had put my career in an incinerator.

"This is the place," Margot said as we headed out to her car at the end of the tour. I knew she'd said that mostly because she wanted a decision made. We'd toured four separate facilities, and I'd deemed all of them lacking for reasons Margot found less than compelling: the wilted iceberg lettuce in the salad bar; the outdated, dusty drapes in the bedroom; the inadequate boardgame selection in the activity room.

We climbed into the car, and Margot refused to start the ignition. "This is it, Babs," she repeated because she really needed this to be it.

"She'll hate it here," I said.

"For a little while." A subtle reference to the diminishing, non-renewable resource that was our mother's memory. "I'll tell her," Margot added, I suppose to sweeten the offer.

"She'll still blame me," I said. "She always blames me."

Margot couldn't argue with that. Our mother had spent decades making it clear that but for the cascade of events that followed Kevin's arrest, she'd—we'd all—have had a completely different life. A better one. To be fair, it was quite the cascade. Along with the loss of Kevin's affection had gone his generosity, and he had the means to be generous.

This, then, became her constant refrain in the years following: that I put Margot up to it; that I never wanted her to be happy; that I chased away the best man she'd ever known; that I had no idea what was happening in that apartment because I was hundreds of miles away. I blew the whole thing out of proportion.

In retrospect the seeds of her Alzheimer's might have been sprouting even then, but by the time Ryan and I moved her into our home, the whole episode had taken on a life of its own.

"Have you made an appointment yet?" Margot asked as she pulled out of the parking lot.

"No."

She took her eyes from the road just long enough to let her disapproval be known.

"I'm going to," I said.

"I can give you the info again," she said.

"I have it."

"Babs it's really important. Especially since—" Her mouth tightened around what she left unspoken.

It was really important because my children only had one parent, now. If they were going to lose another, I needed to plan for that. It was really important because Margot's results had come back negative, though no one had expected them to be positive—at nearly forty, she had no symptoms. Unlike me, who had just forgotten a court ordered deposition of my own client. Who hadn't slept through the night in close to a year. Who sometimes felt *something,* maybe sometimes saw *something, someone.*

"When was the last time it happened?" Margot asked.

"I don't know."

"Yes, you do." Her eyes were fixed on the road as she pulled onto the Eisenhower.

"Last week," I muttered into my lap. "I'll make the appointment."

I pulled my phone from my pocket as if I might make the appointment right then, but when I unlocked the screen, I was greeted by four missed phone calls and a cascade of texts.

> Monika: Hi Babs. Just checking to see whether I have the time wrong? But I don't think I do. Court reporter is here?

> Monika: Could you give me a call when you get a chance?

> Mark: Kelly has explained conflict. I'm covering Flessing dep for you.

> Mark: What do you have reports saved as on sharedrive? I can't find any reports to prep for dep. I need a summary of this case.

Missed call: Mark Johnson
Missed call: Mark Johnson
Missed call: Monika Flessing

Kelly: I am done covering for you. I just got chewed out by Bruce for not telling him I knew you weren't coming in today.

Mark: What year was the first copyright on Tatters of Truth?

Mark: BABS!!! I need the year!

Missed call: Mark Johnson

forty-one

Austin stirs but doesn't awaken. I glance out the window to see that it's dark, but the snow that fell over the weekend has been, at intervals, sufficiently trampled upon or shoveled that I know I can make it to the lake path without incident. I change into my winter running gear, and with my driver's license, my phone, and my plunger in my pocket, I plug myself into one of my running mixes and head out the door. A quick wave to Tyler, and I'm off. Coffee will be waiting for me when I return.

There isn't a soul out. Although my music pulses in my ears and drives my feet forward, I'm aware of the infinite stillness of the city. Unusually so for a Monday, but it's President's Day. Universities, schools, government offices, the post office—all are closed.

The trains observe a holiday schedule, and as I run along Belden, I glance in both directions without even the distant shimmer of a headlight. Once I reach the zoo, I follow the path to the lake. I've politely acknowledged a grand total of five cars, the drivers of which seem surprised to see anyone else out at this time of the morning. They flash their lights at their respective intersections, indicating I have right-of-way. Then not another person in sight on the lake path.

The snow is slush under my feet; I'll have to take off my shoes and socks as soon as I get home, or my feet will turn to soggy blanched prunes that will make my whole body cold.

I pass another runner, heading north. We nod to each other. I've seen him before. We early morning crew get to know each other. He's wearing a new hat. I wonder if it's a Valentine's Day gift from someone, a girlfriend, a wife, a boyfriend. I have no idea who this man is. Just that we observe something of the same running schedule, and unlike much of the city, we don't switch to treadmills in the winter. He passes me, moving on, and I'm back in my beautiful solitude.

I see another runner coming toward me. One I don't know. They're struggling, not the light step of a year-round runner. They have all the gear, though. They're really going for it: the fleece running pants, a quilted winter running coat, a sock hat tucked tightly over the ears, and a winter snood pulled over chin, mouth, and nose. Their lungs aren't used to the cold, yet. It takes a while. Those first couple of weeks of winter running, the Chicago air burns so badly, it's hard to know whether it's frozen or on fire.

We come to our point of crossing, and I nod. It's a woman, judging from her build and eyes, which are the only parts of her actually visible.

Good morning to you, fellow warrior of winter.

But instead of passing each other, she lurches to the side and grabs me by my forearms. She's bigger than I am, not taller but more muscular, larger, and I'm thinner than I've been in years. I lack heft. Plus, the slush under them makes it impossible to stick my feet. I realize the woman is wearing hiking boots. That's what made her running so clumsy. But it's improving her ability to gain leverage as she pulls me toward the lake.

I am frantic, my feet sliding beneath me like a marionette violently pulled across a stage. The lake must be, at most, thirty-five degrees. I'll die within minutes if she pushes me in, which appears to be her objective. My plunger is in the pocket of my coat, but with her fists clinging to my sleeves, I can't steady my arms to reach into my pocket.

I'm in a nightmare—it's the only explanation—the kind where my mouth opens to scream and nothing comes out, my larynx simply refuses to obey. But then it's there, a thin whistle, followed by more substance.

"HELP!" I scream louder and louder, over and over. "HELP!"

The woman drags me toward the lake—chunks of blue-white ice bob in the green-black water, the waves slap the cement and splash onto the path as the wind carries them up and over the pavement. My feet flail like the scarecrow in *The Wizard of Oz* immediately after he's freed of his post.

Suddenly her eyes flash to something over my shoulder, then flash back to the lake, five, maybe six, feet away. Abruptly she releases me, and my feet are lost as I sling-shot to the side. My arms spring out, grasping at the winter vapor as my body slams to the ground. I hear what sounds like a large chunk of ice crashing onto the concrete path.

"Oh shit!" the woman says and turns, running in the direction she came from—a drop-dead, all-out sprint—before she disappears into the zoo.

I hear another woman's voice, soft and familiar but distant. "Babs? Is that you? Are you okay?"

I'm not. I'm not okay. I can't see, and my head feels like it's been split with a meat cleaver. I reach up but can't feel anything through my hat and gloves.

"Babs, I'm calling the police." The woman pulls my phone from my pocket.

"Okay," I say, as if my permission has been sought, and I, ever reasonable, am merely granting it. For reasons I can't explain, I start screaming for help again, despite the fact that help has—it seems—arrived. I begin crying, too, the tears cold against my cheeks as the slush slowly seeps through my running tights.

The woman takes out my phone, and I sink into a darkness so black and cold, I'm certain I'm in the lake after all.

Two police officers flank Austin. Their thick, blue vests and wide tool belts make them appear preternaturally large in the cramped room. Occasional static from a walkie-talkie competes with their hushed voices.

"She runs every morning. Leaves promptly at 5:30," Austin says softly.

A woman, also wearing blue—the same blue Ryan used to wear—walks into the room. She takes a stern edge with the three men already gathered. "Can you take all that into the hall?" It isn't really a question. "Mrs. Aganon is starting to wake up."

"I'm staying," I hear Austin say.

"Who are you?" she asks.

"Her fiancé."

Everything feels fuzzy, including my tongue. "Water," I say.

"I got it," Austin says and pours a cup from a plastic pitcher on a table next to my bed.

The woman leans over me, a small flashlight in her hand. She waves it in front of my eyes, then tucks it into the breast pocket of her scrubs. The two police officers, disregarding her instruction to leave my room, stand back from my bed, observing closely.

"I'm Dr. Engleson, Mrs. Aganon. Do you know where you are?" she asks.

My eyes dart around the room. "A hospital."

"You're at Northwestern. Do you know what happened to you?"

Austin steps closer to the bed, and I reach for his hand. I suddenly feel terrified again, fear gripping me around the ribs. I want to scream for help. "It's okay. It's okay," he says.

"Mrs. Aganon, do you remember what happened to you?"

I feel the tears begin to leak from my eyes. "My head." Each word emerges in coordination with a sudden and pronounced throbbing from that very body part. I reach my hand up and see Dr. Engleson's eyes grow wide.

"Don't touch your head, Barbara."

"Babs," Austin says. "You have stitches, Babs. They're on the side of your head. Don't touch them."

I drop my hand, and Austin puts the cup of water in it. He adds a straw, which he steadies, then brings to my lips. The cold of the water sends another mind-splitting throb through my eye into the back of my skull. I lean back into the pillow and close my eyes.

"What? What is it?" Austin asks. "Oh God. Is she okay?"

"Are we going to be able to get a statement from her today?" one of the officers asks.

"Are you fucking kidding?" Austin snaps.

"Why don't you all go out into the hall?" Dr. Engleson says for the second time.

"I'm not leaving," Austin says.

"Well, I'm going to give her something for her agitation, so she's not going to be very talkative."

"Penny and Colin?" I ask without opening my eyes. A

warmth spreads through my body, and I suddenly feel very tired.

"There," I hear Dr. Engleson say.

"They're at home," Austin says. "The police woke them up when they came to the door though, so they know you're here. I told Penny I'd text her with an update."

I muster a nod of acknowledgement. The police came to the door. They must be terrified.

The ping from my phone wakes me, and I reach for it only to find that someone has moved the whole tray-table back from the bed, putting my phone out of reach.

"Hold on, Mrs. Aganon," a woman in navy-blue scrubs says. "I'll get that for you." She hops off a stool where she's been perched in front of a computer and hands my phone to me.

"I'm Carrie. I'm your nurse today. Is there anything I can get you? Are you hungry?"

> Penny: Austin says you're okay. You're just sleeping. Please text me. Colin and I are worried.

"I have to respond to this," I say. My thumbs tremble over the phone as I work to conjure a voice of reassurance for the sake of my children.

> Me: Just waking up from a nap. Feeling pretty good. Is everything okay at home?

> Penny: When are you coming home? Austin said you have to spend the night at the hospital. What happened?

"Do I have to spend the night here?" I ask.

"For observation," Carrie says. "Just one night. Neuro wants another CT in the morning. They'll okay you to go home if it's clear."

> Me: Just one night. Is Austin there with you guys? Do you want me to call Aunt Margot?

> Penny: Austin is here. He made us lunch and now he's in the office. Colin is really upset. Can we FaceTime?

I reach a hand up to the side of my head, and Carrie steps forward an inch. I drop my hand before touching the bandage.

> Me: I look awful. Didn't get to shower after my run.
>
> Can we talk without FaceTime.

The phone rings immediately. Penny and Colin greet me in unison with a "Hi Mom!"

Carrie sits back down at her chair and returns to her computer screen. This might take a while.

I talk for a few minutes, feeling the exhaustion set in again—the extraordinary energy it takes to pretend everything is fine when I suspect that the breeze I feel along the side of my head is the result of at least some portion of it being shaved. But Colin seems comforted by hearing that I'm under the close supervision of doctors, and they have determined I'll be fine.

"Is that your mom?" I hear Austin in the background followed by Penny's confirmation.

There's another muffled exchange, then Penny says, "Austin's on his way back to the hospital."

I end the call, assuring Penny and Colin that I love them, I'm fine, I'll see them soon. Then, I set the phone on the table by my bed and take a deep breath, exhaling slowly to the sound of Carrie click-clacking on her computer.

"I went ahead and ordered your lunch tray," she says as I shift in the bed, trying to sit up a little straighter.

"Thanks." I examine the buttons on the bedrails, attempting to figure out how to elevate the head.

"Do you want some help with that?" She hops off her chair again, then gives me a brief tutorial on the different buttons and assists in elevating the head of the bed to a comfortable station. "I'm supposed to give those officers a call when you're awake so they can come talk to you. Do you feel up to it?" she asks, and I know that her additional expertise involves a kind of gatekeeping. If I say no, she'll honor that.

"Probably should just get it over with," I say.

She lifts a white object from her lanyard and holds it to her mouth. "Barbara Aganon is ready to give a statement if you want to let the officers know."

A voice bounces back, "I'll call down."

I'd imagined it might take at least a couple of hours for them to rearrange their schedules to meet with me, but the officers arrive in my room within fifteen minutes. Apparently, they'd been biding their time in the cafeteria.

"Ten minutes," she tells them when they walk into the room. The older one gives her a look that suggests he's pretty sure *he'll* be the one to decide how long he gets to speak to me, but I think he probably underestimated Carrie. I bet a lot of people do. Though not for long.

"Hi, Mrs. Aganon. I'm Officer Simonson, and this is Officer Kirk. Can you tell us what you remember about this morning?"

Kirk—the younger one—stands one step back from his partner, observing.

"I was running south along the lake path, and I saw a woman approaching me, and I thought she was another runner, but when she got close, she grabbed me and tried to throw me into the lake. I started to scream, and when I pulled back from her, she let go, and I fell back and hit my head on the pavement. I don't remember really what happened after that."

My lunch tray arrives, rather inconveniently, but Carrie pushes her way to the bed and sets it on the table, rolling the tray over the bed to make it accessible.

"Would you recognize the woman if we showed you a picture of her?" Officer Simonson asks.

"No. She was completely covered. She had brown hair and brown eyes, but she wore a snood—"

"A what?" Officer Simonson asks.

"It's a face mask," Officer Kirk explains. "For keeping your face warm when you run. The bike messengers wear them, too, this time of year."

"And she had a hat on," I continue. "I might recognize her voice, though. And her eyes."

"I'd like to show you a picture, and I want you to focus on her eyes, since that's what you saw." Officer Simonson holds up his phone, and I examine the photograph of a woman, her brown hair matted and tangled, her skin rough and wind-burnt surrounding deep-set brown eyes.

"That's Irene," I say. "That's not her. That's the woman who called you."

"A man named Christopher Jorgenson called us. He said he found this woman crouched over you, and you were screaming for help. When he yelled at her to get back, she ran away. We picked her up about an hour ago, hiding in the zoo."

"No. That's not the woman who attacked me," I say again. "I know her. She was trying to help me."

"Nice of you all to finally take an interest," Austin says as he rounds the corner into the room. "If you'd done your fucking job two months ago, this wouldn't have happened."

"It's okay, Austin," I say, reaching for him. He comes over to the side of the bed and takes my hand.

"How are you feeling?" he asks as if the entire rest of the room has disappeared.

"Like I've been hit over the head by a two-by-four," I say, going for levity.

Austin doesn't think it's funny. He spins toward the two officers. "Where are you in your investigation?"

"They arrested Irene," I say, closing my eyes as a particularly deep throb slices through my skull.

Carrie steps forward. "Mrs. Aganon, if you don't feel up to speaking with law enforcement right now, please say so."

"No. I'm fine... well not fine... but they've arrested Irene, and it wasn't Irene."

"Who's Irene?" Austin asks, glancing around the room.

"She's a woman who comes to the pantry on Wednesdays—"

"She's a woman with a record as long as my arm," Officer Simonson cuts in. "Disturbing the peace, public intoxication, indecency, resisting arrest, breaking and entering, possession, possession with intent to distribute, vagrancy, vandalism... and now assault and battery," Officer Simonson says, sounding very much like he thinks *I* am the problem when really, they arrested the wrong person, and *that's* the problem.

"What? No!" I exclaim. "This is a mistake. It was not her."

"Bee," Austin says gently, his eyes focusing intently on mine. His voice drops to a whisper; he doesn't want to be heard. "Babs, are you sure it wasn't her? You lost consciousness. The man who found you said he thought she'd killed you." He covers his mouth with his hand as if the words shouldn't even be spoken. "You've been through an awful lot today."

"Listen to your boyfriend, Mrs. Aganon," Officer Simonson instructs with condescension.

"Hey!" Austin barks.

"It wasn't her. It wasn't Irene. You have to let her go," I say, feeling myself begin to cry again. "It was a fan."

"Okay, okay," Austin says, placing a kiss on my forehead. "Okay." He pivots toward the officers. "She says it was a fan."

"A what? It sounds like it might have been some kind of gang initiation," says Officer Simonson. "And it's not really safe for a woman to be running at that time of the morning. It's dark—"

Austin glares at him wide-eyed. "Are you kidding me with that?"

Officer Kirk cuts in. "Maybe we should talk to you both tomorrow. After you're home. When things are a little... calmer." His eyes shift to Austin.

"Please, let Irene go. Tell me you're going to let her go." I can't stand the thought of it. Her face appears behind my eyes, the round, wind-burnt cheeks, her hands aged from wear and weather.

Officer Simonson guffaws. "So, no positive ID? Do I got that right? We walk in here with a suspect in custody, and we walk out with nothing? Not even a lead. A white woman with brown hair and brown eyes. That's what we got?"

"You're going to release her, though?" My eyes bounce between the two officer. "You have to do that."

Officer Kirk steps forward, "Yes, ma'am. We can't hold her if you're saying it wasn't her." The statement is equal parts comfort and warning—he wants me to understand the stakes.

"It was not her." I stare at him, unblinking.

Officer Simonson huffs, handing Austin his card. "Call when you get home." He eyes me, the corners of his mouth tucking into a frown—I've let him down, *personally*.

"I'll heat this up in the break room," Carrie says, referring to my lunch tray. Then she picks up the tray from my table and follows the officers out of the room.

forty-two

The younger of the two FBI agents is named Miranda, which strikes me as a bit on the nose for law enforcement, but it's not like she chose it. The older agent is Burt. He's wandering around my living room examining the sheets of music on the piano, the photographs on the bookshelves, the books themselves.

Austin drove Penny and Colin to school this morning, then picked me up from the hospital. He told them I'd be home when they got home and said he could hardly get them out of the car when he dropped them off; they wanted to wait for me, but we didn't want them here when the FBI came over.

Austin walks into the living room with a tray of coffee and sits next to me. He takes my hand in his, and his thumb brushes over the back as he kisses my temple. He can see that I'm anxious.

Burt drags a finger down the spine of *I Am Charlotte Simmons*.

"Have you read it?" I ask.

"No," he says in a manner that doesn't invite trading TBR lists.

"Help yourself to coffee," Austin says.

Burt peeks over his shoulder. Miranda takes out her notepad and flips the cover back, simultaneously clicking the top of her pen in a gesture that's almost graceful in its choreography. The pen is navy blue and says "FBI." In case we've forgotten who they are, I guess.

Burt sidles over to the tray, pours some coffee and cream in a mug, and lifts it to his lips. I sip mine, letting the ceramic mug warm my hands.

"Do you mind if I record this?" Miranda asks, moving a small digital recorder to the center of the coffee table.

"Not at all," I reply.

"When did all this start?" she asks, having absolutely no way of understanding how difficult a question that is to answer. Thankfully Austin steps in.

"It looks like someone took a picture of us while we were eating lunch back in August," he says.

"That was the day you met?" Miranda asks.

"Sort of," Austin says.

Burt gives him a tired expression, and I fill in. "My uncle worked on a television show that Austin was in back in the '90s, and my sister and I met him on the set in 1997."

"But this was the first day since then?"

"Not exactly," I say, and now it's my turn to be on the receiving end of Burt's worn patience. He takes a seat in the wingback chair next to the fireplace in a movement that reflects his appreciation for how long this is going to take.

Austin and I fill them in. The whole interview takes two-and-a-half hours and leaves me completely spent. At the end of it, Miranda acknowledges that despite the number of incidents and the intel Micah has garnered on the Lewnatics, she really doesn't have much to go on. Like Austin, their leading theory is that it's a fan, probably one of the Lewnatics. They suspect it's just one, maybe two, but not a coordinated group. Probably local to Chicago.

They note their difficulty securing cooperation from Facebook in past investigations and ask Austin to help them obtain a list of all of the members of the group. Austin glances at me, a silent question residing behind his eyes.

"My sister used to be in the group," I say, daring only to look at the Midwestern hiking trails coffee table book in front of me. "She left back in December."

"Your sister?" Miranda says, as though she isn't sure she heard me correctly.

"Yes," I say.

"I take it she wasn't the one who tried to push you into the lake?" Burt says.

"My sister has dark brown hair and green eyes. The woman who tried to push me into the lake had light brown hair and brown eyes."

"I see," Miranda says. She clicks the end of her pen and tucks it into a small canvas tote she's carrying. Then she and Burt promise to reach out again as soon as they have any information.

Mid-afternoon arrives, and I haven't moved from the couch except to open the door for Miranda and Burt and to use the restroom when they left.

"I can't believe this," Austin whispers into the top of my head as his fingertips travel the length of my arm. A cup of hot tea sits untouched in front of me. I'm too tired to reach forward and lift it from the table.

Mike texts Austin from the front step.

> Mike: Visitor here for you.

Austin and I glance at each other with shared dread. Reporters? Police officers? Nosey neighbors?

> Mike: Christopher Jorgenson. Approve or refuse.

"How does he know where we live?" I ask.

"I met with him yesterday at the police station while you were at the hospital. He probably saw it on one of the reports."

"Well, I guess we should let him in. I owe him a thank you."

Austin rises and goes to the door, and his low baritone matches a similar pitch on the other side. This is followed by the soft steps of both Austin and a second man crossing into the living room.

His face is as unfamiliar as his voice, but Austin offers the introduction. "Bee, this is Christopher Jorgenson. He called the police yesterday morning and stayed with you until the paramedics arrived."

"Hello," I say, feeling suddenly self-conscious of the uneven fall of my hair as it drapes over the shaved and stitched portion of my head.

"Can I get you anything?" Austin offers Christopher. "Coffee?"

"No. No, I can't stay. I just... I wanted to make sure you were okay. That whole scene was... unnerving."

I know he's referring to the part where he thought—however briefly—that he'd witnessed a murder. I have no doubt it was *unnerving*. It sure as hell was for me.

"I'm sorry for dropping by like this. I hope it's okay," he adds.

"No. It's fine," Austin says, though I'm not sure I agree, and

Austin's voice sounds sort of like he isn't sure either. "We do owe you a thank you."

"You probably saved my life," I say. I'm nearly positive that if Christopher hadn't arrived on the scene, Irene would have saved my life, but I'm tired of having that argument and don't want to have it with someone who'd only tried to help.

"You don't owe me anything. Any decent person would have come running when they heard *that* scream." He seems to shiver at the mere memory. "Did the police find that woman?"

"They got the wrong woman," I say. "The one who was leaning over me wasn't the woman who attacked me. She's been released."

"But... you were screaming at her?" he says and glances at Austin, who now stands on the other end of the couch opposite Christopher. The implied sentiment—she's wrong about who attacked her—is unmistakable, but Austin remains stoic, his expression unreadable.

"Do you know *why* she attacked you?" Christopher asks.

It was a *she* either way, so I decide not to get into the weeds about which *she* he means. I peek up at Austin again, and he nods, apparently having determined the man to be, on the whole, a decent enough guy. Austin provides the same explanation he'd supplied the officers that morning, familiar enough at this point that I almost mouth it along with him. *I used to be on a TV show, and some of the fans...*

"Oh yeah? What show?" Christopher asks in a voice that seems far too upbeat for the circumstance.

Once again Austin provides the name, though with considerably less enunciation than he had with the police.

"No shit? My wife loved that show."

I take a second glance at our friend Christopher, and, sure enough, he does appear to be the right age to be married to a

Lewnatic. Maybe his wife isn't a Lewnatic. She could just be a fan of the show.

"Is there any way you could avoid telling her about this?" Austin asks.

"Of course." He pauses. "Well, she already knows that a woman was attacked at the lake path. I had to call her so she'd know I'd be late coming back from my run yesterday. But yeah, she doesn't need to know... Well, I already told her your name. But I can leave it at that." Christopher looks around my living room, taking it all in. He's going to tell his wife every detail.

"It's just that, Babs has been the target of a considerable amount of harassment, and if this leaks out, I think that will make it even worse," Austin says, pleading our case—in vain, I suspect.

"Worse than almost being thrown into Lake Michigan in February?" Christopher asks.

"Yeah," Austin says, puffing his chest. "They might actually succeed next time."

I shudder, and Austin returns to the couch, pulling the blanket up around my shoulders as if I'd shuddered from cold. Christopher appears to be appropriately shamed, but I still think he'll tell his wife.

forty-three

"Get your hands off me!"

"I guess Margot's met Mike," I say.

Austin gets up and heads for the front door. "It's okay, Mike," I hear him say from the vestibule.

"Babs!" Margot's voice erupts into the front hall. "Babs, where are you?"

"And I guess Christopher told his wife about his Monday morning," I say to Austin, who trails Margot. It's been less than twenty-four hours since Christopher left my house.

Margot strides into the living room and sits down in a chair across from the couch, her face stricken, pale, eyes wide. "What the fuck, Babs?" she offers as her opening salvo. "Why am I learning about this from Instagram?"

"I'm sorry," I say. "I just got home yesterday. We had to talk to Austin's attorney. I was going to call you."

"This happened *Monday*," she says—emphasizing that I've had time to call her. Austin opens his mouth to offer further argument, but Margot catches him. "Do not speak, motherfucker."

"Margot," I say, my voice a warning. "I cannot do this right now."

Austin sits next to me on the couch. "We've talked to the FBI," he says. "They're investigating the Lewnatics." It's a test. If she's truly worried about me—and not about getting caught—this should reassure her.

"This shit is not coming from his fans, Babs. They are crazy, not violent."

Austin steps in. "You don't have any idea what that fandom is capable of, Margot. You've been sitting on one side of it only. The view from my side is pretty ugly."

Margot locks onto him. "Am I wrong? You've had your guy sitting in that group for how long, and have you *ever* seen them orchestrate something like this? Has anything like this even happened before? They hated that fucking Isabelle woman you were dating, and the most they did to her was mail a bunch of picture books to her house."

"They what? Why?" I ask, but Austin seems to know what she's talking about.

"At Christmas," he says as a further indictment.

"I don't understand," I say. "Did she have children?"

"No," Margot says. "She was one."

"She was not—"

"Whatever, Austin. This is not the Lewnatics, and you know it. Who is on your list? Is Samantha on your list; she fucking should be. And Chloe? Kurt?"

"Stop!" I shout at the two of them.

Both Austin and Margot clamp their mouths closed so fast I think I hear teeth clack together, and their eyes shoot in my direction.

"The FBI are going to be a lot better at figuring this out than any of us," I say.

Margot sits back in her chair. She gives Austin one last ice-cold stare, and he shakes his head, settling his focus on the fireplace.

"Regardless of who it is, he's not worth it, Babs." Margot offers this without emotion, as if she were commenting on nothing more interesting than the price of an item on a menu. *That's too much for a burger.* "Since he has come into your life, you have been harassed all over the internet, isolated from your family and friends, and now nearly murdered. Not. Worth. It."

I feel Austin's breath quicken next to me, and I know this is what he fears most, that I'll weigh the risks and benefits as decidedly against him. Just this morning, while standing outside the guest room in the basement, one hundred percent eavesdropping on his conversation with Micah, I heard a side of him I've never heard before.

"You have to find out who's doing this... She's going to get hurt. Or leave. All these years and I'm going to lose her, Micah..." Micah must have offered some words of reassurance as Austin's voice dropped. "Yeah. Yeah. I know..." Another pause. "I know... I just... Micah, this has to stop. I can't lose her."

"This is ridiculous," I say, reinvigorated by her casual dismissal of Austin. "You can't just come here and say these things."

"Like hell I can't." She turns to Austin once again. "She is my sister. She is all I have in this world. No dad, no mom—or at least not one who remembers me. It's just the two of us. It's always been just the two of us. And if she gets hurt because of whatever fucked up world you're a part of, I will kill you with my bare fucking hands."

Ironically, I haven't seen her this angry since she screamed at me from her bedroom at Uncle Leo and Aunt Iris's house in 1997 because I'd gone hiking with Austin Lewis. I kind of thought she might kill *me* with her bare fucking hands then, but she didn't. Of course, I'd locked my door when I went to bed that night.

"Margot," Austin begins. He sounds awfully measured for someone who just received a death threat. "I love your sister. I love her. If anything happened to her because of me, you wouldn't *have* to kill me with your bare fucking hands; I'd do the job myself."

Margot glowers at him from the other end of the sofa.

"Are you parked in front of Lasky's building?" I ask, thinking only of how to get her out of my house.

"It's fine. He doesn't own those spots," she replies.

It is almost certainly not fine. Not with snow on the ground and parking at a premium. Not when Lasky has probably "dibs'ed" every inch of the front of that building.

"Why don't I walk you to your car?" I suggest, rising from the couch. The conversation seems far from over, but I have no energy to continue it. I want to sit on the couch, burrowed into Austin's chest with his arms tight around my shoulders.

"You can't walk me to my car, you're wearing socks. I'll walk myself," she says and gets up abruptly, stomps her way through the living room out to the front hall, then slams the front door behind her.

The house falls into a silence so profoundly still, I nearly jump off the couch when there's another knock on the door. I figure Margot must have forgotten something, but when Austin opens the door, the voice on the front porch isn't hers.

"Your sister moved my lawn chairs and patio table from the street," Lasky says as I join Austin in the vestibule, scanning the front of the house for any sign of Mike. "It's bad enough you've got cops coming to your house, lowering the values of every property on this block. Now your guests are taking up *my* spots in front of *my* building."

Austin has reached his breaking point. "Those aren't *your*

spots, and putting a fucking patio set in the street doesn't change that."

"I shoveled them out; they're mine," Lasky insists, his cheeks turning the same color as his hair.

"What do you mean, you shoveled them? There's three inches of snow on the ground. I own thicker sweatshirts," Austin shouts, throwing his hand in the direction of the street.

"Dibs isn't a thing," I say, and Lasky glares at me. Slowly his expression shifts from ire to confusion.

"What happened to you?" he asks, his tone carrying disgust rather than concern.

"Hey, hey you!" Mike says, bounding up the steps. He glances at Austin. "I'm sorry, sir. I was doing a perimeter check. I thought I heard something in the alley."

"Is that your Pathfinder," Lasky asks Mike, indicating a black SUV parked in an admittedly pristine space on the other side of the street.

"No. I took the 'L'," Mike says, momentarily dazed before taking an open assessment of Austin's expression and addressing him. "Would you like me to remove this man from the property?"

"Yes," Austin says, then slams the door in Lasky's face.

I hear a small commotion on the front step but when I get back to the living room, I see Lasky stalking—unescorted—across the street toward his building, looking furious but unharmed.

forty-four

I flip through the pages of a magazine. Women half my age stare back at me, drenched in white tulle, surrounded by ranunculus and peonies. I know most brides use the internet, now. They have Pinterest boards full of ideas pulled from blogs and websites, virtual scrapbooks and social media influencers. The magazine I'm paging through has a website, too. But I don't have a Pinterest page. I don't have any social media anymore. I have magazines and a wedding planner and need to start thinking about invitations and centerpieces.

It will be a small wedding; we made that decision intentionally. Second marriages for both of us (even if he doesn't really count his first one), but more than that. We've gotten enough attention. The wedding planner promises she can be discrete but keeping it small furthers the effort.

Austin has flown out to L.A. to meet with Micah about the ongoing investigation into my attack and Austin's permanent relocation to Chicago. He needs to sell his house and arrange for his remaining belongings to be sent here.

On top of that, Micah has successfully staved off the release of Kurt Alison's memoir. But the sum total of these things, plus the approaching date for filming, persuaded Austin that he needed an in-person meeting with Micah.

This also prompted what I'd anticipated would be a most uncomfortable conversation: Should we have a prenup? I suggested the formality, thinking of it as the ordinary business of a marriage between two middle-aged adults. I also thought it an important sign of my intent, my sincerity. Besides, I like that I'm financially independent, and a prenup is an outward sign of that. Plus, some version of our 1997 encounter *will* eventually make its way into the fan-chatter, and maybe this will at least provide some insulation against aspersions that I'm nothing more than a groupie.

I was stunned when Austin said, "I already told you: all of me is yours. I mean it." He folded a couple t-shirts and placed them in his suitcase on top of a pair of jeans. I probably should have initiated the conversation when we could sit and discuss it, but something about his movement back and forth from the closet to his suitcase, from the dresser to his suitcase, made it easier to raise the topic.

"But... there's more of you than there is of me," I said.

He tucked several pairs of socks along one end of the suitcase, then paused, staring at me from the other side of the bed. "Everything, Bee. It's yours. If I'm stupid enough to do something that would make you leave me, I deserve to lose whatever you take with you." His face was placid, as if the comment were utterly uninteresting—an observation about the weather. *Lot warmer today than I thought it would be.*

"Sometimes I can't believe you're real," I said. "How are you this... perfect?" The comment sounded small, pithy, but felt existential.

His busied movements stopped. His hands calmly rested on his neatly folded clothes. "I'm not perfect, Babs," he said, shaking his head. His eyes drifted down. "I have made so many mistakes in my life. So many. But not this. Not you."

I stepped back from the bed as if the size of his words were too great for the small space between us. His eyes found mine, small lines appearing at the corners, speaking to days spent in the California sun and a life of past *mistakes* he carried within him.

His lips curved upward, fondly. "Now come here and give me a kiss because I'm going to miss you while I'm gone."

"It's only two days," I said, meeting him on his side of the bed.

He closed the lid of the suitcase and zipped it, then took my hand, his eyes growing sharp as his mood seemed to shift. "Please be watchful," he said. "Check the locks before you go to bed. Make sure you set the alarm on the house. Keep your phone close. *Please* don't run in the dark." He kissed me and dropped his forehead to mine. "I'm going to be checking in on you."

"I know," I said, with a peck to his lips.

"A lot," he said, pecking back.

"That's fine," I said.

He closed his eyes and breathed a sigh that suggested he could have been talked out of the trip to L.A. But an hour later, I dropped him at the airport and returned to my house looking forward to him checking on me as often as he'd promised.

"Ma'am?" calls the security guard from just inside the vestibule of my house. I set the magazine down and step into the vestibule to find David standing on the front step behind Drew.

"He's my friend," I say to Drew, who steps aside and allows David to enter, pulling the door closed behind him.

"Come in. Let me take your coat," I say.

David steps into the front hall a little awkwardly, glancing around as if to get his bearings. "I'm sorry for not calling first. When you didn't come to the pantry again this morning, I started to worry and thought I'd just walk over."

"I'm sorry. I didn't mean to worry you," I say, leading him further into the house. "Would you like some coffee?"

"That would be nice," he says, following me to the kitchen. "Irene told me what happened."

"Is she okay?" I ask.

"Seems to be, but she's worried about you. From what she told me, I understand why. Are *you* okay?"

"Yeah," I say. I pour David a cup of coffee and invite him to sit with me at the kitchen table.

"Where's Austin?" he asks, scanning the kitchen.

"He's in L.A. for a couple days meeting with his lawyer."

David nods and takes a sip of coffee. I see him make a face, then suppress it. American drip. Plus, Austin makes better coffee than I do.

"The best coffee I ever had in my life was in Paris," I say.

David perks up proudly. "When were you there?"

"Hmm. I guess almost four years ago, now," I say somewhat wistfully. *I could live here, Bibs.* "I went with my husband. Just the two of us. Neither of us had ever been to France before."

"What did you think?" he asks.

"I loved it. Ryan wanted to move there."

"Ryan," David says, seeming to understand something beyond just the name. "Where is he now?"

For about half a second, I consider lying, but I don't think I could carry it through the questions that might follow. "He died," I say. "About three and a half years ago. He was hit by a truck while crossing the street at the Fullerton stop."

"Oh my God. I had no idea," he says, stating the obvious. I never told him. "I assumed you were divorced."

"Nope," I say, almost chirping the word.

He sets the mug on the table. "Here I've been complaining about visitation schedules and Andrea's affair, and you must think I'm so rude."

"Why would I think you were rude? I didn't tell you he died. It's hard to explain something like that between handing out sandwiches and pieces of cake."

"Well, I'm very sorry for your loss, Babs. And it's long overdue of me to say that." He takes another painful sip of coffee. "Are you planning to come back to the pantry?"

"Yes, eventually," I say. "I'm up to my neck in wedding planning at the moment, and I got an interview for a teaching position at Northwestern. And I'm trying to keep a low profile until they figure out who was behind that attack."

"They still don't know?" he asks.

"They don't even really have any leads," I say.

"I'm so sorry, Babs." He sets down his mug with some finality, though he's only finished half of the coffee.

"Would you and Madison like an invitation to the wedding? It's not till next year, and it's going to be very small, but I'd love it if you could come."

"We'd love to," he says enthusiastically. "I have a feeling I'm going to be going to the weddings of quite a few of her friends. It will be nice to go to one of mine."

We're quiet for a few moments. David spins his coffee mug on the table. I watch the second hand on the clock over the doorway to the hall.

"So, they really have no idea who attacked you?"

"No," I say. "Though the FBI are involved now so, here's hoping." I cross my fingers theatrically, and David winces like he can't get the taste of the coffee out of his mouth.

forty-five

THE MAIL LANDS ON THE FLOOR OF THE VESTIBULE WITH A CLAP. I HEAR it from Colin's room where I'm putting away laundry and let loose a yelp. I was lost in my thoughts: wedding planning, FBI agents, track season, interviewing, piano lessons, picking up Austin from the airport tomorrow. I'd been hoping for a phone call following my interview at Northwestern, but having heard nothing for nearly a week now, I accept that it must not have gone quite as well as I'd thought, and it's much more likely I will be a receiving a "Thank you for your interest" letter, than a "Welcome to the university" phone call.

Trotting down the stairs, there's no letter from Northwestern. Instead, I see a rectangular, white USPS box, which I initially think is related to Austin's movie. As I pick it up, though, I see that it's addressed to me. I walk into the office and set it on the desk, sitting heavily in the chair behind it. The screen illuminates as the box bumps the mouse, and the nature-scape wallpaper glows in the dim room. I turn on the desk light, and my eyes come to rest on the photograph of Austin and me from Christmas that he framed and placed next to the monitors.

There's no return address. Maybe it's sample invitations. I note the postage sticker: *MediaMail $4.45*. One time, Margot sent me a set of wind chimes for my backyard and mailed them *Media-Mail*. They weren't media, and there was postage due on arrival. The postal service had x-rayed the parcel and knew it wasn't a book. All of which is to say that I think it's probably a book, but it could be a bomb. Or a photograph of Austin fucking some woman a decade ago. Or a catalogue of sample wedding invitations.

"Fuck it," I say and open the box.

The book slides out onto the desk, and I set the box to the side. *Maple Street Mayhem: A Memoir* by Kurt Alison.

So, a bomb of sorts.

The cover is a television screen with rabbit ears. The screen displays the "off air" rainbow bars that run on network television during "technical difficulties." I hold the box up and shake it, wondering if a note will float out, but it's otherwise empty. Upon examining the postage sticker more closely, the box has been mailed from Vaiden, Mississippi.

I flip through the first couple pages, thinking perhaps I'll find a note, but the book appears essentially untouched. A first edition, mint condition, as it were. The dedication is to Nicole, whoever that is. I turn to the first chapter: *Chapter 1: I Am Born*.

"Oh please," I groan. "You are neither Charles Dickens nor David Copperfield, you self-aggrandizing man-child."

I flip through a few more pages, reluctantly admiring the chapter titles as I appreciate that each one corresponds with a chapter title in an existing classic. "A Mad Tea Party"; "Start of the Dream" (technically that chapter is entitled "Daisy and Gatsby: Start of the Dream." I guess Kurt took some poetic license); "What Happened After Dinner"; "In Which We Begin Not To Understand."

Bonus points for creativity, Kurt, but you're still a dick.

I'm preparing to set the book down, when my eyes land on Austin's name toward the middle of the tome. I have reached the part of the book that details the aforementioned *mayhem* of Maple Street.

Kurt begins with an overture of Austin's transgressions—something Austin already warned me of. These include his "obsessive perfectionism," his pattern of quickly cycling through women essentially as soon as they slept with him, "temper tantrums" on set, "pathological vanity" (a phrase I am definitely remembering), his decades-long vise grip on the show, and his sham marriage to "a no-name model whose life was destroyed by Austin's vindictive approach to an otherwise banal Hollywood divorce."

Well.

Kurt begins with a rough sketch of Austin's "discovery." According to Kurt, as a child, Austin wanted to be a pediatrician. He wanted to help people. But in first grade, while Christmas shopping with his mother at Water Tower, an agent gave his mother her card. Austin's mother had been skeptical, but Austin's father saw only dollar signs. Within a couple of months, Austin had started in commercials—first local ads, then very quickly national ads for action figures, toy cars, board games, breakfast cereal.

This isn't entirely unfamiliar to me—Austin told me the Water Tower story. It's the chapters that follow that take my breath away and go a long way to explaining why Austin fought so hard to keep the book off shelves.

Austin was ten when he signed with KidZone, Inc, and by the age of fourteen, he was posing in cheesy, low-quality photo shoots to stock the pages of the teen magazine circuit. That same year, he lost his virginity to a woman (unnamed) more than twice his age, an event Austin described as leaving him (according to Kurt) "wondering whether there were any adults actually responsible for *protecting* him."

Austin told me he lost his virginity to a co-star at KidZone and that it "wasn't great." I'd taken that to mean he lost it to another teenager and neither of them knew what they were doing. That wasn't far from my own experience, frankly. But this. This is new. Or maybe it isn't. Maybe it's not even true.

Kurt's memoir blames Austin's "cliché child-star saga" on his father, whom I know Austin was estranged from right up to the single-vehicle, drunk driving accident that killed him at seventy-two-years-of-age. Austin's father was supposed to establish a trust fund for Austin but didn't. Instead, Kurt writes, Austin's mother discovered and divorced Austin's father for stealing nearly ten years' worth of earnings from their son. Austin attempted to sue, but the money was gone; his father hadn't been terribly good at saving even for himself. The only thing Austin got from the process was his legal emancipation from his parents. At the ripe old age of sixteen, he was an adult.

Austin landed the role of Bobby Martin on *The Maple Street Martins* two and a half years later, at nineteen. Kurt writes (read: gloats) that Austin originally sought the role of the older brother heading off to college; he got the role of a freshman in high school. He might have walked away, Kurt speculates, but he was broke. His age also made his career more than a little precarious. If he didn't transition to adult roles soon, he never would. Thus, the paradox of Bobby Martin—Austin was an adult, no longer a child star; the role though, was a kid.

Kurt writes that he and Austin were friends immediately and nearly inseparable for years. Both were nominated for Emmys during different seasons, though Austin won and never let Kurt forget it.

With the fifth season, it all fell apart. Austin returned to the set morose, argumentative, singularly focused on his own success at the expense of his castmates (or so Kurt says). Although he now attributes that behavior to Austin's compromised mental health, at the time, Kurt assumed it was related to several decisions made by the show-runners that he and Austin both strongly disagreed with.

First, the show maintained the family for a second season in "one year." Meaning, Bobby should have graduated from high school and gone to college, but the writers kept him in high school as if time simply moved more slowly on Maple Street. The rationale was that audiences wanted to see Bobby in his high school football uniform, navigating young love with his high school girlfriend. This also meant that Kurt was "stuck" in college. Kurt refused to renew his contract, and his character was written out of the show with a "study abroad."

Austin considered threatening to walk, too, but negotiated for producer credit and some creative control instead. Still, his suggestions for the fifth and sixth seasons were generally ignored. The plots were saccharine, uninspired, predictable. The show pushed no boundaries, was nominated for nothing, and attempted to mitigate the precipitous decline in viewership by finally letting Bobby go to college during the sixth season. They also wrote in the pregnancy/baby plot for the Martin parents, who by anyone's estimation should have been limited in their capacity to have more children by Mrs. Martin's perimenopause. Even the actress who played Caroline Martin was nearly fifty.

Kurt writes, "If Austin's frustration at the direction of the show was pronounced, it paled in comparison to his depression after its abrupt and unceremonious canceling." With his last major role being that of a high schooler, Austin was never taken seriously for adult roles. The marriage to the model was supposed to help him bounce back, but it was over almost before the ink dried on the marriage license and only worsened his depression.

Following his divorce, Kurt claims, Austin experimented with coke, experimented with women (a lot of them, if Kurt is to be believed), and finally one bleak evening, he experimented with suicide. He then experimented with suicide a second time when he realized that his star had faded so much, the news hadn't even bothered reporting the first attempt. Neither was "successful."

Despite his struggles, Austin managed to negotiate a deal to acquire *The Maple Street Martins*—a deal Kurt claims Austin "froze [him] out of" for the sole reason that Kurt wanted to be an active business partner, rather than a silent investor. Austin eventually threw himself into a career behind the scenes, producing and purchasing several other television shows, as well as managing the legacy of the show that had made them both stars, then made Kurt a nobody and Austin a businessman. Austin accomplished this through an obsessive and ruthless stranglehold on every aspect of his business ventures by way of a "cartel of yes-men, who cater to his every self-indulgent, egocentric whim."

The claim makes little sense in light of Austin having, to my observation, *one* person he regularly seeks counsel from: his attorney, Micah. But Kurt goes the extra step of accusing Austin of keeping even those cast members he did include in his dealings at arm's length through a nesting doll of conglomerates, subsidiaries, and a streaming platform that he alone owns and controls.

I recall the Wikipedia entry concerning Austin's businesses which describes essentially the same thing, but in more generous terms. Peeling back the vitriol, what Kurt describes is just a successful businessman, who probably uses corporate structures to gain a tax advantage.

I flip back to the chapter on Austin's marriage and divorce. It's entitled "Sunday Evening" and the specificity of detail is startling. An empty house, a marriage dissolved, a friendless, desperate, lonely man. Kurt cautions the reader that the night in 2008 when Austin was rushed to Cedars-Sinai Medical Center was no mere accidental overdose. It was a quiet Sunday evening at home, not a raucous Friday night at the clubs. He meant to die.

I understand that Kurt means to wound, embarrass, shame. He means to take the fresh buds of Austin's renewed career and pluck them from the stem before they can bloom. I lift my fingers to my cheeks and find them damp. I brush away the tears and step back in time more than fifteen years, picturing Austin on the other side of the country, believing that nothing of worth lay before him.

The memoir ends with Kurt, who'd spent the previous 327 pages writing almost exclusively about Austin, boldly asserting that he no longer cares about Austin or what he does with his "sad, lonely life." In the end, Austin's career cost him his childhood, his father, and every appurtenance of a man's life—marriage, children, friends, family. Austin is, thus, "little more than the latest example of Hollywood's unrepentant exploitation of children, and the insatiably hungry machine that is fame." Something that, in retrospect, Kurt asserts he's grateful he escaped.

I set the book down on the desk and lean back in the chair. My gaze floats up to the ceiling where I focus on the flawless matte white of the ceiling. On the desk, my phone buzzes. Hoping it's Austin, I read the text.

>Margot: Did you send this to me?

Below the text is a picture of a book: *Maple Street Mayhem: A Memoir* by Kurt Alison.

"We've reviewed the footage from the post office in Mississippi," Miranda says. "From what we can tell, Kurt has never set foot in that post office. Maybe ever. And he lives in Arizona."

"Who sent it?" Austin asks.

He's certain Kurt sent it. When I picked him up from the airport and showed him the book and told him about Margot, that was the first thing he said followed by a request that we call Miranda and Burt. But when I asked him if what Kurt said was true, he broke down. He said he was embarrassed, that his divorce had been a turning point for him. When his marriage ended, he felt like a total failure. The wheels just completely came off.

"We're still not sure. As you might imagine, there are a number of fingerprints on the books and the boxes—including both of yours." Her expression scolds. "But not Kurt's."

"The person who sent them—looks like a woman—paid in cash, didn't provide a return address, and is not identifiable from the footage inside the post office," Burt summarizes. "So this could be just more of the same from your fans." He nods in Austin's direction.

"No," I say. "They sent one to my *sister*. And the memoir is unpublished. Whoever sent them had to get the copies from either the publisher or the author—"

"Babs," Miranda begins—we've all been on a first name basis for weeks now, "they could have been sent by the wife of some low-level IT guys at the publishing house." Not likely, but

I understand what she's saying. She's explaining why it's not enough to get a warrant to search Kurt's house.

"Do you have enough to question him, at least?" Austin asks.

Burt and Miranda glance at each other. Miranda explains, "We're trying to decide whether that's strategically smart. Does it just give him a heads-up?"

"This man was your friend?" Burt asks.

"For years," Austin says, his voice low with regret. "But we haven't spoken in more than a decade."

"Did you sleep with his wife or something?" Burt asks.

Even Miranda is shocked by the question and coughs into her notepad.

"I'm trying to establish motive," Burt says, though I suspect there's a fair amount of lurid curiosity at work.

"He's never been married," Austin says in a tight voice, frustration barely controlled. "He's just pissed. He quit the show after the fourth season, didn't get the same deal on royalties, and he wanted to buy the rights to the show with me back in '03, but didn't have any money."

"That's it?" Burt asks. "A dispute about money? If he's the one behind all this, he's spent months trying to destroy your relationship, and when he couldn't, he hired someone to kill your fiancée. How much money are we talking about?"

"A lot," Austin says. "And it's also what the money represented."

"What did it represent?" Miranda asks.

"His value. Or what he thought his value was. The show was written for him, originally. He was supposed to be the star. But he couldn't carry it. And he couldn't pivot after it was canceled."

Miranda nods, but Burt seems skeptical. He sucks in a quick

breath as if he plans to say something, but then exhales it through his nose.

"We need something else," Miranda says, bouncing her knuckles against her lips, not talking to anyone in particular.

Burt takes a sip of his coffee. "Your attorney blocked the release of this memoir?"

Austin nods. "We threatened to sue the publisher."

"On what grounds?" Burt asks.

"Public disclosure of private facts and libel."

"Public *what*?" Burt asks.

"My medical information. The uh... my hospitalizations. None of that was public." Austin rubs his palms along the tops of his thighs. His eyes focus intently on the flower pattern of the chair Miranda sits in.

Miranda's forehead ripples. "How'd you manage to keep two suicide attempts and a cocaine habit confidential?"

"This was all back in '08. Social media was barely off the ground, and I wasn't famous anymore anyway."

"Then how'd he get that information? Did you tell him all that?" she asks.

Austin laughs. "Absolutely not. I have no idea how he got it."

"That's it," I say. "That's the thread. You need to contact the hospital and ask if there was a medical record request. Then ask who sent it?"

Burt gives me a look like he really doesn't appreciate me telling him how to do his job. He adds, "We should look to see who his sources were for this book?"

"You should look to see who sent the request to that hospital—that amount of detail? He had medical records. And then you should ask them *where* they sent the records," I say.

forty-six

2022

"Try to stay still, Mrs. Aganon." The voice reached me disembodied, as if it had no actual point of origin, but surrounded me.

"Sorry," I said, then promptly grabbed one hand tightly in the other. That probably counted as movement. "Sorry," I said again.

"It's fine Mrs. Aganon. We're going to start now."

"Okay."

"You'll want to keep your eyes closed. The light can be quite bright."

"Okay."

"Try to hold still, Mrs. Aganon."

I'd thought I already was, but now that she'd mentioned it, I could feel my hospital gown tickling my arms and realized I was trembling. "Sorry."

I tried to focus on the whirring around my head, imagined it was breath, as if a PET scanner breathed. I held as still as I could.

When the voice—which belonged to a woman named

Ginny—retuned, she pressed a button and a different whirring sound accompanied my exit from the scanner.

"Are you okay?" she asked.

"Of course, sure," I said, the words expelling rapidly and with artificial confidence.

Ginny extended a tissue. "Here," she said. "It can be an intense experience to be in such a confined space for so long." The line was rehearsed—she'd said it before—but I didn't understand why she was saying it now. "A lot of people cry," she added. "You don't have to be embarrassed."

"I think it was the air in there. Just dried out my eyes," I said.

"Okay," she said. "You can get dressed, and I'll take you to the waiting room. Dr. Eyman will take a look at the scan and we'll get you when he's ready to talk to you about the results."

I returned to a small waiting room designed for patients like me existing in limbo. Two other women occupied the room. A mother and a daughter by the looks of it. The older of the two appeared frail, truly elderly. The younger woman next to her rummaged through her purse until she held up a palm-sized plastic container. A closer inspection revealed it held a peeled, sliced kiwi.

"Here, Mom," said the woman. "Eat these."

"I don't like those," said the older woman.

"Yes, you do. They're your favorite."

"I'm not hungry," she said. "I want dinner."

"It's not dinnertime, Mom. Dinner's not for four more hours. This is a snack."

"Well, I don't want it." The woman turned and faced the television, and her daughter placed the container back in her purse.

She glanced across the the small space between us. "It can be hard, eh?"

"I'm sorry?" I said.

She tipped her head to the side where her mother sat placidly focused on an episode of *Family Feud* with the volume too low to hear either the host or the guests.

"Oh. Right. Yes."

"Is your mother being tested?" She reached back into her purse and retrieved the container of kiwis, pulled off the lid, and ate one of the slices.

"No. She was already diagnosed. Years ago. I'm being tested."

"Smart," said the woman, unfazed by the looming prospect of my cognitive annihilation.

"Aganon," called a woman from the waiting room door.

"That's me." I rose from my chair. "Nice to meet you," I said to the woman as I passed through the door, preparing to conclude what I assumed would be the second worst day of my life.

I'd anticipated being led to an exam room, the paper-covered table, the industrial chairs with their subdued pleather upholstery, the otoscope attached to the wall so the physician could peer into my ears and see the cells slipping out.

Instead, I found myself delivered to an office not wholly unlike the one I occupied in the Loop—smaller, perhaps, and much better organized. Still there were similarities. Degrees adorned the walls, photographs of children and vacations. A computer monitor rested atop the desk.

Dr. Eyman entered the room from behind me, forcing me to corkscrew in my chair to see him before he took a seat on the other side of the desk, wiggled the mouse on his computer, and typed through to my medical record.

"Let's begin with the good news," he said, with a glance around the monitor. "Your PET scan is normal. The genetic testing, too. See, each of us has two sets of twenty-three chromosomes—one we receive from our mother and one we receive from our father—for a total of forty-six chromosomes." He brought his two forefingers together to illustrate the complete parental set. "The kind of Alzheimer's your mother has requires you to have inherited what we call an APOE mutation from either your mother or your father."

I considered stopping him. I already knew this. But he seemed to have a routine, and I hesitated to interrupt it.

"You do not carry this mutation. Your cognitive screening, though, is consistent with memory loss, as are your... reports of..."

"Paranoia," I said. I'd already heard it described as such by the primary care physician who'd referred me.

"And difficulties at work," he added, though I didn't really think he needed to pile on.

"Okay. Sure. All of it." I was being a little argumentative. After all of this, I felt entitled to a diagnosis and suspected I was about to be told to eat better and get more sleep.

"A lot of things can cause poor performance on a cognitive screening." He held up his fingers to let me know I'd be hearing the list. "Poor sleep, poor diet, extreme stress, trauma. Grief." He emphasized the word allowing it to land on the desk in front of him like a clump of wet clay.

When I didn't respond, he continued. "I understand your husband died a little less than two years ago. He was killed in a car accident?"

"Car versus pedestrian. He was the pedestrian," I said.

"How would you say you're processing that event?" He regarded me almost coquettishly, the question rhetorical.

"Fine," I said, even though I'd only stopped waking up in the closet three months earlier.

"Have you spoken with anyone about your loss?"

"My sister has been really helpful. Really supportive."

"Hmm," he replied. "Talk to me about this feeling you have. That someone is watching you."

"It's not always that someone is watching. Sometimes it's just a feeling that someone is *there*. But then when I look around, no one is."

"Who do you *think* is there?" Another rhetorical question.

"No. It's not like that."

"What's it like, Barbara?"

"My name is Babs," I said.

"I'm sorry. Babs," he said. "You know, it's very common for people who've lost a loved one in a sudden event like this, to imagine that person is still with them."

"I'm sorry. What are we doing here?" I asked. "I wanted to find out whether I had Alzheimer's. Because my mother does. It sounds like you don't think I do. So what am I being evaluated for now? In this conversation? What are you evaluating me for?"

Dr. Eyman leaned back in his chair. "I'm trying to help you get answers to why you have started experiencing these... episodes. I think I'd like you to speak with my colleague Dr. Tan. She specializes in complicated grief—"

"A psychiatrist. You want me to see a psychiatrist."

"Dr. Tan is a psychologist. But she works closely with the psychiatric team here at Northwestern and would be able to collaborate with them if you require any medical interventions—"

"No thank you," I said. "I wanted to know if I had Alzheimer's. You gave me that answer. I appreciate the time you've taken. But this is not because of Ryan's death. I mean... the grief, yes. The memory stuff. I'm assuming that will get better. But that feeling—being watched—that was there before. That was before Ryan." I started to rise from the chair, gather my belongings.

"Babs," Dr. Eyman said, rising as well. "I think it's really important that you talk to someone. Especially if some of this started before your husband died—"

"Thank you for your concern," I said again, heading for the door as Dr. Eyman came around from behind his desk. "I really don't have time to take this on right now. I have to get to work."

forty-seven

Austin flies into Chicago for a seventy-two-hour break from filming. When I pick him up at the airport, he looks haggard, tired. Still, as soon as he steps into my car, his hands are frantic, as if he can't decide what part of me he needs to touch first. My shoulder, my cheek, my hand, my waist.

"I can't be away from you like this," he says. "It's unbearable."

This is our longest time apart since October, our longest time apart in more than seven months. I offer an affectionate laugh, but I don't think he said it to be funny. He takes my hand as I pull away from the curb.

"Was everything okay while I was gone? Any episodes?"

"None," I say. "At least none that I know of. And no other attempts to contact Margot. You?"

He breathes a slow breath and loosens his grip on my hand. "Nothing like before. Some hash-tagging. Speculation about what will happen if my career takes off after this movie."

"Margot mentioned that," I say. "Evidently, there was some commentary on Instagram that I am not *equipped* for this part of your journey."

"Oh fuck them," Austin says.

I laugh again. "Those were my exact words to Margot when she told me."

Austin remains silent. It might be more accurate to say that he's remained silent when it comes to Margot since February—since she threatened to kill him with her bare fucking hands. She, though, has remained a reliably forthcoming source of information, trying to remember anything about the group that might serve as a lead for Miranda and Burt. That hasn't helped thaw the ice between her and Austin, and my previous worry that my sister was secretly in love with my fiancé, has been replaced with my worry about her seething, unadulterated rancor for him.

"Micah said there was a post last week with the Lewnatics about you going shopping at Oak Brook. The administrators banned every single member involved in that thread," Austin says. "They've taken a pretty hard line."

"I guess being contacted by the FBI will do that," I say, referring to Miranda's request to the six administrators of the group for the list of current members.

"Any word from Northwestern?" he asks.

"No," I say. "And the position's not posted anymore. They've obviously made a decision."

"I'm sorry, Bee," he says.

I shrug, casually, but I'm still smarting from the rejection. I'd thought the interview went well. "They could at least send me a rejection letter. Kind of unprofessional."

We pull into the garage twenty minutes later. We'd spent some of the drive from O'Hare focused on happier topics—the trip to Rome, the end of Penny's track season, Colin's Spring recital. But we both know that we won't be able to relax—not truly—until we know who was responsible for the attack in February.

Penny and Colin are waiting for us when we walk into the kitchen. They haven't seen Austin since he left for L.A. at the beginning of May. Colin has peppered me with questions almost every day about who Austin's co-stars are, when the movie will be released, whether we'll get to go to the premiere together.

"Hey guys—" I say, prepared to be the buffer between their enthusiasm and what I sense is Austin's need to use these few days to rest.

He stops me with a light touch to my forearm, and when I turn to him, he is effervescent. "Let me grab dinner, and I'll meet you in the dining room and tell you all about it," he says as if he's read their minds.

Penny and Colin scamper into the next room where I can hear them whispering excitedly. I'm worried for him though. I feel almost protective. We need each other acutely, fiercely, and he needs sleep.

"We have time. And it's a big deal to them," he says, reading my mind as well.

He heats up some lasagna, then sits down at the dining room table where he somehow finds the energy to tell two hours' worth of stories to my absolutely entranced children.

Austin has his hand under my shirt when his phone pings.

"No," I groan as he lifts his lips away from my neck.

"It might be someone from the team. I said I'd stay available," he says. The angle at which he reaches for his phone plunges his hips against mine, and I wrap my legs around his waist trying to pull him back to me.

"It's 5:30 in the morning there. What could they possibly

need at 5:30 in the morning?" I ask as he pulls his phone off the nightstand.

He reads the text and grows instantly serious. "Miranda's at the door. Mike wants to know if he can let her in," he says.

"At 7:30 on a Saturday?"

He rolls away from me, taking his phone (and my hope for a very different start to the day) with him.

"Tell him to let her in, and we'll be down in ten," I say.

We dress quickly and step out into the hall to find both Penny and Colin emerging—bleary eyed—from their bedrooms.

"Is someone here?" Penny asks.

"One of the police officers who's been helping us," I say, heading for the stairs. "You two stay in your rooms. We'll come and talk to you when she leaves."

Penny glances at Colin. "We'll wait in my room."

Downstairs, we direct Miranda to the kitchen—presumably out of range of my kids' curious ears. We sit at the table.

"Can I make you some coffee?" I ask. I'm just being polite. I hope she says no, and she does.

"I can't stay long. I just wanted to tell you as soon as we knew. We arrested Kurt last night. I'd assume the news will break some time today."

My hand shoots up to my mouth as if I'm trying to keep myself from saying anything, but I'm speechless. Austin takes my other hand in his.

"We conducted a search of his apartment, too. Confiscated two computers and several documents," Miranda says.

"Was it him?" Austin asks. "All of it? It was him, wasn't it?"

"Not all of it," Miranda says. "That's been the most challenging part of this. Your fans are..." Her eyes slide to me, and I know she's talking about some of their less charitable commentary on everything from my career (*I think she got fired. She must not be a very good lawyer.*) to my running times (*She's not very fast for a former D-1 runner.*) .

"A lot," I say, helping her out.

Miranda nods. "He impersonated you," she looks to Austin, "to obtain copies of your medical records from your hospitalizations. That's how we got the search warrant." She nods at me but keeps her eyes on Austin. "You were right. When we contacted the hospital, they said the only person to request your records in the past fifteen years was *you*. But the records were sent to a FedEx seventeen miles from Kurt's house." She shakes her head. "It's always something little like that," she says. "Some little detail." She's almost wistful.

"Anyway," she goes on, "we managed to recover a few things from his computers already, and there were quite a few images of you both. Including the photograph of you, Babs, from your backyard."

"He was *here*?" Austin asks, obviously shaken.

"Or someone was on his behalf," Miranda says. "We're going to interview some of the neighbors to see if they recognize him... I mean... not from the show. But if he was canvassing your house, maybe they saw him."

"How did he figure out who I was?" I struggle to form a coherent question. "That was... we'd only gone out twice by that time. How did he even know about me? How'd he find Margot?"

"We think he was actually embedded in that Facebook group," Miranda explains. "The Lewnatics?" She says it like maybe we're unaware. "He was posing as a fan in there. Put together a whole profile and everything, pretended to be some woman named Kami Anderson. That profile is almost completely blank. Just a photo and a couple of memes about the show. But he used it to infiltrate the group and gather info. He also had the photograph of you both from Tufano's." She shoots

Austin a tense stare. "We suspect he was watching you very closely. Do you have any idea why he would do that?"

"I'd assume because he knew about the movie deal and was trying to pick the right moment to publish his memoir—torpedo that project."

Miranda bobs her head back and forth as though this is a plausible, though not completely satisfying explanation. "Could be."

"It was a woman who attacked me at the lake, though," I say. "Was that him, or—"

"Yes. He hired her. Paid her a pretty sum, too. But she seems to have disappeared. We have no leads on her other than the wire transfer."

"Wow," I say. "Okay. So that's it?"

"Well, pretty much. We're still going through his computers, and he is—as you might imagine—not talking. We've reached out to his agent and his publisher, but they haven't gotten back to us yet. I'd imagine they'll lawyer up pretty quickly, too. But if we're right that this was predominantly coming from Kurt, it should stop now. Or the worst of it should." Miranda raises her eyebrows in Austin's direction; there's nothing that can be done about the petty meanness of his real fans.

Miranda rises to leave, and Austin and I stumble to our feet. "I can't imagine what all of this must have been like for you both." She pushes her chair in under the table, and we start walking her to the door. It's hard to make my feet move. I manage it, though. We both thank her for coming to tell us in person. Austin follows closely behind me. At the door, Miranda offers an awkward wave, though it's not really good-bye.

"I'll be in touch as they recover more from the computers," she says, then turns and heads to her car parked across the street in front of the fire hydrant. Who's going to ticket a cop car, I guess.

"It's over," I say as we stand in the vestibule. I am in shock.

Austin pulls me into his arms. I feel him vibrating against my chest, and I'm afraid to draw back and look at him. Afraid he'll see my tears and know how scared I've been.

Then I hear him. "It's over." And I can tell from the way his voices cracks over the words that he's crying, too.

forty-eight

THE BROWN LINE—OR RED, I CAN'T BE SURE—RATTLES THROUGH THE night, across the blocks that separate my house from the tracks. It must be close to two in the morning because the trains are spaced out, interrupting the silence maybe every fifteen or twenty minutes. I have to listen closely to hear them, not like when Ryan and I first moved in together, and our apartment was right on Sheffield—trains loud enough to rattle the glass in the windows and force us to pause and play back whatever we'd been watching on TV.

The sounds of the city are the sounds of nearly my entire life. Cars, voices, trains, dogs, glass hitting the metal dumpsters in the alleys. I roll onto my back, picking out shapes in the shadows on the ceiling, and I think about all of the sounds of my life in this house. Babies crying and giggling. Ryan and I fighting and making love. The creaks and groans of the wind and rain. Penny and Colin bickering or laughing at something on TV. Colin at the piano. My sister and me at brunch in the kitchen. They're the sounds of my family; they're the only sounds I love more than the sounds of the city.

"Hey. Are you still awake?" I whisper, turning my head to

Austin who is most definitely not still awake. His flight back to L.A. leaves at 7:30 a.m.

"Hey. Austin. Are you still awake?" I ask just a little louder.

He mumbles inaudibly in his sleep and throws an arm over his forehead.

I scoot my feet across the bed, until they meet with the side of his calf. He rolls to his side and reaches for me in his sleep, and I burrow into him as he tosses a heavy arm across me. Under the covers, my hand slides over his chest, resting on his ribs, then slowly tracing the side of his body down to his hip. I threw on my t-shirt and underwear after we made love; he quickly fell asleep naked. I know he's tired. I should let him sleep.

"What time is it?" he mumbles.

"I don't know. Around two, I think." I drop my hand to his crotch, and he draws a quick breath as his arm tightens around my side.

His eyes open, blinking sluggishly as a lopsided grin pulls at the corner of his mouth. "Are you having trouble sleeping?" he asks like he might have a solution to that problem.

Under the covers his fingers trace the side of my body, sliding up to my shoulder and down again. It should tickle, but instead it just makes my body throb in places he was already more than attentive to last night. I didn't know my body was this greedy thing that could take and take and still want more. I lift my fingers to his mouth tracing the line of his lips, the cupid's bow, the texture of an emerging shadow along his upper lip and jaw.

"I want to talk to you about something," I whisper and return my hand to his hip.

His smile fades as he sees my face, which I know, even in the dark is more pensive than provocative. "Is this the kind of thing we should talk about at two in the morning before I go out of town for two weeks?"

"No. Probably not," I say reluctantly and snuggle toward his chest. I might be able to fall asleep if he holds me close.

"Where are you going?" he whispers into the top of my head. "You can't just leave it like that. I won't be able to sleep. What is this about?" He tries to push me back from him so that he can see me.

"You make me nervous," I say. "I don't always say the right thing with you." The dark, it's made me honest. I tent my fingers against his chest, then flattened my palm again, my fingertips brushing the errant strands of chest hair.

He doesn't say anything, and his breathing has become so calm, his chest moving under my palm, I wonder whether he's fallen asleep again.

"Hmm," he says at last. "You know, one of the reasons I fell for you so hard, back then—now, too, I guess—I just felt like I could talk to you. I could just be me. You can talk to me, too. There is no *right thing*." His eyes are still closed, which combined with the dark and his words gives me courage.

I rest my hand on his chest, feeling his heartbeat, strong under my palm. He opens his eyes, looking greedy, too.

"I wondered—and I know we've only talked about this a little—but I think I'm ready to sell this house. I think I'm ready to buy something with you." I press the pillow down under my cheek, which gives me an unobstructed view of him. "The past few months have been really hard—to say the least. I feel like with the police getting Kurt, with us getting married, with your movie... I want to start fresh. I want a place for *us*."

"Are you sure?" he asks as if he kind of can't believe it.

"Well, I need to talk to Penny and Colin; this will be hard for them, especially Penny, and I don't want to rush it. Take our time. Find something really perfect. For all of us."

Austin adjusts his head on his pillow, and his eyes trace the shape of my face, but he says nothing. The silence is unnerving, and I regret bringing up the topic at two in the morning before he goes out of town for two weeks.

"How long have you been thinking about this?" he finally asks.

"I guess about thirteen hours."

I feel his body shake with laughter, then his lips find the top of my head again. "I love you so much, Bee," he says, still laughing. "I really do. I wish..." He stops, his words skidding to a halt. Even his breath stops. He pulls back from me. Partially he's tired —so am I—and the fatigue creases his forehead and the corners of his eyes. His jaw tightens and relaxes as he stares at me, and he could be brokering an international peace treaty for as serious as he is.

"What?" I ask.

His jaw stops its movement, and his eyes hold to mine. "I wish I'd fought for you. Then. I... I should have fought for you."

"Austin," I say trying to warn him off whatever he might say next. I understand the hypothetical he's toying with, but there's no way for me to toy with it, too.

"I should have fought for you," he says again, but pulls me into his chest as if he knows there's nothing I can say in response. "Yes," he says finally. "I'll call Jenna on the way to the airport."

forty-nine

The Harold Washington Library is one of my favorite buildings in all of Chicago. The gothic roof, green above the imposing red brick, is unlike any other building in the entire city.

Admittedly, I'm partial to libraries, though.

After I dropped Austin off at the airport, promising him that I'd text him the minute I heard anything from Jenna, I took Penny and Colin to school, went for a run, then showered. As I stood in my closet tossing my running clothes into the laundry basket, I had an idea of how I might spend the first day of the two weeks Austin and I will be apart.

I walk up to the circulation desk. A real librarian sits on the other side of the counter. No work-study students at the Harold Washington Library.

"Hi," I whisper.

"Yes?" the librarian replies, her voice only slightly louder than mine.

"Hi... I'm wondering if you have the DVD of the first season of an old TV show from the 1990s called *The Maple Street Martins.*"

She groans, then chuckles.

"What?" I ask, matching her smile. When it comes to the legacy of Austin Lewis, I've learned it's hard to know what to expect.

"We definitely have that on DVD," she says. "All six seasons, actually."

"What? What's funny?" I try to sound curious rather than defensive, which is what I feel.

"Oh, let me tell you, there's nothing funny about *The Maple Street Martins*," she says even though I'm pretty sure she'd just been laughing. She gets up from behind her desk, and I see that her tag identifies her as Terese. She looks about my age, but I suspect she's not a fan, both because she can laugh about the show and because she doesn't appear to recognize me.

"Follow me," she says, stepping out from behind the desk.

As it turns out, *The Maple Street Martins* have been a real pain in Terese's ass. She takes me to the television section of the DVDs, walking her fingers across the cases until she lands on a box of three discs: Season 1, a gift of the estate of Selma Ritner.

Noting my confusion, she explains, "The DVDs are really expensive for libraries to license. These were donated about three years ago, and it caused quite the kerfuffle when we got a full set."

"Kerfuffle?" I ask.

"Yeah. They're supposed to be in circulation, but we don't allow people to check them out. You have to watch them while you're here. They're technically part of the rare objects collection because you can't get the complete set on DVD anymore."

I consider asking her whether they should be kept behind the reference desk with the grad school test prep books, but those books probably aren't very valuable anymore because everything is online.

"The fans of this show are just awful," she continues. "Sorry if you are one." She appears chagrined, like she said more than she meant to, but I shake my head.

"Not a fan. Just doing a little research," I say.

"We had a few fans throw a real fit about the fact that these aren't part of our digital collection, and they can't be streamed through the library app. But of course, they just want to burn them which is a felony." She seems ready to say more but must have decided against it. "What research?" she asks instead.

"What?"

"You said you were doing research. For what?"

"Oh." I scramble for an explanation. "I'm writing an article for my alumni magazine on what life was like in the late-90s when I graduated from college. Thought I'd say something about this show, but I didn't watch it back then."

"That's fun." She hands me the box for the first season. On the cover is a very young Austin Lewis and his TV-family. I can't help but smile.

"I'll show you the viewing rooms," Terese says.

I place the first DVD in the tray, select the second episode, and press play.

I only have time for three episodes. I have to get back to my car and pick up Penny and Colin. But I binge episodes two through four and promptly know I'll be coming back until I've finished the series. By the end of episode four, I'm hooked.

Caroline Martin is possibly having an affair at work—a nice twist on the unfaithful husband trope. Katy Martin is being bullied at school *by her teacher*. Daniel is trying really hard to overcome his demons and meets a history professor who recommends he be tested for dyslexia (which he's diagnosed with in episode four). Rachel seeks her parents' attention in a multitude of ways but is lost amid the needs of both her younger sister and her "troubled" older brother.

And Bobby. Bobby is the most interesting part of this show, and I don't think I'm saying that just because I'm biased. His navigation of the early-nineties high school is riveting. I already see the rough outlines of discussions about sex, AIDS, rape culture, racism and police violence, sexuality and gender-identity, things that didn't even have names in 1993 when this season aired.

I check my watch to confirm I don't have time to watch just one more episode, or maybe one more scene from one more episode. I don't. But I come back the next day. And the day after that.

By the middle of the second week, Terese knows I'm not doing research. It doesn't take a person six hours a day of watching episode after episode of *The Maple Street Martins* to write a feature for an alumni magazine. By Tuesday, she's unlocking the viewing room like the request constitutes a personal betrayal. For as much as the Lewnatics are capable of, I can understand how my ostensible affiliation with them doesn't warm her heart.

But I can't help myself. I watch episode after episode, forwarding one to the next the minute the fade-out music cues. With each episode, Austin ages before my eyes, slowly evolving into the man I met in the summer of 1997. Meanwhile, Daniel becomes an advocate for more accommodations for people with learning differences. This embarrasses Rachel, whose middle school friends see Daniel on the news and start teasing her. Bobby is no longer embarrassed of Daniel. By the middle of the fourth season, his plot revolves almost entirely around his on-screen romance with high school girlfriend Beth—they're thinking of having sex, but they're being smart about it, discussions of consent and birth control, of waiting until marriage but knowing that almost no one does. The show still pushes boundaries, but I can see what both Austin and Kurt meant about the Bobby-centric plot lines and the way the show slowly became more derivative melodrama than cutting-edge cultural commentary.

In the penultimate episode of the fourth season, Beth and Bobby have sex. *Skip.*

In the final episode, even though I see it coming, I'm still gobsmacked when Beth tells Bobby she's pregnant (condom mishap apparently—I didn't watch the previous episode), and he scrabbles his savings to pay for her abortion. They don't say the word *abortion* on the show. I can't imagine getting that word onto primetime in 1996. But it's clear that's what happened. Beth and Bobby lie to their parents about spending the night at friends' houses. Then, the two walk into an anonymous looking brown stone building, Bobby with his hand at Beth's back. The season four cliffhanger. The next season, Bobby will remain in high school, for his second senior year. This is the season he was filming when Margot and I visited the set. The sixth season will end it, but the fifth season will begin the decline. It's hard to believe and yet, just like Beth's unintended pregnancy, I see it coming.

I also see why Kurt was so pissed by that point and actually feel kind of bad for the guy; there are entire episodes (plural) in which he doesn't make a single appearance. Everything revolves around Bobby.

I lean back in the chair in the viewing room as the credits float up the screen on the final episode of season four of *The Maple Street Martins*. I have some things to think about—like how I'm going to tell Austin that I'm now a fan of the show (or at least the first four seasons; apparently the next one won't be great, and the last one will be truly terrible). But I feel like the breath has been pulled out of me. The viewing room is hot, my cheeks flushed.

I glance at my watch and still have an hour and a half until school pick up. I could start season five, but as the white printed letters of cast, crew, and music crawl up the screen, I find myself thinking about what the fuck happened to Austin Lewis that he couldn't break through after this. Even as the show started to fall apart, he didn't. His acting remained solid. I think about the movie he's filming and whether that talent is still there. Probably.

We'll need more privacy. The new house is a good idea for several reasons.

I exhale heavily into the room, allowing my arms to fall limp at my side. I feel my eyes glass over—strained for sure from watching entirely too much television over the past week and a half, but also heavy from the weight of my thoughts.

And that's when I see it.

At the end of the credits, with the anti-piracy warning. A logo. I recognize it instantly. I've seen it on correspondence and pleadings, in discovery and emails: Closed captioning available in French, German, Italian, and Spanish. © InterVids.

My first instinct is denial. It has to be a mistake. I pause the screen, unable to come up with an explanation: *The Maple Street Martins* was one of my clients? Well, more accurately, one of my client's clients. I was the attorney who enforced the copyright for the foreign language captioning of *The Maple Street Martins*.

I examine the DVD cover for the date. Several are listed, and it's hard to tell, even for me, what they designate. The copyright of the first season would have been 1993. The DVDs look like they were copyrighted in 2010, but that doesn't mean that's when the captioning was copyrighted. InterVids became my client in 2008. Right after Penny was born. I worked my ass off for that client. I made partner because of that client. And in

August of last year, I lost my job because of that client. And then forty minutes later, I met Austin. Again.

My mouth is dry, and I have trouble swallowing.

Austin.

The name creeps through my mind like a dream fading with the morning. I remember some of the pieces, but they seem unordered, disconnected from the story that made sense in my sleep.

Austin.

I was the attorney who managed the copyright on the translation for the international distribution of *The Maple Street Martins* DVDs. I would have done it for every single country the show has aired in since 2008. For nearly fifteen years, I was InterVids. And then my associates were InterVids.

I've been staring at the back of the DVD case for twenty minutes, the logo of my most lucrative client paused on the screen in front of me. I force my feet to move, my legs to hold me up. I take the discs and place them on a tan, metal book cart, which isn't where they belong. They're supposed to be returned to Terese at the circulation desk so that she can ensure they haven't been stolen.

I leave the library.

I pick up my kids from school.

Nothing coheres.

fifty

"Mom? Mom, are you okay?" It's Penny.

We're eating dinner and despite not having a job, and my fiancé being out of town, and there being precious little to occupy my time, I've only managed to prepare the culinary delicacy that is spaghetti with tomato-sauce-from-a-jar. I've failed to ask either of my kids about their day at school and really haven't offered a single verbalization since sitting down at the table. I look at the plate in front of me and see that I also haven't taken a single bite of the food.

"Hmm?" I ask, even though I heard her.

I need more time to answer even that simple question. Am I okay? Not to sound like a lawyer, but that probably depends. I try to create a scenario in my head in which Austin doesn't know that I was the attorney who managed the copyright infringement on the foreign language captioning of the international distribution of *The Maple Street Martins*. Until he fired me. Or his company did. Or his company's company did. I wonder whether there are enough layers between InterVids and Austin that Austin conceivably might not know. After all, his was just one show. That client had over two thousand holdings.

"Are you okay?" Penny asks again.

Colin puts down his fork and awaits an answer.

"Yes. Just distracted. Tired, I think."

I force small talk. Are you excited for summer break? Have you cleaned out your lockers? Do you have homework tonight? Probably should go do that.

Penny and Colin finish their meals and take their plates to the sink, then head up to their rooms. I go to the office and close the doors. I text Mark.

> Me: Hi. It's Babs. New number. Do you have a minute. I need a favor.

My phone rings, which is more than I'd expected in response to my text, but I answer.

"What the fuck is going on with you?" he asks as soon as I answer. "I've been trying to get ahold of you for months. My emails are bouncing back, your phone is disconnected, you're not on social media anymore. And then Kelly tells me someone tried to kill you while you were running along the lake in February?"

"I need a favor," I say as if it's possible he thought I'd texted to discuss the various events he just recited.

"What kind?" he asks, his voice still elevated, the question taking the form of a demand.

"I'm getting married—"

"You're getting married?" he asks, incredulous. "How do I not know this? I thought we were friends."

"Are we? What kinds of texts have you been sending the number I no longer have?"

"Fuck you, Babs. I've been worried about you." The two statements seem at odds with each other, and I think it's more likely he's insulted than worried. How dare I fall in love again and it not be with him?

"I need a favor, and you owe me," I say.

"I owe you? For what?"

"For all of it," I growl and am met with nothing more than the sound of his breath against the phone.

"Now's not a good time, Babs," he says, finally.

"Why did you call me, then?" I ask.

"Because I figured it must be an emergency if you were calling me."

"It is an emergency," I say. It kind of is. I have about two and a half days to get as much information about InterVids's connection with Austin as I can. I already have questions for Austin, but I know you don't show up to a deposition before you've completed initial discovery.

"Fine." I hear a door close in the background.

"I need to know when *The Maple Street Martins* became a client of InterVids. Do we have their client list from '08? Not the firm's clients, InterVids's clients. Our client's clients."

"That Martins show was an InterVids client?" he asks.

I feel at least somewhat vindicated by the fact he also doesn't know. Of InterVids's two thousand products, we would have enforced the translation and dubbing copyrights but would have done so as a bundle—all shows combined, listed in an appendix. Did I ever read that whole list?

"Apparently," I say. "Do we still have the InterVids client list for the years we represented them?"

"I don't know, Babs. They pulled all their files out of the share-drive when they fired us. I don't know what's in there now. Pleadings and correspondence maybe. I'd be surprised if they left anything proprietary. Why do you want to know?"

"I can't tell you," I say.

"Are you poaching that client back? Are you going to open your own firm?" He's on alert.

I hadn't thought of that particular cover story, but it's a

good one. "Yep. And don't say a fucking word. Just get me the client list."

"I don't know if I can do that," he says. "I really don't know if its still there. I'll look tomorrow when I'm at work. Maybe it's attached to a motion or something."

"Thank you, Mark. I really appreciate it," I say.

"I have to go," he says and ends the call before I get a chance to say good-bye.

My phone buzzes again, and I jump. It's Austin FaceTiming. Sweet Jesus, his timing. This will be the greatest performance of my life, which isn't really setting the bar very high.

"Hieee!" I say, already flubbing my lines.

"Hi?" he replies. "Everything okay there?"

"Yes. I'm just excited to hear from you. I missed you today." I can do this. I can do this.

"I missed you, too. Take a look at this view." He turns his phone, and I see the ocean and the horizon, already turning pink. It's after five there.

"Where are you?" I ask.

"My hotel," he says, turning the phone back around toward himself. He sounds so happy; this must be some kind of mistake. "What did you do today?" he asks, and I almost throw up.

"Watched TV," I say. "Went to the library."

"Sounds like you took it easy. That's good."

"How's filming going?" I ask.

"Good. We're not done yet today. I have to go back. We're filming a night scene. I can't talk for long. I just wanted to call and tell you I miss you and I love you and I can't wait to see you this weekend."

"I miss you, too," I say. It's easy to deliver that line because, still, it's true.

"Think of me tonight?" he says, sounding just a little wicked.

"I will," I say, trying to sound seductive. He laughs so I probably didn't exactly nail *seductive*. "Think of me?"

"Babs, I can't *not* think about you," he says, and I wonder how I can possibly love someone so much and trust them so little. "Love you. Sleep tight," he says.

"I love you, too," I say and watch his face disappear.

I return my attention to the computer in front of me. I could do nothing. And if I do nothing, I will learn nothing, I will know nothing. I will be in love with someone who is in love with me, getting married, going to Rome, buying a house. I will be Austin's wife.

I google InterVids, but I already know what I'll find. The company doesn't maintain a true website. The street address of their physical office is the only thing Google has to say about them. They don't need more than a mailing address—they don't sell anything on the retail market so don't advertise anything. They exist for the sole purpose of arranging for the international distribution of U.S. media products. That includes television shows, movies, video games, some audiobooks, limited run series. We managed the copyrights for translation and closed captioning, images on boxes and book covers, remastered products, variations in packaging to target foreign markets. InterVids embedded anti-piracy software and monitored the market, and we wrote cease and desist letters, filed restraining orders and occasionally, infringement suits. But never once did I do that for *The Maple Street Martins*.

I sit back in the chair behind the desk, looking at the blurry white building corresponding with the address for InterVids. It's possible. It's possible Austin doesn't know. If *The Maple Street Martins* never had a problem, never blipped on InterVids's infringement radar, I never would have interacted directly with that show. I'd never have had any reason to know they were one of my client's clients and neither would he.

I obsessively pick through my memories of Austin's and my interactions. Had I ever mentioned the name of the client I'd lost? Had I explained in detail what it did, what I did for them? It could be a coincidence. Maybe even a happy one. *Oh my gosh, can you believe... all these years...*

I close the browser and set my computer to "sleep." Then I get up from the office, go to the bathroom in the hall, and vomit.

fifty-one

I WAKE THE NEXT MORNING AND RUN AT MY OLD TIME—5:30 A.M. Austin asked me not to, but there's no reason he needs to know, and I suspect we aren't in the practice of telling each other everything. I return home, shower, take Penny and Colin to their last day of school for the year and head directly back to the library. I don't watch the DVDs; I'm there for the library's internet. I don't want any search history, not even a cookie, attached to my home computer.

> Me: What was the name of InterVids's in-house counsel? We took her to all those Cubs games.

Mark: How the fuck would I know that? That was your client.

> Me: It was your client too.

Mark: Melissa something.

> Me: Monika.

> Mark: Flessing. What are you up to?

I set my phone down and google the hell out of Monika Flessing. I desperately want to call her, and I briefly consider whether I can do so under the pretense of "catching up." But if she's as closely connected to Austin's businesses as it appears, I can't be confident she won't call him and tell him I've started asking questions. So, it's just me and Google.

Monika Flessing is in-house counsel and the registered agent for accepting service of process for InterVids. That's all I can remember about her. Well, I remember some other stuff too because I had to sit through more than ten years of Cubs and Bulls games with her as part of "client entertainment." So, I know she's married; she lives in California; she has three boys; and she's approximately five years older than I am. I also know that she doesn't read, doesn't belong to a church, and doesn't maintain any social media presence at all (not even a LinkedIn account). I don't know what else I'm looking for, what else I want to know about her. I suppose I want to know whatever I can find out.

Google tells me only that Monika Flessing is an attorney licensed to practice in California. The California Department of Professional Regulation tells me she has been licensed to practice in California since 1995, which makes her more like seven years older than me. She passed the bar when I was graduating from high school, and it might not be the first bar she passed. But I don't even know enough about Monika to know if "Flessing" is a married or maiden name. I don't know if she's a native of California. I always assumed she was just spectacularly boring. As I struggle to find additional modifiers to add to her name, I begin to think perhaps she's been spectacularly guarded.

I wrack my brain until the sliver of a memory of her

husband percolates up. Greg. His name is Greg. Last name, unknown. I google him under the assumption that his name is Greg Flessing and get lucky. He's an attorney, too. Works for the firm of Baird Barner & Coolidge also located in L.A. His profile resembles mine—a waxy, posed photo surrounded by a professional biography. According to his bio, he graduated from law school in 1993. NYU. I note that Baird Barner & Coolidge has offices in L.A., Chicago, Atlanta, and New York. They also have an office in Vevey, Switzerland, which I assume is really a partner's vacation home serving as a business write-off. Bruce did that with a home in Boca.

I resign myself to both Monika and Greg Flessing, like InterVids, being dead ends, when I remember that Austin's sister is an attorney in New York. I click the New York office for BBC and search for "attorneys by last name", clicking on the "Ls." Lewis? Her first name is Ellen, and as I turn her name over in my head, I'm pretty sure Austin said her last name was Lewis. I needed it for the guest list. But my search returns only one Lewis at BBC New York: Jodi. From the looks of it, Jodi is a baby associate.

Best of luck to you, Jodi. It's a long slog to the top in Big Law.

Back to Google. New York + Baird Barner & Coolidge + Ellen... Google suggests Klein. I click. Ellen Klein, Partner at the New York office of Baird Barner & Coolidge is, without question, the woman in Austin's family photographs.

She graduated from NYU Law in 1994. It takes me a minute to connect the dots. It isn't a direct line, Austin's sister to Monika's husband. And there is still the possibility I'm wrong. Maybe I have the wrong Greg Flessing. Maybe Monika's Greg is one of the other five thousand hits Google returns. Maybe he owns the heating and air conditioning company. Maybe his last name isn't even Flessing. Maybe it's Schumacher.

I'm thinking about this when my phone rings. It's Mark.

"Hey. What did you find?" I ask.

"Are you marrying Austin Lewis?" he whispers. "Is that who you're marrying?"

"Why are you whispering?" I'm whispering because I'm in a library.

"Because I feel like I'm not supposed to be doing this!" he hisses. "Are you marrying a client?"

"He wasn't our client. That's what I'm trying to figure out."

"I don't understand."

"I think Austin knew I was handling the copyright on the captioning for his show. And I think he hid that from me. I don't understand why he would do that."

"Maybe because he knows you're not supposed to fuck your clients, Babs. How long has this been going on?"

"No! You don't understand. I'm not even sure if he *was* my client." I attempt another explanation, but don't know where to start. The meeting in college? The reunion in Starbucks?

"I don't want any part of this," Mark says. "I'm out."

"What do you mean, *you're out*? Just tell me what you found. They're *my* files," I say.

"Not anymore."

"Fine. They're the *firm's* files. Whatever. What did you find?"

He pauses, then I can almost hear him make a decision. "I have one list attached to one set of discovery from 2015. *The Maple Street Martins* isn't on it. And by the way: titles that begin with 'the' aren't alphabetized under 'T'. This list has easily 200 titles that begin with 'the' all alphabetized under 'T'." His voice elevates with indignation.

"I didn't alphabetize the list, Mark. It came to me already compiled. Page after fucking page." Now I'm indignant. I was a reference librarian; I know how to alphabetize titles. "Can you email me the list?"

"Babs. No. This list is proprietary."

"Mark," I say, calmly. I'm not above begging, but I really don't want to.

"Babs," he returns as if it's a roll call, then adds, "It's not my fault you can't remember who your clients were."

"This isn't my client. This is my client's clients. And the only time I ever paid attention to the individual name of an InterVids product was if there was some issue with their copyright. Like, the Spanish dubbed version of that *Green Lantern* cartoon was always showing up on pirated websites. I was constantly writing cease and desists for that show."

Mark's quiet on the other end, waiting for me to either say something or end the call.

"Where did the files *go*?" I ask.

"What do you mean where did they go?"

"What firm picked up InterVids? Is there a transfer letter to the new firm?" I ask. I hear him typing.

"Um... Jesus!" he exclaims. "They went with the L.A. office of Baird Barner & Coolidge. Kind of a big gun for a niche client. I wonder why they would do that," and before I explain, he says, "Oh, wait, I guess it makes sense. That was their original counsel before us anyway. So, they just went back to their last firm."

"It's Austin's sister's firm," I say, supplying the missing piece.

"His sister's a lawyer?" Mark asks.

"I need another favor," I say without answering his question.

"Okay." He's already hesitating like he knows this one will hurt.

"I want a cell number," I say.

"Google it," Mark says.

"I don't know where she lives."

"Google her name," he says in a tone he usually reserves for underperforming associates.

"I have. Do you still work with that guy who handled the Rybarczyk case? Can you have him get it for me?"

"Not unless I absolutely have to," Mark says. "Who's number do you want?"

"Samantha Mason. Austin's ex-wife."

Mark doesn't respond right away, but I know he's still there. "I'd rather email you the InterVids product list," he says.

"Tell him I'll give him $50,000 if he can get me a phone number by close of business."

"Babs, this is not a good idea." Mark speaks slowly, calmly, but his voice is filled with dread, and also, he isn't wrong. "If you're paying fifty-grand to track down your fiancé's ex-wife, that's enough for you to know you shouldn't be with him. You don't *have* to talk to her; you need to end the relationship."

"All due respect, Mark, but I'm not taking relationship tips from you. I'll give you a finder's fee if your guy agrees. Five thousand dollars?"

"I don't want your fucking money. If you want your fiancé's ex-wife's phone number and you want to pay fifty-grand for it, I can set that up. As they say in this city: I know a guy."

"I want the number," I say. I know it's crazy, and that Mark is right, but I have to know. I have to understand. I can't end my relationship with Austin on a weird vibe or some strange business dealings.

"I'll text you the info for the wire transfer. He's going to want the money before he starts the search," Mark says.

"Half to start. Half when I get a phone number," I say.

Mark doesn't respond. He simply ends the call. Three minutes later, he texts me the info for the electronic transfer.

My next call is to Rishi. I need him to move some money, which is what he does for a living. Specifically, I need him to move fifty-thousand dollars into my checking account. And he is going to want to know why. For this, I step into one of the library's private reading rooms and close the door behind me.

When he answers the phone, I tell him I need the money for wedding planning and house hunting, but he doesn't buy it for the length of time it took me to utter the words.

"Does this have to do with Austin, and you're afraid I'll tell Margot? Because what you're asking me to do right now is technically as your financial advisor, so this would all be confidential. I couldn't discuss this with Margot."

I consider this for a minute. "Yesterday, I learned that Austin's show was one of the shows that was handled by InterVids, or it might have been. I'm trying to find out as much as I can about when and how and why InterVids became my client."

"What's the fifty-K for?" he asks.

"A phone number."

"Whose?"

"Austin's ex-wife's. InterVids became my client about a year after Austin's divorce." My phone buzzes interrupting the conversation. It's Austin. "I have to go. I am directing you to transfer $50,000 into my checking account."

I hear a reluctant "Okay, Babs" as I end the call with Rishi and pick up the call from Austin.

Austin asks what I'm doing. I tell him, reading. I ask him what he's doing. He says he just finished meeting with Micah about both the movie and our wedding. He's walking back to his car. We talk a little more about how much we miss each other, how much he can't wait to come home tomorrow.

I don't know how to explain this other than to say that when I say I miss him, I'm telling the truth. And when I say I love him, that's the truth, too. And when I get off the phone, my heart aches with how certain I am that something is very, very wrong.

I put my head down on the table in the small room and start to cry. A thousand images of Austin flash behind my eyelids: him behind the desk in my home office, curled up next to me on the couch, standing guard by my hospital bed, getting dressed in my closet, sitting next to me at Starbucks. I sniff back the tears and focus on the carpet between my feet—navy and maroon threads in a repeating geometric pattern.

On something that seems like a whim, but under the circumstances absolutely is not, I decide to call Northwestern. It takes a few transfers, but eventually I'm connected with Cheryl in Human Resources.

"Hi," I say, my voice sounding nasally through my tears. "I'm calling to follow up on the posting for an adjunct instructor in copyright law."

"That position's been filled," she says quickly. "But thank you for your interest—"

"No," I cut her off. "I applied for the position and interviewed, but never heard back—"

"Letters went out May seventh," she says with all the efficiency of someone speaking to someone who no longer matters.

"I didn't receive one," I say.

She exhales into the phone, annoyed. "What's your name?"

"Barbara Aganon."

I hear her typing, then she clears her throat. "I show your application was withdrawn on March sixteenth?"

"By whom?"

"By you," she says. "Via email. I'm sorry, could I ask for the last four of your social? I'm not comfortable continuing this conversation. I'm sure you understand."

"2589," I say. "But it's fine. You've been very helpful. Have a nice day." I end the call before she can request more information.

I open my email on my phone and look in both the "sent" and "deleted" items folders. Nothing.

"Kurt?" I ask the room. Why would *he* care? And notwithstanding all of his surveillance, I find it hard to believe he could log on to my email from Arizona without me receiving a *new device* warning.

But Austin could. From my computer in the office. With the ID and password he watched me set up in December.

Questions batter around my mind, crashing and colliding with a reality I thought I understood, a person I thought I knew. Why wouldn't he want me to work? Or is it just Northwestern? He wouldn't want me to work at Northwestern? It's my *alma mater,* and it's part-time.

My heart stops.

I call the Office of Alumni Affairs. A woman named Alicia answers. I introduce myself as "Babs Aganon, alumna."

She asks if I'm calling in response to their request.

"What request?" I ask.

"We sent you an invitation maybe four or five months ago," Alicia says.

"To what?" I am truly confused but suspect that whoever has been sending messages using my email has also been deleting them.

"An invitation to make a gift to the endowment," she responds, her voice far too chipper for my mood.

"I'm not calling about that," I say, thinking I probably do need to make a gift to their endowment. "I would like some more information about a scholarship I received when I was a student at Northwestern."

"Do you remember the name of the scholarship?" Alicia's voice has descended maybe half an octave. She's ready to return to her sales pitch but has a feeling that's not what this call is going to be about.

"The Big Shoulders Law Foundation."

I hear her clicking a few strokes into the keyboard, then she says, "That technically wasn't a scholarship. That was a privately funded gift."

"What's the difference?"

"A scholarship comes from the school. This gift came from an individual. It was processed through philanthropy," she says.

"Who was the individual?"

More key-clicks, then, "The donor asked to remain anonymous. We never learned their name. They only made the one gift to the school. They've refused requests to make another, even when we had prospective students who satisfied their criteria. Anyway, we worked through their attorney to set up the fund."

"Who was the attorney? The one who set it up?" I brace myself to hear Monika Flessing or Baird Barner & Coolidge.

"I'm not sure we're allowed to provide that information," Alicia says, and so help me God, the only reason she isn't giving me that information is because she likes being in a position to say "no" to people.

"Oh, that's too bad. I wanted to use that fund to make my own donation. I was hoping whoever set up my scholarship could help me set up another one."

"It's not a scholarship; it's a privately funded gift. Are you saying you'd be interested in funding The Big Shoulders Law Foundation?" Her voice has traveled back up the octave.

"Maybe. It would be easier if I could just work with the same team that set it up the first time."

"The firm was Rey & West," she says. "Do you need their number?"

"Sure. Save me the trouble of looking it up," I say in a tone so sweet it hurts my teeth.

She gives me the number with an enthusiastic, "Looking forward to working with you on this."

I block the number on my phone and dial the number Alicia gave me. Not surprisingly I'm directed to voicemail. More surprising is the outgoing message:

"Hello. You have reached the voicemail of Micah West of Rey & West—"

I hang up before he can tell me to leave a brief message with my name and contact information.

I put my head down on the table and sob until the snot drips from my nose in a thin, clear line, and the tears pool on the table, and I feel sweaty from the effort of weeping, and broken from the emerging realization that when it comes to Austin Lewis, there are only lies and no truths.

fifty-two

SAMANTHA MASON LIVES IN AUSTRALIA. IN PERTH, SPECIFICALLY. THIS is both good and bad. It's good because it means I can call her at night, and it will be morning for her; I don't have to wait until (my) tomorrow. It's bad because it sure does look like Austin's ex-wife went to literally the ends of the earth to get away from him. She really couldn't have gotten any farther away and remained within the English-speaking world.

Perth is fourteen hours ahead of Chicago. It's 8:36 p.m. in Chicago, making it 10:36 a.m. in Perth. That's the perfect time for someone to receive a phone call from their ex-husband's new fiancée. I'm not surprised when the call goes straight to voicemail. I leave a message introducing myself, explaining that I'd really like to speak with her "about a private matter," and requesting that she please call me back. An hour passes with no return phone call. I call again and leave another message. Another hour goes by. I send a text.

> Me: My name is Babs Aganon. Please call me. I need to speak with you.

> Samantha: I can't talk to you. Leave me alone.

Well, that's something. At least I know I have the right number.

> Me: I'm engaged to Austin Lewis. I need to talk to you.

> Samantha: I know who you are. Leave me alone.

I channel my inner Margot.

> Me: No. I will keep calling and texting you until you talk to me.

No response.

> Me: I am not beyond getting on a plane and flying to Perth.

My phone rings. The number says "unavailable", and my phone has assigned it a "spam risk", but I have a feeling I know who it is.

She doesn't say hello. Her first words are, "I have a family."

"I do, too," I say. See, we have something in common already.

"How did you find me?" she asks.

"I know a guy," I say. "I skiptraced you."

"You *what* me?"

"I hired a private investigator to get me your contact info," I explain.

"Austin's going to find out."

"What would he do if he found out?" I ask.

"To *you*? Nothing. I can't imagine him ever doing anything

to hurt you. I'm pretty much screwed though, so thank you for that."

"Maybe I can protect you. Maybe we can work together to figure some things out." I don't know enough to know how to bargain with her, and she starts laughing on the other end of the line in a low scoff that says, *You don't even know enough to know how to bargain with me.*

"Why don't we start with what you know, and I'll fill in the gaps? If I'm going down, I might as well go down big," she says.

I clear my throat. "I know that Austin seems to have intersected with me in ways I can't explain. His attorney is the same attorney who set up a fund that paid for me to go to law school twenty years ago. The registered agent for one of my former clients is married to a man who works at the same firm as Austin's sister. That was my largest client, and losing that client cost me my job last year, which happened on the same day I ran into Austin at a coffee shop across from my office. I think *The Maple Street Martins* was a client of one of my clients. And I know he never told me any of these things. Not over the past twenty years and not over the past ten months."

"Hmm." She sounds impressed. "I had to divorce him to get that much information about his business dealings."

The questions swim in my head, and I hardly know where to start. "I don't understand the why," I say.

"The why?"

"Yeah," I say. "I don't understand why he wouldn't tell me this. I don't understand why he paid for me to go to law school."

"I mean, he's totally obsessed with you," she says with more than a hint of derision. "He has been for decades. Or, I guess on and off. But certainly on during our marriage. If you can even call it a marriage."

"I still don't understand," I say. This isn't going the way I thought it would.

"Look, I don't have any idea what happened between you two, how long it lasted or whatever, but I get the feeling that he was trying to move on by the time I started dating him, and he could not. Part of that was because of the internet and social media. We got married right before that took off, and I think if it weren't for that, maybe we could have made a go of it, but there was just no way. Not with pictures of you right at his fingertips." She's rambling and reminiscing and not really making much sense. But for as much as she didn't want to take my call, she does want to understand why her marriage failed, and I think maybe I *do* understand how we can bargain.

"It sounds like you might have some questions for me. Maybe we can fill in some gaps for each other," I suggest.

"When did you first meet him?" she asks. She hasn't agreed to a trade, but I think she's playing ball.

"In 1997. We went hiking together." A very abbreviated version of that day.

"How long did you date?" she asks.

"We didn't," I say and am met with absolute silence from the other end of the line. "He asked to see me again, and I think he hoped we could maybe travel back and forth to see each other—I was in undergrad in Boston—but I said no. I was already seeing someone, and I honestly wasn't so sure about the idea of dating someone famous. I felt like I might not be cut out for it." It seems like I'm still not.

"When did you start seeing him again?" she asks. I think of saying it isn't really "again" because there wasn't an initial "seeing each other," but that seems a small point, so I say, "In August, when he was in town for his mother's funeral."

"You didn't have an affair with him in '07 or '08?" she asks.

"No. I had a baby in '08. And not Austin's." I laugh, but it probably isn't funny to her.

"Well, that kind of makes sense, too, I guess," she says.

"What does?"

"So, in 2005, he asked his agent to fix him up," she begins. "Austin had this extensive list with these very specific requirements. He wanted someone who wasn't a huge celebrity, and honestly, he couldn't have gotten a huge celebrity anyway. *He* wasn't a huge celebrity." I can almost hear her rolling her eyes as she says this. She might be a lot of things, but during this conversation, she is undeniably Austin's ex-wife. "He wanted someone who was tall and thin, 'built like a runner,' he said. She had to be at least five years younger than he was. He wanted blonde hair and blue eyes. It felt all very mail order."

"I'll say," I mutter.

"My agent sent his agent a photograph of me, and then we went on a date. That date felt more like an audition, but I don't know what to say. I just totally fell for him, and I ignored all the red flags. My agent said it would be good for my career which was kind of sputtering at that point because I was too old to model but hadn't managed to break into TV or film. I'm sorry, I'm rambling. Is any of this helpful?"

"Yes," I say because, my God, is it. "When did the problems start?"

"Really, the problems started with the way he was going about looking for a girlfriend, but if you're asking when I knew there was something seriously wrong with him? Maybe a couple months after we were married. We got married pretty quickly, so some of this started before that, but I was trying to build a marriage, and that's not at all what he was trying to do."

"What was he trying to do?"

"The only way I can explain it, is that he was trying to cast someone for a role. He was trying to cast *me* in a role, but I didn't understand what the role was. So, I was just being me, and that wasn't making him happy. I thought we were maybe going to try for a baby, so I stopped coloring my hair, and he got very weird about that. I gained a little weight after we got married—I mean, I was stress eating because he was so difficult, and I wasn't modeling anymore, anyway, and man, he got me a personal trainer *likethis*." She says it like it's one word. "I know it sounds weird, but I was crazy about him. I'm sure you can understand why." I can. "I just did whatever he told me to. It probably didn't help that growing up in this industry, I was used to men telling me what to do and just doing it without asking a lot of questions."

I'm actually beginning to feel pity for her, and if she weren't giving me so much of the "why" that I asked for, I'd feel bad for tracking her down and calling her in the first place.

"So, it was probably about a year into the marriage, late-2006 or so, that I started to think he was maybe having an affair. It just didn't make sense to me that I was bending and twisting myself in literally every way he told me to and he still didn't seem to want me." She sounds like she's started crying. I know almost nothing about her, but I hope she has someone in her life who positively adores her.

"I did all the things you'd do if you thought your spouse was having an affair. I stood outside doors and listened to him on the phone. I read his text messages. I went through his computer, through his email. I followed him to Chicago once in 2007, and all I could piece together was that he seemed to be obsessed with some attorney there and was trying to give her a bunch of business. I assumed at the time it was because he was sleeping with her, or... I guess... you. But no?"

"No," I say. "That's right before I landed the InterVids client, but all of that happened through some woman named Monika Flessing. I didn't know Austin was connected with her until yesterday. If Austin had tried to connect with me at that time... that could not have been worse timing. I was trying to get pregnant in '07, had a new baby in '08. I got InterVids right around when I came back from maternity leave. Then I was gearing up to make partner. No. I wasn't even thinking about Austin at that time." I was barely thinking about Ryan, which became its own problem later.

"Well, when he came back from that trip, I confronted him and accused him of having an affair. He didn't deny it. He just said he thought I'd had one too, which I hadn't. But he got to the courthouse first with the filing and alleged infidelity, which was totally unnecessary. He could have just listed irreconcilable differences like everyone else, but I was just really too hurt and sad to fight back."

"I'm so sorry, Samantha," I say, and I mean it sincerely. I feel some responsibility for breaking up her marriage. For the better part of fifteen years, she's imagined I had an affair with her husband, and that's why her marriage fell apart. "Hey. Did you have any problems with his fans?" Austin said that's why she moved to Australia. It sounds like she moved there for a few reasons.

"Oh, yeah. Some. The Lewnatics?" She definitely isn't into puns.

"Yeah."

"What a stupid name," she mutters. If things had been different and I'd met Samantha instead of Austin at Starbucks, we'd have hit it off. "It was harder to do that stuff back then. It was all on message boards, not Facebook groups. But there were a few pretty nasty threads dedicated to how much I sucked. How I wasn't really his type, and he was just doing it for publicity, and it wouldn't last. It probably wouldn't have stung so badly if I hadn't thought he agreed."

She pauses, and the line hums for a few seconds.

"Well, this has all been pretty interesting," she says, and I sense that she wants to get off the phone.

"Wait!" I say. "You said you figured out a lot about his businesses during the divorce?"

"Oh right. Yeah. *I* was pretty depressed, but my lawyer wasn't." She chuckles at this. "She requested a complete production of Austin's business dealings, all of his holdings, every bank account, every shell, every partnership. Literally everything. She alleged that Austin had failed to make material disclosures during the negotiations of our prenup, and I was entitled to half of those assets he hadn't disclosed."

"Smart lawyer," I say, admiring the strategy as I recall Austin's breezy dismissal of my suggestion that we have a prenup.

"I know, right? So, that's when I realized that most of his business dealings are held in a company called RealReel."

"They are?" I ask. "I did a pretty heavy amount of googling and never came across that entity."

"They're located in Vevey."

"Switzerland?" I suddenly remember the BBC office in Switzerland. More than a tax write-off, it seems.

"Yeah. RealReel owns All-In Productions, which is the entity he uses for his producing credit. And it owns a company called Mapletown Marketing that he runs a bunch of other crap through. And RealReel owns an international distribution company called InterVids."

"It *owns* InterVids?" If that's the case, Austin wasn't the client of my client. Austin *was* my client.

"Yeah. That's why I thought you'd continued to see each other over the years. Why else would he give you all this business?"

"Indeed," I mumble in response to a question for which I have no answers.

Samantha doesn't elaborate.

"Hey Babs," she finally says. "I'm really glad you called. I mean, I've violated the hell out of my non-disclosure agreement, but—and I know you probably don't want to hear this—but I loved him. It wasn't just a business arrangement for me. And for fifteen years I've wondered who you were and why you would do this to another woman, or to *your own* family. When I saw that you two were officially together and out as a couple, it really just opened up old wounds for me. And... I don't know. It's just nice to know that you're not what I thought you were."

"I'm sorry I made you violate your NDA." I can't think of what else to say.

"It's okay. It feels worth it." She laughs—a single burst that recognizes the strangeness of our kinship.

"Maybe I'll come to Australia and visit you," I say, knowing that I will never do that. This will be the last time I ever talk to Samantha Mason; we will never meet, and that's probably for the best. She doesn't respond anyway. The conversation is over. She's told me what she knows. I've answered her questions. We're done. We say good-bye and end the call.

fifty-three

IT'S AFTER MIDNIGHT. I TURN OFF THE LIGHT NEXT TO MY BED AND SINK down under the covers. In my head, I see a timeline of my relationship with Ryan. 1997. 1999. 2009. At every point that my relationship with Ryan was threatened, Austin was there. In the shadows. By way of his corporate agent. By way of a wholly owned subsidiary of some wholly owned subsidiary of some company tucked away in Switzerland.

The offer that was too good to pass up at Northwestern, I paid for that with two years of a painful breakup with Ryan.

In 2009, when I was a new mother trying to keep both my career and my marriage on track, Austin was there. Or his company was with its multi-million-dollar book of business, and they wanted me, so I was going to just one more Cubs game, just one more Bulls game with that pedantic woman, who I now realize was really Austin.

He was there when I was chasing partner, slamming me with work that took me away from Ryan and Penny, and I was at the office until eleven at night writing cease and desist letters for the pirated versions of cartoons and movies.

Every low moment, every fissure in my relationship with Ryan, Austin was there.

I no longer feel my heart breaking. I am enraged. I am molten lava in the form of a woman.

The phone buzzes on the table next to me. I resolve that I will not answer it if it's Austin. I am asleep if it's Austin. But it's Margot.

"I have called the police," she says without saying hello. "I want you to know that I have done that."

"On me?" I ask, thinking this has something to do with the lengths I've gone to track down Samantha.

"No."

"Babs?" It's Rishi. I'm on speakerphone. "I want you to listen to me. Are you awake?" I don't know this side of Rishi. Rishi is tall stalks of willow next to a pond, bobbing back and forth in the breeze. But Rishi is not willow tonight. Tonight, he is the wind.

"I'm awake. I haven't fallen asleep yet." I glance at my phone. It's 1:52 a.m.

"Austin owns InterVids," Margot says.

"He owns it through a holding company located in Switzerland," Rishi adds.

"RealReel," I say.

"Yes. How did you know?" he asks, suddenly sounding confused.

"How did you know?" I ask.

"Kurt's book," Margot says. "The nesting doll companies. Mapletown Marketing."

"We'll explain more later," Rishi says. "Mapletown Marketing made a single electronic transfer of $475,000 on October 12, 2020. Don't ask me how I know that."

"Okay," I say.

"And another $525,000 on November 3, 2020." They're quiet, waiting for my reaction.

"That's the day after Ryan died," I say. "Who was the transfer to?"

"Another account, no name attached. I couldn't find the holder. But I'm guessing that on November 2, 2020, they were driving a truck filled with the broken pieces of a sidewalk."

"That's kind of a big leap," I say.

"Is it?" Margot asks.

I don't answer.

"Babs," Margot says. "David's on his way over."

"What? No."

Rishi ignores my protest. "He'll stay with you tonight, and then you and your family are coming to our house tomorrow."

I don't argue further. I don't tell him it isn't necessary. I don't tell him I'm fine. I open the door when David arrives and sit with him at the kitchen table until morning.

The next day, I don't meet Austin at the airport when he returns from L.A. Miranda and Burt do.

six years later

fifty-four

I STUMBLE INTO THE KITCHEN AND THROUGH THE DINING ROOM TO THE living room where I stand at the window next to the piano and stare across the street. The fire hydrant has been painted so many times, its nubby little cap resembles a scoop of ice cream. Mint. No sign of Lasky. The students who rent his building are all parked along the curb. Or I presume they are. I don't actually know which cars belong to which people. I couldn't tell you who is home and who is not, who has a guest staying over, who is parked illegally. I couldn't tell you that based solely on the make and model of the cars along the curb. But Lasky could.

The streetlights cast their blue-white hue on the sidewalk. The yellow warmth of lamps glows through the windows of the houses along the block. I hear Olivia, David's daughter, skip down the stairs.

"Hey Babs," she says cheerfully. She has no idea.

"Hi, sweetie. Are you hungry? I'll get dinner started here in a minute."

"Sounds good," she says. "Did you get Dad's text?"

I reach for my phone in my pocket and realize it's in my coat which is in the garage. "Shit. I missed it."

"His flight's delayed, but he's still getting in tonight. He said he'll take an Uber home, so you don't have to drive all the way out to O'Hare in the middle of the night."

"That's thoughtful of him," I say, hearing my own robotic, monotone voice.

"Are you okay?" she asks.

I turn to her and smile, knowing it's not at all persuasive. "I'm fine. I just have a lot on my mind right now. I'll get dinner started."

She shrugs and scampers upstairs to her room. I hear her door close in the distance, leaving me to my thoughts, which are indeed a lot right now.

I gaze out the living room window onto Seminary Avenue. David comes in through the garage and takes his shoes off next to the door. His roller bag glides along the hardwood floors and stops at the foot of the stairs. He must have caught sight of me sitting in the dark, looking out the window at something and nothing, like my mother used to do.

"Babs," he whispers, "what are you doing still awake?" He glances briefly up the stairs, I'm sure wondering whether Olivia is also awake, but she's been asleep for hours.

He rights his suitcase, lowering the handle, and comes to sit with me on the couch. The moment his body presses into the cushion, I fall against his shoulder.

"What's all this, love?" he asks and wraps an arm around my shoulder. He smells like stale coffee and recycled air. He must be exhausted. He'd flown to Paris to visit his brother for his birthday and was supposed to get into O'Hare by two this afternoon.

"I met with Miranda and Burt today," I say.

"I thought that was next week. I was going to go with you."

"They called this morning. Lasky's talking."

David's chest expands with a single, cleansing breath that he exhales with a *hmm*.

I continue staring through the window, and David's arm tightens protectively around my shoulder.

"Austin was watching for years," I say. "He came to town every time Monika did. And he was here the night Ryan died." The words fall out of my mouth like marbles—heavy, noisy, clattering to the floor and rolling away.

"Why didn't they figure this out six years ago?" David asks. The accusatory tone of his voice contrasts with the dull, round shape of my words.

"They were focused on the money," I say, poorly summarizing Miranda's response to that very question, which I'd posed to her in equally accusatory terms this morning. "They were looking for bank records, electronic transfers, tax returns."

David brings his lips to my temple. Across the street is the Resident Permit Parking Only sign that the alderman agreed to at the request of the FBI in exchange for the city prioritizing the ward in the construction of new wheelchair-accessible sidewalk ramps, which appeased the business owners, who were pissed about the Resident Permit Parking Only signage.

Hashtag Chicago.

All of this, so that the FBI could persuade Lasky to testify about nearly fifteen years of observations of Austin Lewis parked along the street. Watching. Studying. Waiting. All those times I was so certain someone was there. For years. Someone was.

The fire hydrant that Austin occasionally parked his rental cars in front of, where he repeatedly garnered the attention of the vigilant landlord, glows under the streetlight. No one is parked there now. No one has been parked there for a long time.

For some months after Austin was arrested, the street was packed full of TV news vans and reporters. They blocked the hydrant and the alley, and knocked on my door, and followed my kids, and for a solid three months, I lived in hell. All three of us did.

I tried to protect Penny and Colin from as much of it as I could, but between television and school friends, they learned everything. Every sordid detail, every truth, every lie about the man who had been their mother's client, and boyfriend, and fiancé, and very nearly their step-father.

Austin was charged with tax evasion. That's it. That's all they could get him on. And he pleaded out on the charge. He was sentenced to ten years. The prosecutor said he thought Austin would serve less than half that.

I wasn't surprised. I saw the direction things were headed pretty early on. The man who drove the truck that killed Ryan had long since disappeared, not unlike the woman Kurt hired to attack me. Micah West provided contracts for the 2020 purchase of two television shows that were added to InterVids's inventory for distribution in Spain. These, he told the FBI, explained the wire transfers from Austin's company in Switzerland. The dates were a coincidence. Combined with the statements given to the police by the long-gone driver that showed he was hysterical and crying, that Ryan was texting on his phone, and that he stepped out against the light on that dark, rainy November night, the prosecutor said it was more than enough to establish reasonable doubt. It was enough, frankly, to establish reasonable doubt in *me*.

The stalking claim was even weaker. The only admissible evidence they had that Austin had interacted with me in any way was that he paid for my entire law school education and, for more than a decade, gave me my most lucrative book of business. Both acts, the prosecutor explained, would probably be interpreted by a jury as kindness—more so because he'd done them anonymously, asking for nothing in return. Honestly, I began to have second thoughts myself. Was I overreacting? Was this stalking? What really was the difference between him following my life through Monika, and me following his through Instagram?

Miranda said the Lewnatics saw things in much the same way the prosecutor warned a jury would. More than that—the prevailing narrative was that I drove the man crazy. I gaslighted him. I happily took the money from his business and led him on for years but never loved him. In short, the Lewnatics are lunatics.

"They want me to meet with him," I say into David's chest.

He responds exactly as I imagined he would, shooting forward from the couch cushions and twisting so that he's facing me, eyes wide in horror. "They what?"

"It's a stupid plan. It's not going to work," I say, slumping forward. "They think if I say I still love him and offer to get back together with him, he'll tell me the truth about everything, and they can charge him with the rest of it. The stalking... Ryan."

"You're married," David exclaims. "*To me*," he adds as if I might have forgotten.

One corner of my mouth inches up; I'd pointed out the same thing.

"Are you going to do it?" he asks, reclining back into the couch and taking me with him.

I rest an arm around his waist. "He'll know I'm married. He'll know I married *you*. It's not going to work. He won't tell me anything."

We sit for a few more minutes, David's lips against the top of my head in a prolonged kiss. I can hear him breathing and picture his face—eyes closed, his cheek coming to rest where his lips had been as if sealing the kiss to me.

"Come," he says eventually and rises from the couch. "Come to bed, love. We don't have to sleep. But we both need some rest."

fifty-five

I LOOK AT MY WATCH. I NEED TO LEAVE, OR I'LL BE LATE. I'D WRITTEN to Austin and asked him to give me thirty minutes of his time. I don't understand what happened, I wrote. I still have questions. Would he consider it?

"Yes," he replied within three days of getting the letter. He signed his letter "Love always, Austin." I shivered when I read it, but I showed it to Miranda and Burt, and both of them nodded to each other as if they'd fully expected it.

I didn't lie either. I do still have questions, and I don't understand what happened. When I picture the last thirty years of my life, I imagine Austin as a cat, and me with the illusion of free will when really, I was nothing more than a small felt ball, bouncing in whatever direction he batted me. Even now, I wonder which of us will actually be manipulating the other when we meet.

I let him select the location, and he chose the shelter at Promontory Point. Outdoors. Cold, but empty. I arrive, park my car, and walk alone under the viaduct. The FBI placed microphones in the shelter and in the zipper of my coat. I know they say criminals are stupid, but I can't imagine Austin being stupid enough to confide one fucking thing in me. I half expect him not even to show up. Or to sneak up behind me and kill me as I'm walking under the viaduct.

On impulse I turn around and look behind me. Nothing. I close my eyes and shake off my nerves and see Austin and me walking hand-in-hand under this viaduct seven years ago. I feel his hand cupping my face, his breath against my ear. The promise of that time in my life, my optimism then, constricts around my ribs like the medieval tools of torture that tightened one clockwise turn at a time.

I lean against the wall of the viaduct. I can't do this. I can't look at him and pretend I love him when I hate him so much now and loved him once in equal proportion. I wish he were dead, and there was nearly a year when he was my entire life.

I bend over, resting my hands against my knees, gasping for breath.

"Babs!" It's him.

I turn my head to the side and see him running toward me. I want him to look worn. I want him to look like he's spent six years in prison, eating gruel and tarring the roofs of prohibition-era buildings. That was a different movie, I guess. He looks fine. More than fine. A few years older. Well dressed. He made a ton of money with the QAnon movie. The overlap between "Rich" and Austin resonated with audiences. I'm surprised he wasn't nominated for an Oscar. He could have accepted it from prison.

He's with me in seconds, bent over next to me, his hand on my back. I know the expression he wears, this anxiety and his chivalrous knight-to-the-rescue routine.

"Are you okay?" he asks.

I want to tell him to get his fucking hands off me. I want to smash his face into the concrete walls of the viaduct, but I can barely breathe, and instead, he's picked me up, an arm under my legs and another around back, and I remember this. I remember his chest and his arms and the way his body smells. Not his detergent, not his aftershave or soap, but some scent under that that is his only and that lingered in my house, and in my bed, even after I washed the sheets until one day, I called Restoration Hardware and told them I was redoing the room from floor to ceiling.

He carries me not to the shelter where the microphones are, but to the playground on the other side of the bike path. There's a picnic table there. I still have the microphone in my coat, but I've already messed this up.

He sits me down on the bench and straddles the wooden planks that comprise the seat. He waits for me to compose myself.

"I don't want to talk to you," I say.

"Okay," he says, but doesn't move to leave.

It takes more than a few minutes to gather myself. I see my children. I see Margot. I see what he did to us. I examine the grain of the wood in the picnic table and try to call back the lines I've rehearsed—the lines Burt and Miranda wrote for me.

When they handed me the first script, I laughed. "You must be kidding," I said. "He'd never believe I'd say something like this."

They let me re-write it, but it's still not great.

"I miss you," I say, which isn't as hard to say as I thought it would be because, in a way, I do. I miss what I thought he was. "I still love you."

He's silent for a beat. Then he sniffs. Maybe from the cold, maybe it's a laugh. "No, you don't," he says. "You're working with the FBI. They've reopened Ryan's case."

I tense immediately, and my eyes shoot in his direction. My chin starts to tremble. This was a terrible idea. How could I have been so stupid?

His eyes bore into mine, and my breath emerges in ragged staccatos. It's forty-seven degrees, but it could be seventeen below.

"See," he says. "That's not love. That's not why you're here."

I start to rise. I'm prepared to run. I'm always prepared to run.

"Sit," he says calmly, almost kindly. "You have questions. I can't answer all of them. But I'll answer the ones I can."

It takes me another minute. I have to remind myself that even if we're not in the shelter, there are still armed agents hiding in the women's restroom there, and they've probably realized I'm on the other side of the path. I have to assume they're keeping an eye on me.

I clear my throat. If we're off script, I'll ask the questions that matter most to me.

"How much of my life was mine?" It's an enormous vulnerability to betray, but I can't help it. In addition to the sense that I haven't actually been living *my* life, I'm overwhelmed by the fear that my life has been a lie. Did Northwestern really want me? Was I even a good lawyer? Why is my daughter's name Penny? And how could someone who said he loved me, have caused me so much pain? "Why would you do this to me? Why would you hurt me like this?" A more ambiguous question that is paradoxically an easier place to start.

Austin gazes at me, his brows knit together as if the questions wound him. "Babs," he says, and I know this voice, this low, near-whisper. "I never wanted to hurt you. I just—" He searches for the words. "I just wanted you. I still do."

This stuns me. "I can't trust you. How do I know what's true?" I ask, reconnecting with words I've rehearsed that unexpectedly have turned out to be exactly what I would say.

"It's all true, Babs. God, I fell for you immediately. I thought about leaving this business for you. I would have moved to

Boston for you—or Chicago. I thought the reason you didn't want to be with me was because you didn't want the pressure of the fame and the spotlight and all that. I didn't lie to you. You lied to me," he says.

"How so?" I demand.

"You didn't tell me you were already in love with someone else."

I feel the guilt instantly. I didn't tell him this. In fact, I hid it from him. And while it's true that I wanted no part of the *Tiger Beat* scene I saw my sister immersed in, when it came down to it, I was just already in love.

He can see my shame and continues. "I came out to Boston," he says. "I bet you didn't know that."

"I didn't," I say quietly.

"That September. I was going to fall on my knees, profess my love, shower you with gifts. But when I finally found you, I think it was after track practice—"

"Cross-country," I say reflexively and regret interrupting him. I know where he found me. Probably walking to the cafeteria with Ryan, which is what I did nearly every day after practice in the fall of 1997.

"When I finally found you, you were with Ryan. I'll be honest, I didn't think that would last. I figured I could bide my time and wait for him to go to medical school, and you'd move on. If you were... distractible enough to fool around with me during one summer between school years, there was no way you were going to make it through an entire year apart."

This comment stings. It's probably intended to. It's hard for me to know whether Austin is trying to plead a case of love or inflict a world of hurt. Maybe both.

"The scholarship," I say, now understanding. "It was about keeping us apart." I drop my head into my hands. "Why didn't you make your move then?" My voice is a provocation. I could have followed up with "Chicken?"

"I thought I had time," he says. I hadn't expected him to respond at all, but he continues. "I thought I could finish the show I was working on, let you sow your wild oats, which you appeared to be enjoying doing, and then when you got all of that out of your system, I'd find you in Chicago right where I put you. But you didn't even make it to graduation before you were back with him. I never had a chance."

"And InterVids? Why did you give me that business?" We're getting closer to topics he'd probably rather not speak on. "Please," I say. "You don't know what it's like. I don't understand *my own life*."

He drops his head shaking it back and forth. I'm just beginning to think he's said all he's going to, when he lifts his eyes pleading with me. "I didn't mean for it to go on like it did," he says. "I thought for sure that with you working so hard, Ryan would leave you for one of the women he was sleeping with."

My body jerks back at his reference to Ryan, to affairs. Plural. Women? This was the worst of my fears, and he has confirmed it as casually as if he were talking about Ryan's favorite movie. I've lost track of the conversation, but Austin has continued talking.

"...then I'd stop sending Monika out, and we could reconnect. But instead, *you* started fooling around with Mark. I thought your marriage was over, but Ryan took you back. My mistake has always been thinking I should be patient, wait for an opening. But an opening never came. Once you had Colin, I knew it was over for me. You were never leaving Ryan. I figured there was a decent chance Ryan would eventually leave you, but I couldn't wait my whole life for that. So, I gave up. Monika gave me updates on you, and it was nice to hear that things were going well. I wanted that for you. I just wanted that for you *with me*. But I gave up on it."

It's an extraordinary amount of surveillance. Far beyond what I'd imagined, and I'm coming to understand that there has been very little of my adult life that I have lived out of the supervision of Austin Lewis.

"You were always there," I say. "I could *feel* it. I thought I was crazy."

He shakes his head as if there's no way to make me understand, and I think there probably isn't. "*You* were always there," he says. He pauses, catches his breath, then his eyes meet mine with so much intensity I think the blood has stopped moving through my veins, and he says, "You are my sorrow. You are my grief at what I could have been. I could have been your lover, your partner, your husband, the father of your children." He looks out toward the shelter. "I almost was," he says as if he's reminding himself.

His eyes wander back to me, and I see something like hope in them. Can he possibly think? Does he truly believe?

"I waited for you for half my life," he says as if it has only just now dawned on him. "Half of my life. I thought if I could just get the timing right, if I could just be in the right place at the right time—at your aunt and uncle's house, in Boston, at your law school, your firm. But it was never the right time. It was never *going to be* the right time for me. For us."

"You did it, didn't you," I say, finally. The reason I'm here. "You had him killed. Ryan." I'm feeling the momentum that comes with clarity.

"I did not kill your husband, Babs," he says. "I have done a lot here that you are entitled to be angry about, but not that."

But of course he would say that.

"At the very least, you were glad he died," I say, directing every ounce of hatred I can muster at him. "How did you celebrate that news?"

Austin is still. He doesn't argue with me. He is stone. And then, "Babs, he was never good enough for you. How could you be with someone like that? Someone who demanded your loyalty but gave you none of his. He was cheating on you when you were pregnant with Colin. Hell, he was cheating on you when he died. Do you really think all those late nights were him doing tonsillectomies? In the middle of a fucking pandemic? Hospitals canceling appointments left and right, and he's coming home in the middle of the night two, three times a week?"

I can't help myself; I want to be angry at him for the accusation, but I just start to cry. "Stop," I say, my voice wavering. "Stop."

"He never knew what he had. I knew it from the minute I first saw you. I would have given you everything. Anything you wanted—anything—I would have given it to you. I *still* would." He pounds his fist on the picnic table, and I jump. Out of the corner of my eye, I see movement between some of the cars parked along the playground's perimeter. He sees it too, and his eyes dart around, then he places his fist in his lap.

I look at him, at his eyes still that crisp cornflower blue, at his lips, lips that have tasted my body, my mouth, that have curled around my name in the most intimate of moments.

"All I wanted was my own life," I say, "And you took that from me." I get up from the table.

"Babs!" he calls after me, but he doesn't follow.

fifty-six

A COLOSSAL FAILURE. I ELICITED NO USEFUL INFORMATION, AND IT seems likely there's a restraining order against Austin in my future. Maybe he'll move to Mexico. Maybe David and I will move to Perth. Maybe I'll let Margot kill him with her bare fucking hands.

The piece I can't move beyond, though, is the creeping feeling that he was right when he said Ryan was having an affair. In telling me this, Austin has murdered Ryan twice: once when Ryan and his whiskey-ocean eyes were pulled under the wheels of that truck, and again as he rewrote my marriage, planting seeds of doubt when there is no chance of ascertaining the truth, or atoning and reconciling if the worst of it is true.

David finds me. I am collapsed on the burnt caramel couch. I am heartbroken. He calls Margot, and she comes over. I hear them upstairs.

"I don't know what to do for her," he says.

"I told her not to go see him," she says. "Why did you let her do that?"

I wish she could be soft. Just sometimes.

David doesn't argue with her; there's no point. I hear her feet on the stairs, then she's sitting with me on the couch.

"I had questions. I felt like I couldn't move on if I didn't get answers," I say preempting her.

"You can't even know if he told you the truth," she says.

"He said Ryan was having an affair," I say. "Affairs, actually."

Margot doesn't blink. "Do *you* think he was?"

"I don't know. I always wondered," I say.

Margot nods, a gesture that's not entirely comforting at the moment. But then she says, "I always thought of him as just ridiculously smitten with you. Always."

I think back to the funeral. It was small because of COVID. Maybe ten people. But there was nothing unusual. Nothing at the gravesite or at Margot's house. Nothing when I cleaned out his office. And nothing since. If he was unfaithful, the other women haven't so much as hiccuped in the time since.

"What?" Margot asks, seeing my forehead crease and my jaw tighten. "Are you remembering something?"

"Kind of." I'm remembering that I have all of the belongings that were on Ryan at the time of his death in a banker's box in my laundry room. I haven't looked at them since they were handed to the funeral home by the hospital where his body was taken by the EMTs, who were too late to do anything other than scrape him up off the pavement and state the obvious about him being dead.

I get up from the couch and walk down the hall to the laundry room. Margot follows without saying anything. I find the box on a shelf in the back by the water heater. I take off the lid, and Margot encircles me in her arms. She is soft. I sniff as the tears tip over the edges of my eyes and fall down my cheeks into the box.

I can smell him. He's still in here. In his coat and hat and gloves. I pull his navy-blue wool coat to my face, and suddenly he's standing beside me. I can hear him.

"I could live here, Bibs," he says in Paris.

"Love you, Bibby," he says as he walks out the door on his way to the Red Line.

"Will this all be okay?" he asks when we were just kids.

I don't know anymore.

Margot sits back on the ground, her legs crisscross-applesauce, as my kids used to say.

I pull out Ryan's backpack, unzip it, and look inside. Pens. A pad of paper. His readers are still in their case. He wore contacts but had started wearing glasses when he read. I loved it when he wore them at home. With the gold flecks of his blue eyes bouncing off the tortoise shell, I was instantly back in those days at the university library. I pause at his lunch tote. Empty. I almost can't make sense of it—of the extraordinary ordinariness of his last day on this earth.

I set the backpack to the side and wipe the backs of my hands across my cheeks as if new tears won't simply replace the ones I've displaced.

His phone. That's what I came for. I pull it out of the top pocket of his backpack. The battery is dead, has been for years. I crawl over to the wall and plug it in, using a charger from the same pocket. It takes a couple minutes for the screen to light up. The wallpaper is me at the lake house in Michigan.

There's no cell phone service; no one has paid this bill in a very long time. But I type in our anniversary, and the phone opens all the same. All the apps are there. Outlook, wallet, Facebook and Instagram, browser, encrypted HIPAA texting app, audible, zoom, a couple of games. I connect to Wi-Fi, and the phone begins to vibrate, speaking into the past. I open the HIPAA texting app. It's as expected. Consult requests, communication regarding medication orders, scheduling issues with the OR, discussions about vent allocation to the adult hospital.

Email is similar, full of meeting requests (some of which continued to come in for the brief period when his battery was alive, but he was not), emails from research partners, a revise-and-resubmit on an article that was never published because its author, Ryan E. Aganon, died. His personal email is much the same. Simply a snapshot of his life. Emails from our kids' school about the upcoming holiday vacation schedule, a quote from a contractor for a repair to a leaky window.

There are no texting apps other than the HIPAA app and the one that came with the phone. I'm reassured by this as I don't have to navigate the waters of "automatically disappearing messages" and what it means if one's husband has such an app on his phone. Mine did not. I open the text app and look at the cascade of people who texted my husband on his last day of life. Me. A lot. I smile nostalgically at this. Our back-and-forth banter throughout the day. A couple of work friends asking if anyone wants to eat lunch together. Cancellation of a well-child checkup for Penny "in light of rising COVID cases." There's nothing. Nothing that even hints at so much as a flirtation at work.

I see his wallet at the bottom of the box and set his phone down. It continues to charge for really no good reason. The wallet holds thirty-seven dollars—who knew?—his driver's license, and two expired credit cards. I pull out the receipts tucked in against the cash and flip through them. Gas stations, hospital cafeteria, hospital gift shop—replaced a phone charger and bought a bag of Chex mix—coffee purchases. If Ryan was having an affair, he could have taught a Master Class in how *not* to get caught.

I think about my own stupidity: in 2010 it was email, not text. And mine was chock full of "Can't wait to see you" and

"I'm so glad we're working together on this client" and "I don't think I've ever met anyone like you." And eventually, Ryan suspected enough to come to our bedroom and stand at the foot of our bed while I sat against the pillows reading.

"Do I have anything to be worried about with you and Mark?" he'd asked, and I can hear his voice and see his face like we are having that conversation right now. I couldn't even answer him. I just started to cry, and he knew. It was one kiss, but it was almost more.

"You are the love of my life, Babs," he'd said, his eyes taking on a liquid quality I'd never seen before. "But I will leave if this continues." Then he walked out of our bedroom.

Next to me, Margot has started organizing the items I've removed from the box. She hasn't said anything, but she's letting me know it's time to go back upstairs. It's time to leave the life I had and go back to the one I have. She knows I didn't find anything, and she knows that an absence of proof isn't proof of absence, but it will have to be enough.

She takes my hand as we walk upstairs and sit together on the couch, and I look out the window onto Seminary Avenue. David brings us tea and kisses me on the cheek. Then he leaves the room, and I hear him in the kitchen, pacing in front of the patio doors.

"I don't think he was cheating on you, Babs," Margot says gently. "I really don't."

I don't respond. I don't think he was either. But that's no longer what I'm thinking about. I'm thinking about the cascade of texts on his phone. The most recent of them, the last text he read before he died, was from me two hours before he was hit by the truck that killed him.

I'm thinking about how his readers were in their case in his backpack, not in his coat, or more to the point on his face, which they would have been if he'd been trying to read texts on his phone.

I'm thinking about the fact that on a rainy night in November, Ryan's phone was somehow not damaged—not so much as a crack in the screen—when the truck drove over him, and he lay in the street with buckets pouring down on him from the heavens.

And all of this, I am certain, means he was not looking down at his phone when he stepped into the crosswalk. His phone was in his backpack with his readers, where it has been since the day he was killed.

I'm not sure it's enough for a jury: the statements that Lasky will offer, Austin's statements at the park, combined with what's left of Ryan in the banker's box in my basement. I'm not sure it will be enough for a jury. But it's enough for me.

the end

acknowledgments

I wrote *Fan Base* over about six weeks when I was on a self-imposed forced absence from revisions of *Load Bearing*. The seed for this novel was all of the celebrity-normal romances at that time and my desire to play with that trope. (I'll refrain from saying more to avoid spoilers for people like myself, who read the Acknowledgements before finishing the book.) The central story came pretty easily, but not much else did, and I put the manuscript away for almost a year after writing it. It felt incomplete, and I couldn't figure out what to do with it.

Then, when I published *Load Bearing,* several friends asked me whether that book was a "beach read"—I'd published it in March, which, in retrospect, did set it up for spring break reading. I responded tongue-in-cheek that *Load Bearing* was a beach read if it was read on a beach. But I know what people meant, and I returned to *Fan Base* thinking, **This** *is a beach read; I'll finish this.*

I sent that first draft to my favorite beta reader, Silja Koivuniemi, who had some solid ideas for directions I could take it in, where it needed to be developed, what was working and what was not.

And so the revisions began.

Without subjecting you all to the painful process, I will simply say that writing a "beach read" is much harder than I thought it would be. To craft something that is simultaneously a bucket full of snack-sized candy bars, but also substantive enough to be satisfying is really difficult, and I have a whole new respect for those who have mastered the genre.

Consequently, this story has endured multiple revisions, and I have many people to thank.

Thank you to my first round of beta readers: Chloe Barnes, Kayla Davenport, Ailsa McIntosh, Susan Morris, Casey Reiland, and Veronica Wiley. A huge thank you for the manuscript assessments by Kim Long, Sydney Weinberg, and Abigail Fenton and to my second round of beta readers Gabriel Bosslet, Melody Chu, Erik Ives, Scott Reisfeld, Dennis Smithenry, and Lynn Wohlwend. And much thanks, also, to my writing group, Mid-World Arts.

Thank you to my unwavering cheering sections: my Marshmallow Peelers: Emily Beckman and Katy Head; and the incredible community at Barre Ripple. I wouldn't have made it through the past year without you.

Thank you forever to my children and to my husband, Steve, without whom I would never have moved to Chicago, which remains to this day my favorite city on the face of the planet. Seminary. *Sniff sniff.* Also, sorry, Steve, but there are no box scores in fictional baseball games.

Finally, I would like to offer up an intention to those affected by the wildfires in California. I was in final revisions of this manuscript when the fires erupted there, fires which have displaced thousands and thousands of people and destroyed everything in their path.

More than half of my family reside in California, and my husband spent his undergraduate years in that state. For those parts of this novel set in California, I relied on memories of time spent with family and friends from San Diego to San Francisco. Indeed, one of my favorite stories is a cross-country road trip my husband and I took from Indiana to California when we'd just started dating. By the time he dropped me off at my aunt's apartment in Santa Monica, we'd spent fully four days together in a 1989 Honda Accord, and I was pretty sure our relationship had run its course. Twenty-four years later, I'm happy to say it is still going strong. But to see the absolute devastation of my family's and friends' homes, of places that carry so much meaning to people I love—I can only say that my heart breaks.

Climate change is real. The effects of it are all around us in a multitude of ways. The earth rages, while conservative politicians deny the science and frustrate efforts to address the impending existential disaster. They do so with a willful ignorance and an unapologetic cruelty, and they are not fit to lead.

about the author

Jane Hartsock is a Hoosier by birth and by choice. She resides in Indianapolis, Indiana with her husband, their two children, and one poorly-behaved but well-intentioned Irish Terrier. She is a Bioethicist and a Medical Humanities professor. *Fan Base* is her second novel. *Load Bearing* (2024) is available on Amazon, IngramSpark, and at a number of independent bookstores around Indianapolis.

If you enjoyed this book, please consider leaving a comment on Amazon or Goodreads. And feel free to connect with me on social media to discuss books I've read and how much coffee I've consumed.

www.ingramcontent.com/pod-product-compliance
Ingram Content Group UK Ltd.
Pitfield, Milton Keynes, MK11 3LW, UK
UKHW021323180426
11947UKWH00017B/1402